MARIE NDIAYE was born in Pithiviers, France in 1967 to a French mother and Senegalese father. She began writing fiction at the age of ten and her first novel was published when she was just 17. She has written six novels in all. *Among Family* (*'En Famille'*, 1990) was her fourth novel and is the first to be translated into English. She is published in France by Les Editions de Minuit and has been widely translated throughout Europe. Marie lives in Normandy with her husband and their young family.

# AMONG FAMILY

## Marie NDiaye

*Translated from the French by*
*Heather Doyal*

**Angela Royal Publishing**

Published in the United Kingdom by
ANGELA ROYAL PUBLISHING LTD
P O Box 138
Tunbridge Wells
Kent TN3 0ZT

First published 1997
1 3 5 7 9 10 8 6 4 2

Copyright © 1997 Marie NDiaye
First published as *En Famille* © 1990 by Les Editions de Minuit
English translation © 1997 Heather Doyal

A CIP catalogue for this book is available from the British Library
ISBN 1-899860-40-1

Typeset by Nick Awde/Desert♥Hearts
Cover design by Nick Awde/Emanuela Losi
Printed in Great Britain by BPC Wheatons Ltd, Exeter

# CONTENTS

# PART ONE

PART ONE

# ONE
## *Among Family*

When she arrived in front of her grandmother's house at the end of the village, the two dogs she had so often petted in the past, now old and blind, summoned enough strength to throw themselves furiously at the gate. Every time she tried to poke her face between the bars, they barked with a violence she had never known in them before. She called them softly by name. They redoubled their fury. She put down her suitcase, hoisted herself onto a large rock at one end of the gate — out of reach of the dogs — then squeezed her chest between two bars and shouted towards the house for someone to open for her. She was upset that the dogs had not recognized her, seeing it as a sign of serious failure on her part.

One of her uncles appeared on the doorstep. What's he doing at Grandmother's today? she wondered, laughing quietly to herself because he had lost a lot of hair. Her last visit seemed recent enough for her uncle to look the same and for the dogs to remember her.

The balding uncle held a glass in one hand and in the other a pie he was munching, without worrying about crumbs. He ordered the dogs to be quiet, then asked her what she wanted.

"George, it's me, your niece!" she said, smiling. She reached out towards him despite the pain the bars caused her at the slightest movement. Breathing was difficult; but could she just stay outside the gate like a stranger, humiliated by the dogs? She had never to her knowledge done the family any wrong and had always fussed over the dogs during her visits to Grandmother. Maybe they were angry with her for something she did not know about. That was probably it! That's what she was up against.

Her uncle looked her up and down indifferently then frowned. He did not make the slightest move to greet her, just swallowed a last mouthful, emptied his glass, shrugged, then returned slowly to Grandmother's house. The door slammed shut. Uncle George had once given her a long-haired doll that she still had. She thought the news would travel fast that George had left her outside, and the whole family would make him feel ashamed of it for the rest of his life. She freed one arm and pressed the bell. Contorted, her waist crushed between the bars, she held her finger on the bell as the dogs went mad and hurled themselves at the gate. Out of the corner of her eye, she looked at her suitcase, buckled carefully yesterday for the long trip, abandoned now on the pavement.

At last the door opened. She was surprised to recognize several aunts, uncles, and cousins, crowding onto the steps, not daring to come down into the yard. Their dresses were bright, their suits dark with white shirts buttoned to the neck. Her cousin Eugene was there, with his shiny curls — the two of them had sometimes stolen a kiss in the shadow of a wardrobe. Suddenly she remembered that today was Grandmother's birthday. Busy with her preparations and engrossed in the bright idea that had taken hold of her, Fanny had forgotten. But she had not been invited anyway, and the family had gathered to celebrate without noticing that one of its members was missing — one who had never done the family any wrong, who had never, even at a distance, spoken ill of them. Hadn't she always taken great pains to cover up how strange the family seemed to her, how insulting and hateful they were towards her?

Even so, they had not invited her to Grandmother's birthday party, and now they were leaving her to hang on the gate, half-strangled by the bars. And the way they were looking her up and down with those cold, puzzled stares!

Only Eugene was smiling at her, vaguely. He was wearing a short, tight-fitting jacket which he delighted in smoothing over his chest with outspread fingers. From a distance his flattened locks looked like a shiny helmet which he kept stroking with the palm of his hand, wiping the grease on his trousers. He soon lost interest and disappeared, with a half-turn on the toes of his boots. Hesitantly at first, a woman broke away from the group and approached the gate. She silenced the dogs with a click of her tongue and said at last, 'Yes?'

'Why didn't you let me know you were celebrating Grandmother's birthday today? After all, Aunt Colette, I am your sister's daughter! Help me down!'

Aunt Colette stepped back, as if shocked, then blushed and clumsily opened the gate.

'Look here, Fanny,' she began, grabbing her niece awkwardly by the hips.

'My name isn't Fanny, Aunt Colette! Have you forgotten everything? But it doesn't matter, call me Fanny. I needed a new name anyway,' said Fanny, pleased.

'Oh,' said Aunt Colette, who was trying to smile.

Wanting to appear friendly, she picked up Fanny's suitcase; Fanny jumped joyfully to the ground, and they entered the yard while Uncle George held back the dogs. In spite of their feebleness, their usually docile natures and the trust they had always shown her (hadn't she played with them throughout her childhood?) the dogs seemed to want to attack Fanny, who was smiling and fresh, now almost eighteen years old. George looked at her with bored indecision, but Fanny ignored him, even neglecting the customary gesture of going, as his niece, to kiss him. Until now she had thought him the most easy-going of her uncles. Inside the house her indignation grew, and she turned towards Aunt Colette with reproachful eyes. But Colette had dumped the suitcase and slipped away. Fanny stood on tiptoe and called in vain, she could not see her, even though Aunt Colette was a large woman and wore a blue-sequined dress for the party. Fanny remembered having seen that dress before and felt moved by it.

As they did every year, the whole family had gathered together. Never before had Fanny forgotten either her grandmother's birthday or the party organized in its honour, and she realized what a mistake, what bad behaviour, even what hostility towards her grandmother — whom she did however love — this slip represented. Since they hadn't seen Fanny, no one had bothered about her, and Aunt Colette — usually so particular — had even mixed Fanny's name up with some other Fanny, some Fanny she had read about in a book, since she did not know anyone by that name in real life. Would there be room at the table for her or would she have to eat in the kitchen with the children? That would mortify her to tears because then she would get the leftovers, the dregs of bottles, the plain tarts; she would suffer the same humiliation they had put her through once before just to punish her. She headed for the dining room (having left her suitcase in the hall, well-hidden behind the coats) and noticed several children she did not know; they had to be from some remote branch of the family. She looked at them severely. Not one of them had offered her a cheek to be kissed or even greeted her.

She passed her cousin Eugene. He was whistling and pulling the legs of his tight-fitting trousers until they covered the tops of his boots just right. Seeing Fanny suddenly look unhappy, he smiled mockingly and gave a slight bow. She grabbed him by the arm and asked him whether he at least recognized her. What must he think of her since she — despite her correct attitude, her usual good-nature, her respect for the family and traditions — had not been invited for Grandmother's birthday. She shook Eugene, bringing her face close to his, then pinned him against the wall.

'Of course,' said Eugene, 'of course, I recognized you. What did you think?'

His smile made Fanny doubt that he was telling the truth. She gave him a thump. Cousin Eugene protested and broke away, laughing.

'I never know when to believe you!' said Fanny, furious. Growing more and more angry, she stared at Eugene's moist lips. What had she done to make the family distance itself from her, irrespective of what it owed her? She had been thrilled by every birth, had never said a word against anyone in the family...

She hurried back to the hall, opened her suitcase, took a photograph out, and slipped it into her pocket; then she returned to the dining room where the family were starting to take their customary places around the long table decorated with flowers. As Fanny was going around, smiling, to kiss each person, she noticed Aunt Colette watching her from a corner. Aunt Colette's face bore an expression of worried surprise and total incomprehension. Why is she looking at me like that, Fanny wondered, when everyone else is kissing and greeting me the same as ever? Robert wanted to pinch her cheeks; everyone thought she looked well. She felt completely reassured when they asked for news of her parents who were both kept away by their occupations, the difficulties of travelling, perhaps weary indifference. But no one addressed her by name, and when she said she would answer to Fanny from now on they assented in silence — only Aunt Colette sighed. An extra place was set, and Fanny took her usual seat. Grandmother, she was told, had retired to her room; Fanny could see her after lunch. Fanny smiled at everyone, anxious to show that there was no reason for them to think she had changed or that she differed from what a family member should be, even though she felt the need to compensate for her parents' absence. On her sturdy shoulders she carried the guilt of their neglect. Eugene is popular, thought Fanny, seeing him yawn, and free to behave badly. No one can find fault with him, because his mother and father are here. Hadn't they passed on to Eugene all the appropriate family features? Her cousin Eugene looked like their late great-uncle. Now he was getting up from the table without saying a word and going out to smoke in the yard, scuffing his boots along the floor. Aunt Colette, who was seated next to Fanny, pointed to her husband then whispered, 'Eugene is our son.'

'Of course,' said Fanny, 'why wouldn't I know that?' And she thought of Eugene's moist lips. But Aunt Colette did not seem to hear her — as soon as Fanny spoke, a slight smile slid over Aunt Colette's taut features as she focused on an invisible point in space. She frequently stopped eating to explain something Fanny had always known, recounted in detail some incident the whole family knew, and showed no surprise when Fanny irritably finished the story for her, but added softly, 'One needs to know all that.' These pathetic stories! Who knew better than Fanny minor family events and everyone's names? Whose memory was more reliable? Whose recollections more accurate? But Fanny's parents were not above reproach. No doubt scornful of Grandmother with her narrow ideas, they unashamedly refused to trouble themselves with the birthday and did not even bother to apologize.

At the end of the meal, as the cake and coffee were brought in, Fanny took the photograph out of her pocket and leaned it up against her glass. It showed her at age three or four in the arms of her smiling, gentle mother, who was as pretty then as Fanny today, but without such bright eyes. Aunt Colette bent over the photograph; the others craned their necks to see. To Fanny's great satisfaction, Aunt Colette passed the photograph on and each person glanced at it discreetly then quickly handed it to the next, without comment. At least, thought Fanny, they must recognize Mother. In spite of her mistakes, she is still tied to each of them. Her mother's name was actually mentioned, even fondly sometimes. Someone whispered his regret that Fanny had not remained the same as the girl in the picture. Despite all her smiles and her eagerness to please, no one addressed her directly. They glanced at her with embarrassment, but the conversation did not interest Fanny who only listened out of duty. They started to talk about the days when the photograph was taken. Fanny related a childhood memory. It was about the river, the little dancing bridge. But did they see clearly all that Fanny described, or did they simply recognize her right to express herself the way people sometimes do in books — with pretty images and enthusiasm? They smiled gently when they saw her become emotional. Aunt Colette grumbled that she did not remember a thing Fanny was talking about. But no one, not even the old people present, could have contradicted Fanny, whose memory was limitless and sharp, who knew the recent past more precisely than those who had lived it.

Eugene came back from the yard to eat his share of the birthday cake and a large slice was put aside for Grandmother. Remembering their kisses, Fanny enjoyed watching her cousin Eugene. Since the trip would be long and she needed a loyal companion, she made up her mind to take him along. It was time to tell the family about her plans. The children had left the table; the adults had settled back in their chairs, eyes half-closed. The left-over gravy was hardening on the scattered plates. Only Eugene and Fanny were fidgeting in their seats. Cousin Eugene sighed loudly, his gaze dull. He was wearing a tight black sweater and a chain belt. He had recently acquired a small, fast car, which gave him confidence. Suddenly Fanny got up, startling her neighbours. She announced that she had something important to say and must ask each of them for help — not for money (she had noticed their frowns) — but for information about Aunt Leda, her mother's sister.

'No one knows where Leda is,' said Aunt Colette, appearing worried.

'I've never seen Aunt Leda,' said Fanny, 'either in a photograph or in person, because she hasn't come to a single birthday party. Perhaps she doesn't even know these parties take place here every year. How could she when no one has seen her or spoken to her since we started celebrating Grandmother's birthday? I've heard you talk about her sometimes, though. You regret not knowing what has been going on in her life, but you accept her as part of the family, just the same as if each of you saw her every day of the year and she hadn't let you down by not keeping in touch. You seem as fond of her as if she had shown some affection in return, which she hasn't. Fine. Aunt Leda has the privilege of being loved by everyone despite her negligence and indifference towards you. As for me, I don't belong here, even though I always believed I did until just now. I am at best tolerated — all I have ever done is to imitate, and that couldn't fool you for long. You saw it before I did. But I'm aware of my mistakes, or those of my parents. All my misfortune is because Aunt Leda was not informed of my birth, as all of you were, even though Aunt Leda is my own mother's sister. Even so, you were present at the official dinner given to welcome me into the family when I was four months and seventeen days old — I still have some of the little gifts from it. Leda, of course, was absent, though no one cared. No one tried to find her to tell her that her first niece had just come into the world, and if Leda happened to still live in our town at the time — since no one knows where she was living, she might have been right by us, rubbing elbows with us without our even suspecting it — perhaps she even learned of it from the newspaper, like anyone else. Things were not done as they should have been on such an occasion and my parents are very much at fault in this, although they don't realize it. Each of you has wronged me a little. Didn't you pretend to welcome me, yet at the same time make it obvious my rights were limited? That is made clear today since you quite simply forgot me. All I can do now is find Aunt Leda. Then,' concluded Fanny with a smile, 'we'll organize a second meal in honour of my birth, and Leda will be at the head of the table, flanked by my parents. Unfortunately, their mistake can only be half undone because now I'm eighteen and I've already paid for everyone's lack of concern with a lot of unhappiness and problems.'

Fanny sat down again and crossed her hands on the table. She bowed her head slightly but beneath her lowered lashes her eyes were passing quickly from one person to another. She saw that Eugene was gazing into space with a deeply bored look, his teeth gleaming in his gaping mouth. Had he at least heard her out?

'Poor Leda didn't do much with her life,' said Aunt Colette.

They all started to talk about Leda, but they did not say anything that could help Fanny or that had anything to do with what she had just said. She remained silent, as though all this were no concern of hers. With her sweeping, nervous gestures, Aunt Colette, without realizing it, was gradually pushing Fanny towards the corner of the table. She insisted that Leda had run away with a man to a strange village, that there was nothing out of the ordinary about Leda's story, which was even vulgar in places. Aunt Colette wasn't sure of Leda's age — her own sister. But she firmly believed that the man whom Leda had run away with had a lot of money, something Leda had always coveted, having neither skill nor education, neither wit nor true beauty. Some of the family muttered their disagreement. Even Uncle George appeared angry, with his puffed neck. But Aunt Colette was insistent; she was Leda's sister and had known her best. She had forgotten Fanny's presence at her side; her hands waved back and forth with such gesticulations that Fanny had to keep moving her chair to avoid being hit.

'Do you have any idea which village Aunt Leda went to?' asked Fanny when Aunt Colette had stopped talking.

'No one knows where she is,' answered Aunt Colette, without looking at Fanny. She quickly added that she found Fanny's intentions confusing and that she herself did not understand what Fanny needed and had no means of helping her. After all, each of us is responsible for what happens to us. And if Fanny had been forgotten, as she claimed, it was no doubt due to the bustle of the preparations. Hadn't Fanny herself forgotten Grandmother's birthday? With that Aunt Colette turned to Eugene, who was yawning, and scolded him for a wine stain on his pale trousers.

# TWO
## *Grandmother*

When, at last, everyone had risen for a short stroll around the yard or to play cards in the living room, Fanny went to see her grandmother. She was resting in her room, which opened directly into the narrow, smokey kitchen where two girls, hired for the day, were doing the last of the dishes. Since the bedroom door refused to close more than three quarters of the way, you could see Grandmother's big bed from the kitchen and, right at the head, a shock of grey hair. Fanny pulled a chair up to the bed which was so high the edge came up to her chin. Grandmother sat up, pulled at the ties which drew the neck of her nightdress together and stared curiously at Fanny. Fanny got up to kiss her on the cheek. The terror in her grandmother's eyes made Fanny think she must be on the brink of death. Fanny was astonished, almost horrified. Presents tossed on the bed made her feel ashamed — she hadn't brought anything. Last year she had given her grandmother a beautiful book about nature because her mother, who hadn't been able to come, had asked her to. This made up a little for her neglect. Today she came with empty hands and without the least excuse for her parents who were not frightened that Grandmother was about to die — since they had a million things to do, a million worries to keep them busy! Responsible for Fanny's unhappiness, they feared nothing so much as boredom, lost time, pointless activities — not even death itself, whose face, it seemed to an amazed Fanny, she was seeing right here.

Grandmother, her mouth open, did not return Fanny's kiss. Her glance was alert again. She called Fanny by her real first name and said that she was very happy to see her. In the dark room, the shadows of the heavy furniture seemed to swell, swallowing up Grandmother, whose pale face, like a carcass stripped of flesh, was barely visible. With a rush of affection, Fanny wanted to take hold of her grandmother's hand, but she felt along the quilt without finding it, and her grandmother did not offer it to her. Next door, the girls, talking loudly and clattering the dishes, could hear nothing from the bedroom, so Fanny's grandmother asked her all kinds of questions. She asked Fanny how her studies were going, what she planned on doing in the future, what she had been doing for the past few years, things she should have known the answer to since Fanny had always kept her up-to-date on what she was doing. Her grandmother wanted to know every detail about even the smallest event. She pulled at her nightdress ties as if to urge Fanny to tell her more.

'Grandmother, that's all done with!' exclaimed Fanny, exasperated. She would leave that very day, she announced, to look for Leda. She would not come back until she had found her. She would rather die during the search than come back to a life that had not gone right from the beginning. A life warped by laziness and forgetfulness, filled until now with sad, confused stories that would take only half a page to tell. She was hanging on to the side of the bed with both hands, tilting her face towards her grandmother, who drew back slightly. Couldn't the intolerable uselessness of Fanny's life be explained by some curse Leda had put on Fanny before fleeing, believing she had been forgotten by her own sister? Fanny's mother and Leda had once been close and for a long time had the same hairstyle: two braided sections rolled above their ears and held in place with golden hair slides. The previous day, before leaving, Fanny had got *her* hair cut very short, thinking that the style would be dignified for travelling. She was only taking black clothes on the trip, with not more than two or three pieces of jewelry. She wanted to know her grandmother's opinion and above all to get her approval. But how tiny Grandmother was! Lost in that huge bed! There was not a glimmer of peace in Grandmother's dark look, but a terrible, vague fear, and she had lived so many years, she had seen so many things, even death more than a few times! Fanny shivered, feeling her confidence in Grandmother slowly weaken. Grandmother, baffled, knit her brow and scrutinized Fanny. At last she said that she had never heard of aunts or any other family member having to be informed of each birth, especially if there had been no news of them for years, as had been the case with Leda. Obviously Leda couldn't care less about Fanny. No one could blame her any more than they could blame Fanny's parents for not trying to find Leda. If Fanny thought she was unhappy, it certainly was not due to any negligence when she was born, since no one knew of any such mistake. Surprised, Grandmother said that she did not think Fanny's parents had done her any wrong, but had raised her the best they could.

'They couldn't care less about your birthday!' Fanny couldn't help bursting out. Carried away, she continued, pounding on the edge of the bed: 'They run down the whole family, not sparing anyone. But everyone loves them anyway, everyone thinks about them, but no one pays attention to anything I do. I guess you don't know it, but you all punish me for every single thing my parents do wrong.'

Grandmother shook her head and seemed to sink slowly under the sheets. Thinking that she was tiring her, Fanny stopped talking but still trembled with anger. Her grandmother asked who had made her think that Leda's absence, years ago, had affected her life. Fanny answered that it had to be — it was fate. She had been aware of it for a long time, while everyone else had gradually forgotten it. 'You too!' she said sadly. 'I thought you at least...' She shrugged in resignation. Grandmother was just like all the rest! But Grandmother clung to ancient superstitions, absurd beliefs, she really believed the improbable stories she had told long ago to put Fanny to sleep, murmuring them with respect and fear. Now Grandmother was looking at Fanny compassionately! She gently asked what all these misfortunes were that Fanny complained of.

'That's just it,' said Fanny, irritated by the questions, 'there's just *nothing.*'

The door suddenly opened; one of the kitchen girls appeared, her hair dishevelled, her face bright — earlier she had tipped a bowl of gravy down the neck of one of the old cousins. 'Can we go now?' She was gone before Grandmother had a chance to answer, and Fanny, hearing the girl laugh next door with the others, felt a painful twinge of envy.

'Yes, I thought you at least...,' she repeated mechanically. Deeply disappointed, she looked at the crucifix above her grandmother's head. She had hoped that news of the trip would bring encouragement, some concerns and many congratulations, because the venture seemed reckless and the cause noble and worthwhile. Grandmother practiced numerous religious rites and believed in fate. Hadn't she once talked in veiled terms — with a look of true fear and familiarity with the supernatural — about a neighbour she believed bewitched?

Fanny thought about her cousin Eugene and wondered whether to take him along, to put her trust in him. Then, as her eyes alighted on her grandmother's emaciated face, Eugene's soft, warm lips crossed her mind and she no longer doubted he would make an obedient, honest and courageous companion.

Fanny sensed that Grandmother's end was near and did not want to leave yet. She succeeded this time in taking her hand, which she held firmly. Grandmother was having trouble breathing but could still smile. She talked about the meal held in honour of Fanny's birth and how Leda — because no one had told her about it — had not attended. She remembered some details very well: for the first course they had eaten head of veal, which Grandmother had not liked. In a corner of the room in her little veiled crib, Fanny had cried throughout the whole thing.

'Anyway,' said Grandmother as she withdrew her hand and slid it back under the sheet, 'did we really have the meal for Fanny's birth or was it to celebrate her father's promotion to manager of that important company where he worked?' His salary had doubled, everyone had congratulated him, deservedly so, and Fanny's mother had smiled with delight, letting it be known that she had contributed more than a little to her husband's success.

Grandmother coughed, making Fanny tense with pity. She got up to plump the pillows and gently raise her grandmother up. Beneath her fingers she felt cold skin and sharp bones. Since her grandmother asked her to, she knotted tight the nightdress ties. Then she walked around the room, bumping into all sorts of furniture that she did not remember ever having seen: a writing desk with lots of drawers, an easy chair, a huge wardrobe which divided the room and two others crammed against the wall. She had remembered a spacious, airy room! On a small table, photographs were displayed in frames. Unable to see them clearly, Fanny grabbed them all and stuffed them into the waistband of her trousers, pulling her sweater down to hide them from her grandmother who, at the other end of the room, had closed her eyes, her head drooping onto her shoulder. Grandmother's body was shaking as if terrified. Fanny sat down again and asked her if she had a photograph of her daughter Leda. But her grandmother did not. So many years had passed since Leda's departure, she admitted, that bit by bit she had forgotten what Leda looked like and even began to almost doubt Leda had really existed, although she sometimes thought she heard Leda outside the shutters at night. Then I imagine Leda never left. Maybe I pass her in the street without recognizing her — my own daughter!'

'My parents have hurt me so much I'll breathe for the first time when they die!' exclaimed Fanny.

# THREE
## *The Departure*

She went to find Eugene who was idling around in the yard with the dogs, bored. The dogs had been tied up; this time they just growled at Fanny, whose stomach tightened. She drew Eugene into a corner and made him sit right next to her on a bench. She reminded him of similar days, in the past, when they had kissed awkwardly on this very bench. Eugene smiled with a somewhat haughty expression, tossing his head back to chase a lock of hair from his face. He casually stretched his legs out then yawned. Fanny nudged him in the ribs.

'Are you coming with me?'

'Where to?' he asked, suspiciously.

She grumbled at him for not listening. Eugene was so absent-minded and lazy, he got tired so quickly you could hardly finish a sentence before his mind had wandered off. She told him about the trip she was planning and announced that she needed a reliable travelling companion, someone who would obey her every command, never deserting her — at least not before she met up with Aunt Leda. Her tone was insistent because she could not think of anyone except Eugene who would agree to follow her like this. She pressed against him and gripped his hands so tightly in hers that he could not move and gasped for breath. Her mouth was now so close to his half-open mouth that their lips brushed together as she spoke. But Eugene restricted his answers to a few noncommittal 'hmm's'. He grimaced skeptically, and Fanny felt deceitful, two-faced, even though she had hidden nothing. When she voiced her thoughts, they somehow seemed to twist into lies!

She remembered that Eugene aspired to some high post, with a spacious office all his own from which he would manage a few dozen employees, while gazing at the town below from a picture window facing the undulating, hazy hills. He wanted to be in business but had no idea how to get started. Sometimes he blamed his youth, sometimes his lack of funds. Fanny quickly assured him that Leda would do something for him if she had married a rich man as people said — she could not refuse to help him since he was her nephew.

'She must have influence by now,' said Fanny, narrowing her eyes as she pulled at Eugene's arm. 'She'll have no problem giving you a little push!'

The dogs had started to growl more loudly and they leaped in

Fanny's direction, to the end of their chain, until she thought it would drive her mad.

'Stop it, will you!' she shouted, tears welling in her eyes. Then to Eugene she said, 'Those two used to obey my every command!'

Still clinging to Eugene, who seemed to be thinking things over, she sat feeling sorry for herself for some time. Finally, without enthusiasm, Eugene said, 'So, when do we leave?'

'Today! Right now!' said Fanny, jumping to her feet.

But Eugene was worried about his mother, about a date he had made, his friends, all sorts of things.

'What a full life!' said Fanny, jealously.

Eugene scratched his head and almost seemed to be regretting his decision already. Fanny gave him thirty minutes to go and tell Aunt Colette and to take care of everything else by telephone. She added that she had a little money and would buy him whatever he needed on the way.

After Eugene had left, Fanny took the photos out of her belt. The sky was grey, the village consisted of low-roofed houses that were brownish, dry, and closed — like the faces that occasionally appeared from behind a curtain in a ground-level window — and darkened by a heavy, humid fog. From her bench Fanny observed it all through the gate. She found the scene majestic and hoped the ancestral home would be handed down to her some day.

In the first photograph, Eugene was posing next to his parents, who each rested a hand on his shoulder. Behind them smiled two cousins, whom Fanny did not know very well. They were also accompanied by their parents, who were only distantly related to Grandmother. Fanny was a little surprised to see their picture displayed in Grandmother's room, on the table facing the bed. The second picture depicted a group of children. She recognized Eugene in one corner, looking sullen. All the first cousins were gathered together in this photograph, taken in Grandmother's yard. She searched for herself, but she was missing. That bothered her a little. Although she did not remember the scene, she told herself that she might be hidden behind the tall, smiling girl in the front row who held the two dogs — then only the size of fists — in her arms. Seeing the dogs in the last picture infuriated Fanny. I walked them so often, she thought. I cleaned out their kennel so many times! She rose and, without thinking, picked up a sharp stone and threw it at the dogs. She struck the gentler one in the eye. Both dogs howled. Worried someone might appear, Fanny escaped to the house. Wouldn't they accuse her of having come to cause a disturbance, since they hadn't bothered to invite her and found things just fine without her? In the hall, where she had left her suitcase, she met Eugene. He waddled towards her — his hands in his pockets, his short jacket tight across his chest — and told her everything was arranged.

'Have you got any money?' asked Fanny.

'None at all!' He seemed proud, and this irritated Fanny, because while she had been telling him that Leda would take on the task of helping him become somebody, she had begun to believe it herself. From this point on, Fanny decided that since she and Eugene both had as much to gain from the trip they should share the expenses.

'Won't your mother give you anything?' she insisted, unthinkingly.

'Her!' exclaimed Eugene, throwing up his hands. Aunt Colette was so angry she had turned away when he had tried to kiss her. He had heard her mutter all kinds of curses against Fanny. The rest of the family, who were taking a stroll around the yard, joined in and wished Fanny to the devil! Uncle George, in a gesture of anger and contempt, had ripped in two the picture Fanny had absentmindedly left on the table.

'No point in going back in,' said Eugene, seeing Fanny about to dash inside. 'They'll throw you out. My father and some of the others are guarding Grandmother's door so you can't say goodbye to her. Anyway, she's asleep.'

He sounded smug, as if everything had turned out the way he wanted, and now seemed so impatient to leave that he paced between the front door and the cloakroom without giving Fanny a thought.

'Let's go,' she sighed, sadly. She grabbed her suitcase and pulled her coat tightly around her. In the yard she avoided looking at the dogs; their silence frightened her, so she rushed past. A heavy, icy rain was falling.

'My car is over there, out front,' said Eugene, shivering.

'But we're going on foot!' exclaimed Fanny. Incredulous, Eugene stopped dead. Fanny could only come up with vague reasons — such a voyage could only be made on foot, taking their time, facing all kinds of difficulties head on. She was convinced this was the only way and insisted, even though she could not give the exact reasons — which were probably long forgotten. She took offense at Eugene's surprise without knowing why. Eugene kicked angrily, tapping one boot against the other.

'I can't believe it! That's the best I've heard yet!' he exclaimed.

His wet jacket seemed to be shrinking and judging by his quick, irregular breaths, was about to strangle him. He glanced from his car to Fanny's determined expression and back again. Fanny got an umbrella out of her suitcase and calmly opened it. As he looked at her, pride prevented him from returning to Grandmother's house where everyone would think that he had given in to his mother's wishes.

'Twenty miles or so won't kill us,' said Fanny, sheltering him with her umbrella. Since she was holding the umbrella, she gave him the suitcase to carry. They set off. Eugene looked back at his car several times, slowed his pace and sighed, calling himself an imbecile under his breath. He ignored Fanny's cheerful promises that as soon as Aunt Leda had found him the excellent position he deserved, he would have a new car — or two or three — parked at his front door if he wanted, all of them more powerful than this one. She held him firmly by the arm and to make up for the roughness of her grip, gently stroked his wrist with her slender fingers.

They crossed the village at a good pace. Their footsteps echoed in the silence, causing a few faces to appear at the lighted windows. They disappeared like shadows the moment Fanny raised her eyes and although Eugene insisted that such and such an acquaintance of theirs had been watching them for several minutes, had sometimes even given him a discreet wave that he had not been able to return, Fanny saw nothing and believed Eugene was playing tricks on her. At one point they thought they saw Aunt Colette. She emerged from an alley and shot into a house with closed shutters — right in front of them! Eugene paused to call her, then shrugged. They continued on their way, telling each other it could not be her, feeling nevertheless a little troubled. Fanny clung to Eugene more tightly. Under the pretext of keeping him warm she pressed a fleshy hip against his. Eugene started to grumble about the cold, the rain, the darkness, about being hungry already. They had not even left the village before he started complaining that Fanny's suitcase was heavy and cumbersome. It kept hitting him in the legs and cutting into his hand. Finally, he talked about throwing everything into a bundle, which would be easier to carry. Fanny lost her temper. All her things would get crumpled or lost. Eugene went quiet and Fanny had to put all her effort into conversation, fearing that silence would allow Eugene's bad mood to weigh on their every step. She let him know that they were heading for her father's village. She had some important things to discuss with her father, not having seen him for a long time, mainly out of resentment. Most importantly, from a little secret investigation into his mail, she had reason to believe that he knew which direction Aunt Leda had taken when she left, long ago. But Eugene's jacket was too tight and he was too busy trying to unbutton it with one hand to listen to her. As soon as he had his jacket open he was numb with cold. He cursed. They would have to stop. Night had fallen and they heard thousands of soft sounds rising from the countryside, making them strain their ears uselessly. Sometimes a car passed them and Eugene would sigh, stepping sullenly out of the way at the last minute. His pride was bruised as he moved onto the verge. Fanny caressed him, kissed his cheek. She kept circling him, smoothing his hair back, adjusting his belt. She listened to his complaints and soothed him, saying, 'Yes, yes,' gently and brightly. Heading towards her goal, she could not care less about the rain!

They weren't getting any further though. She tried to lend Eugene a sweater and he let himself be talked into it, then complained that it was too tight. Finally, he dug in his heels, put down the suitcase, crossed his arms and announced he was quitting. He stared at her accusingly, as if she had tricked him into dragging behind her down these hard roads. Fanny blushed, not doubting — although she could not remember how — that she had inadvertently lied to him. From head to toe she was nothing but lies, from the moment she was born! Behind them, footsteps echoed. Suddenly a man wearing a long, black raincoat appeared, a flashlight in his hand — it was Grandmother's neighbour. His starkly lit face frightened them, as if it were floating in the night. Eugene threw out his chest and got up the courage to step forward, still dragging his boots. The man thrust forward a wad of money, which was rolled up and held together by a rubber band.

'From your mother, and double if you come back,' he said to Eugene with a laugh.

'I can't be bought!' exclaimed Eugene. He was about to refuse it when Fanny intervened, unable to stifle a little cry. She accused Eugene of recklessness and whispered to him to take the money, which in no way obligated him. She grabbed Eugene's arm and pushed it roughly towards the wad of money. The man handed it over and disappeared, so quickly that Fanny, suddenly remembering they didn't have a flashlight and that the cars were too few to light the way for them, did not have time to beg him to sell them his. Eugene, however, had forgotten that he had refused to go on. Flattered, he made fun of Aunt Colette's fears. He almost became angry, thinking that Aunt Colette did not care about his future and would rather keep him at her side, in a state of mediocrity, than see him leave to pursue some chance at success, no doubt dreading that he would come back changed. Then he got worried. He became silent, and Fanny thought she saw a flicker of deceit, a mysterious, calculating expression cross his dark, half-closed eyes. She pressed against him and soon forgot about it.

Now the moonlight showed them the way, and since the rain fell less heavily, they livened up and began to chat happily. Fanny envied Eugene who had always seemed firmly planted — growing strong on stable ground that he was not scared to abandon or to disown, knowing full well that it would always be his. Eugene was talking a lot, not worrying, but making plans, even using fancy words sometimes. He was describing his future life as he saw it and dreaming of a wide roll-top desk.

At Fanny's suggestion, they compared memories. But whether Eugene did so unwillingly or whether Fanny overrated the importance of events and went out of her way to cling to trivialities, Eugene could not recollect a single scene that she described. Fanny almost lost her temper and insisted that he had played a part in everything she was telling him, long ago, during the numerous vacations spent together at Grandmother's house.

'I really don't remember,' said Eugene over and over, puffing out his cheeks.

Painful situations, humiliating little episodes, a discussion in which she had made a fool of herself had tortured Fanny for years, while no trace of them remained in Eugene's happy memory! At the thought of her useless regrets and shame, she resented him and felt herself weigh more heavily on his arm. What surprised her most, though, was that she had no memory whatsoever of what Eugene started to recount in great detail. With a vague foreboding that he would accuse her of lying or of letting down the family, she was too frightened to admit her forgetfulness. Perhaps Eugene would then turn away from her with the greatest disgust, even though *she* had to accept the thoughtless way he had forgotten *her* memories, and all because *his* birth had taken place with a full observance of traditions. But wasn't he decent enough in looks and character to do without traditions, glowing with perfection as he was?

Fanny wisely brushed aside the subject of memories. Finding nothing to say to each other, they walked in silence. From time to time, Fanny dug her fingers into Eugene's arm, pinching it, making him angry. To get back at her, he threatened to throw the suitcase under the wheels of a passing car. She cajoled him and fussed over him. They felt closer.

They became tired and stopped at a service station where Eugene purchased crackers and a garlic sausage. Fanny bought a society magazine of which she had not missed a single issue for years, because she liked to compare her own inexpressible life with those of famous people and forget herself in dreams that were a little morose. Following the service station attendant's directions, they reached a nearby hotel. They would be able to leave early the next day and arrive at Fanny's father's house before lunch.

Perched right next to the road and violently lit with neon signs, the hotel was full of identical business travellers, seated at tables, white napkins tucked in their collars. They stared curiously at Fanny and their looks seemed so serious, their expressions so solemn, that she suddenly felt transformed into some enormous error in taste. At her side, Eugene only met with indifferent glances. Once Fanny was seated with Eugene, at a table set out of the way, some of the businessmen went as far as moving their chairs back to examine her more easily. Having finished their meal, they crossed their legs and lit cigars. Little by little the smoke veiled their plump faces — which were obstinately turned towards Fanny — and blended with the confused chattering. A sour-tempered waitress came to take Fanny and Eugene's order. It seemed she waited as long as possible before coming over to their table at last, nonchalantly, perhaps in the hope that these two would be intimidated and slip out without asking for anything. But Eugene was hungry. As for Fanny, the stares of the commercial travellers, at home here, forbade her to leave had she wanted to. Eugene wanted everything at once — fish soup, squids fried in olive oil, hearts of palm in a vinaigrette sauce, stewed eels and two or three desserts. Fanny made do with a piece of sole and a drop of red wine. She spoke quietly, her head lowered, but the waitress repeated her order in a thundering voice, causing a stir among the salesmen. Embarrassed, Fanny took a sidelong glance at Eugene. Wasn't he ashamed of being with her? He was absorbed in studying the menu and did not notice anything. He cried out with delight, 'That's got to be good!' slapping his thigh.

Later, he fell asleep as soon as his body hit the double bed and took up so much space that his little pointed behind bothered Fanny until morning. With a big, blissful smile on his face, he talked in his sleep about a girl Fanny did not know.

# FOUR

## Fanny's Father's House

The heat was suffocating after the cold of the night before. In her father's village, they freshened up at a fountain. It was siesta time. Eugene was sulking because he had not eaten lunch. He had wolfed down the sausage and crackers that morning, then dragged his feet, complaining that Fanny was walking too fast. To save his strength, he said, he kept throwing the suitcase in front of him, picking it up, throwing it again, and Fanny had let him do it, worrying that another quarrel would delay them more. But she was furious. Eugene is nothing but a brute, she told herself. He doesn't understand anything about this trip and has no idea of the dignity, the solemnity, the humility needed to carry it out. My cousin Eugene is nothing but a leech!

As they were entering the silent village, she grabbed Eugene's arm and did not loosen her grip until they arrived at her father's house. Eugene seemed to like being hung onto this way. She put on bright red lipstick, gently pushed Eugene back a little, then rang the bell, trying in vain to hear some noise behind the high wall which circled the house where her father had been living for some time, now that he was rich. She had not seen him for years and wondered if he would recognize her or whether, seeing her, he would knit his brow, doubtfully. Rich and highly regarded as he now was, couldn't he suspect her of trying to pass herself off as his daughter just for money and indignantly throw her out? She regretted that at Grandmother's house she had not dared take the photograph of herself in her mother's arms, the photograph Uncle George had ripped up without any right. That photograph, though not a very good one, was the only proof she could have offered, simply because her father, esteemed by everyone these days, would not have been too suspicious or dishonest to acknowledge Fanny's mother, then pretty, happy, tenderly loved. Fanny, for her part, was sure that this was her father's house. It was the biggest in the village, the most modern and the most private.

After a long moment, a servant in a smart uniform opened the door. 'You are no doubt Miss Fanny?' he said, sullenly.

'That's not my real name!' exclaimed Fanny, both surprised and delighted.

The servant shrugged. Large brass buttons fastened his red jacket. He took the suitcase from Eugene, who had approached curiously, and all three crossed the dry garden, which was planted with shrivelled bushes. Without saying a word, the servant left them in the marble hallway. Then a door opened and Fanny's father stood there. Through the doorway she caught sight of a large unmade bed, a woman who looked at her blankly and a little white dog wrapped up in the sheets. Her father's life was more unknown to her than a complete stranger's!

'So, it's you,' said Fanny's father. He kissed her mechanically while she hugged him with enthusiasm. Relieved, wanting to impress Eugene, she even gave in to an old, forgotten wish and pulled playfully on her father's beard, which was thick and black just as she remembered.

'That'll do, that'll do,' said Fanny's father in a bored tone.

'How about some lunch?' said Eugene.

With sudden attentiveness Fanny's father led them into the kitchen, ordered the servant to heat up the leftovers from lunch, then disappeared, slipping away silently. Fanny noticed, as he left, a gesture he used to arrange his hair, which seemed remarkably thick, shiny, and wavy. She gave Eugene her share of the meat.

'Who told you to call me Fanny?' she asked the servant, who paced up and down the kitchen, yawning and twisting his brass buttons.

'That's the name I've heard them use for you,' he answered indifferently. 'Unless I'm mistaken and it wasn't you they meant when they spoke of Fanny. Now, was it Fanny? I don't remember for certain.'

'What an ass!' exclaimed Fanny angrily. 'How can anyone have such a bad memory!'

The servant pursed his lips and said nothing more, not even answering Eugene who was worried about dessert, and he took Eugene's plate so abruptly that a little gravy spilt on his trousers. Does my father really know who I am? Fanny wondered anxiously. He had recognized her, but was it really her he thought he had kissed, Fanny as she really was? And if he noticed his mistake, if Fanny proved to be very different to what he had thought, and if their relationship seemed suddenly improbable, even weak — to the point that he would say to himself, 'Who cares?' — couldn't he accuse her, not of fraud, but of betrayal, hypocrisy, and reproach her for her long silence, when she had knowingly distanced herself from him, her closest relative? Almost as a reward for not saying anything bad, she expected family to give her a warm welcome.

'Do they often talk about me?' Fanny asked the servant. She leaned forward and stroked his knee to make him forgive her earlier rudeness.

'I already told you,' he grumbled, 'I don't know if it's you they're talking about when they mention this Fanny.'

'It must be me,' said Fanny after some thought, 'since my name is Fanny.'

'I'm not even sure,' continued the servant, 'that they were talking about Fanny, or even that the name Fanny has ever been mentioned here. So how do you expect me to know whether they were talking about you? Who are you anyway?'

'I'm Fanny!' shouted Fanny, irritated.

'Oh, Fanny, that doesn't mean a thing!' he retorted.

'I'm none other than Fanny,' she said stubbornly, 'and that would be enough for you if you were reading my story in a book.'

'No doubt,' he answered with conviction.

With that the servant became silent, his face calm and satisfied, as if he had solved the problem in his favour and there was nothing more to say.

'Ignoramus,' Fanny muttered under her breath.

'Since you're talking with your father,' said Eugene, 'I'll leave you alone and sleep for a while.'

'But this isn't my father, it's the servant!' Fanny laughed indignantly. Offended, the man turned his back on her and pretended to look out of the window. As for Eugene, he shrugged and yawned widely. In all honesty, it didn't matter to him which one here was Fanny's father. Noticing a couch in the corner of the kitchen, he went to lie down. His eyes closed, he snored gently, his half-open lips swollen and full.

# FIVE

## *In Front Of The Television*

Fanny joined her father in the living room where he had summoned her for afternoon tea, since that was the least he could do for his visiting daughter. In a dry tone, he sent back the servant with the brass buttons three times in a row after he brought dirty water or unsuitable cups or too little tea. Now that she found her father to be so difficult, so coldly authoritarian, although she did not remember ever having heard him give an order to anyone or even raise his voice before, Fanny suddenly felt the pride of a true daughter. She could not expect, though, that her father's prestige would reflect onto her, whose name people were not even sure of, or that the servant would serve her with as much humble respect when he had just seen her eat in the kitchen. Fanny was not at all sure that the servant with brass buttons really knew who she was, although he had called her Fanny just like everyone was supposed to now, but perhaps in his case it had just been a mistake, confusion, and perhaps he thought she was an unimportant guest. Oh, if only I'd kept the photograph! thought Fanny, keeping her head up and trying to hold onto her dignity.

Fanny's father switched on the television. It was time for an important football game. They both stayed in the expansive living room with huge furniture, under the seascape of a sinking steam-ship that decorated a whole wall-panel. Fanny's father followed the game attentively, exclaiming at times and automatically drew Fanny's attention to what was happening, forgetting who she was and her lack of interest in football. Surprised, Fanny watched his profile. He was a complete stranger to her! Everything around her seemed strange, enigmatic and embarrassing, as though it were clamouring, 'But where are *you* from?' in an outburst of vicious joy. Fanny wanted to assert her rights! She could not prove that she and her father were linked by a mysterious understanding, nor that they had lived happy moments together at the time when the photograph was taken, memories that escaped her today but that the photograph could have vouched for a tiny bit through its warm glow, the relaxed scene, the mother's loving smile. Who could attest today that her father had once pinned his greatest hopes on Fanny? Or, she suddenly wondered with alarm on discovering he had such a long nose, that she was really his daughter? She remembered nothing of their common past and could not reproach him for anything whatsoever.

Fanny's father drank his tea in silence. He turned up the sound on the television. The woman in her robe, carrying the little dog clasped against her cheek, appeared timidly at the door. 'Do you want...' she began, without seeming to see Fanny. Fanny's father did not even look at the woman but impatiently waved her away. Yawning, he stretched his whole body. Fanny boldly told him her plans, she begged him to confide in her all he knew about Aunt Leda, his sister-in-law. Had her father ever told her the shortest story, handed down from his own experience for her protection? Had he ever told her about their ancestors?

'It seems to me,' said Fanny, 'that you might have an idea of Leda's whereabouts.' Had her father ever helped her by sharing his experiences? Had he ever, as was his duty, instructed her in family history? Fanny cuddled up to him, watching intently for his answer. The look he gave her was so cold that she felt like she had committed some great indecency, as if, forgetting all morals, she had provocatively rubbed herself against a stranger. He was her father, though, living in this huge house which she had recognized immediately.

'I've always done what I should for you,' he said at last, bored. 'I've closely monitored your education. As for money, you've never gone short.' And with that he stared at the television screen, twisting to get away from Fanny without showing it. Fanny exclaimed that he had always acted in his own interest, for his own pleasure, for the approval of his colleagues; out of laziness he would not bother with the most necessary rituals unless he had something to gain from them. His sense of duty was never strong enough to make him do anything that did not directly benefit him, even if it would have put her on the path set out long ago and allowed her to gaze at her surroundings with clarity and confidence, giving her the choice of distancing herself, knowing fully why, saying 'This isn't the path I want to follow, nor the tradition I want to carry on.' Instead, she regretted what she had missed through fated blindness. She knew nothing of her ancestors, except that she desperately regretted not knowing them. And the family, stupid but justified, considered her impure, an intruder with limitless pretensions. It was her father's fault, because he did not care.

'What nonsense!' exclaimed her father, irritated. Just then his team, his very favourite team, made one mistake after another, then the screen became blurred and nothing was audible except indistinct shouts. Fanny's father slammed his cup down and turned towards her. What a strange face he suddenly had, now that Fanny couldn't remember anything precisely. 'If that's how it is, get out of here! You're nothing to me.' He was so angry he grabbed Fanny's arm to pull her up. With his other hand he pounded the television set. His furious, disorientated glance shifted from the screen to Fanny's face, and he abruptly let her go, saying, 'Get out of here,' then turned away, the matter closed. Fanny rushed out. She heard giggles and sighs coming from a corner of the hall.

'I thought you were sleeping,' she said to Eugene, whom she found there, his hair dishevelled, still smiling towards the door through which the woman with the little dog had, on seeing Fanny, discreetly withdrawn. 'Take my case. We're leaving.' Fanny pushed Eugene. Silent and tight-lipped, she roughly smoothed his hair down and wiped his face with her handkerchief. Eugene was sorry to have to leave so soon a house where he had been made so welcome. He really couldn't care less about finding Leda when it was so easy to enjoy life. His satisfied expression and his glowing cheeks disgusted Fanny. But she was scared of losing him! 'What about your roll-top desk?' she asked gravely. She did not wait for Eugene's reply because someone was calling her from the other end of the hall. It was the servant with the brass buttons. His finger against his lips, he gave her a crumpled old postcard, making all sorts of gestures to beg her not to say anything to the master of the house. According to him, this card had been sent by Leda some years ago from a little town where she had stayed, although he could not prove it since Leda had not written anything on the back, not even her signature.

'You don't even know exactly who I am,' whispered Fanny, 'if I'm really the person matching the name you've given me, or if you've ever heard this name uttered, and yet you're sure my Aunt Leda sent this blank card, this dirty scrap of cardboard! How do you explain that?'

'I don't know,' said the servant, shrugging his shoulders. 'I suppose it's my job.' Then he disappeared in the direction of the kitchen. Happy, Fanny examined the postcard — it showed a church in a sunlit square that reminded her of Grandmother's village with its narrow pavements, its few gloomy shops with grey roughcast fronts which, due to a lack of inventiveness and stinginess, were never brightened by even the smallest geranium — its bright pink would have appeared an odd cheeriness there. Fanny actually preferred things as they were, with not a single flower. She put the card away tenderly and rejoined Eugene who was going out.

'Aren't you going to say goodbye to your father?' asked Eugene, astonished.

'He threw me out,' said Fanny.

'Even so, it's still polite to tell him goodbye.'

'Do you know now who my father is?' asked Fanny. 'He's not the man with the brass buttons and white sideboards that you saw in the kitchen.' But Eugene was already thinking about something else and had a dreamy expression on his face. Fanny shouted, 'You dog! This is my father's house! Where did you think you were?' She viciously pinched his neck, while Eugene slid his tongue back and forth over his lips. His jacket was crumpled, his trousers shiny, strands of his hair, stiffened with gel, were standing up in peaks from his skull. Suddenly affectionate, Fanny took the suitcase from him and clasped his arm. She obligingly explained where they were heading next.

# SIX

## *The Bus Trip*

The road to the town where Aunt Leda had mailed the postcard was so long and the air where Fanny's father lived so hot, so heavy, and for a long time, advancing slowly in the red dust, they risked coming across so few places to drink or rest, that Fanny agreed to take the bus. Otherwise Eugene would not have gone with her. He was more independent now, quite full of himself, due to the hearty welcome he had received at Fanny's father's while she had been sent away without even a handshake. Seeing them greeted so differently, wouldn't people think that he was the son and Fanny the stranger? Now he freely declared that it did not really matter to him whether he became director or president of whatever and that he was not even sure he wanted Aunt Leda's help if they found her, because then he would have to be accountable to her, show himself to be serious and hard-working — in other words, deserve what she had done for him. He wanted nothing other than to live peacefully and to be lucky sometimes. He would have been perfectly happy to stay at Fanny's father's forever, eating and chatting in the coolness of the kitchen with the servant in the red jacket, enjoying himself with the gentle woman with the little dog, without a thought in his head.

'What about me?' said Fanny. 'Don't you love me a little?'

'I'd love you,' said Eugene, 'if you were less selfish and hadn't brought me along just to keep you company and carry your suitcase.'

Since Eugene's voice sounded serene and detached and since he appeared relaxed as he looked at their surroundings and even at her, Fanny preferred not to answer him. She made do with hugging his arm under hers, thinking that her cousin Eugene had a simple mind and mediocre ambitions. Wasn't he dreaming of taking her place at her father's house, making his niche in a corner of the kitchen? He would have become the son or the servant with equal satisfaction. In contrast, Fanny judged her father harshly, telling herself: It would have been better if he hadn't recognized me and had convinced me that I'd come to the wrong house!

They waited a long time on the side of the road for the bus. Eugene was sitting on the suitcase; Fanny was pacing up and down, unhappy without knowing why, her eyes dazzled by the bright colours of the village houses. Suddenly it occurred to her that someday Grandmother's house would surely be left to Eugene. She might get some pieces of furniture, old things full of secret sufferings which would fall into dust almost as soon as she had reconstructed their family history, making her think that she had not known how to conserve them. Eugene's rights took precedence over hers because his start in life had lacked neither conformity nor basic decency. He was loved by the family, who no more expected to know him than to be able to trust him. It was to him they would give the old house. 'Anyway, that's how it should be,' Fanny told herself, feeling completely distraught, gazing at her cousin's innocent face. The heat and boredom were dragging Eugene down. He had rolled his clingy jacket up; his tight sweater was stained with sweat and sausage grease. He was breathing heavily. Fanny thought she truly loved him, but even more she loved their link of kinship — which could not be denied, even though the day before it had worried her that their childhood memories had not coincided. She wondered vaguely if Eugene hadn't just told her some old dream.

An old bus stopped in front of them. They sat down in the only seats that were left, all the way in the back. Women with loud voices and strong necks, men smoking silently, chickens with their feet bound, shut into baskets or wedged into the hollows of deep laps, here and there a well-behaved child, and a strong, unknown smell — all these surprised Fanny and Eugene. Intimidated, they dared not speak. The language they heard was foreign to them. Inspired by the slightest shadow of a memory that she could not quite grasp, Fanny vaguely remembered having known this language long ago, or in a past life, and she suddenly felt a kind of nostalgia. But was it long ago or during another life? Was it really she or some character from one of the countless books she had read, with whom she identified without knowing it in the muddled memory of a similar situation? She felt on the verge of understanding what was being said, unsure if even that were real or imaginary, and she suffered from her confusion, thinking of Grandmother's village and of the poor, simple house at the end of the high street. She put her arm around Eugene's waist and whispered in his ear, 'Do you understand a word they're saying?'

'No, of course not,' said Eugene. 'How could I? It's not my language.' And he shrugged his shoulders, surprised at such a question. Suddenly, a swarm of women surrounded them. For a little while they had been turning towards Fanny, examining her with curiosity, laughing among themselves and looking at her, their eyes perplexed. They had risen and were approaching now to touch her. They were clutching at Fanny's arm and shoulder when a jolt almost hurled them to the ground. They cheerfully asked questions. Fanny heard her father's name. The women's faces were friendly and attentive. From their shimmering skirts arose indefinable scents as if to intoxicate her. Did they want to let her know that they knew her father and who she was? Fanny became afraid and huddled against Eugene. If these women, grasping at her with a troubling freedom, knew Fanny, it was because she had something to do with this place, yet she had forgotten it — she thought she had never before come to her father's house, the prettiest in the village, yet she had headed towards it without hesitation, guided by intuition.

The women were surprised when Fanny did not answer as they patiently kept on with questions in their language which was curiously laden with mysteries as familiar as fragments of dreams. Half-collapsed onto Eugene, Fanny stiffened. She saw leaning towards her the wide-eyed faces of an alien world, friendly, wanting to draw her in and make her their own with a great maternal kindness. Eugene grumbled that he felt smothered. At last, Fanny managed to look straight ahead with so much coldness that one by one the women moved away, disappointed. From among the folds of their clothing, their numerous adornments, Fanny thought she heard cruel murmurings. Didn't her father have a woman just like these under his roof, the one Eugene had dragged into a corner, who perhaps would have eagerly seized Fanny and pushed her to betray the family and Grandmother's dear village? Fanny had made a mistake in coming to see her father because, with the exception of the servant with the shiny buttons, he had surrounded himself with strangers who in all truth were hostile towards Fanny and perhaps, like these women, wanted to win Fanny over, capture her even. As she was, she was hated everywhere! 'I made a narrow escape,' she murmured to Eugene. And she added, in a rush of love, 'I can trust in you. We're equals.'

As she was looking out of the window, the countryside changed abruptly. It was raining on the slate rooves, on the muddy road, in the little enclosed gardens. The filling stations were already lit up. From time to time large, vague slums of trailers with closed doors stretched out before them, or never-ending motorcar graveyards, and Eugene would name some splendid carcass or other. As they entered towns, illuminated supermarkets, which were announced several times in giant letters on posters spread with feasts, delighted Fanny, who smiled gently on recognizing everything. Little by little the bus emptied, they were soon alone. Fanny pressed her forehead to the window, next to Eugene's. Now she congratulated herself for having been thrown out by her father like an intruder. But the coldness of the family and of Grandmother's village, the meanness of the dogs had disorientated her at first and filled her with despair! Yet she understood now — it was because she was not complete.

36

Dusk was falling. The driver turned on the radio and a song that Eugene liked muffled the sound of the rain. Fanny outlined her intentions to her cousin.

'You know, there's one thing I don't doubt — I won't stop until I've found Leda, our aunt. Nothing else matters unless it serves that goal, that duty. And, you know, sometimes I think I was born to look for Leda, so all my little wrongdoings are justified in advance. Only, I still have some questions. Since no one ordered me to do it, could I be making a mistake in searching for Leda? Wasn't it fate that my parents neglected to invite Leda long ago? Wasn't it in the true scheme of things for Fanny to be outside of this family's history? Couldn't it even be for my own good — no one suspecting it, but each acting as he was meant to — that Leda was absent? Am I not in the process of disturbing what is most dear to me, the great established order and tradition, by believing that people messed it up? You see, all these questions float around in my head. Because if I'm following the wrong track in all this, I'm lost. Yes, Eugene, if I'm wrong, there will be nothing left for me to do but die. What if Leda herself causes my downfall? What if she turns out to be a huge, terrible disappointment? Will she really be my aunt? Will I be able to tell for sure? Because now I'm nobody except the person called Fanny searching for Aunt Leda.'

'If you go far from me, it won't be happily...,' hummed Eugene along with the driver who was swaying to the music. Eugene's face bore an expression of enraptured concentration. At the chorus, which the singer screeched in a high-pitched voice, he could not help smiling, he was enjoying himself so much.

# SEVEN

## *The Bus Trip (continued)*

On the outskirts of a village, the driver stopped and Aunt Colette got on the bus. She was carrying a shopping bag full of vegetables and wore the blue-sequined dress which Fanny remembered her wearing for the birthday party. The rain made the dress shine all the more — it was, Fanny noticed, lightly printed with crescent moons. Aunt Colette sat up front. 'She hasn't seen us,' whispered Fanny.

'It's me she's here for,' said Eugene, proudly. 'It doesn't matter where I am, she doesn't let me out of her sight.'

'I'm telling you, she hasn't seen us,' insisted Fanny.

Aunt Colette's wide shoulders were rocking under the thin material of the dress. You could guess the colour of her soft skin, where Eugene still cradled himself sometimes when he was worried about the future. Fanny wondered anxiously what Aunt Colette was doing in this lost corner of the world. She was carrying vegetables as if returning from the market. From her shopping bag, which she had placed in the aisle, protruded three mackerel heads, dripping with blood.

Fanny wiped the misted window and saw Grandmother's village. They were just passing the church, which looked like no other since it had been coated right up to the steeple with a layer of cement so it would be sure to last several more centuries.

'Here we are, back at Grandmother's!' whispered Fanny, astonished.

'Mum hasn't gone home then,' remarked Eugene, calmly.

'But this isn't the way we're supposed to go!' cried out Fanny.

Up front, Aunt Colette, as if deaf, did not turn around, did not even move her head. She was perfectly immobile in her best dress which she steadfastly lengthened or shortened each year according to fashion and less out of vanity than out of respect for social rules. She did not seem to be cold even though she was dripping wet.

At the next stop, not far from Grandmother's, she got out into the rain and disappeared quickly down a little street — she was running, slipping away like a shadow.

'Mum must hope I'm coming back,' said Eugene, suddenly sad. 'That's no doubt why she's stayed on at Grandmother's.' He added with a sigh, 'What if we said hello to them?'

'That's impossible,' said Fanny. 'We can't see them again before we find what we're looking for. Just think that you'll come back a manager or a head clerk, at least a foreman, whereas until now you haven't even been able to hold down a plain old employee's position.'

Eugene scowled. Fanny leaned on him and stretched her legs across the aisle. She eagerly gazed at the dreary shop fronts, at each gate, every face where she thought she perceived the family traits which she wanted her own to have, even if the face were reddened and impassive. She no longer found it odd that the bus was crossing Grandmother's own village when she had thought they were going in the opposite direction. But contemplating Grandmother's imminent death, she anxiously wondered if it would even be possible for her to enter the village when Grandmother was no longer there. Grandmother's unquestionable authority had protected her for a long time; her presence as they both walked in the streets had always kept Fanny from suspicious questionings. When Grandmother was gone, how would Fanny prove that she had been her granddaughter and had the right to claim to be from the village, her only home? She wasn't in any of the photographs displayed in Grandmother's room! People would laugh in her face when she declared that she had been born here, that she knew better than anyone the narrowest alley, each crevice in a wall, and that the village appeared in her dreams with supernatural accuracy.

Fanny got up, approached the driver and asked him if he was really driving them towards the market town from where Aunt Leda had sent the postcard a few years previously. He nodded as he applied the brake. 'What's more, here we are!'

They were only a few minutes from the village and could see the steeple just ahead.

# EIGHT
## A Village

Neither Eugene nor Fanny knew this little town. The bus had stopped on the church square, which Fanny recognized from the postcard. She felt moved by it, as if it were glaring proof of Aunt Leda's existence and of the deep necessity of her trip, whatever its outcome. She shook Eugene who sat in sulky silence, and ignoring his grunts, rubbed his face with her handkerchief. 'What filth!' she cried, joyfully. Then she could not help planting a big kiss on his glowing pink, rather soft mouth. Eugene indifferently let her, his thumbs crooked in the pockets of his fitted jacket. Night was falling; the rain had stopped but Eugene was shivering. He wanted to eat at once. Fanny took advantage of his distraction to kiss him again, and Eugene did not even seem to notice. His lips were so soft, puffed like little cushions, that Fanny could have kissed them like this thousands of times without tiring! In a giddy spell, she suddenly envisioned herself mysteriously attached to Eugene, her own lips glued to his indifferent ones. In her lack of restraint, she had forgotten Aunt Leda, even her name, despite the fact that she had become Fanny's sole reason for living. She felt a momentary disgust, detached herself from Eugene and, with her toe, kicked the suitcase over to him. He obediently picked it up and they turned down the first street they came to.

What Fanny had thought to be a large market town turned out to be a village hardly any bigger than Grandmother's and similar to it in almost every respect. In its main street, as night fell, more and more lorries passed, so heavy and so fast that their turbulence made Eugene and Fanny stumble, and they huddled against the walls which were sometimes so long that they seemed to be walking down a corridor, dazed by the roar of the lorries. The shops had already closed and Eugene was in despair. His longing for a slice of liver paté in a hunk of bread became so violent that tears sprang to his eyes. He even lost his temper and scolded Fanny for never thinking about provisions and for keeping the money — which was both of theirs, since he had entrusted Aunt Colette's roll of bills to her — in a secret place unknown to him. Fanny did her best to calm him with gentle words and vague promises. Under the pretext of soothing him, she stopped to kiss him full on the mouth, lustfully. Then she became angry with herself, because how would she ever get very far in her search for Aunt Leda if Eugene's lips stopped her at every step? What if she gave in to her desire to hole up with Eugene in some cramped hideout, where, without talking to him, without seeing his eyes, she would be happy just clinging to his body, which was as soft as a rag doll? Would she ever reach her goal? Could she even hope to find at last the true existence that she so wanted, having read the detailed story in every book and magazine she had glanced through, when someone like Eugene was capable of immobilizing her through the sole attraction of spineless indifference and tender, passive lips? Aunt Leda was perhaps far away, so far that it would take all Fanny's energy to find her and recognize her! Just as importantly, Fanny had to make Aunt Leda recognize *her* too, which could turn out to be difficult, if not impossible, in which case she would have nothing left to do but disappear.

Following the main street, they soon came to the end of the village where the line of street lamps ended. They could already hear the noise of shutters being slammed shut for the night and sometimes, beneath a window, the muddled sound of harmonious voices which they guessed, after a moment of uncertainty, came from a television set. A few dogs howled at the passing of a vehicle that was so heavy it shook the ground. Since a child was walking towards them and they still had not passed anyone, Fanny leapt in front of him, grabbed his thin shoulder and bent down so her eyes were directly level with his. In her joy at getting her hands on a villager, however puny, however weak, she almost shouted and placed her hand heavily on him as if begging him not to disappoint her. 'Have you heard anyone talk about Leda, my aunt?' At the same time, Eugene asked in a high-pitched voice, 'Do you know a place to eat around here?' Fanny repeated her question, shaking the boy a little to make certain he understood, and Eugene immediately copied her in an even shriller tone. It suddenly occurred to Fanny, as Eugene placed an authoritative hand on the boy's other shoulder, that without even realizing it Eugene could become her most dangerous enemy unless she put him in his place, made him walk behind her and looked at him as little as possible so she would even forget his features. Because she was now under the impression that Eugene's pink flesh was relentlessly hounding her and might cause her downfall, just like his whinings and his voracious appetite. Yet he was as indispensable to her as her own shadow! Calmly, the boy answered that all Fanny had to do was follow him — he was going precisely to the place where someone called Leda was often mentioned, and she might well be the one Fanny was looking for. Then he turned to Eugene and assured him that there would be room for him at the table there. He opened wide the shopping bag on his arm — a dozen shiny eggs that he was bringing for an omelette for dinner.

'Let's go!' exclaimed Eugene.

'Yes, let's go,' said Fanny firmly, not wanting Eugene to imagine he had made the decision, and she pushed the boy in front of her in the direction of the village, but he skipped off to the left down the dark road towards the countryside from where arose the roar of continual traffic, as though it were its true cry, as natural as the clamour of wheat in the fields. The boy advanced nimbly, closely followed by Fanny. She felt Eugene's breath in her hair and feared that if she slowed down he would take the opportunity to pass her, because he was asking questions the child could not hear, about the meal and about the bed he might be offered at the same place. Eugene was exhausted and cursed Fanny. He deliberately harassed her — treading on the heel of her shoe, or throwing himself against her to make her stumble, claiming with a chuckle that he had tripped. Fanny angrily pushed him away — she almost hated him now that she had her back to him and nothing reminded her that it was Eugene, her cousin whom she had once dreamt she might marry, not realizing then that at Grandmother's very house, everyone, right down to the soulless dogs, would one day refuse to let her in. 'Yet I walked those dogs and cared for them so many times!' thought Fanny. But since Uncle George had slammed the door in her face, maybe the dogs had done nothing but obey the family's tacit orders. The family were so certain they should exclude Fanny that they had even managed to forget her existence, her name, and the respect that she had always shown, knowing the history of each one of them better than the very person concerned. Yet she felt such blind affection for the family!

They passed a pigsty. Deafened for a long time by the gruntings of the startled beasts, they crossed a pea-field, and another field that would have been a shortcut except that Eugene, hindered by the suitcase, got tangled up in the high stalks and they had to stop to disentangle him. He took advantage of his lamentable situation to scold Fanny for not even letting him say hello to his mother on the bus. He reminded her that she had left her own father's house without saying goodbye to him, a thoughtlessness that deeply disgusted Eugene, whether Fanny's father was the man with brass buttons or the other one. Furious, Fanny pinched Eugene's waist, but he only sniggered at her defiantly. She would have continued to rough him up but for the thought that, in spite of everything, she could not run the risk of losing him in her tracks — cousin Eugene, on her arm, represented her surest tie with the family.

# NINE

## *The Pastis*

They followed the boy into a yard scattered here and there with piles of garbage, scrap metal and broken toys, which the child dodged through despite the darkness, holding his eggs up high. From the carcass of a car half-buried in the mud, a big yellow dog jumped, snarling. There were several rabbits in a sorry-looking, lopsided hutch which stunk so strongly of urine that Fanny held her nose. The child proudly exclaimed, 'This is our place!' Then he jumped the few steps to the house and suddenly seemed so offhand that Eugene and Fanny felt forgotten. Hadn't they themselves made the boy appear, as if by magic? They had clutched the boy's shoulder as if for their common good, shouting in his ear without thinking of his discomfort.

A little angry, they too entered the poorly constructed house. It was made of prefabricated walls on a foundation of rough concrete blocks. A fat woman was shuffling towards them. In the harsh light from the ceiling bulb, she seemed so disproportionately wide, and her bare arms extending from her flowered blouse so thick, that Fanny shrunk back, thinking it was Aunt Colette who had set a trap for her. She looked for the boy, but he had disappeared among the numerous children who were running, jumping, or simply sniggering in a corner of the room. They were shoving one another and giving Fanny wicked looks as they skirted the wall — hands behind their backs, chests thrown out with vile impertinence — or rolled on the hideous tiled floor, their limbs stretched as if on a soft lawn, distastefully squealing with delight. The boy could be any of these excited brats, so numerous and so fidgety that you could not look anywhere without your eyes alighting on one. And you were never sure whether the child you had observed for a few seconds had not been replaced without your noticing by an identical child, whose sex was just as indefinable, who shouted, giggled or whined in the same tone as the first. All these children no doubt appeared in the dozens of photographs pinned all over the papered walls.

'There were only twelve eggs!' muttered Eugene despondently. But Fanny couldn't care less about the omelette and thought only of Aunt Leda. She confidently approached the woman, poked her finger at the enormous, ill-defined bosom and said with determination, 'Now, missus, tell me please where Leda, my aunt, went. Unless,' she added with sudden hope, mixed with fear, 'she's still here?'

43

'As to that, no,' said the woman. She calmly shrugged her shoulders then turned her slow body towards the kitchen, shouting through the racket for someone to bring the eggs. Without looking at the child or losing her good-natured expression, she shook her leg to loosen a toddler who was clinging to it and kindly left him her old slipper. She was perfectly serene, young still. Two kids, doubled over with laughter, pretended to catch the long brown pony tail which hung to her waist, but Eugene dashed forward and swatted them. The prospect of a meagre dinner when he was dying of hunger produced in him an irritable, trembling anger. They were standing in the doorway and had not noticed a man sitting in the back of the room at one end of a table which was covered with miscellaneous objects. He cleared his throat to make his presence known and offered them a drink. He was short and slight, taking Fanny aback a little — her own father had always had a broad chest and hard muscles.

The man ceremoniously served four drinks. Eugene and Fanny sat down, and Fanny put Aunt Leda's postcard on the table. It showed the church square and its parched cemetery. Before she could stop him, and before the man had even leaned forward to look at the postcard, a child sprang up like an evil spirit from under the table, grabbed the postcard with a burst of laughter and scrambled away with it, followed by a merry little troupe, which quickly gathered around him and hid him from sight. Fanny could not suppress a cry of rage. But she did not move because the man found it hilarious, and his wife, who had returned from the kitchen, laughed too, carrying Eugene away with her so he too burst out laughing, banging his fist lightly on the table. Fanny was agreeably drawn into the harmonious atmosphere of the little house. She smiled and downed her drink in one gulp. Her cousin Eugene and the man, whose eyes were bloodshot, began telling dirty stories which greatly amused the woman even though her husband was talking about his youth and his success with women. Eugene bragged, all the while tugging at his tight-fitting sweater. Fanny regularly caressed him attentively or made dry remarks to make it look as if Eugene belonged to her. He didn't care whether she cuddled him or ignored him, his only thought for the moment was to impress the couple with tales of his exploits. He smoothed his chest and his sticky hair, wriggled in his excitement, and threw in obscene language with affected naturalness.

The man poured four more drinks and the woman opened a packet of potato crisps. She flung a few generous handfuls to the children, who pounced on them so noisily the adults could not hear one another any more and the children had to be threatened with the strap — 'I'm going to get out my little friend!' said the woman — or kicks to their

44

behinds. Hardened and insolent, the older ones just sniggered. They seemed to be made of thick leather, insensitive to knocks or falls, as if they had endured so much that the thought of violence tantalized them — across their pointed little faces there sometimes slid a wicked expression of sly desire. They skirted the walls without taking their eyes off the table, from where the danger might come. But the children were forgotten, the adults were quietly enjoying their aperitif, confiding more and more intimately as the glasses emptied. Fanny would not give up but kept returning to the subject of Leda. Finally, with a deep sigh, the woman said they had indeed known Leda some years previously when she had lived here for a while, having nowhere else to go. In the next room they had a photograph of Leda reading. Fanny jumped with joy and wanted to run to get it. The woman added that Leda was so fat then that fitting all of her into a photograph had been difficult, and Fanny exclaimed, astonished, 'I was told she was as thin as Mother!' But the man vigorously contradicted Fanny. He had caught a glimpse, purely by chance, of one of Leda's breasts, he admitted subtly, his face reddening. Leaning eagerly towards him, Fanny asked what her Aunt Leda's breast was like. The man could not find the words to describe it, so he raised his hands to caress an invisible form and smiled and winked at Eugene, but Eugene, being Leda's nephew, looked away. Yet Fanny felt a sharp pleasure in knowing that the man had seen Aunt Leda's breast and had perhaps even touched it, thus proving better than anyone the physical reality of Aunt Leda. Even Grandmother, when Fanny had left her, had shamefully admitted doubting Leda's existence at times, although in her dreams she heard her bang urgently against the shutters.

Under the pretext of going to look at the photograph, Fanny arranged to be alone with the man at the end of the hallway leading to the bedroom. During this time Eugene was setting the table, and the woman was breaking the eggs. With her voice lowered and an encouraging smile on her lips, Fanny pressed the man to tell her everything he could about Leda's unknown body. She made a few remarks to refresh his memory and leaned towards him so her own body was clearly lit by the bare light bulb dangling on a long wire from the ceiling. Her heart beat rapidly because she felt strongly that this puny man had been nearer to Leda than he had dared to admit in front of his wife. Perhaps he had even pinned Leda against this very wall, covered with old, flowered paper. Perhaps he had buried his fingers and his burning face into Aunt Leda's unimaginable flesh. The mystery surrounding Aunt Leda so obsessed Fanny she became dizzy.

Because he had been drinking, the man chattered incoherently. He reached his hand towards Fanny, who straightened up and unhappily

45

stepped aside. 'I can't get anything out of you,' she grumbled. He had been taken in by her accommodating manner and was shocked. He shouted out that he was just a railroad man and she a damn slut, leaning over him like that only to move away as soon as he approached her. He became angry and confused. Fanny stamped her foot, then rushed into the bedroom and locked the door. She muttered insults against the man and all the inhabitants of the house who had rubbed shoulders with Aunt Leda but were incapable of telling anything about her — the simplest words escaped them. She, Fanny, only asked for a few precise words to describe Aunt Leda! With growing jealousy, she thought of the man. What had he held between his big, clumsy hands? How had he looked at Leda, her back to the wall, which might have been decorated with a floral pattern, or with hunting scenes like in the living room? Clenching her fists, Fanny vowed to force Eugene to join her, even if he thought the family had been right to throw her out like a stinking corpse.

Noticing that they had left her alone, she examined the bedroom, furnished simply with a bed with an orange chenille spread, two green plastic stools and matching night stands. In the middle of the bed was a big carnival doll with its dress spread out, perhaps giving the room a bit of character in the woman's eyes. Fanny opened a drawer and took out a framed picture where she could only see a blurred grey mass. At the bottom she read the name Leda. She could not help exclaiming, 'So this is my aunt!' She squinted in an attempt to make out her aunt's features or at least the silhouette of this grey form spread over a whitish background, until she realized that some kind of magazine was opened out, hiding Aunt Leda's head and shoulders, so that she could just barely make out her fingers, the hem of her skirt and a lock of hair that sprouted over the top. Could it be that Aunt Leda was in the habit of reading the same magazines as Fanny, about princesses and movie stars? A little disappointed but very excited, Fanny pulled the photograph from its frame, folded it and slipped it into her pocket. Back in the living room, she sat next to Eugene at the table where the older children had taken seats and were stuffing themselves with omelette and bread, while the younger children were eating either seated on the floor or sprawled on a couch facing the television. Bent over his plate, Eugene was silently wolfing down huge mouthfuls and ignored Fanny as though her conduct towards the scrawny-necked man had offended him personally — or perhaps her cousin Eugene, who loved to chat and laugh loudly, was angry with her because their host was now sullenly, grudgingly silent, feigning disinterest, yet rather scornful towards them. With a smile the woman served Fanny her share of the omelette. Her ponytail bobbed with such liveliness on her back that Fanny moved away from Eugene towards the woman, whose tired, strained face beamed with limitless kindness and bore the same quiet attentiveness as during her husband's bawdy stories. Sometimes an expression indicating her complete awareness of the unavoidable end fleetingly crossed her face, quite abruptly, as if it had suddenly occurred to her that this miserable existence would finish, just as it had begun, in poverty and hardship. Fanny saw, though, that the woman summoned up enough indifference to serve the omelette carefully, scrape out the frying pan, mysteriously delight in who knows what, cuddle the children, and give those who needed settling down a few good taps with her slipper. But since that action, like everything else, was futile, in view of the poor life she was forced to lead and the violence she had suffered, and which showed in the lines of her face, she looked about her sadly and resignedly, said to her husband, her gaze distant, 'What do you expect...,' and let herself drop into a chair, listlessly scratching her calf, in sudden hopelessness.

# TEN

## *A Dream*

After the omelette, the children gulped down big bowls of milky coffee, then the woman signalled to Fanny to follow her into the bedroom. They sat side-by-side on the bed, in front of the dusty carnival doll. The woman put her arms around Fanny and pressed her mouth to her ear. She sighed because she had to admit something she would have preferred to keep secret. In a high-pitched voice that irritated Fanny's ear, the woman told her that having dreamt of Leda only last night, she felt obliged to recount this dream — a number of clues might have slipped in which Fanny would easily recognize and which might help her follow Leda.

'Hurry,' said Fanny, full of sudden hope, 'I'll find what I need!'

So the woman leaned towards one of the night stands and took out a stained piece of paper torn from a notebook where she had scribbled down the outline of her dream that very morning, worrying that she would forget. 'But how did you know that I existed and that you would meet me?' Fanny asked, astonished.

'I really thought it my duty to know it,' the woman quietly replied, filling Fanny with joy. She no longer thought of the ache the woman's voice caused her eardrum as her damp lips tickled Fanny's ear and her soft skin irritated and squashed down the blond hairs in it. Interrupting herself frequently to glance perplexed at her paper and struggling to decipher her own handwriting, the woman told her dream. She admitted that in this dream she had been Leda. She had possessed neither Leda's features nor her body, yet she knew with deep certainty that she was Leda, living in the village M. not far away and, apart from that, leading just the same life as here, where she took care of children and household duties. But, she said, people called her Leda without her feeling surprised, and she had Leda's character, but without its changing her.

'And the same husband too?' asked Fanny with distaste. The woman said yes, and Fanny, disgusted, stared at her reproachfully. What right did this woman have to insult her aunt, burdening her with a husband such as her own, without embarrassment and — a half-smile on her lips, her voice becoming more insistent — even seeming to find amusement in it?

Fanny sighed. The woman's delicately perfumed perspiration was dripping from her neck onto Fanny's, but since she was rendering her a great service Fanny decided to excuse it. The end of the dream, several lines more, was illegible. Leaning over the paper together, they guessed the shape of a letter or word, but the woman immediately rejected every suggestion with an ostentatious and proud gesture that irritated Fanny all the more because her hostess insisted she did not remember in the slightest what she had dreamt then written. She delighted in exclaiming in an overwhelmed voice, tapping on the already soiled paper, 'All the same, everything is there! The truth really is there!'

Finally, apologizing for her carelessness, she carefully put away the paper as if it had somehow appreciated in value, though it was really of no further use.

'Where is the village M.? I've never heard of it,' said Fanny as she got up.

It was, however, quite nearby, the woman asserted, and it was strange that Fanny, who claimed to be from these parts, did not know it.

'Well, no,' said Fanny defiantly, 'I don't know it!' Then, thinking she saw a glimmer of mistrust cross the woman's eyes, all her pride deserted her at once. She sat down and squeezed up against the woman, who sat stiffly, staring straight ahead. Fanny almost begged the woman not to doubt her intentions just because of deceptive appearances and meaningless contradictions, when all she knew, all she loved from the bottom of her heart, was right here in this very region. What more could she say since the family was relentlessly determined to misjudge her? How could she prove her good will towards the family when they refused to listen to her, fearing trouble because of her unusual presence and the uncertain circumstances surrounding her birth? It made no difference that she was calm, humble, respectful, or that she was more worthy of trust and affection than her cousin Eugene, who carelessly blasphemed and had already called Grandmother — Fanny trembled with shame and sadness at the thought — an old witch.

'Nevertheless,' insisted the woman, 'if you've never heard anyone mention the village M., which is known to everyone here, there's really something strange going on.'

Eugene must know this village, thought Fanny with ferocious jealousy, in spite of his indifference and his sniggering. Yet no one has even mentioned its name in front of me! She would end up not even believing herself! When Grandmother died, the troubled family would tactfully look away and let the dogs devour Fanny! To cure her of her intolerable pretensions!

49

# ELEVEN
## *Eugene Runs Away*

At nightfall Fanny and Eugene were kindly led into a children's bedroom. Two brats were put out of a small, squeaky bed that was given to them with apologies for having nothing better to offer. They bunched up in it, half-dressed because ten or so of the biggest brats were sleeping in the room, watching them with curious eyes in the light of the full moon, and they dared not remove all their clothes in spite of Fanny's desire to do so. The children were whispering and laughing quietly. One of them made a hooting sound that was softly echoed by ten excited little voices. Then they played a farting game. Eugene thundered, 'For God's sake, if I have to get up...!'

'It's useless,' murmured Fanny, 'we'll have to put up with them until they fall asleep.' She in turn felt overcome by a joyful excitement, a fever that made her hot. As if to stop Eugene from getting out of bed or because she was uncomfortable pinned on the edge, she wrapped her arms and legs around him, blinding him with her hair, then got him by the ears and, making the whole bed creak, slid onto her cousin's stomach, where she stayed flattened like a toad, her body heavy and her cheek pushed so hard against Eugene's lips that he could neither speak nor breathe. 'Eugene, I love you,' said Fanny, happily, so glad to hold her cousin in her arms that she did not think of the discomfort that he doubtless felt. She went as far as to tell herself that she could have spent the rest of her life like this. Carried away, she gently pressed harder against Eugene's flabby body, pulling at his ears and nibbling his neck, inconsiderately. How she loved him! She felt like she was embracing Aunt Colette's vast flesh, Grandmother's cold skeleton, even the carcass of the rough, old dogs! How she loved them, all of them! A violent slap on her back took her breath away. Eugene had disentangled his fists and was furiously hitting her. She set her jaw and rubbed herself against him until she hurt. Eugene arched his back, and they both fell entwined into the space between the bed and the wall. Immediately, the kids jumped out of their bed and gathered noisily around them, without getting too near. Ten pyjama-clad silhouettes, as nimble and slight as puffs of wind, impalpable yet clearly outlined, danced slowly, unreal figures, strangely cautious. Eugene kept hitting out, trying in vain to bite Fanny's cheek, which was still stuffed in his mouth. At last, not because of the pain, to which she was indifferent, but because her joy had diminished and the intoxicating certainty of holding Eugene — the whole family and the dogs and even those dead long ago — was also fading, Fanny jumped up to chase the children away, then got back into bed. Eugene silently hauled himself up soon after. She wanted to hug him, but he pushed her away with disgust, and Fanny fell asleep.

In the morning the window was banging.

Eugene had run away across the pea fields, taking with him the money that had been locked in the suitcase. Fanny's head spun with despair. Forgetting her shoes, she straddled the window and ran all over the fields, shouting 'Eugene, come back! Have you forgotten everything? Eugene!' She stumbled, her body shaken, and jumped from row to row — from a distance she looked joyful. The children laughed to see her prancing about so strangely! Fanny cried all day long, then got angry, only to start sobbing again. Her sorrow at having lost Eugene was made worse by the absurdity of a companionless voyage — she did not remember ever having read of such a thing being done, in the real or imaginary past.

# TWELVE
## *The Village M.*

Although Fanny's hosts had admitted that they struggled alone to feed and educate their numerous brood with a little less than was needed and without any luxuries, they insisted on giving her money for her trip to the village M. where the woman had dreamt Leda lived and where Fanny hoped to get news of her aunt, if not to find her in person. She hugged everyone, then left on foot, carrying her suitcase. She still felt bouts of grief when she thought of Eugene's silky lips or her own unseemly solitude, or when she stopped to massage her hand, which ached from the handle of the suitcase. She remembered with what touching obedience Eugene had always taken charge of the suitcase, despite his laziness. What had she done to make him run away like that? She had stretched herself out on him and handled him a little roughly, but, being her cousin, couldn't he feel how much, suddenly, she loved him, and the whole family? How she wanted to mix her imperfect flesh, her troubled blood with his? How she, snuggled against him, had wanted to become Eugene himself, to have for parents Uncle George and Aunt Colette, whom no one ever said anything about except that they were 'fine people'! To become perhaps one of the faithful dogs...

Fanny sat down crying on a milestone. In a little mirror that she had, she looked at herself with disgust, even though she was pretty, as people had often told her — but no one in the family, since for them Fanny's face was nothing other than strange. The cold made her start walking again, and she worried about Eugene. Had he bundled up enough? Now she felt sorry for him for not knowing the necessity of the search for Leda, of sticking to that at all costs, for not having known to set his mind on that one goal, which at least swept away the temptation of depression. Eugene had dreamt of a desk the size of a bed, of respectful employees whom he would have treated with kindness, of pink hills floating on the clouds! Poor, poor Eugene, thought Fanny angrily.

Holding her collar with one hand, she stepped briskly towards the edge of the road. With desolate reverence the wind whistled across the dismal expanse of wheat fields, beet fields and monotonous fields of corn, across the dismal flatness of unending pea fields and huge, monotonous fields of lonely sunflowers. Fanny feared rain, from which no tree, not a single copse would have protected her. But she already saw the cemetery of the village M., separated from the village Fanny had just left by a strip of road and surely hardly any further from Grandmother's village, which Fanny had only left a few days previously, thinking she was leaving it far behind her. She hurried happily on with the hope of Leda. She recalled the woman's dream with such colourful accuracy and so many details that the woman herself had been incapable of giving her, that it now vaguely seemed her own dream, fallen somehow into the hands of a stranger. In this dream Fanny *was* Leda! I'll question each inhabitant, Fanny told herself, and perhaps it will turn out that one of them is Aunt Leda or knew her well. I know so little about Leda, and people have told me such different things about her that Leda could, after all, just as well be a man or anything else. What do I know about Aunt Leda? Where have I ever seen her face? Nothing's certain! Only this, a mistake was made regarding her when I was born, a mistake that piled misfortune on my poor head.

The sky grew heavy; now huge drops were falling. The deserted road glistened and Fanny ran forward clumsily. In front of the cemetery enclosed in high, cemented walls, was a new housing estate where all the houses had grey shutters and brown tile rooves. In their narrow forecourt was a kennel, and despite the rain, nasty little dogs rushed out and howled for a long time as Fanny passed.

The street was empty. The walls were grey roughcast, just like in Grandmother's village. The windows, with carefully closed opaque curtains, had no sills. The pavement was so narrow that Fanny had to hold her suitcase in front of her with both hands. Also, just as in Grandmother's village, the road cutting across the church square had prevented the installation of benches or the planting of a tree at the foot of which people would have met. Oh, Fanny thought contentedly, how well I know all this, how familiar everything is! She entered the café opposite the church — the Coq Hardi, where, according to its sign, one could eat as well as drink. There was no one in the room. Fanny shook off the rain, making her chair creak, she felt a fleeting pang of despair as she thought of Eugene, then despised him.

A girl arrived, dragging her feet. 'My name is Fanny,' said Fanny, amiably, 'and I would like two fried eggs, a sausage and some beer please.' A scowl settled on the girl's face. She had not bothered to come to Fanny's table when she first saw her, and now she sighed loudly as she rubbed the counter with the corner of her apron. She shook her lifeless hair with an air of intense weariness, and her whole being, a little heavy, a little flabby — the flesh on her arms and her hips wobbling gently — suddenly seemed burdened with such a weight that

Fanny blushed, worried that she might be the cause of it. But the girl waved vaguely, shrugged her shoulders and headed towards the kitchen. The hem of her ugly skirt hung down behind her. I'm bothering her, Fanny humbly told herself, but why? Oh, I've got to make friends here, so everyone will open their door to me. I'll learn how to convince them I'm from around here. One day they'll say to me with a smile, 'Here is your Aunt Leda!' At this idea, Fanny could not help closing her eyes with happiness, but she wondered, with a perplexed shiver: then who will I be, with Aunt Leda at my side? What will the family do? What if they refuse to acknowledge Leda? What if the dogs throw themselves growling at the gate when Leda arrives? Fanny shuddered and quickly chased away this thought.

Fanny slid her suitcase under the table, then made herself adopt a casual expression so no one would notice her fears, which would hardly be in keeping with her insistence that she was practically at home here, in this village which so resembled Grandmother's.

What makes me doubt I belong? Is it because people mysteriously persist in convincing me that I can never be anything but an outsider around here? Is that what alarms me, or is it that I'm not completely sure that I'm getting anywhere and it makes people suspicious? Oh, I don't have any idea. I have so much vested in this that I may be blind at times. If all these villages make it clear that I positively cannot belong, whatever proofs I produce, whatever knowledge I show of everything that happens, for the simple reason that it just can't be, well, I'll never be from anywhere. Besides, if I don't find Aunt Leda it's useless for me to return to Grandmother's village, the family will just triumphantly insist they were right.

Fanny glanced around the room, which was darkened by the rain. It was early afternoon and as dark as sunset without it being at all depressing, just as in Grandmother's village where a heavy greyness seemed to make people look down at the rough, plain ground. From the low, dirty ceiling hung strips of fly paper. The neon lights were getting dirty. An old forgotten garland rustled gently in a current of air. The pale green walls were splattered with yellowish stains at the level of the tables, which were covered with oilcloths patterned with faded blue and white squares. Through the narrow windows, all one could see was one side of the church on the other side of the road — totally without charm. A persistent odour of burnt grease, dark tobacco and dirty dogs poisoned the air and almost made Fanny faint. She had never stayed in the café-bar in Grandmother's village, Georgette's Place, as long as in this one, the Coq Hardi, where she had already been waiting for half an hour.

When the waitress came back, Fanny had dozed off. The girl woke her by kicking her chair and slammed down a mug of beer, and two fried eggs and a frankfurter on a chipped plate. Fanny thanked her excessively, held out her hands to help, then shrank back, looking down, fearful of getting in the way.

# THIRTEEN

## *Lucette*

This heavy girl, proud and stocky, with broad shoulders and a firm step, but a quite slender face, a straight nose, thin lips, and big, well-spaced eyes, started pacing back and forth with large furious steps in the little room, without paying attention to the fact that whenever she banged against the tables she caused Fanny's table to vibrate so that Fanny would have to stop eating, watch for the waitress to pass into a clear space, and hurry to swallow a mouthful, all very discreetly. The girl's incensed manner frightened Fanny, as did a certain way she had of curling up her lip or of tossing her hair back as if she wished her head would go with it. The girl, however, did not even deign to glance at Fanny, whom she sometimes indifferently brushed against, jostling her table, her chair, the end of her suitcase in her mania to move on. When Fanny had finished — with great difficulty since the sausage tasted so bad — she leaned back in her chair and timidly said, 'What's your name, if I might ask?'

'Lucette!' shouted the girl. She stopped dead, walked up to Fanny, sat with one thigh on the table and crossed her arms. She stared into Fanny's eyes, which were full of respect and hope. 'You know,' said Lucette quickly, without losing her enraged expression, 'you know, I can't be at the oven and the coffee-maker at the same time. I can't wait tables in the dining room and work in the kitchen at the same time. No, this can't go on. I'm a waitress, and that's enough. I can tell you it's not nothing, especially in the evening. I hate cooking, messing with food, and I wasn't hired for that. What I like is to be in the dining room, to take orders and to serve. When I'm not running around I'm sitting on that tall chair, at the back there, spreading out my skirt, keeping an eye on the room and joking with the customers, as it should be. Oh, I don't miss a thing. I cross my arms on my chest, like that. I have to close my eyes because of the smoke, and I watch everything without looking like I do. As soon as a customer calls out something, sometimes even before he opens his mouth, I spring to his side. More often than not I know exactly what he wants, because I've watched him so closely that I sense his desires.'

'Really!' piped up Fanny, admiringly.

'Yes, yes. It's just like that,' said Lucette, who was suddenly reminded of Fanny's presence. 'The kitchen isn't my business, and if this carries on I'm going to take off. Oh yes, that's what will happen if the boss keeps refusing to hire someone.'

'If you leave,' said Fanny, 'I'm sure they'll have a hard time finding a waitress as worthy as you.'

'That's what I tell her, and she's well aware of it. Only she can't make up her mind, it's too much for her, she has such a hard time letting go of her money!'

'Can't she hear us?' murmured Fanny.

'She's asleep,' said Lucette contemptuously. 'In any case, that wouldn't stop me from talking. Oh, I thought I'd go mad when you asked for sausage and eggs! Do you think it's good for the prestige of an establishment if the waitress smells of stale grease? Look, a little egg yolk has splashed on my blouse. Do you think that looks good when I'm bringing the aperitif?'

'Certainly not,' agreed Fanny, who thought, however, that the Coq Hardi's dining room was sufficiently smelly and dirty that no one would notice the smell of Lucette's hair or be offended by some stains on Lucette's dubious-looking clothing.

'Now, I'm desperate!' exclaimed Lucette, pounding on the table. 'I might as well tell you, I cried while cooking your eggs, my situation seemed so wretched to me, so far from what I'm meant to be. I'm so humiliated! Yes, as soon as I'm sent into that revolting kitchen I feel like I'm dying of shame.'

'That's terrible!' cried out Fanny, sincerely touched. She wanted to take Lucette's hand, but the whole time she talked Lucette flung her hands about with sweeping, indignant gestures, and she did not in any case understand Fanny's intention but, engrossed in her own problems, looked her up and down. Beneath the light-coloured nylon of her blouse, her sturdy shoulders rolled like waves, her soft chest violently rose and fell. The rain battering angrily against the window-panes became more intense. In the dining room, which was so dark that Lucette's features were indistinct, some fat flies stuck to the honey-coloured fly-paper and struggled for a long time; others were circling Fanny's plate and dipping into a small puddle of beer. Fanny placed complete faith in Lucette, no longer doubting that as strong as she was, working in the village, she must know Aunt Leda, whatever she might be. Her heart skipped beats as she thought: And what if by some miracle Lucette... It occurred to her also that since Eugene had taken everything she had practically no money, just enough for her meal, and nowhere to sleep. She needed to be in this place!

'I can help you,' she said, approaching Lucette as near as she dared.

'Help me, what do you mean, help me...' Lucette was distracted, having completely forgotten Fanny, and was swaying to the rhythm of

57

the raindrops drumming against the panes and the low door, and twisting her calf in its black sock. Above it her pale knee extended as if strangled — round and fat. She was lost in her bitter thoughts, when her eye landed by chance on Fanny. She was completely taken by surprise to see her and could not repress an impatient grimace. Beneath Lucette's rather stupid gaze, Fanny felt crushed, cut down, nothing seemed as important to her as pleasing this powerful and difficult girl. To give herself courage, she stared at a leafy pattern on Lucette's skirt.

'In return for food and lodging,' she said very quickly, 'I could replace you in the kitchen. If the boss agrees, I ask no more, that shouldn't be too expensive.'

'Well, fancy that! And you'd know how to do that?' said Lucette, amazed.

'I can do everything,' said Fanny, looking modest.

'Even regional dishes?' Skeptical, almost scornful, Lucette raised her eyebrows, crossed her arms, and swung her leg hard, though it was weighed down by a big lace-up shoe.

'I've often watched my grandmother,' said Fanny without looking up.

Then, as if moving on to important matters, Lucette dryly asked, 'Head of veal?'

'With strawberries, I let it simmer for three good hours, with thyme, lots of thyme.'

'Stew?'

'With stock, potatoes, a little red wine.'

'Here we make hare pie, and jams.'

'Oh,' cried out Fanny, enthusiastically, 'I helped make rhubarb jelly just last summer. As for the pie, I can skin the animal, and I know to put in half pork and some parsley.'

'Yes,' said Lucette, 'but what about egg custard, do you know how to make egg custard?'

'I've often made it.'

'You'll have to stuff pastry puffs.'

'With veal sweetbreads and mushrooms, in a seasoned white sauce.'

Fanny was almost disappointed when Lucette stopped questioning her, so affectionately did she remember what she had watched Grandmother do countless times and what her mother had forgotten, feeling nothing but irritated disdain for those old practices carefully passed down. By teaching Fanny's mother these recipes and making her faithfully repeating them, hadn't they tried to drag her back to the very place she had fled? With a sort of fear, boredom, and repugnance, Fanny's mother now always found a way to avoid Grandmother's birthday, burdening Fanny's guilty conscience with further shame and instilling her with the habit of making up for it with a display of respect, especially towards Aunt Colette.

Lucette seemed convinced. She would speak to her boss as soon as she woke up, and she already felt certain that Fanny would be taken on under the conditions she had proposed, which were very reasonable. The deal being finalized so easily, Fanny had started to kick herself for being too reasonable. Lucette, she noticed with a little bitterness, seemed very satisfied at the idea of no longer suffering in the foul-smelling heat of the kitchen, almost proud, as if she had conquered Fanny's reservations or as if this meek and eager Fanny were her own creation. Now she had taken on an air of amiable superiority, which distanced her even more from Fanny. She sat day-dreaming on the table, her hands on each side of her thighs holding her skirt with a great show of dignity. Her head was slightly thrown back and her sparse hair fell straight and thin in a cascade down her back. On Lucette's bare knee, which was blond and pale, Fanny gently laid her chin, without Lucette's even noticing. In the past Grandmother's dogs had stretched out their muzzles just like this on Fanny's thigh, out in the garden in summer, in quiet abandon, devoted. She already despises me a little, thought Fanny, because I'm going to take on a task that disgusts her. So be it. It doesn't matter. I'll be able to make her know Leda...

'I need to explain what you'll have to do,' said Lucette without looking down at her. 'I can go ahead and do that, since the matter's in the bag; the boss has her faults but she's never refused me anything as long as it doesn't cost her a penny and it suits me. It's straightforward. You get up at seven o'clock. You accompany the boss to the market, to the shops, to the farm for the eggs. On the way you decide the menu with her. You come back without dawdling. You sweep the dining room, you polish the bar, you wipe the tables. You check that none of the bottles are empty or low. You put on the kitchen apron hung on the door. You prepare the lunch dishes. At noon you write down on a pad all that I call down to you from the dining room. You place the full plates on the stairs. That way I won't ever have to set foot in the kitchen! To save time, do the dishes as you go along. You clean, you tidy up, you take off the apron. It'll be about four o'clock. You are free for an hour and a half. You go and rest, that's the best thing to do. Don't undress! Don't take off your shoes! You'll risk falling asleep. You come back down to get dinner ready. Everything will be just like the afternoon, only there will be more people. At eleven o'clock you're finished. Then, Fanny, before you go up, if it tempts you, you'll come have a drink in the dining room, with the customers! One! At the boss's expense!' Lucette burst into joyful laughter. She jumped to the ground and took Fanny by the elbow. With her other hand she affectedly plumped up her hair, completely free now of the mundane problems which would occupy Fanny, and said, 'I present to you the kitchen,' in a voice changed so egoistically by pleasure and disgust that Fanny purpled with shame and suddenly felt her flesh very inferior to that of Lucette. Lucette dragged her towards a small door by the bar that was blackened with grime all around its handle. A few steps plunged down towards a sort of tiny cave where Fanny ventured alone with Lucette directing her from the top of the staircase, where she blocked the dwindling daylight. 'Never,' she called out with voluptuous frivolity, 'never again will you see me in the kitchen!' Then there was a noise behind her, and Lucette turned her head and called out some words of welcome. She carefully closed the door before leaving, and Fanny had to feel her way along the greasy walls to find the light switch. If by some miracle, she thought despondently, Lucette should lead me some day to Aunt Leda... and if, by some miracle, Lucette herself, perhaps... She sat down on a step and cried a little, out of pique, thinking of Eugene. How threatening and unapproachable this Lucette was! She seemed, in her disturbing yet fascinating elation, to possess divine powers that had escaped poor Fanny. Fanny did not doubt the necessity of fearing and respecting Lucette as long as she had no other contact in the village, for now Lucette seemed to be its queen and keeper. Just as Lucette had integrated her into these premises, wasn't it in her power to send her packing for the slightest displeasure Fanny gave her?

The hostile neon light filtered through a layer of dirt. A small basement window at pavement level was the only opening in the room. Through the bars she saw a pair of legs pass, and wellington-clad feet suddenly leapt into a puddle, splattering muddy water across the window pane. In the corner was an old blackened stove with crusted hotplates, and a sink filled with greasy dishes which Fanny undertook to wash straight away. The tiled floor was so sticky she had to move around very carefully. Revealed as though it were Lucette's dark secret, the suffocating filthiness of the kitchen revolted Fanny yet pleased her at the same time, even though, thrown into it without warning, she felt even more looked down upon than she had been by the family for her incongruous presence. Thinking of the family, Fanny sometimes despaired. What if, after all, it were less difficult to find Aunt Leda, wherever she might be in the world, than to ever be received with dignity by the family, or for Uncle George to cry out, 'There's my niece!' or for Aunt Colette to call her by her first name? Would it ever be any less difficult to receive even the smallest sign of gratitude from the dogs?

# FOURTEEN
## *The Boss Accepts Fanny*

Just as Fanny was starting to wash the floor, a tall, skinny woman opened the door. Fanny, pleased that the owner had found her hard at work, blushed slightly and, on her hands and knees in soapy water, pretended to be too absorbed in her work to notice. The woman studied her. Even Aunt Colette, thought Fanny, glancing back and forth, has never stared down at me from such a height nor with such disbelief. It must be that strangers are so rare in this village. Let's hope Aunt Leda believes in my existence when I introduce myself to her, since I no longer have anything to prove it — that blasted idiot George tore up the only photograph I had. Anyway, my father accepted me as his daughter whether he recognized me or not, and even whether or not he remembered that my name has been Fanny for only five days and that he once gave me a completely different name that no one in the family ever knew how to pronounce correctly, except for Grandmother...

The woman motioned to her to come up. Fanny scrubbed a little more, then wiped her already swollen hands. A vicious dog, glued to the window, was watching Fanny with his chops curled up, furious that he could not jump at her through the windowpane. Fanny turned away in fear and anger.

Upstairs, Lucette dominated the room from her favourite chair. She had spread her skirt, a leafy green and yellow print, showing a little thigh. She bestowed a distracted smile on Fanny, then a wide and glowing smile at a table of lorry drivers who were calling her Lulu and joking with her. The room had suddenly become dark because of the lorries parked from one end of the café to the other. The boss turned on a bright light. Fanny approached her humbly and said to this tall, lanky woman whose expression was glum and suspicious, 'My family lives not far from here. I promise you'll be pleased with me.'

Shrugging, the woman put her hand on Fanny's head, made her turn carefully, uttered a few 'hmms' as she examined her back, her waist, and her hips, which she poked with her finger, then glanced at Lucette who looked dull-witted yet imposing, indifferent to what was happening on this side of the room. The woman said tonelessly, 'You'll do fine,' and gave Fanny a little pat on the neck. Fanny thanked her, sincerely grateful, knowing she now belonged. On the other side of the room, Lucette was laughing contentedly. Not one of the three men had turned towards Fanny, yet they were laughing with Lucette, and one shouted out, 'So she says her family lives around here! Anyone can say that, can't they? Who's going to check?'

# FIFTEEN
## *On The Right Track*

Later, Fanny took advantage of the lorry drivers' unexpected departure, followed by the owner's, to hang around Lucette. She took out the photograph of Aunt Leda reading — a plume of hair and the hem of a skirt — and held it out to Lucette, imploring her, 'Lucette, do you know anyone who looks like this woman, my aunt?'

'Yes, quite possibly,' answered Lucette after glancing at the picture. She raised her wicked, disdainful eyes, uncrossed her legs and, without even realizing it, crushed Fanny's hand which was clinging to the seat. Lucette's chair was so high her legs swung more than a couple of feet above the floor.

'Yes, that could be,' she repeated, casually. 'Across the county there's a woman called Leda who might be the one in the picture.'

Fanny almost burst into tears. She clung tightly to the seat and stammered excessive thanks, while Lucette, feeling magnanimous, smiled briefly then mechanically pocketed the photo, crumpling it. Fanny dared not ask for it back, though it saddened her to lose it so soon. She did not complain either when she discovered that her suitcase had disappeared, but turned away so Lucette would not see the redness mounting in her cheeks. She was ashamed of the mistrustful thoughts that popped into her head. After all, she owed the people here — hadn't they, after the usual precautions, treated her less like a stranger than her own family had on Grandmother's birthday?

# PART TWO

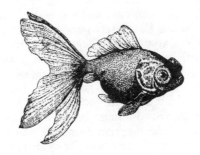

# ONE

## *In The Kitchen*

Grilled cutlets, roast beef, rabbit stew, chicken casserole, roast turkey, pink trout in butter sauce, boiled brains, fancy salads, devilled eggs and then crème caramel, chocolate mousse, apple pie, plum pie, and on Sundays a perilous egg custard and an unbelievable peach melba; such was the menu at the Coq Hardi every week, without a day's rest. In the mornings Fanny ran around the village on the hard pavements of packed, frozen earth, harassed by the foul weather, scared she might be overwhelmed with business and would fail to please, rushing into the kitchen just when Lucette finally got up in a bad mood, noisily demanding her breakfast and often suffering from dangerous bouts of depression which she vented through brutal, angry gestures she never bothered to explain. Under the grimy neon light, which at dawn turned the basement window into a dark hole, Fanny chopped, sliced, peeled, washed and scrubbed with anxious fervour. When around noon Lucette started to shout down orders from the top of the stairs, she never showed more than her impatient feet, which, to Fanny, looked stern in their big boots. Fanny had oil ready in the pans for cutlets and steaks, the daily special was heating gently, and she went up to the first step so she could hear Lucette better. Lucette would not repeat herself under any circumstances. Sometimes Fanny leant her whole body along the staircase, pressing her worried face as far forward as she could, even brushing the toe of Lucette's boots with her forehead, seeing a daring flash of firm, rough flesh under Lucette's musty print skirt. Sometimes Fanny could not be at the base of the stairs when Lucette called out the orders, or Lucette talked too fast or with her face turned towards the dining room so Fanny did not understand. Even if she dared ask Lucette to repeat an order, she would never have time before Lucette — who never lingered and hardly even stopped — spun back towards her customers. Besides, to do so Fanny would have to come out of the kitchen, be it just a little, climbing the few steps to Lucette's level because her own voice did not carry. Could she clearly justify such a bold move? Wouldn't Lucette's surprise at discovering her suddenly in front of her, drawing attention to a breakdown in their system, be enough to make her lose complete control and any leniency towards Fanny? Fanny decided she still could not take the slightest initiative, feeling that although she was useful here and a voluntary worker, she was tolerated out of generosity. No doubt lots of the village girls envied her place, she who had less right to it, coming from no one knew where. She sensed the limitless power of Lucette, who even dominated the owner.

So when she missed some words, after an instant of terror and helplessness, and a desperate homesickness which made Grandmother's village seem lost forever, Fanny rushed to the first dish she came across, filled a plate, and placed it at the top of the stairs on the chance that she had the right one. In the smoke-filled furnace of a kitchen — her hands crossed over her greasy apron and pressed resignedly against her stomach — she would watch for Lucette's arrival. Because if the dish was not right, Lucette would simply flip it to the bottom of the stairs with the tip of her boot. Then she would wait for Fanny's new offering without saying a word, while Fanny rushed so much she forgot to breathe. The heavy smells suffocated her, but she ran back and forth across the little kitchen, her only thought being to please Lucette. Lucette stood waiting at the top of the stairs in offended silence, a contemptuous look on her face. The second plate might well be rejected in the same imperious manner, or even more violently. Fanny moved aside so she would not get splattered. But the shame of it. Even Aunt Colette would not have inflicted such shame on her, not even to test her. What had given Lucette the idea of outdoing her family in this respect? She thought some close link must exist between Lucette and her search for Aunt Leda. Perhaps this village was really Aunt Leda's village. Perhaps Lucette herself... These thoughts tugged at Fanny. She promised herself she would be even more devoted to Lucette in the future, Lucette who might be able to lead Fanny right to her goal, through her influence, her knowledge of the village, the simple mystery that surrounded her person, so similar in certain ways to, say, Aunt Colette, who, in her blue dress decorated with little moons, rarely left Fanny's thoughts.

As soon as Lucette had turned on her heels, proudly bearing the dish she had ordered, Fanny hastily picked up the scattered pieces of plate, wiped up the gravy, and threw the chunks of meat back in the cooking pot. But Lucette was already back, wanting this, demanding that, and Fanny had to rush to the dish cupboard then to the ovens to the harsh commands of the invisible Lucette, whose feet tapped impatiently at the top of the stairs. Fanny hardly took time to eat. She had lost all taste for food and nibbled at a bread-crust that she kept in her apron pocket just to keep up her strength. A crust lasted her two days. She happily gave her share of food to Lucette, whose hunger was never satisfied.

When Fanny looked up at the basement window, she saw, lying against the window and baring its teeth as soon as she looked at it, the huge, yellow dog that had frightened her on the first day. Only a little winter light radiated from the window. The dog stole it from her. He was there every day at dawn. But Fanny never came across him during her outings in the village. She was sure that if she ever did he would attack her ferociously, since he gave her the evil eye the whole day, scratching aggressively at the windowpane with his paw, growling relentlessly.

'You'll see, I'll turn you into a casserole!' shouted Fanny, irritated when on her way down the stairs in the morning she noticed the dark mass of the yellow dog behind the window. Then she stopped thinking about it, because work took up all her time and energy. But the dog's gaze pressed on the back of her neck, and she trembled to think of the day when he, or another, would finally punish her. 'What can you explain to dogs?' she muttered. 'I played with them, I cleaned their kennel without shame, but as soon as the family turns its back on me, they devour me...'

In time, Fanny built up her confidence. She crawled to the top of the stairs when Lucette was not there and spied carefully around the dining area where she was not allowed during the day. Crouching behind the crack of the half-open door, she decided waitressing at the Coq Hardi would be much better for collecting information about Aunt Leda, simply because she would be in contact with such a large number of people. Her behind-the-scenes kitchen job which, despite everything, she was beginning to like, isolated her from village life. So many lorry drivers stopped each day, so many sales reps travelled the region, that it made Fanny's eyes blink and her mind cloud as she stared and tried to follow the comings and goings of so many different people in the smokey little dining room — coming in and going out non-stop, calling to one another, hurrying so much, eating so quickly that having hardly sat down they were already back on their feet, wiping their mouths to leave while still gulping down the last bites. Some of them worked straight through lunch, so the tables were strewn with files, papers leaned against bottles, where they got sprayed with gravy or wine without it seeming to bother the overweight, reserved men, who consulted the documents while they ate silently and swiftly, swallowing without even looking at their plates to see what Lucette had served them. Fanny never recognized anyone, although the crowd regularly consisted of the same customers and Lucette often greeted each one by first name.

Very happy now that she was only the waitress, Lucette, her hair done with more care than before — tied back in an old plaid ribbon — was amiable and prompt, yet serious, severe even, and she moved around the dining room with heavy, fast steps, her wide eyes shining with joy and attentiveness. Behind the counter the boss was napping, confident in Lucette. Fanny felt envious. If I don't become a waitress what's the point of staying here... And the Coq Hardi's dining room, over which Lucette proudly reigned, with its stained walls, its low ceiling, its poor light, dimmed even more by the lorries waiting outside the windows and the thick smoke of cheap cigarettes, became the object of Fanny's desire. She began to hate her little kitchen into which no one descended, and she became more bold and hasty, going to the top of the stairs as soon as Lucette had left. One day she thought she recognized someone among a group of salesmen. He was clutching a large woman whose accent was from the capital, and both of them were eating in this uncomfortable position — it was Uncle George himself. Since her uncle sold toiletries door-to-door, this could be him. But Fanny only observed him, uneasily, from behind. She closed her stinging eyes for a few seconds; during this time Uncle George and his companions disappeared — to Fanny's great regret since she was just getting ready to run and embrace him, savouring in advance the impression she would make. I'll let Aunt Colette know one or two things about her dear husband, she thought excitedly. If she doesn't know about it, I'm guaranteed her appreciation.

Lucette suddenly noticed her. Putting down her tray, she pounced on Fanny, grabbed her by the shoulders and pushed her to the bottom of the stairs, without even worrying about the plates filled with steaming lamb stew that Fanny had placed at the top. They clattered downstairs and the red-hot gravy splashed Fanny.

'Never!' shouted the indignant Lucette, 'never should you leave your post! Never should you come upstairs when we're open! Do you want to ruin everything? Is that what you want? To mess everything up so much that we'll never get straightened out?' Fists on hips, she stamped her foot angrily. A crowd gathered. Customers with napkins still tucked in their collars strained to see and threw wary looks at Fanny, who had slumped to the floor. Lucette claimed them as witnesses. Murmurs of approval surrounded her and she calmed down. Though Fanny's whole body ached so much she could barely open her mouth, she took advantage of the calm and said, 'Tell me, Lucette, do you know George R. who was here just now?'

'George? Yes, of course, he's a regular. He sells soaps,' said Lucette, shrugging.

'He's my uncle!' exclaimed Fanny, hopefully.

'Your uncle? Huh!' exclaimed Lucette, laughing contemptuously, without Fanny being able to tell whether her disdain was directed at Uncle George or whether she simply could not believe Fanny was telling the truth. Lucette waved the customers away then bent down to whisper, 'How could you have that man for an uncle? I don't believe a word of it!'

'But it's true,' said Fanny, defiantly.

'Anyway, he's often talked to me about his family, but he has never mentioned you.'

'That's because I have a new first name,' answered Fanny, irritably. Seeing distrust darken Lucette's round face, Fanny became silent and looked down. Lucette hmm'd, unsure. She added in a matter-of-fact tone, before rising, 'George is one of us.'

I've got to become a waitress, Fanny thought as she lay motionless on the cold tile floor, her face grimy, or I'll never get anywhere, because who will see me down in this hole? Who will even remember I exist except that damned spiteful dog? Aren't I from around here just like George? Won't anyone ever say that about me? It's even more true of me than a lot of people, than my cousin Eugene who hardly shows any respect... At the thought of Eugene, Fanny got excited. Whenever she had felt like it, even at the most inopportune moments, Fanny had given him such rough kisses they had made Eugene stagger, as well as a lot of prodding and affectionate slaps which he had taken very well. For as long as she could remember, Fanny would willingly have married Eugene. Except that Aunt Colette would undoubtedly have violently objected. But if Fanny brought back Aunt Leda, surely the hostility towards her would evaporate, because a cruel mistake would be erased along with the negligence of Fanny's parents, who could not care less about the family or its acceptance, or even Grandmother herself and who felt for the village only a slight contempt, an irritated disdain.

# TWO
## *Evening In The Village*

After work, instead of going upstairs to drink a glass of brandy with Lucette before bed, and even though it was after midnight, Fanny decided to visit the woman called Leda whom Lucette had talked about. But Fanny's schedule would always make it either too early or too late. It so happened that the boss was absent this evening — she could not prevent Fanny from going out but would certainly have suspiciously asked her where she was off to, since bad conduct on the part of her employees could always reflect on her establishment. Fanny tolerated being picked on for her actions more than anyone, especially Lucette! She was grateful to this woman, who did not pay her, for having taken her in without insisting she be from the village and without holding her in low regard for this reason. Having shown up without proof of anything, without a single family photograph, she was not offended when she was mistreated once she had been taken in. Besides, Fanny liked Lucette and did not dislike the owner, although neither one believed her when she talked about her close ties with George or the immediate family. Both of them half-smiled, and Lucette whistled disbelievingly or got irritated, calling Fanny a liar, wanting to make her ashamed of her pretension and anxiety. Because it did not really matter to Lucette that Fanny had no relatives in the region, a fact that seemed obvious considering Fanny's appearance, language and character, which were in every respect so different from Lucette's. Fanny did not even have the intimate and precise knowledge of the geography of the area that Lucette, having been born in the village, had without ever having gone anywhere.

Fanny hastily put the old raincoat on, then she went out, teased by Lucette who pretended to believe that Fanny was going to meet one of the travelling salesmen. It was raining hard. Tall street lamps lit the centre of the village and outlined in white the concrete church, the highway, which was wide and newly-tarred, and the disused bus shelter provided long ago by a bank whose name could still be read on the roof, a name familiar to Fanny since Grandmother had always deposited her savings there. Beyond, the black and silent houses stood with closed shutters. Before she set off, a publicity poster on the facade of the Coq Hardi caught her attention for a moment. Her cousin Eugene, Eugene himself, with his shiny hair, his tight sweater, was smiling at her from the poster, looking both insolent and elegant at the same time. Her cousin Eugene! With his full lips, which had been reddened a little! Dumbfounded, Fanny remembered that Eugene had dreamt of becoming an actor, and here he was showing the whole village his gleaming teeth; here he was, stupidly delighted, unruffled and joyful under the cold rain, pointing with his index finger to the four letters of a hardware store; here was Eugene succeeding at last and without the help of either Fanny or any Aunt Leda. Fanny knew the reputation of this store where all the men in her family — with the exception of her father — got their supplies. Fanny felt piqued. Eugene was so lucky to have found this way to show himself off, and it nettled her a little that through a picture of him alone, his silent, likeable face, he was extolling the merits of a store where it was a real monthly treat for all the uncles to go.

She turned away from the poster and narrowly missed tripping over the big yellow dog from the basement window, as it rose, growling, onto its hairless paws. It had appeared without warning, and she screamed with fright, then hurried away, pulling her raincoat hood down over her forehead. The pattering of the rain stopped her from hearing any other noise. Fanny glanced fearfully behind her. Undisturbed by the weather, the dog was following, its thin flanks swinging. It appeared so ugly, suddenly, that Fanny gained confidence. She stopped and let it approach. She kicked it violently under the muzzle, thinking: another will take its revenge! — then pushed it to the ground, deaf to its yelping. The dog now seemed old and tired-out. Was it really a threat or had she been mistaken? It might have made a more reliable and faithful companion than Eugene, who'd had ulterior motives for going with her. Already tired out from her struggle with the dog, she finished it off with a kick in the stomach, then with the tip of her toes slid the heavy, rain-soaked carcass from the sidewalk into the gutter, where the gushing water carried it gently away. She ran away guiltily, but comforted herself with the thought that she would no longer be afraid to look up at the basement window. This ugly beast had made her toil in the kitchen even more difficult! Besides, one summer's day in the yard, hadn't she seen Uncle George coldly shoot his most faithful hunting dog then dump its body on a manure pile because it had just devoured three chickens? He had not eaten lunch with any less appetite than usual, and Grandmother's dogs always jumped with joy at the sight of him and greeted him by licking his hands. If her uncle George — who knew how to handle dogs — did not hesitate to punish them with death, neither he nor any other member of the family would blame Fanny for killing this filthy animal.

The rain was pouring down harder when she stopped in front of

Leda's house, at the edge of the village. From time to time a roaring lorry passed or a single car slowed behind Fanny, tempting her to jump in; she was so cold now she would have done so shamelessly, without worrying about the driver's reaction, if she had not so strongly desired to meet at last someone called Leda, who might even be her aunt — couldn't Aunt Leda be anywhere?

Leda's house was part of a housing estate and had beige-coloured roughcast walls and garden gnomes in the flower beds. A bright light shone through the French window onto the road, and as Fanny approached she saw a living room filled with furniture, a woman in her robe watching television, and a budgie. She took shelter under the porch and rang for a long time. A dog barked in the distance. How much time, thought Fanny, how much time will it take me to recognize my Aunt Leda, if it's her? Will I know for sure that it isn't her or if I'm mistaken in thinking it is? Surely I'll just know. Oh, if only Lucette hadn't kept the photograph! If only I'd dared to ask for it back!

The door finally opened. Trembling with emotion and numb with cold, Fanny almost collapsed onto the woman's breast, but she controlled herself and greeted the woman calmly. The woman was holding the edges of her robe together. To reassure her, Fanny stuffed her fists deep into her pockets, then regretted not having taken off her hood, which covered her face down to her eyebrows.

'Is it possible,' she asked, with difficulty because she was completely stiff with cold, 'that you are Leda herself, my aunt? My name is Fanny.'

'I don't know anyone called Fanny,' muttered the woman irritably.

She was in her forties, her hair was tightly curled, and she looked neither like Fanny's mother nor Aunt Colette, though this hardly worried Fanny.

'But I have nieces, yes,' added the woman, to seem willing.

'Oh!' cried Fanny, 'that means you could be my aunt, because I didn't tell you my real name, which could be the name of one of your nieces, who could be me. You see, I can find my Aunt Leda here just as well as anywhere; it's very possible.'

Very excited, Fanny suddenly pushed her hood back and held out her hands to grab those of the woman, her cheeks reddening with emotion. Her dishevelled hair was sticking up in little pointed tufts, and she was stamping her feet without realizing it, she was so hopeful, wanting to go into the house.

'Well then, what's your real name?' asked the woman curiously.

'Oh, I'm not supposed to tell! I'm only supposed to be Fanny, you know. Just imagine this name was given to me like a character in a book or a soap opera and don't wonder about it any more than you just did when watching television.' She leant forward and whispered in a contrite tone, 'Anyway, my real name is so strange you'd have a lot of trouble pronouncing it.'

'In that case,' the woman sighed, 'I have no way of knowing whether I'm your aunt or not.' She was about to shut the door, but Fanny insisted, 'If Grandmother is your mother...'

'My mother just died.'

'My God! What if Grandmother died while I've been gone!' moaned Fanny, appalled, and with guilt and shame she suddenly remembered that she had forgotten to worry about how near death Grandmother had seemed on her birthday. The idea that Grandmother could already be buried, without her even knowing, without her even thinking of it — she was so distracted and thoughtless — made Fanny's legs weak. She wanted to beg the woman to let her in, but the woman was tired of all this and had already slammed the door shut. Fanny slumped against it. Grandmother had her place ready in the village cemetery: a dry plot of earth in one corner, under the breeze-block wall which remained unshaded since there was no foliage, not a single cypress tree, just a huge granite cross that could be seen from all ends of the region, not a single bush, hedge, or even flowers. Fanny had not thought Grandmother immortal, having seen the terror in her eyes last time, but she had vaguely imagined that Grandmother would not die until she had brought Aunt Leda back, that she would wait to die with Fanny there — she was her grand-daughter after all — to see her with her eyes closed, her hands crossed, to kiss her with dignity on the forehead in front of Aunt Colette, who would be attentive and sad, everything as it should be. But if Grandmother had already been laid to rest, Aunt Colette had undoubtedly taken great pleasure in noting Fanny's absence, and she had every reason! Crouched against the door, Fanny wrung her frozen hands, and her shame was so overwhelming that she moaned a little, without even realizing it. So she had perhaps failed Grandmother twice, first on her birthday, then at her moment of death — and she had been surprised, upset, that Grandmother did not have a picture of her displayed in her room! In any case, even if Grandmother were not dead, Fanny was just as guilty for having forgotten to worry about her. Yet she loved Grandmother more than anyone! Without her, who in the village would not regard Fanny as a stranger if she could no longer point at the house and say, 'My grandmother has always lived here'?

She got up with difficulty. Through the picture window, she saw the woman settled once again in front of the television. The fact that the woman had refused to let Fanny in seemed to prove that she could not be her Aunt Leda; anyway, she really seemed to look too different, her face not in keeping with the common features of the region. Fanny left in the rain and passed through the deserted village again. Suddenly, a man appeared in front of her, carrying the body of the yellow dog. Surprised, Fanny jumped aside with embarrassment. He wanted to speak to her, but she lowered her head and ran hastily away.

*The following evening* — As soon as the boss had gone upstairs to bed, Fanny slipped on her raincoat and Lucette's big, black wellingtons. She joked a little with Lucette and, to put her in a good mood, thanked her for her silence and for the loan of the wellingtons and pretended to find it really funny when Lucette spoke in convulsions of laughter about a travelling salesman with a drooping moustache, a regular at the café whom Fanny had gone to meet each evening on the bench in the bus shelter without daring to say so. This salesman, whom Lucette wanted to believe was Fanny's lover, she came to understand was none other than her Uncle George.

'You don't have to pretend he's your uncle, go ahead,' said Lucette, amused and disdainful at the same time. 'I understand these things, you know!'

Fanny reproached herself for perhaps having let slip an unfortunate, unintentionally ambiguous word or two, which had led her friend Lucette's malicious mind to this shocking assumption, though she felt vaguely flattered by it. In her head she also apologized to her Aunt Colette — but from now on her aunt's pitiless face hardly ever left her dreams.

She slipped out discreetly, glancing at Eugene's big white face, which was still intact, then darted into the street. It rained all day during this season. If I question every inhabitant of the village, which must add up to about two hundred people, I will surely come across Aunt Leda — whoever she might be and if it's true she lives here — or at least someone who will know how to help me. She strode quickly on, making a lot of noise in her wellingtons. The dim light from the street lamps splashed onto the greyish walls, and the narrow brown doors sank deep into the shadows. As soon as she spotted an orange or bluish glow through the slats of a shutter, Fanny stopped and knocked vigorously. Often, inside, a dog would bark threateningly.

*Fanny interrupts a T.V. show* — An impatient face would appear behind the windowpane, and, distrustfully, a hand would push lightly on the shutter. Leaning her hooded head forward into the window, Fanny could just make out a big colour television screen. While she was explaining what she wanted, the person would frequently turn towards it, no longer listening and pulling on the shutter so Fanny had to jump back to avoid being struck. Then the person would turn back to Fanny, irritated by the interruption, and Fanny would repeat, 'If you aren't my Aunt Leda, do you know her or anyone here who can tell me about her? People call me Fanny...' without success. Incredulous denials would be muttered, and the window and the shutters would slam shut as Fanny hurriedly withdrew.

*Fanny is invited in* — Having seen a light, Fanny opened the gate to a farm. A boy, sheltered under an umbrella, was crossing the yard. He rushed by without seeing her and jumped when Fanny grabbed his sleeve.

'Do you know...,' she started. The boy carried on walking, so Fanny skipped after him, careful to dodge the ribs of his umbrella. She could not speak because the boy was charging with such determination towards the house with lit-up windows. He grabbed Fanny's elbow roughly and pushed her towards a sort of shed, to one side.

'Wait in there,' he said, 'I'm going to get someone.'

Fanny was contented with this promise. For the first time she had been allowed in, albeit into a dark and foul-smelling shed. At the end of her refuge, three big dogs were sleeping, chained. Fanny crouched down by the door and watched them out of the corner of her eye. But her stare seemed to wake them. They growled at first, coming as far towards Fanny as the short chain allowed but barely brushing against her. Fanny did not move, too aware of how unhoped-for the invitation to wait in the shed had been to dare thwart fate, or some inhabitant of the farm, by taking shelter elsewhere or waiting in the rain. She huddled against the wall, her hands behind her back, her face carefully held up. One of the dogs barked and tried to bite her boot; Fanny stayed still, pleased just to be there. She scrunched up her toes to avoid getting hurt if, by dint of pulling and strangling themselves, the dogs succeeded in catching hold of the tip of one of Lucette's wellingtons. Now they were howling, as if Fanny's unexpected and remarkable presence had aroused an old hatred. In the same way, Grandmother's familiar dogs had barked at Fanny on the birthday, although they had loved her before and she had not been any different that day.

Long hours passed, the dogs were wearing themselves out, the grey dawn appeared. No one had come, and Fanny saw the moment approaching when she would have to get back to the kitchen at the Coq Hardi. Without hope now, she slipped out of the lean-to into the pale, cold, early morning drizzle. The boy, bucket in hand, was crossing the tarred farmyard. Fanny ran to him and grabbed the tail of his jacket.

'Oh!' said the boy, 'I forgot you last night.'

'What about Leda?' murmured Fanny humbly.

'Leda is our dog,' said the boy in a knowledgeable tone.

'But who else?' begged Fanny.

'On my honour, I don't know any other.' The boy looked at her attentively, smiling gently and running his tongue over his lips to let Fanny know, under her hood, that he was not indifferent to her. He waddled on, making the bucket squeak, and tried several times to wink at her.

*Fanny meets another aunt* — The shutter opened after Fanny had been drumming on it for several minutes, bruising her fist, and Aunt Clemence's small, pinched face appeared, suspicious and framed by the pink baubles on her old-fashioned nightcap. Fanny cried out with surprise; as for Aunt Clemence, she calmly recognized her niece, whom she avoided calling by name. She gave Fanny a reserved yet polite look. Aunt Clemence had never been very affectionate, preferring Eugene who refused to kiss her, however, since she had the shadow of a moustache.

'It's rather late for a visit,' scolded Aunt Clemence.

'You *have* moved then?' exclaimed Fanny.

'Look, I've lived here for twenty years.' She laughed a little at the strange idea that she could have changed village.

'I'd forgotten,' said Fanny, embarrassed. 'It's that everything looks the same. But, quick, reassure me! Is Grandmother still alive?'

'Of course!' Aunt Clemence was shocked, and her thin lips tightened.

'May I come in?' asked Fanny.

'It's after midnight. Your uncle is asleep.'

Fanny apologized profusely, then, under the pretext of the rain coming into the living room, Aunt Clemence, as slight and pale as an apparition, closed the shutter without inviting Fanny back the next day.

*Fanny comes across Lucette* — Wearing only a teddy, her hair tangled, but with full cheeks and a ruddy complexion, Lucette was leaning out of the window despite the cold and was taken by surprise when Fanny came to knock at such an hour on her own fiancé's shutter, since Fanny did not know him.

'What have you done with your salesman?' she asked, smiling broadly.

Fanny stammered, she did not know that a fiancé of Lucette's lived here. Behind, in the brightly lit room, the young man, naked to the waist, was stretched out on the couch, watching the silent images of a television screen. 'Is he from the village?' Fanny could not help asking. He was. He was a pleasant and quiet young man. Lucette loved him well enough. Fanny left enviously, dreaming of her cousin Eugene. He got on so well without her; perhaps, there in the village where he lived with his parents, he had already found some Lucette or other, whom Aunt Colette would welcome with the greatest satisfaction!

*Christmas evening* — Although it was a special evening and Lucette was insistent on lending her something suitable to wear, Fanny really wanted to keep her old raincoat and the black wellingtons, because it was snowing and the pavements were slushy. Down the whole length of the street, right to the end of the village, shutters had been left wide open and fake candles shone brightly. Numerous figures moved behind the curtains, and Fanny saw joyful silhouettes in festive dress dancing about and children in bright outfits cavorting from one room to another. In the empty street, shouts rang out. Somewhat intoxicated by the festivities, Fanny strode on, stepping high in her wellingtons. Then she noticed a woman approach a window then turn away, hands on hips, wearing a billowy blue dress scattered with little silver moons, moving gracefully, her hair done in a different style — it was Aunt Colette herself, or a full-figured woman who looked very like her. Fanny pressed her forehead against the glass and called, but the woman was already leaving the room where bustling, happy people were crowding in. It was Aunt Colette's holiday dress and the same heavy, brisk walk! Fanny did not see Aunt Clemence or anyone else she knew. She remembered, however, how surprised she had been, last time at Grandmother's, by the new faces among the children. The family was so enormous that there was always some cousin or other from a distant branch of the family whom she had never met. Aunt Clemence could very possibly be busy at this moment in another part of the house, in the kitchen probably, where she had always set her heart on helping on busy days. But since she did not appear and Aunt Colette still had not reappeared, Fanny, seized with cold from head to toe, knocked on the windowpane, timidly at first then more violently, but to her great disappointment, neither of her aunts appeared. Intrigued faces strained towards the window; a stern-looking man walked towards Fanny while adjusting the knot of his tie and could have been taken for Uncle George if it were not for his protruding stomach. The living room, like Grandmother's and like those of almost all Fanny's relatives, was covered with dark, excessively complicated leafy patterns stretching right to the ceiling. It was suffocating. Famous pictures decorated the walls, along with canvases embellished with appliqué, next to decorative plates which were overflowing with large sea shells and varnished starfish. I find all that more beautiful than anything, thought Fanny. At Grandmother's too the centre light is a real yoke with eight little flame-shaped bulbs!

The man wiped the condensation from the windowpane. Without opening the window, he irritably shouted a few curt words, among which Fanny made out 'family holiday,' then he drew the curtains, and though it was unlikely she would be struck this time, Fanny nimbly withdrew. The church bells rang out for mass. In an instant the lit street filled with a crowd, suddenly appearing from the houses scattered along the miry road. Fanny noticed Lucette, with pink sequins in her hair, on the arm of her young man. Fanny flattened herself against a door, afraid she would be pushed, and the owner of the house, dressed in all her finery, passed unexpectedly in front of her and gave her a reproachful look. The whole village streamed in the direction of the church; the children were dragging their toys; in the greyish snow some loose dogs were frolicking. No one paid any attention to Fanny. How she had once enjoyed accompanying Grandmother to midnight mass! The whole family would go together, and on the way Uncle George would taunt the old pastor. Fanny, who could not receive communion, would sit on her bench — a little jealous but grateful that the walls of the little church welcomed her with such discreet kindness — to wait for Eugene to rejoin her, his hands clasped, his eyes lowered, his cheeks puffed, a look of feigned contrition on his face.

Alone now, Fanny left the doorway and hurried towards the church. The doors were closed, the church square deserted. She pulled one side of the double door and almost made a young man fall who was leaning against it on the inside.

'Don't come in, there's no more room, everyone's suffocating,' he whispered in an authoritative tone. And he closed the door himself, leaving Fanny outside.


*The next day* — Early in the morning, after crossing the village which was heavy with sleep and quiet domestic comfort, beneath the snow-filled sky that was even darker than the dull grey facades, Fanny knocked at the house where, yesterday, she thought she had seen Aunt Colette flit across the living room. She waited for a very long time before a pyjama-clad little girl with a determined expression finally opened the door. The little girl willingly answered the questions Fanny sternly put to her. It turned out that the woman in the royal blue dress was a certain Aunt Paulette, who was well-loved by the little girl, her niece, and that at dawn she had headed to the nearby village where she lived with her son and husband, whose respective first names the child

79

did not know since she had never met them because of an old disagreement between them and her father.

'Could it be,' exclaimed Fanny, grabbing the child's dainty head, 'that you're making a mistake and that the aunt is called Colette instead of Paulette? Oh, you don't understand,' she added irritably, seeing the little girl gape at her. 'But, you know, that could well be. People your age often confuse things. Go on, tell me that you have an Aunt Colette. Think!'

The little girl's face hardened; she suddenly raised her chin towards Fanny and shouted, 'Paulette, Paulette, Paulette!' Then she slammed the door as hard as she could. Fanny went on her way. In any case, it's Aunt Leda I'm looking for, she thought. Wouldn't she have been more alarmed than happy to run into Aunt Colette now, having nothing more to take pride in than her miserable cook's job at the Coq Hardi, and no longer knowing anything about the family, not even Grandmother, whom she had left in the worst state to come and stay in this village where they treated her even more indifferently than anywhere before. In the face of such inconsequence, Aunt Colette would certainly have shown her definitive contempt and would have congratulated herself on Eugene's absconding, regardless of the fact that he was undeniably Fanny's first cousin.

# THREE

## *In The Bedroom*

The room was long and narrow and looked out on the din of the street.
It was just large enough to squeeze in the double bed which could only
be reached from its foot. Fanny and Lucette both slept there — a
second bed would not have fitted — a fact that made Fanny a little
uncomfortable at first. A bright pink plastic chair, a white wooden
chest-of-drawers, a Greek carpet with beige, thick shag that was now
crushed and dirty were all the room's furnishings, yet one could not
take a step without bumping into something. The old wallpaper,
printed with brown diamonds and orange circles, was blistering at the
ceiling. The window was high, but they never opened it because of the
noise. On the first day Lucette had grabbed Fanny's suitcase and,
having no desire to share the cramped chest-of-drawers, shoved it
under the bed, from where Fanny had to pull it out, not without
difficulty, each time she needed an article of clothing. The slightest
pressure on the mattress prevented her from getting the suitcase out;
consequently, Fanny could not touch it when Lucette was asleep and,
since she dared not ask her to move, could not even get to it when
Lucette, totally unaware of Fanny's predicament, was simply sitting on
the bed. It was extremely rare that Fanny, who was working much
longer hours, found herself in the room during Lucette's absence;
what's more, Lucette hardly ever sat anywhere in the room other than
on the bed. The suitcase was inaccessible almost all the time, and
Fanny put little effort into her appearance, wearing the same old grey
trousers every day and a sweater permeated with greasy smells, for
which Lucette, from high on their bed, sharply rebuked her. Fanny's
respectful affection for Lucette prevented her from suspecting that
Lucette wickedly enjoyed her discomfort or from even considering that
Lucette, for never having noticed that she prohibited use of the
suitcase, might not be as scrupulous and thoughtful as Fanny liked to
believe.

Besides, it seemed that Lucette continued to think of the room as her
own, and she only left Fanny the little space which she did not think to
use or which did not suit her need for comfort. When they both
returned to the room for a brief rest during the slack period of the
afternoon, it went without saying that Lucette, who liked to spread out
and move as she pleased, would occupy the double bed alone and

Fanny would settle for the thick part of the carpet, between the chair and the chest-of-drawers, along the wall. Fanny appeared to have become so accustomed to this little corner that Lucette would sigh when she saw her settle down there, as if she envied Fanny this privilege. That bothered Fanny, because she did not want to be envied by Lucette. But if Lucette let Fanny sleep beside her during the night, the ordeal was so great that Fanny would have preferred her little patch of carpet, if she were not afraid of offending Lucette and that Lucette would then forbid her both the bed and the carpet and make her curl up on the chair as punishment. In her sleep Lucette totally forgot Fanny's existence; she pressed against Fanny, pushed her, struck her, rolled Fanny against the wall, squashed her with all her weight, smothered her, elbowed her, and pressed Fanny's cheek against the wall all but cracking her skull; and she kicked Fanny, suddenly threw her sharp hips into Fanny's stomach, and in her dreams screamed cries that kept Fanny awake for a long time. Fanny stifled in Lucette's bed. Her friend Lucette's flesh filled all the space; she seemed to have limbs everywhere, to the extent that Fanny no longer knew where in the bed her own body had fitted, disappearing into and under Lucette's body, which had no limits and gave off a strong odour. Several times Fanny thought she would die of asphyxiation against the wall. But she was somewhat grateful to Lucette for not being disgusted and not caring whether or not the body next to her came from the village. Lucette never hesitated before rolling onto Fanny, and Fanny loved her for this reason, despite the difficulties she suffered.

Lucette was untidy and Fanny's arrival made her even more careless. Each evening her clothes lay wherever her whim had led her to scatter them. Sometimes Fanny found it difficult, despite the ridiculous size of the room, to find Lucette's hair ribbon or her panties or her bra, which Lucette threw into the most improbable spots, incapable of guiding Fanny in her searches afterwards. Lying down, she would wave her hands, saying in a weary voice, at random, 'Look over here then... or maybe there...,' and she enjoyed watching Fanny as she crawled under the bed or shook the rug out. Fanny liked to render these little services which put Lucette in a good mood and undoubtedly, though Fanny really never felt quite sure, would not make Lucette regret for a second having accepted her in the village. She also washed Lucette's underwear, scrubbed her back and legs under the shower, and made up her eyes for her, complimenting her all the while.

# FOUR

## *Lucette's Contempt*

It always remained impossible for Lucette to comprehend the value of Fanny's venture. Fanny had to resign herself to being nothing more to her friend than the Coq Hardi's unfortunate cook and accept Lucette's condescension towards her for occupying a position she had so hated in the past. What could Fanny say?

# PART THREE

# ONE

## *Lucette Slips Away*

One evening, Fanny found her place in Lucette's bed occupied by Lucette's fiancé. He stuck his delighted face out from under the sheets while Lucette, cozily buried with only her face showing, winked at Fanny, who did not say a word. What would Aunt Colette think of her niece if she could have seen the trust with which Lucette, with all kinds of strange expressions, now invited Fanny to join them and with an imperious gesture threw back the blanket so Fanny could slide into bed next to her? The boy himself, a native of the village, turned smiling to Fanny, encouraging her to take up their hospitable offer. But neither Fanny's terror of Lucette nor the young man's kind welcome could overcome Fanny's image of Aunt Colette asking the horrified Grandmother and the entire family, 'So now what am I to do?' She turned her eyes away from the bed and lay down on the carpet, furious with Aunt Colette who surely did not invade Eugene's thoughts when he was alone with whatever girl he had taken up with in the village. Aunt Colette no doubt troubled only Fanny! Aunt Colette, who had not even recognized her, had got her first name wrong and had gone into a rage to have her thrown out!

The bed shook violently, and Lucette and the boy were suddenly on their feet. Lucette, stark naked, hurled insults, flung the window open into the cold, leaned far over the ledge and angrily started to throw the young man's things out, while he tried to hold her back. Trousers flew, then a shoe. The fiancé tried to grab Lucette by the waist. Fanny saw her chance to please her friend. She too jumped up and with all her strength lunged at the boy, throwing him a punch in the back that made him groan. He fell onto Lucette with Fanny crushing him, and confusion followed. Fanny was boring into the small of the fiancé's back, pushing hard enough to bruise him, when Lucette toppled, screaming, over the windowsill.

# TWO
## *Fanny Becomes A Waitress*

After the death of her friend Lucette, who was buried at lunch time in the dry, desolate cemetery on the outskirts of the village, near the new housing estates and the little supermarket with the flashing sign which had just opened, Fanny replaced her, for pay this time, and also arranged for a girl who had recently come to the village to work in the kitchen. The girl had just arrived from a distant region and was marrying a local fellow, a relative of the owner. Having little interest in this stranger, Fanny proved hardly less authoritarian than Lucette had been. It particularly displeased her to learn from the young woman that she knew Fanny's father — she had been born and raised in the same region as he. Thinking she was pleasing Fanny, she tactlessly confided in her that she had guessed at first sight Fanny's relationship to this eminent man who, in this humble young woman's eyes, was Fanny's rich father. She would never have imagined that Fanny was from a neighboring village just like this one, nor that she had there a dear grandmother, with dogs! Her surprise offended and frightened Fanny who became stern and haughty, but without managing to silence the young woman who did not understand and showered her with excited tales from home. Would she tell the whole village about the strange dried-up shrubs planted in Fanny's father's garden or the curious reddish colour of the earth there, so strange that people stared at it warily? The young woman thought she was helping her new friend out and, in any case, enjoyed talking about a region she already missed. She might describe in detail the garment Fanny's father wore, which no one here knew, piquing their curiosity and most certainly ruining Fanny's efforts to make people see her as someone from here. The young woman must feel no shame! She was utterly proud and insisted everyone know which mysterious place she had come from and, on account of her illustrious father, that Fanny was from there too. In an attempt to keep her quiet, Fanny forbade her from coming up into the café, and when the young woman crossed the dining room in the evening after work, Fanny followed on her heels right to the door, staring at the girl to stop her from saying a word. After she had left, Fanny lightly uttered a few contemptuous remarks about her, to which no one paid attention, so little was the interest in the cook at the Coq Hardi.

Fanny enjoyed her job as a waitress. She wore Lucette's beige blouse and, after alteration, the green and yellow skirt with all the pleats, which Lucette had loved to spread around her on her raised chair. Fanny flung herself whole-heartedly into the job; she remembered the regulars' first names; she was obedient and level-headed.

Twice a month Uncle George stopped in for lunch, parking his little travelling-salesman car in front of the window. He sat at his regular table and ordered veal casserole. Looking a little different in his steel gray suit to how Fanny remembered him, having always seen him on holidays, he took soap samples out of his suitcase and handed them out around him. A good chap. Uncle George showed no sign of recognizing Fanny, his niece. Fanny did not doubt that he still bore a grudge against her for having taken Eugene with her. This was his way of punishing her. But how indifferent and passive his glance was when it happened to land on her! Where on earth did he find the strength to look so coldly at his own niece? She hovered around George, brushed against him with her sleeve, had fun spiriting away his little bars of soap and giving them back to him with huge bursts of laughter. One day she called him 'uncle' without getting any reaction. When he called her Lucette she exclaimed, 'I am Fanny, Lucette isn't here any more!'

'Oh, alright,' agreed George, courteously.

Could he really be her Uncle George? She watched him from every corner of the room. In spite of the irreproachable professionalism which she tried to show at all times, the service she gave other customers when George was having lunch came second to her uncle's wishes, to the pace of his meal. Fanny hardly took her eyes off him and hesitated for a long time before leaving his table. Even if he was pretending not to know Fanny to express his displeasure, at home he could enjoy the satisfaction of claiming that his niece treated him with exemplary respect, reminding Aunt Colette that such respect was typical of Fanny, who, long conscious of the imperfection of her birth, had always humbly striven to be forgiven and to make amends for her parents' negligence.

Gradually Fanny became bold enough to call George nothing but 'uncle', and she made a show of addressing him with familiarity. But he did not seem to notice, only mindful — when he was not eating — of arranging his multicoloured soaps on the table, putting them in precise piles, bowing his head so low over his work that you could only see the balding top of his skull. Since last time Uncle George had lost another good handful of hair! Fanny could not help singing Uncle George's praises to the boss and the cook, greatly surprising the young woman, who thought Fanny's father much more impressive than this unobtrusive travelling salesman. Moreover, neither of them wanted to believe this customer was Fanny's uncle, the first because she never saw him show Fanny any particular interest, the second because she could not imagine that Fanny was related to such an insignificant individual, someone who looked just like any other man from the region.

A storm broke. The neon lights — which were always turned on at noon during this season — went out. Uncle George was finishing a crème caramel. He took advantage of the darkness to stretch his hand out towards Fanny, who was standing next to him. Fanny trembled with joy, thinking he was going to speak at last. She leaned towards her uncle, who murmured, 'In my car, now.' George firmly gripped the delighted Fanny's elbow and they went out. They skirted around the restaurant in the little courtyard where he had parked his car that day and, at Uncle George's instigation, they both got into the back seat which was scattered with crushed soap bars. Uncle George said nothing, but began to breathe heavily and clasped Fanny in his arms. Oblivious to her discomfort, he squeezed her hard, causing sharp pains in her nose which was crammed against his curiously fragranced neck. Amazed, however, she let him do it. After all, wasn't it vital that Uncle George could in no way complain about her to Aunt Colette? Wasn't it vital that he agree to recognize her some day, a thing he would be more willing to do if Fanny was always obliging with him? George was grinding against her bones in silence; he finished by drooling a little on her shoulder, and she gently extricated herself while he caught his breath, one hand on his heart. 'If you speak to my aunt,' said Fanny, 'make sure she knows that I abandoned my post to come here with you.'

'Of course, of course,' answered George, with a lost look.

Uncle George must have changed his route because, to her great regret, Fanny did not see him again. She consoled herself with the certainty that he must have given an excellent report of her to Aunt Colette. But just as she had failed to glean the slightest information about Aunt Leda, no one among the Coq Hardi regulars — whom Uncle George had frequently treated to bars of soap — could tell her what had become of him or anything at all about him. What's more, her new position as waitress failed to bring Fanny all the advantages she had expected.

# THREE

## *Fanny Starts Dating*

Since this time of year left him idle, the young man who had led Fanny into the dog kennel one rainy evening then had looked at her insistently despite his having forgotten her the whole night, went to see her at the Coq Hardi, where he ended up spending entire afternoons. He would seat himself at the end of the room, order a beer, and watch Fanny, whose pleasure in meeting him again grew, even though she only half-liked his sullen features. She made certain that he had really always lived in the village. He had a slightly red face and seemed older than he was with long, thin sideboards that devoured his cheeks and at which he constantly tugged. He rarely knew what to say. But, for Fanny, his being from the village was a quality worth all others. What use would an outsider have been to her, whomever he might be? Such a person would have distanced her forever from the villages; the family would no doubt have welcomed him politely, but he would have indirectly reminded them of Fanny's defect. Fanny smiled at the boy whenever she dared. She thought his watching her at work put a sparkle in his gloomy eye. She was flattered that he liked her, despite everything, and felt grateful. As he was content for a long time to just come and sit at the café, quietly gazing at her, she decided to speed matters up. Awkwardly but firmly, Fanny put her hand on the young man's thigh, concealing her action from the other customers, and looked at him suggestively — although close up she found his face less appealing. His attraction to her was no longer as distinctly evident in the depth of his pale pupils where only a slow desire was now awakening now.

'Come on, take me to your parents' house,' whispered Fanny.

'They're not expecting us,' he answered, surprised.

'It's out of the question for me to go out with you or simply to talk to you if you don't introduce me to your parents, if you don't take me to your home straight away,' insisted Fanny.

She was ready to withdraw her hand while the stunned boy was still thinking it over.

'You see,' added Fanny, 'your parents' faces, their behaviour, the general atmosphere in your home are as important to me as your own charm, which would no longer appeal to me if certain external conditions weren't fulfilled. It's essential, you see, that I please your parents as much as you.'

'What does it matter?' exclaimed the young man, appearing somewhat offended.

'People like you can best judge what I can claim in my family, in this region, which is mine, even though no one will admit it. If your parents like me, Aunt Colette will like me for the same reasons. If you feel affection for me, I can just as well seduce my cousin Eugene. Perhaps,' cried Fanny, shrilly, 'the mistake of my birth isn't permanent. What if I never find Aunt Leda? There might be other ways. I have to find out.'

She roughly caressed him, worried that she had said too much and he would take fright.

'Our dog's called Leda,' he murmured, mechanically.

'Even so, she can't be my aunt,' laughed Fanny.

'I would like,' the young man added seriously, 'our dogs to make friends with you because they are good animals, you'll see.'

'Oh, dogs are too ungrateful,' sighed Fanny.

Then, since people were coming in, she took off across the room, wearing the smile which she had learned from Lucette and turned into her own, just like the skirt and blouse — it was not unusual for an absent-minded customer to say Lulu still, fooled, Fanny assumed, by the green and yellow leafy pattern. She was, after all, none other than Fanny.

Later, she made certain that she left the café at the same time as the boy. She took his arm, cuddled up to him and accompanied him to the farm. If only all the villagers could see her like this! Fanny was so proud that she deliberately dawdled and turned her head this way and that.

The parents were sitting at the kitchen table. Their hands lay idly in front of them, and they seemed to be quietly waiting for their son and Fanny, who sat down silently. The young man got out glasses and a bottle of liqueur wine. Down to the smallest detail, the parents were exactly as Fanny had imagined, thinking of members of her own family. They could have been part of her family just as they were. In their ordinary faces, a little sullen and distrustful, she saw the familiar features of uncles and aunts, and she even had to pull herself together to remember who they really were and hold back her affection. The mother was wearing a floral apron with familiar patterns, the father blue canvas overalls — displayed on one strap was the name of the store which Eugene still pointed to with his inviting finger in the poster on the Coq Hardi's facade. On the rounded kitchen cabinet were a calendar decorated with kittens, a gilded frame holding the photograph of the radiant young man in uniform, and crocheted doilies. Fanny would not have felt more at home in Grandmother's kitchen. Leaning back in her chair, she smiled broadly at the parents. She must marry this boy as soon as possible! The two old people, who still had not said anything and had simply waved away the wine that their son offered, took turns mumbling remarks which seemed to embarrass him and which Fanny could not understand no matter how hard she tried. She pricked her ears, but their strong accent — more pronounced than Grandmother's — prevented her from distinguishing one word from another. What's more, she was under the impression that they meant to be heard only by the young man. Her intent smiles remained unanswered, her affable looks met with a similarly reserved and prejudiced expression.

'They're asking,' the young man snapped at her, 'why you killed one of our dogs one night. My father saw you.'

'Oh!' cried out Fanny, 'if I'd known it was yours I'd have sooner let it eat me alive!'

Dismayed, she wanted to apologize. But the mother had crossed her arms over her apron and the father was scratching his elbow, staring at the table.

'They also wonder,' the boy continued, staring into space, 'why you dress exactly like the old waitress and find it strange that you could want to be taken for her. When my mother sees you through the café window, for a second she always thinks you are Lucette. That troubles her and makes her angry with you.'

'I was just trying not to change things,' mumbled Fanny.

The mother tutted and slowly shook her head, her lips pursed, her mind made up. The father reached forward to move the bottle a half-inch on the table, and the son got up and offered to see Fanny home.

In the café, which was closed now, she embraced him. Perhaps all was not yet lost — as exhausted as the yellow dog had been, wouldn't he have died by now anyway and already be forgotten? Even though she felt his reluctance, Fanny enticed the boy, not to her little room where she was afraid the noise would awaken the boss, but into the kitchen, which was still hot from the day's cooking. She made him lie down on the tile floor and pressed against him. The smell of grease filled the room and permeated the young man's skin. Then something scratched at the window. Fanny thought she saw the silhouette of a big, motionless dog staring at her, its tongue dangling. She closed her eyes, then opened them again. As she had hoped, she no longer saw a dog but just the cold glimmer of the street lamps and a few drops of rain on the windowpane. She shook the young man, whom the heat had lulled to sleep in her arms. He woke, ashamed, and could not be persuaded to stay any longer. He left without even kissing Fanny, disgusted by the filthy stains on his clothing, his back covered with onion peelings and grease spots.

He did not show his face in the café again. Fanny went and hung around the farm, not because she missed the boy but because she was overwhelmed by the idea of everything she had lost. She dared not go in because of the parents. She saw him, ran to him and hung on his neck.

'None of that,' he said, extricating himself, 'you know only too well that it's impossible after what you've done.'

'My uncle George acted just like that!' shouted Fanny.

The young man replied that he couldn't care less about Uncle George and continued calmly on his way.

# FOUR

## *George*

Just when Fanny remembered that she had a fiancé whom she had not exactly split up with before leaving home but had quite simply forgotten, he came in. He was wearing the same clothes as the last time and was exactly as Fanny pictured him in her mind, where he had suddenly reappeared for no apparent reason. His name was George and he was the same age as Fanny. She blushed profusely as he walked up to her, smiling happily and proudly. He had a broad chest and a handsome, confident face. He looked so like Fanny that they had often been taken for brother and sister — a fact that disturbed her. She found the memory humiliating and muttered sharply, her face turned away, 'Well, what do you want?' as he stood and blocked her path.

'But it's me. Don't you recognize me?'

He called her by her old name, tenderly drawing out each consonant. 'I don't want to hear that name any more!' exclaimed Fanny in horror. She looked carefully around her; with the hubbub and business of lunch, George's words could not have reached any ears but her own. 'I'm Fanny now, try not to get it wrong,' she said bitterly. George nodded good-naturedly, then, since Fanny said she had to work, he started towards an empty table, but she held him back and declared that under no circumstances could he sit down in the dining room, his presence would embarrass her too much. The boss was already turning her indifferent gaze on them. A few customers, as they waited for their meal, quietly watched them. What would they think, all of them, if they learned that this boy had been Fanny's fiancé and undoubtedly still considered himself as such? Would they believe for another second all that Fanny had declared about Grandmother's village and her own family? There was no comparison between him and Uncle George. Exactly where *this* George came from Fanny had never known anyway, and now she was too scared to ask him. George, her fiancé, did not come from anywhere! Not knowing what else to do with him for now, she took him to her room. To be absolutely certain that he would not appear downstairs, she locked him in, despite his protests and promises.

George explained that he had come to look for her. He had gone to Fanny's father's house and the servant had sent him to the village in the postcard. From there, he had arrived directly here, after meeting the same people whom Eugene and Fanny had met, and was only a little surprised that such a long journey had led him just a couple of miles from her Grandmother's village, from where he knew Fanny had set out. Intensely worried, George paced up and down the room. He reminded Fanny of the marriage plans they had made before she had fled, of all the promises and demonstrations of love which Fanny could not remember and could not imagine having made.

'Come on, you're exaggerating,' repeated Fanny, smiling indulgently. All she remembered of George was a remark Aunt Colette had made, one day when Fanny showed her a photograph of her fiancé: 'If you hadn't told me who it was,' exclaimed Aunt Colette, 'I would have thought it was you!'

Now George's face filled Fanny with disgust. But George would not leave. Mad with disappointment, he grabbed Fanny, calling her a traitor, using her real name as he shook her and shoved her about. How strange his words and actions seemed! But George, still hopeful, refused to leave. He slept on the carpet, at the foot of Fanny's bed, and let himself be locked in the bedroom when Fanny left in the morning. She did not want him to be seen in the village streets either, where people might guess his acquaintance with her or believe that he was from her family — if they did not quite simply mistake him for her. If she had time, she took the leftovers from lunch up to him; she scolded him and kicked him when she found him lying in her bed. One day, to Fanny's great relief, George disappeared without her seeing him leave. Since no trace remained of his visit, Fanny soon forgot him just as if she had never had anything to do with him.

# FIVE
## *Aunt Colette's Village*

Since Fanny had arrived at the Coq Hardi, the rain had only let up briefly to give way to some short-lived snow, and now it was raining and raining again so that the weak light seemed to become dimmer and the days shorter.

A lorry parked in front of the café and Fanny greeted the driver, whom she did not know, as he came in. As she walked up to the table, she glanced out of the window. On the lorry, inscribed in big brown letters, were the words 'LEDA Transport'. Fanny pulled up a chair and sat down opposite the man, gracing him with her most engaging smile; he responded with surprised, flattered pleasure. Didn't his ruddy face bear the same eager and paternal expression as Uncle George's when he had grabbed Fanny in the back seat of his little car, where for the first time he had allowed her to imagine that she would perhaps one day be his niece in spite of everything, that after all she was forgivable? He had embraced her not without a certain family affection.

Fanny pressed the man with questions and learned that the head office of LEDA Transport was located in the village where Aunt Colette and Uncle George had always lived! What's more, he was going back there and, since she begged him so plaintively, he did not see any problem in taking Fanny there at once.

Fanny grabbed the man's sleeve and asked, 'What is LEDA Transport? Why that name?'

'It's my boss's name.'

'Could your boss be my Aunt Leda?' exclaimed Fanny.

'I don't think so,' said the man, who did not understand.

He added, for the satisfaction of stating something he was sure of, that a secondary character on 'White Coats', a television series he was watching at the time, was called Leda, a beautiful, middle-aged woman with red hair. Then he got up and Fanny hurried to fetch her suitcase. The boss was not around, so she could leave quietly, and she clambered up next to the lorry driver for whom she already felt a deep gratitude and that special affection for the round, purple faces of the region — so different from George's slender and noble face!

On her way to Aunt Colette's village, she was happy to leave this one. No one had told her anything about Aunt Leda that had not confused her a little, talking, for example, about a dog with that name;

and Aunt Clemence, like Uncle George, whose presence here had disconcerted her, had finally turned out to be deceptive and disrespectful, which made Fanny sadder than if they had shown her open hostility. She definitely intended, once she had arrived and if Uncle George had neglected to do so, to let Aunt Colette know how devoted she had been to her husband by leaving her job for him in the middle of lunch. What's more, the next time she visited Grandmother, she would not miss the chance to sternly inform her of Aunt Clemence's bad manners. Fanny delighted in everything she would have to tell everyone. Her close interest in family matters and her keeping Grandmother and Aunt Colette informed could only be to her advantage. Eugene, on the other hand, was content just to use the family without giving back the consideration it deserved.

Fanny settled comfortably with her suitcase on her knees and the collar of her raincoat turned up high on her neck. The man chatted as he peered at the road through the heavy rain, and Fanny, who was not listening, responded with occasional exclamations. At one point he stopped on a dirt track and turned towards Fanny with a big, benevolent smile, an affectionate look. He became so like Uncle George that it disturbed Fanny. He grabbed her clumsily, and Fanny hurriedly asked herself what she could gain from this unexpected encounter — perhaps he would introduce her to the boss called Leda. He squashed her against the window just as Uncle George had done, or as Lucette had against the bedroom wall, and shook her in every direction with such heavy, clumsy movements that Fanny had to stop herself from resisting. Each person here can be useful to me, she thought, and even though this is my home, it's not my place to tell other people how to act. I should be submissive and unassuming, happy simply not to displease. The sky was so grey and the downpour so heavy that she could hardly see. The man's features became blurred; when he sat up and finally let go of Fanny, she could no longer tell who he really was because of all the other faces mixed in her memory, all going out of their way to take advantage of her. To avoid letting Uncle George's name, or that of her own father or her cousin Eugene, slip from her mouth, Fanny said nothing. Happy and more relaxed, the man chattered on and drove fast. In Grandmother's village they passed in front of her house. The shutters were closed, and the house looked deserted, abandoned. She promised herself to ask at the first opportunity for news of Grandmother. But for now, she had to admit, a more urgent mission awaited, because she was heading towards Aunt Colette's village where LEDA Transport was located, a coincidence that was so encouraging Fanny barely kept herself from assuming her troubles were over.

They reached Aunt Colette's village a few minutes after passing through Grandmother's. In the middle of the open fields, silos marked its boundary. The church without a weathervane overhung the main road, which had eaten up the pavements. Aunt Colette's village looked so much like the neighbouring towns that Fanny truly believed she had remained in the same place, until she recognized the grey-blue walls of her uncle and aunt's house where she had often come as a child. The lorry driver dropped her off not far from it, and Fanny was sorry he drove off again before seeing her knock at the front door, because she wanted to prove to him that she really had family everywhere she said she did! She ran under the porch to find shelter from the rain. The street was silent and empty; the cars that were flying past in a steady stream did not break the endless, pervading torpor, which seemed to emanate from the vast grid of fields, perpetually crossed by isolated combines. She pressed the doorbell; Aunt Colette's door opened and a girl Fanny did not know answered her greeting.

'I'm Aunt Colette's niece!' announced Fanny straight away.

'She's not here,' said the girl, whose face was pretty but nothing out of the ordinary, 'neither are George or Eugene.'

'Well, where are they then?'

Fanny seemed so disappointed that the girl became concerned. Fanny scrutinized the girl's movements and the expressions on her pleasant face. Could this be Eugene's fiancée? Could she have already moved in here? The girl was in her slippers and her hair was wrapped around big multi-coloured curlers. Kindly, she explained that Aunt Colette had left the previous day for the capital, where she was staying with her sister, Fanny's mother.

'Nobody told me that!' exclaimed Fanny, vexed.

As for Uncle George, he was travelling the region as his job demanded; he wasn't expected for several days. Even Eugene was out in search of some job or other — his contract with the hardware store had not led to anything, said the girl, who could not help pursing her lips and wrinkling her brow with disappointment.

'If only he'd listened to me,' said Fanny, 'if only he'd stayed with me!'

But the girl shrugged indifferently. She displayed her lack of concern at the prospect of rivalry with Fanny so cruelly — hadn't the girl more than likely heard several things about Fanny to reassure her? — that Fanny, who was tightly buttoned into her raincoat, felt crushed. She looked at the girl — who must have pleased Aunt Colette — with admiring respect, a sudden affection, complete humility. She was invited in. The girl offered her tea and shuffled comfortably in her slippers. Fanny sat down in the kitchen, at the table covered with an oilcloth, and, beneath its considerable wear, she recognized the pattern of leaves, acorns, and mushrooms that she had enjoyed analyzing with Eugene in days gone by when she had been taken to play at her cousin's, from time to time, on Sundays.

The girl silently bustled about. She used each object as Aunt Colette would have done, with casual familiarity. Fanny dared not move, although she really wanted to look in Aunt Colette's living room to check whether the collection of little folk dolls, each a prisoner in her round plastic box, was still in the display cabinet; whether Uncle George's three rifles were still hung against the wallpaper with the country pattern, above the sideboard holding the precious holiday dishes and old wedding presents; and, most importantly, whether on top of the television set they still had a certain photograph of Fanny as a child, laughing and hugging one of Grandmother's dogs. But the girl did not suggest they leave the kitchen. She no doubt would have been shocked, and might even have reported it to Aunt Colette with a snigger, if Fanny had got up and started to poke around without her permission. She poured the tea into a holly-patterned cup, pushed it towards Fanny, then sighed heavily and started to take out her curlers. She placed them one after another on the oilcloth, and her tightly curled hair suddenly made her face look mature and weary. Wasn't this Aunt Colette herself, in the dim light? How right it was that this very girl was engaged to Eugene and loved by Aunt Colette, instead of Fanny, even though she was a member of the family! Because wasn't this Aunt Colette herself?

Fanny informed the girl, who politely pretended to be interested, that she in turn would go to her mother's, in town, and would join Aunt Colette there; then Fanny left her and set off to find LEDA Transport, whose headquarters the lorry driver had told her she would find at the end of the village. Fanny had to cover a good half a mile in the rain before reaching it. Bordered by a cornfield and a two-lane road, it was a sort of run-down warehouse flanked by a shed that served as an office. In the shed, a lone woman was typing under a light bulb hanging from the ceiling.

'I would like to meet your boss,' Fanny, intimidated, broke the silence. 'I have been told he is called Leda.'

'No, no, not at all.' Annoyed to have to turn from her work, the woman spoke in a brisk, peremptory voice. 'He's called that, but Leda is the name of the business not our boss's name. LEDA stands for Loyalty, Endurance, Discipline, Ambition. You've been misinformed.'

'Then Leda's nothing and nobody?' asked Fanny, surprised.

'Nothing and nobody,' answered the woman with satisfaction.

'Nevertheless, Leda exists, even if you can't tell me anything about her!' protested Fanny.

'What Leda? I haven't heard anyone mention any Leda for the thirty years that I've lived here.'

And the woman, plunging back into her work, cut Fanny off and seemed to forget her presence completely; so Fanny left and slowly made her way back to the village, in the increasing darkness. Numb and exhausted, she passed Aunt Colette's house where a bluish light glowed. The pavements were still deserted; the only café and the little grocery shop, its display window sullied with undecipherable graffiti, were closed.

# SIX

## *Fanny Leaves*

She arrived at the train station, bought a chocolate bar and a ticket, and waited on the desolate platform for the next train to the capital, where she had spent her entire adolescence with her mother. Not remembering a single family member ever visiting them made it all the more difficult for Fanny to imagine Aunt Colette there. Aunt Colette hated to travel, to leave her house, to needlessly spend money. Fanny dared not hope that Aunt Colette had made the trip to see her, Fanny; that would have meant that Uncle George had not mentioned his reunion with her at the Coq Hardi and that Aunt Colette pined for her niece so much she had decided to take the train to find her, which was not likely. Besides, even though Aunt Colette did not openly disapprove of her sister's behaviour, it was even harder to imagine that she would undertake a trip just for the pleasure of her company. Fanny was impatient to know the motive for Aunt Colette's trip. Believing Aunt Leda to be at the centre of everything, Fanny imagined some fatal connection between Colette's expedition and Aunt Leda.

Fanny got onto the train alone. Some people were sleeping on the orange plastic seats. Frightened someone might steal her suitcase from her, Fanny sat on it and dozed off. When she awoke shortly before dawn, she was stretched out on the floor among apple cores, paper wrappers and wads of chewing-gum; her suitcase had disappeared and so had her raincoat, although she had not removed it. She had dreamt that Eugene was tenderly slipping it off her! She searched the three empty carriages — all the passengers had got off before the capital — and she stepped on so much litter that her shoes were covered with it. Through the dirty windows, a mild day was breaking over the sprawling suburb. The air trembled with drizzle. New towers appeared to sway, and cranes were already moving. Alongside the track, a window lit up and Fanny caught a glimpse of silhouettes, a man in his kitchen, as the train blared and its blast of air made the curtains flutter all along the blackened facades. Fanny shivered. Was there any reason to believe that Eugene had come, as she had dreamt, to take her raincoat and snatch her suitcase at the same time, then had slipped away? Should she rush after him? Thick streams of smoke rising from a burning rubbish tip obscured the dawn. Now the train was passing over a major road, and Fanny leaned out in the hope of spotting Uncle

George's vehicle in the stream of greyish cars. From above they seemed to move slowly and silently, as if in a dream! Identical houses, neat little gardens enclosed by hedges passed by; ill-assorted constructions of strange and unexpected new towns scraped the sky, and a large concrete statue of a suffering prisoner blocked the light for a while; mysterious warehouses, uniformly corrugated iron on uneven ground, stretched out next to the river and the bare grass. In front of the supermarkets, which were gradually opening now, long lines of shopping trollies were parked one inside the other; cars were arriving already, and boots gaped open and were methodically filled. Then a tunnel muffled everything, and the train entered the station, beneath the drizzle resounding on the glass roof. Fanny jumped out onto the platform, which was crowded with working people coming from the suburbs. Dragged by the flux, she took a few steps towards the exit and suddenly bumped straight into her mother. It really was Fanny's mother, in a new coat, a brown fur! It took them a few seconds to recognize each other, and they were too surprised to think of hugging straight away. Fanny thought her mother looked like an elegant bear in this coat which she had never seen before and which surprised her.

'Unfortunately, my little girl,' exclaimed the mother as she brandished a tartan suitcase, 'I have to be off. I'm catching a flight in an hour!'

'But you've never flown before,' said Fanny, taken aback.

'Yes, yes, but that's how it is. Today I'm catching a flight.'

She took a key from her pocket and shoved it into Fanny's hand.

'Go home; you'll find Aunt Colette. I still don't know exactly when I'll be back. 'Bye, my little girl. Imagine meeting you here!'

# SEVEN
## *At Home*

Fanny left the station, thinking that she would have liked to accompany her mother wherever she was going, as in the old days, but it was typical that her mother had not suggested it — perhaps she knew, anyway, from Aunt Colette that Fanny had set out in search of Leda and respected her undertaking. Immediately Fanny headed northwards, to where her mother lived, next to the ring-road, in a vast housing development with unfashionably bright-coloured walls, on the first floor of a high building not far from a car factory; a neighbourhood equipped with every convenience, as she delighted in pointing out. Grandmother had often repeated it with satisfaction, although she had never come there. But her mother's wise choice of such a practical place, which she did not have to leave to go shopping, to the cinema, or to her place of work — a stylish hairdressing salon — earned her the family's grudging approval. For them such ingenuity, such resourcefulness made amends for many past mistakes — though they pretended to attach little importance to it, they boasted that Fanny's mother decidedly knew how to get her own way, how to set about things. How proud Fanny had been, when she arrived in the village, to have once lived in this housing development! At that time her mother's glory had completely enveloped her, because she had made her way in the mysterious city — though not without losing her head and her good sense a little.

Fanny hurried through the wide streets, dizzy at the very idea of seeing Aunt Colette again so soon. She was almost running and at this moment felt not in the least tired or worried. But she found the flat empty. In her own bedroom, where her mother had probably put Aunt Colette, only a shopping bag remained, which she remembered seeing on her aunt's arm. Fanny opened it at once and was disappointed to find nothing but a dog-eared photograph. In it Aunt Colette was barely visible, half-reclined on a couch, with a strangely youthful face and wearing a thick fur coat similar to Fanny's mother's coat; she was firmly holding the two lapels between her thumb and her forefinger. Although she did not like this picture, Fanny put the photograph away in the back pocket of her trousers. She had to keep in mind that access to Aunt Leda now depended on Aunt Colette, she could not hope to flush Leda out as long as she did not know where Aunt Colette was, and besides, Aunt Colette's unexpected absence weighed on her. Even when she succeeded in laying hands on whatever Aunt Leda was — Fanny sniggered bitterly, thinking that she could have presented some dog to the family and said, 'Here is Leda,' without their taking the slightest offence as long as the animal turned out to be docile and a good hunter — what would victory mean to her if Aunt Colette was not there to respect it? Fanny no longer knew where to look for Leda; her dreams of the last few nights had not revealed any sign as far as she remembered. Perhaps Aunt Colette, who was surely better disposed towards Fanny today than she had been during Grandmother's birthday lunch, would help her. But Fanny anxiously wondered if Aunt Colette would come back; she hadn't left any clothes or any sign of having been there, except the old shopping bag and the photograph. Fanny's mother, as usual, had deceived her or made a mistake through carelessness and haste. Fanny would not have suffered if she never saw her again. Without meaning to, her mother had so far done her less good than harm, such was her indifference. Yet Fanny's shame would have been greater still if her mother had decided not to come back from her trip and to cease any relation with the family. It was fortunate that, in spite of everything, the family kept more authority over Fanny's mother than she imagined!

Fanny proceeded to wait for Aunt Colette; she left her bedroom for her and made herself a bed in the living room.

# EIGHT
# *The Housing Development*

*The flat* — Fanny's mother's satisfaction with her flat was also firmly based on the fact that for the privilege of living here she had to pay much more than her relatives spent each month in the villages, where she would not have found anywhere to rent, not even a big place, for as high a price as her noisy, dark little flat. Even Grandmother sometimes boasted that her daughter had to spend half of her salary for such a roof over her head. She herself would not have been able to make such a sacrifice, no more than the rest of the family, who were flabbergasted and congratulated themselves on their own luck, but still admired, even envied this expense, which seemed to prove that it was not granted to everyone to live in this place — you had to either deserve it or possess such remarkable faculties that for some obscure reason you preferred it to any other. If the family had come, Fanny's mother would no doubt have attributed its inability to see the smallest advantage in living in one of these buildings — in a large, decrepit development, in the constant rumbling and fumes of the roadway — to its ignorance and lack of refinement. The living room looked onto the ring-road, and for this reason, despite the noise, Fanny's mother thought it the most pleasant room in the flat, because from the couch she enjoyed watching cars speed by towards town, sometimes even witnessing some spectacular accident. In this modern living room with deep, comfortable chairs, and shelves strewn with exotic little knick-knacks, it was never boring, even though the windows could not be opened.

*The supermarket* — Fanny's mother's choice of this exact lodging had been influenced by the location of the supermarket at the foot of the block of flats, which aroused the envy of all the women in the family. At dawn, in front of the locked doors of the long, never-ending supermarket, patient groups formed and waited, freezing in the winter morning cold, right in front of the shop window, as if, knowing full well that they would arrive too early and perfectly aware of the hugeness of the shop — could anyone claim to have already explored the whole place? — they wanted to be sure of having a place or to experience the unique, exhilarating pleasure of being the first to slide along the clean, new-looking tiled floor, to push without hindrance the big, still-empty trolley with squeaking wheels along the stretch of aisles between the shelves which had been mysteriously refilled since the previous day, or as if, which was even more likely, they hoped against every past experience that they would be among the first to reach the check-out counters and that the interminable lines would not form before they reached them; lines that always, whatever the hour, whatever the number of people you thought you had seen enter the supermarket, wound from one end of the shop to the other, or snaked in complicated scrolls, without anyone being able to explain where so many people came from, so many different faces, nor for what strange reason, the sun having hardly risen, they suddenly found themselves reunited there and beaten again to the check-outs, which were so numerous that the eye could not take them all in at once — an entire life in the development would not be enough for one to claim to have paid at each of them at least once. More than anything Fanny had loved to accompany her mother to the supermarket. They always arrived at opening time, ate lunch in the cafeteria upstairs, and stayed until evening; it was a real holiday, and Fanny could not have said which was more exquisite, the supermarket holiday or Grandmother's birthday party.

*The hairdressing salon* — In the past, Fanny had taken almost as much pleasure in going to meet her mother at the end of the day at the hairdressing salon. The salon was located on the same huge strip of hard-packed ground as the supermarket, beneath an overhead subway track. Sometimes, when Fanny's mother was in the mood to enjoy herself, they went from the hairdressing salon straight to the supermarket for the sole pleasure of looking at some new product. They would have dinner there, although the food was not that great, but even Fanny's mother loved the up-beat musical atmosphere of the cafeteria.

The hairdressing salon was always full. There were always so many people of all types and ages at the entrance that it had become necessary to build a corridor narrow enough that two people could not stand in it side-by-side. This was to control and hold back the crowd, because if it pushed into the reception area fights would surely break out. At the end of the corridor was a barrier, and it was Fanny's mother's responsibility to operate it as wisely as possible. That was her job. When she saw that a hairdresser was about to finish with her customer, she lowered a lever and allowed in as many people as there were free hairdressers — who only had to worry about their work and were not even supposed to look up. Constant attention was demanded of Fanny's mother, and a sharp eye, since more than fifty hairdressers were working in the salon. She stayed on her feet for eight hours at the barrier, one hand on the lever, wearing an elegant pale green uniform. She was proud, as was Grandmother, who was informed of every detail, that no one ever noticed a single trace of weariness on her pleasant, smiling face, which she tilted imperceptibly to greet each person who burst from the corridor, reeling a little, propelled, once the barrier was open, by the weight of the crowd piling up in the shaft, who muttered unhappily when the barrier clanged shut again.

*The cinema* — As for the supermarket and the hairdressing salon, Fanny and her mother only had to cross the road to go to the cinema, which they visited on some Saturday nights. They never bothered to consult the programme, because they knew what kind of films, if not exactly which, were being shown at the Eldorado, and both of them happened to like violent stories about karate experts or brave policemen with hard, cynical faces. They arrived early to reserve the best seats in the middle, and Fanny was most happy when, after the customary humming and hawing, her mother called the usherette over and proudly offered Fanny a chocolate ice-cream bar with hazel nuts, advising her to make it last. The seats, which had been reupholstered in an old orange fabric, were wreathed with little yellowish stains and covered with writing conscientiously etched in indelible ink. The loud squeals of young people, getting over excited at the back or laughing constantly, sometimes drowned out the dialogue, so Fanny and her mother never minded seeing the same film again, from one Saturday to another, and tried hard to figure out the plot. They really enjoyed telling people that they had succeeded in watching a film three times in a row without realizing that it was the same one!

*The park* — On the other hand, Grandmother was not aware that for complicated reasons the project for the landscaping of a beautiful green area between the supermarket and the overhead track — which had been announced a long time ago — had not been carried out. Fanny's mother hardly complained since she would not have had the time to stroll around the park, even on Sundays, when she ironed the week's laundry and watched a particularly entertaining television show.

# NINE

## *Aunt Colette Does Not Return*

Fanny waited for Aunt Colette for as long as the food lasted in the refrigerator and the kitchen cabinets. Prudently, she did not leave the flat: if Aunt Colette came back during her absence, perhaps to retrieve the photograph of herself in a surprising fur coat, and left before Fanny's return, Fanny would not have forgiven herself. Besides, she would have given the photograph back to Aunt Colette without hesitation, without even asking for a word of explanation, she felt so embarrassed by such a picture of her aunt seated on an unknown couch. For the moment, Fanny held onto the photograph and felt too responsible to keep it anywhere other than on her person, in one of her trouser pockets.

Neither Aunt Colette nor Fanny's mother showed up. Her mother must have abandoned her job at the hairdressing salon. It was lucky that Fanny had bumped into her in the train station and been able to get news of her — her mother would have allowed herself to catch the plane, to just clear off, having completely forgotten her daughter. The fact that Fanny had not planned on returning for some time made no difference, her mother hadn't bothered to leave even a short note on the kitchen table, a fact that offended Fanny, who saw it as a sign of an increased lack of concern. What must Aunt Colette have thought, observing how her sister lived? Did it make her take a more lenient view of Fanny? But Fanny knew they would forgive her mother and yet grant her nothing, despite all her efforts to be perfect, loving and repectful where the family was concerned. Fanny was, to all of them, twice as guilty as her own mother, although she had rarely acted badly. This was the family's harsh law.

# TEN
## *A Job*

When she ran out of money, Fanny found work at the fast-food restaurant in the development. The restaurant was situated at the bottom of a fairly new tower, on a big paved square, where the wind blew. Its presence was announced by tall, flashing pink letters, visible right from the centre of town, and by a giant balloon, marked with the same bloated letters. The balloon was light and fanciful, and floated from the top of the slender tower which seemed to have been built solely to allow it to fly so high. For as long as Fanny remembered, the balloon had served her as a landmark; so, when she needed a job, she naturally headed towards it, confident to see it so bright, so pink, circling gracefully, full of promises. But Fanny disliked leaving the flat because she was certain that Aunt Colette would choose this precise moment to come back, only to leave again. Unless the persistent cold persuaded her to stay a while? But when she saw that Fanny was living there, wouldn't Aunt Colette prefer to avoid her? Could she have the slightest desire to meet up with Fanny unless she had something to scold her for? Fanny did not see anything Aunt Colette could scold her for after the attentions she had lavished on Uncle George and since Eugene had returned to the fold — besides Eugene, as Fanny persisted in thinking, had perhaps stolen her suitcase and her raincoat from her on the train, although she had not actually seen him and had not found a plausible reason for such a daring act. The only thing she could do was to try to get home early every evening, even if it meant running all the way through the streets, which were identical to one another, where she still got lost sometimes, between the grimy buildings. But her shift, which started at around eleven in the morning, lasted well into the night, not that there was a clause in her contract to that effect, but people kept coming in all the time and it would have been inappropriate to stop abruptly, following out-dated rules which would have hindered the smooth operation of the business. Fanny understood, as had been stressed, that business demanded sacrifices. She had been placed in the preparation of hamburgers, where about thirty young people were already bustling about. She was made to wear a pink and white striped smock and a floppy-eared cap bearing her name, Fanny, and the name of the restaurant. She stood behind a long counter, just beyond the cash stands, which were almost as numerous as those in the supermarket. When she happened to look up, she had a global view of the dining room, and the customers could just as easily watch her work; — they rarely forewent this entertainment, some of them going so far as to perch on the seats, chewing slowly — despite the double ban on putting one's feet on the solid pink plastic furniture and unduly lengthening the time they took to eat. Fanny's neighbour stuffed bread rolls with a ground meat patty which Fanny then garnished with tomatoes and pickles amid such a din — monotonous tunes, which Fanny could not get out of her head, wailed from the restaurant's own radio station and peppered her dreams at night — that it was impossible to start up the slightest conversation. This of course, was good for work. A conscientious young woman, dressed in a darker pink, strictly supervised the production of the hamburgers. On a heavy slate which hung around her neck, she noted in white chalk the first names of the employees she had judged the best in the categories of enthusiasm, efficiency, cleanliness, good manners and smile. At the first sign of flagging, she would erase a name with one swipe of a fat sponge which she brandished in her other hand and called 'my little soul'. Employees singled out for recognition had the luck one morning of discovering their faces displayed above each cash stand, in a gold frame decorated with fake laurels, and the satisfaction of putting on a special outfit for ten days — a silver-coloured smock gathered in a belt with a buckle in the shape of two angel wings. Most importantly, they could now hope to become cashiers more quickly, a position sought by all and which everyone agreed held a degree of dignity. As a result, the young woman was unanimously courted and flattered. During the big party which the restaurant organized each summer, where a good number of badges and tee-shirts were handed out, there was not a single employee, male or female, who did not fight over taking her arm, offering her an ice cream cone, or making her laugh with jokes and gossip.

# ELEVEN

## *Aunt Colette?*

One day when Fanny raised her head, as she did once or twice an hour to rest, she suddenly noticed Aunt Colette in a fur coat coming into the dining room and heading straight for the cash stands. When the two lapels of the fur coat fell open, the unlikely blue of Aunt Colette's holiday dress sparkled briefly. Fanny could not hold back a cry. She dropped rolls, tomato and onion, despite her colleagues' astonished protests, and started to go round the long counter, which seemed endless. She did not take her eyes off Aunt Colette. Why, there was Aunt Colette ordering a hamburger, one hand clutching the top of her coat in a manner Fanny had never seen before and with an impatient expression on her face, which was, however, very familiar. Fanny made no headway, even though she was running. Some obstacle kept cropping up to hold her back: a group of employees blocked her way as a joke, her cap fell off, slipping under her foot; and as for the counter, it stretched out further and further, and Aunt Colette became smaller and smaller and more distant with each step! Soon Fanny could no longer see her. When she finally made it to the other side, Aunt Colette had disappeared, no doubt taking her meal with her since Fanny did not see her seated at any table. Despairing, she slowly returned to her post. Her escapade earned her the wiping of her name from the slate and a harsh reprimand. But how could it be explained that now every time Fanny raised her head she saw Aunt Colette come in, in the same article of clothing, only to leave almost immediately, passing through so rapidly that Fanny did not even have time to dash forward? Aunt Colette always seemed upset and annoyed, as if she were angry at being seen in such a place but could not avoid it. Despite her repeated appearances in the dining room of the fast-food restaurant, Aunt Colette never showed up at Fanny's mother's flat, and neither did Fanny's mother. But Aunt Colette must have been living in the area to appear so often in this same place, motivated by intentions that Fanny, who thought about it constantly, could not work out. If Aunt Colette had learnt of what Fanny was doing, was it conceivable that she was getting a kick out of tormenting her in this way? That she deliberately did not acknowledge her but pretended not to see her and ran away before Fanny could reach her? Ten, twenty times a day, Aunt Colette came in then hurried back out, wide and heavy as she was, always wearing the long coat, which she tried desperately to prevent from falling open. Fanny was scared that people would begin to find her aunt's conduct — which they must have noticed — suspicious, and that shameful questionings would land her in trouble again. But it was so difficult for her not to look up!

# TWELVE

## *Fanny And Her Colleagues*

Fanny's arrival had not inspired any particular curiosity. Most of the employees, who lived in the development, bore features so like hers, that she sometimes thought that she saw George or herself reflected in some colleague or other and had to do a double-take or lose herself briefly in thought to make this illusion vanish. People were surprised, however, that she was called Fanny; they laughed outright when she tried to describe Grandmother's village, and never wanted to believe that it was her village or that she had such an ordinary individual for a grandmother. Laughing, they demanded she admit her real first name.

'I'm Fanny and none other than Fanny!' she would cry out, blushing with helplessness. For several girls around her to have the very name she was hiding, the name her scatter-brained parents had chosen for her and which Aunt Colette had forgotten, would have been enough to make Fanny conceal it, since it seemed to her that these girls' faces differed so little from her own that, were she to be addressed by that name, she would merge with them without even noticing it and no longer remember that she was Fanny, Aunt Colette's niece, Eugene's cousin, according to her true nature. They were anxious for her to forget it — that's why they wouldn't believe her! While the girls were assembling various hamburgers, with knowing expressions on their faces, they would make fun of Fanny for inventing such an extravagant ancestry. They called her 'sister', refusing to doubt that Fanny was one of them. Eugene had never said 'my cousin'! They imagined that some stupid vanity, a shameful self-disgust, made Fanny create so many tall tales and such a fuss. The irritable pity that she aroused in the most indulgent of her colleagues only increased when Fanny pulled from her pocket the folded, dog-eared photograph of Aunt Colette in a fur coat, and presented it as the unlikely proof of her story.

# THIRTEEN
## *Brief Return*

One lunch time, Fanny saw her mother suddenly come in, wearing the same outfit as at the train station and casually swinging her handsome Scottish suitcase. She joined the line in front of one of the cash stands and stared at the illuminated board which displayed all the different kinds of hamburgers the restaurant offered. Fanny, having asked permission, was able to join her mother before she had given her order.

'Well, my little girl!' exclaimed Fanny's mother, barely surprised. She wanted to kiss her but was hampered by the suitcase and the ample fur sleeves on her new coat. Smiling, she blew some kisses into the air. 'Imagine meeting you here!'

'Where is Aunt Colette?' asked Fanny, her arms crossed over her apron.

'Oh, well, listen, I have no idea! I've just arrived from the airport, and I leave again in two hours.'

'Aren't you going to see Grandmother?'

'I don't have time! What's the point? Has she changed?'

'She's going to die!' whispered Fanny, her knees trembling with rage.

'You're exaggerating!'

Fanny's mother bought two thick hamburgers and two servings of chips, then looked at her watch, put down her suitcase and, lifting the paper bag up high, gave Fanny a little peck on the cheek. She turned and walked towards the exit where a man whom Fanny did not know, but who was a little like her father, took her arm; they left, Fanny's mother's curled hair bouncing gaily on her collar. Then Aunt Colette came in, fleetingly. The two sisters did not seem to see each other. As for Fanny, she had already gone back to her counter. Knowing that Aunt Colette would fly off at a run, having barely reached the cash stand, she did not move but suffering, her skin burning, tried not to look at her.

# FOURTEEN
## *Fanny Becomes A Cashier*

Since Fanny's attitude and work had been perfectly satisfactory and in view of the tacit rule that young people with the most pleasant faces would never be kept too long making hamburgers — even if it meant leaving some essential post vacant and relentlessly pushing back those with unattractive faces — Fanny moved to cash register number ten, under a higher arch and with the added duties of friendliness and servility. It was forbidden to smile without showing one's teeth, which must be gleaming and perfect; to utter, whatever the circumstances, the word *no*; to lean or relax against the cash stand; or, finally, to say anything at all that could keep the customer — who, in any case, should be allowed no more than forty-five seconds — one second longer than necessary. Fanny eagerly moved up to this new post. But it was maddening fate that from the day when she appeared, fresh and polite, behind the cash stand, Aunt Colette never again, in one form or another, set foot in the restaurant, although Fanny had noticed her the day before, thirty or more times, in her coat or simply her blue dress, coming in without reason, venturing a few steps, then hastily disappearing. Now that Fanny was in a position to talk to her, Aunt Colette had slipped away! Although her mother had not come back, Fanny could not help seeing a connection between her visit and Aunt Colette's sudden absence, although she had to admit that Aunt Colette had not followed her mother immediately. But if her mother had seen Aunt Colette, she might well have influenced her in some way, advising her sister to stay away from Fanny, as a general precaution, having perhaps heard how Fanny had behaved at Grandmother's birthday party or imagining Fanny would ask her aunt annoying questions, or even forbidding Aunt Colette to continue to persecute Fanny, if that had been Aunt Colette's intention. Perhaps Fanny's mother had naively declared, 'My little girl has nothing more to atone for! She loves and respects the family much more than I, she concerns herself with Grandmother while I take off, without telling anyone, with the first man who comes along!'

'That's right, that's right. Who cares more about the family than Fanny,' Aunt Colette would have replied.

Since Aunt Colette persisted in staying away, Fanny got tired of being on the lookout for nothing and started asking about her two aunts, Leda and Colette, timidly at first, then with every customer, thinking it would be stupid to see so many people pass through without trying to benefit from it. 'Do you know Aunt Leda? And where is Aunt Colette now?' she would quickly whisper, her lips moving imperceptibly, as she gave back change. But it was so noisy that people rarely heard her or even noticed that she had spoken. When they understood, they shook their heads and puffed their cheeks. 'You've never even met anyone by that name? Not even an animal?' Fanny would insist, discouraged. 'Not even a dog?' Her words were drowned out by the staccato music, or a cheerful, really witty commercial for the restaurant, that made everyone around smile. 'Not even a dog?' Fanny would repeat, but no one knew these two names. At the same time, when she dared, she would show Aunt Colette's photograph. A man thought he recognized his couch and made a dirty remark; from then on Fanny kept the photograph hidden. Besides, since the picture was unclear, couldn't it actually be her mother, whose features, though finer, were not that different from Aunt Colette's? Fanny's mother had inherited the pleasant, broad family face, whereas Fanny, to use Grandmother's expression, took after her father. Neither Aunt Colette nor Aunt Clemence had ever considered her as pretty as one of their other nieces, who had long, pale cheeks and a small, proud nose which was straight and insolent and always seemed to say, 'Yeah? What?' Fanny would not even have allowed herself to mumble such an impertinence in Aunt Colette's presence!

# FIFTEEN

## *Reunion*

A determined-looking George was suddenly right in front of Fanny and firmly gripping the cash stand.

'It's you again!' exclaimed Fanny, who had prepared to speak about her aunts, and irritably tapped on George's fingers.

'What information can *you* give me?' she sneered at him.

'I came to get you,' said George, calmly.

His familiar, resolute face infuriated Fanny. He was wrinkling his brow just as Fanny was doing! She leaned forward and slapped him in the face, then blushed because the management might have noticed. She ignored George, who did not say anything, and took the next customer's order. Her own cheek was stinging!

'Will you clear off?' she muttered, as soon as she could. But George just stood back a little and did not move. Then Fanny felt ashamed and pretended not to see him, worried that someone might suspect a relationship between them.

At the exit, George took her arm and drew her to one side. She softened, because it was night — no one would recognize her or, in any case, tell her and George apart.

'Come to our house,' he said, tugging her, 'my mother and my sisters are waiting for us.'

'But, my poor George, can't you tell me anything about Aunt Colette!'

'Yes, I can, in fact.'

He smiled confidently, without letting go of Fanny. He was wearing the same clothes as before: a bright blue nylon jacket, which was done up to the chin and tight around his slim waist, baggy velvet shorts, and boots like Eugene's, with pointed, turned-up toes. Fanny hesitated, sighed, then followed him, with George keeping a firm grip on her arm.

# SIXTEEN

## *Among Family?*

George lived in a large block of flats on the edge of the development, scored on each floor by narrow galleries so long that two people could hardly see each other from one end to the other. In these dark corridors, lit from morning on by electric lights, the children had made play areas, because the huge car park in front of the building, constantly filled with hundreds of cars, and the ring-road behind, prohibited them from playing outside. George led Fanny to the fifth gallery. Despite the lateness of the hour, some children were still dawdling in the hall; they stood firmly on outspread legs, narrowed their eyes and stared at Fanny arrogantly.

George's four little sisters, who had changed considerably since Fanny had last seen them, jumped on her neck. George's mother kissed her with emotion.

'Good evening, my child,' she said, before addressing Fanny with her real name. Fanny said nothing. George delightedly showed her the changes they had made to the flat; he was as relaxed and happy as if she had only left the day before. George's mother showed nothing but affection towards Fanny. Whenever Fanny moved she followed on her heels, anxious that Fanny should not want for anything. To be nearer to her, she perched on the arm of the best chair in the living room, where she had seated Fanny, and from time to time gently stroked her head. She enquired with concern after Fanny's parents, having forgotten nothing at all about them, and was particularly pleased to hear news of Fanny's father, although she had never met him. In front of the window the four sisters tilted their charming faces, which seemed to grow heavy from all the smiles they showered on Fanny at every word. Fanny ate dinner; they stayed up in her honour.

'What about Aunt Colette?' she whispered in George's ear, when his mother was in the kitchen.

'Yes, yes, later,' he answered with a grimace.

Fanny stayed the night in George's room, despite her disdain. He agreed to give up his bed for her and went to sleep next to his mother, not, however, before demanding several kisses, which turned Fanny's stomach. How proud she had once felt to be kissed by one of the most handsome boys in the development, one of the most sought after! Her repugnance dated from the instant she had decided to leave in search of

Aunt Leda, understanding that for her family she was an outsider whose presence they had only tolerated. She had not said a word about it to George; he would have tried to stop her, not because he loved her, even if that were likely — although Fanny couldn't care less — but because he would probably have worried that Fanny would enter into a world where he would not have had the advantage, despite his good looks. What was George to Fanny, compared to Eugene, who, as if being Aunt Colette's son were not enough, would one day live in Grandmother's house?

Nevertheless, Fanny had not slept so well in a long time. Every evening George came to wait for her at the restaurant exit and she willingly accompanied him to his mother's flat, where she ate dinner surrounded by care and friendship. The four little girls pressed around her. Fanny loved to hug and fuss over them, they were so sleek and pretty. But, to Fanny's great worry, George always pushed back the moment of revealing what he knew about Aunt Colette. George insisted on more and more prolonged kisses!

One evening, when Fanny was talking about the villages and Grandmother, George's mother did not pay her as much attention as usual but reduced her replies to polite nods. She did not even ask any questions, but soon unconsciously interrupted Fanny to ask if she had seen her father recently and if he was well.

'Who cares if he's dying!' Fanny said impatiently. 'What matters to me is for Grandmother to hold out.'

George's mother was deeply shocked, speechless. Her mouth pursed a little. Evidently, Fanny was a traitor in her opinion. But what could Fanny betray? George's mother took her by the shoulders and hugged her to her breast.

'Come now, don't speak to me about those people any more,' she said severely.

'That's my entire family!' Fanny indignantly replied.

'We're here,' said George's mother.

The four sisters jumped on Fanny, clung to her clothing, hung on her neck; one of them even wrapped her legs around Fanny's, and they rubbed their little rounded foreheads on Fanny's cheeks and shouted, 'We're here, we're here, we're here!'

'My real family lives in the villages, out there,' Fanny insisted, half-suffocated by the little girls' passionate affection.

'Of course, of course,' said George's mother, becoming more distant.

'What your family really thinks of you,' George then said, with a cryptic smile, 'I know, because your aunt visited me.'

'Aunt Colette came to visit you?' cried Fanny.

'Oh, she made a special trip.'

Fanny abruptly disentangled herself from the little girls, grabbed George's ears, as she used to by way of a joke, and shook him, her nose against his.

'And what did she tell you?' she demanded, in a changed voice.

'She wants you to marry me, as planned, and stop chasing after her son.'

'But Eugene is my cousin!' moaned Fanny.

'That's how it is,' said George, coldly.

# PART FOUR

# Aunt Colette's Accusations

Aunt Colette and Fanny were out in a small boat beneath the gentle sun on the big lake, deserted during this season and surrounded by high blocks of blue glass flats and majestic old houses. Aunt Colette had grabbed the oars and, with vigorous strokes, was boldly putting a distance between them and the hut from where they had rented the small tired boat which took in water a little. She had hitched up her fur coat and placed her feet, clad in heavy ankle boots, on the cross-plank, leaving no room for Fanny whose feet were getting soaked in the pool of water. Although she was shivering, Fanny hardly worried at this moment about falling sick; she could not even have cared less about death itself. Wrapped in her fur which was wadded up in places, Aunt Colette soon got hot and passed the oars to Fanny. When they were in the middle of the lake, she ordered Fanny to stop. They were alone on the bare lake, even the swans and ducks had taken shelter for the winter. Not a single face looked out of the windows of the houses on the shore, the new glass facades sparkled, the colour of water, and hid from view the office workers they knew were there — rushing along the halls, going up and down in the lifts, milling behind the reflective, polished surface. A distant relative, Aunt Colette seemed to remember, was a secretary in one of the towers. Aunt Colette leaned back, placed her arms on the sides of the boat, and looked Fanny sternly up and down.

'I have to explain to you,' began Aunt Colette, 'the reasons which have led me to a certain decision in your regard, which I will make known to you last. No, no, don't ask me now what it's about, you must know what you've done wrong so that you find my decision just. If that's not the case, it will be that you haven't heard me right. But this decision is irrevocable, I'm simply trying to justify it to you so you won't be able to complain of having been mistreated, in other words, to shut you up. Then there will be nothing more to discuss.

'Definitive measures in your regard became necessary because you spread trouble in our family, a thing that no family, as you know, is obliged to accept. We claim no responsibility for your misbehaviour. Since the beginning we have of course, since you are my sister's daughter, considered you as one of us, a fully-fledged member of the family, not because we had noticed something different about you and agreed to disregard it, but simply because we did not notice anything which singled you out. You were, for us, your mother's daughter, and what's more, a fairly charming child, in every way just like your cousins. Look, I have here a snapshot which proves that.'

Aunt Colette showed Fanny a photograph where she saw herself among other little girls next to a well, with her hair arranged like theirs. Just as Aunt Colette had said, she looked so like them that she could be taken for their sister, even though the picture was blurred and any little girl dressed and combed in the same way would no doubt have given this impression.

'It's true, I was hardly any different then!' exclaimed Fanny, delighted.

'It's too late to be thrilled about it,' said Aunt Colette, as she put away the photograph. 'But you understand, we had no reason to regard you as an outsider since nothing made us think you were one. Whether we did not see what was there or whether there really was not anything unusual about you then doesn't matter. Even today I can't make up my mind about that, although I lean towards the first hypothesis. We loved you and welcomed you, as was our duty. But what is strange is that the difference in you, which we didn't notice, you apparently became increasingly conscious of as you grew up, forcing us to discover it in spite of ourselves. You used every possible means to make us set you apart when we wanted no better than to continue to treat you impartially, when we did not dream of changing our attitude towards you, having no grounds to do so! I don't know what made you ashamed in the first place of what you were, shouldn't I say of what you thought you were, or what you took it in your head to believe you were? Because who were you really at the time? Who even remembers? Your mother herself would hesitate to say! You astounded and embarrassed us with your excessive humility. You intentionally positioned yourself in photographs so you would be half-hidden. You wanted to be served last and seemed always to apologize for putting us to any trouble, for appearing before our eyes, for my calling you my niece, for your very presence among the family, which was so normal, yet you seemed secretly to want to be excluded at the same time as you dreaded such an outcome; had it occurred, you would have simply found it just. Your behaviour troubled us, we no longer knew what to think; because you insisted on making us see it, we began to see what had escaped our notice before. How could we not be influenced by your shame? We became more restrained with you. Is she right? Is she really different? We could not help wondering as soon as your attitude began to convince us. Maybe we even started to feel contempt for you, egged on by your constantly putting yourself down, a certain ridiculous way you had, when we wanted to kiss you, of only giving in reluctantly, as if you were alarmed at the danger we risked by touching our lips to your skin. You succeeded in twisting our judgement. We got in the habit of thinking of you as someone basically strange and, I have to admit, hardly deserving of our respect. Look at this picture!'

In the photograph which Aunt Colette held out, Fanny, her hair tied in scraggly bunches, stood far behind Eugene and her three cousins, who wore their hair long and straight. Her head hung and she looked distraught and out of place. It seemed unbelievable that she had once resembled the other children and had grown up in the same place. Fanny sighed without saying anything and Aunt Colette continued.

'Once you had reduced us to setting you apart in our minds and having little regard for you, then pride took hold of you; only then did you rebel against our distrust of you. Having done everything to alienate yourself from our affection, you bore a grudge against us for no longer loving you as plainly as before and for seeing an intruder in you from then on, which you irreparably became. You silently blamed us for abandoning you! You tried to get Grandmother on your side, since she was weaker and more lenient. You tried your best to become her favourite through thousands of little attentions! At the same time you tried to be like us, you wanted to restore yourself to the family and for us to forget this thing that made you stand out in spite of yourself. Oh, what delusions! My poor niece, how pitifully you tried to copy us! You borrowed your oldest cousin's voice inflexions, another cousin's odd habit of scratching her nose, you cursed like your uncle, you wanted to wear Eugene's old clothes even though they were dreadfully tight on you. Added to that you became touchy and proud. And who were you fooling? Grandmother, perhaps, who in any case hardly needed it. But these extremes made the rest of the family even more uncomfortable than before. We no longer saw anything except what separated you from us. And sometimes, when we looked at you sitting at our table, we wondered with surprise what you were doing among us before we remembered that you were my sister's daughter, a fact that seemed more and more mysterious to us although we could not deny it. You had started out, unfortunate girl, as an anomaly; you transformed yourself into an offence, for which we all, in some way or other, bore the shame. Do you know that we hid your existence every time we could? Admittedly, you went for walks in the village with Grandmother. But do you know what she said about her relationship with you? Oh, I won't tell you, no. Am I being cruel? I only want to enlighten you. I'll keep quiet about that.'

'There's nothing I respect more than the family,' murmured Fanny, mechanically, her hands clenched at knee level on the oars.

'Oh, that's not enough! It will never be enough from you!' shouted Aunt Colette, impatiently. 'Look what you've become. Look how you have allowed the very thing that distanced you from the family to grow!'

A new photograph showed Fanny in the full glare of her distinction, a grown girl now, next to her thin, pale cousin, whom Fanny eclipsed with her height, her vigorous complexion, her unique features. Aunt Colette became so angry she made the boat rock.

'You must understand, I think, that in return for what can only be called our sacrifice, yes, because we kept you among us and have always received you courteously — oh, you want to deny that now? — in return for these efforts, we expected from you, at least, a certain self-effacing manner, a certain discretion — dare I say it: a perfect insignificance, so that we could at least forget you just a little. That would have made up for a lot of your faults. Who knows? Perhaps we would even have been grateful to you. Could you hope for anything more? But blind arrogance pushed you to every extreme. You crushed, that's the word, crushed my Eugene with your school achievements. What good did it do you? Did it gain you the family's respect? It was just the opposite of what we wanted from you! Instead of keeping a humble profile next to your cousin, you made a fool of him with feats that he could not keep up with, feeding our bitterness. People thought you were pretty. They hardly complimented your cousins. Oh, people probably said you were "cute." Your cousins' true beauty was less plain to the eye. Was it your place to be the prettiest? There was nothing in your face we could either understand or appreciate. You hardly looked like us, that we were sure of. You started chasing after Eugene round every corner. You threw yourself at him and kissed him, there was no way he could resist you — don't deny it, I saw the two of you. Intentions towards my Eugene! It was one thing to invite yourself to our table, but to give yourself our son! Was that conceivable? You can pride yourself on having tormented me!'

'I didn't know,' Fanny ventured.

'That makes no difference. My health was affected by the worries you caused me. I feared that you would drag my Eugene beyond the limits set for him by his love for me and his deference towards the family. At last, you introduced to us a young man from your own kind, George, who looked surprisingly like you and visibly made for you, even nice. After choosing him, you tossed him aside. He made you ashamed like you made us ashamed in the village, without anything to justify your embarrassment except a stupid presumptuousness — it seemed to you that George did not attest too well to your place in the family, which you thought you had to constantly prove. You didn't care what we wanted, which was to see you stay with George, where you belonged. What good does it do to mix opposites? It isn't that you thought George unworthy of you, just that in your eyes he did you no good, while Eugene, your cousin, was useful to you.'

'How can I give up Eugene?' Fanny dared whisper. Aunt Colette grew so angry again that she leaned forward sharply. A few black strands escaped from her bun and stood straight up on her scalp.

'You impudent child! Who do you think you are? What are you today? Can anyone even define what you are? Are you anything? Are you even someone about whom anyone can say precisely: she is so, from such and such a region, that's her origin? Are you nothing definable? So you want my Eugene? But you know, I did not even recognize you on Grandmother's birthday and I gave you the first name that came into my head, one I had read the previous day in a second-rate novel. Perhaps that's all you are, perhaps you don't exist any more than that minor character Fanny in that flimsy book, which, what's more, I tossed aside — it's probably stuffed under my bed with the fluff and your uncle's magazines! What did we call you before? I don't even remember! Did you have a name? See, I'm not even convinced of that.'

'I've forgotten it too,' said Fanny, quickly, to please Aunt Colette.

'You poor girl!'

Aunt Colette, sickened, seemed no longer to know where to look. With a gesture she commanded Fanny to take up the oars.

'You made one final mistake,' she continued calmly, 'that I find unforgivable — stupidly trying to find Leda, my sister. What harm did you do? Oh, it's only serious, really, because you're involved, that's how it is. What do you hope to change in the state of things? My girl, that's life. Everything you do is subject to the most severe judgement. You should have kept out of things. Do you belong in the village? You're the only one who thinks so. Wanting to find Leda, you accused your mother of negligence. Still, that's nothing. But you seemed to claim knowledge of Leda, since you hoped to find her in some corner of the world and persuade her to listen to you. Where did you get such confidence? Who ever told you anything about Leda? Answer my question, please.'

'No one,' mumbled Fanny.

'Could you be sure we wished to see Leda again and that you wouldn't upset us by wanting to bring her back?'

'No, but...'

'Did you know, honestly, that we didn't see her every day?'

'No.'

'If we suffered from Leda's silence, if there was a silence, should the prestige of bringing her back among us fall to you, the outsider?'

'I don't know,' said Fanny.

'Wasn't it wrong of you to choose yourself as the messenger between Leda and her family?'

'Perhaps.'

'If it turned out that Leda was not worthy of our affection, was it your place to bring it to our attention?'

'I really don't know.'

'Finally, don't you think you usurped the right to involve yourself in this matter?'

'Leda is my aunt, and I thought...'

'You're too sure of yourself,' cut in Aunt Colette, dryly. 'Leda is your aunt as long as we wish it, and you were my niece before I decided otherwise. That's the point I wanted to get to. We forbid you, Fanny, to appear again among our family where we have decided, for our own protection, you no longer belong.'

Fanny made a gurgling noise. She dared not stop rowing and could not wipe her tears, which dribbled from her chin and made her nose swell, disturbing Aunt Colette, who fixed her gaze on the shore.

'The novel,' Aunt Colette added, 'was called *Lovers without a Homeland.*'

When Fanny and Aunt Colette had returned the boat, after making a complete circle of the lake and a brief stop on a little island in the middle, Aunt Colette, who was satisfied with the outing, took Fanny to a nearby refreshment room, where several children, accompanied by their parents, were drinking cups of chocolate. She offered Fanny a cup, then, generously, a cream cake. Sitting by the window with her aunt, Fanny savoured the moment. This surprised her, since just a few minutes ago she had wanted to throw herself into the water.

# PART FIVE

# ONE

## *Return To The Village*

When Fanny arrived in Grandmother's village, loaded down with a new suitcase in which she had put all her meagre possessions, the annual watercress fair was in full swing. Larger than life characters in cardboard costumes were moving heavily along the streets, making the excited children laugh or run away. They announced the programme in deep voices and called out advertisements for the supermarket which at long last was going to open nearby. In front of the church, trout fishing had been set up, and on the village common were dodgems and a shooting gallery. Men were trying their hand at shooting, aiming for so long before firing that they wore the spectators out — although such ceremonials had convinced them of their talent. Not without emotion, Fanny recognized in their strained faces that masculine expression which is a mixture of detachment and seriousness, of composure then of displeasure, when they blamed the mediocre quality of the weapon after they had missed the bull's eye — an expression which she had always seen borne by the men in this place, whoever they might be. It was duplicated, barely altered by the lower stakes, on the ruddy faces of the young lads who were racing around the bumper car track, half raised up in their cars, steering with one casual hand. They appeared blasé, as if pushed on by the sole desire of relieving their boredom, but took intense pleasure in crashing headlong into a car driven by a girl, to make her giggle and impress her. Girls in stiletto heels, and with bleached, tightly curled hair, hurried with small steps to the cars, their hands in their jacket pockets. When a boy accompanied them, they submitted to his masculine desire to drive, and let themselves be shaken and rattled about, screaming a little to flatter him and make him put all his honour into the fray. Other girls, with pink make-up, were waiting at the side and chewing gum. Deafened by the music, they were enjoying the moment and seemed to want to stay there forever. Some made themselves comfortable and removed their shoes.

Fanny moved forward into the lingering and satisfied crowd. Here and there she recognized some of the heads which turned towards her, indifferently or with a somewhat gloomy curiosity, empty of memories. But I recognize them, thought Fanny, surprised, and it's not long since they saw me! Then an idea chilled her: Grandmother must be dead now. She turned, half-running, towards the cemetery. This part of the village was deserted, and just like long ago in Grandmother's yard, always beneath a dull sun at this heavy hour of early afternoon, she could hear the mysterious cooing of the turtledoves which she never saw. The familiar sound crushed her. Without any doubt Grandmother was dead, and in one stroke Fanny was uprooted from the village. Sure of what she would see, abruptly Fanny stopped running and retraced her steps. She walked up to Grandmother's house. The gate refused to open. She rang. No dog barked. Suddenly Aunt Colette was on the threshold at the other end of the yard, her arms crossed over a flowery apron.

'Well, what is it!' she called out.

'It's me, Fanny.'

'Oh, yes! But now this is Eugene's home,' declared Aunt Colette, proudly.

'I would like to come in,' said Fanny.

'We'd rather not.'

Aunt Colette went back in and slammed the door. In one corner Fanny noticed a beautiful brand new dog kennel which had a little sloping tiled roof and was festooned with imitation ivy. Fanny did not see the dog and assumed he was in the house — a privilege which Grandmother had never granted her own dogs. 'Eugene has moved in,' mumbled Fanny. 'Is it too late? What if he's married?' She was standing on tip-toe on the narrow pavement to scrutinize the windows in search of some clue, when a cyclist swooped past and almost bumped into her. Then dozens of sweaty, deeply concentrating men on bicycles flashed by, and Fanny was suddenly surrounded by a crowd who had run from the fair booths, as they did every year, to watch the winner of the race — a butcher by trade, the same one again, on his top quality, sylph-like bicycle, fragile and almost impalpable between his wide, muscular champion's legs — receive from the mayor's hands a bottle of good wine and ten pounds of sugar. They jostled Fanny as if she were invisible, and she tried to extricate herself from the group of enthusiasts who were yelling in front of the gate. She knew them well, they had changed so little! But on seeing her, no one cried out, 'Hey, look, it's Fanny!' or any other name they could have given her. Fanny was suffocating, squeezed between two of Grandmother's neighbours. One of them was kneading her arm without even realizing it!

'Please, Mr. Lagneau,' complained Fanny. He looked down at her, wrinkled his brow as if wondering what on earth she could be, grumbled angrily for having to move, and squeezed over just enough that Fanny, with difficulty, could prise herself free.

'When I was with Grandmother,' muttered Fanny, 'you didn't peer at me like that. Nothing seemed more natural than seeing me here.' She retrieved her suitcase, which had been trampled on and smashed in on one side. Hadn't even the grocer, an affable and dignified lady whom Grandmother had always gone to for her provisions, just jumped on the suitcase with both feet, for no reason, without even deriving any particular pleasure from it, since she did not even seem to have noticed? Fanny planted herself right in front of her, but the grocer's eyes passively and politely slid over her forehead and cheeks. Too well brought up to show any bothersome curiosity, the kind shopkeeper — to whom Fanny's face meant nothing, although she had greeted her only last year — preferred not to see her. She did not even hear the few words of apology which Fanny addressed to her for having blocked her view.

At the ground floor window appeared Aunt Colette, Eugene, and Uncle George, their three faces pressed together, turned towards the podium where the prizes were being distributed.

'Eugene!' shouted Fanny, happily. Surprised, he winked at her and gave her a quick smile, which bathed Fanny in a warm, pleasant feeling.

But Aunt Colette shouted harshly, 'Are you still there? Well, I never! Why don't you get out of here!'

Fanny pretended not to understand. She turned her back to the house and shifted her attention to the podium. Suddenly a rotten plum smashed against her neck then another in her hair. 'Sss, sss,' hissed Aunt Colette, as if to chase off a wicked animal, and continued to bombard Fanny with old plums. Eugene was laughing so hard he got the hiccups. Uncle George was smiling indulgently and stroking his moustache; his glance met Fanny's without the slightest embarrassment. All around, the onlookers were equally amused. They were confident that Aunt Colette would not have fun at the expense of someone who did not deserve it. They moved away from Fanny, who was jumping left and right to avoid the stream of plums, but Aunt Colette was a good shot and rarely missed — Fanny's face was already dripping with sickly sweet juice. Mr. Lagneau was laughing harder than anyone. It seemed he finally saw what Fanny was and what use she could be put to. Hadn't Mr. Lagneau, in the past, made her a bow and arrows, only too happy to give her such pleasure to oblige Grandmother, his neighbour?

'Mr. Lagneau, I'm Fanny!' she told him, when she landed next to him, panting.

'I don't know any Fanny!' he guffawed, thinking it a joke.

At last Aunt Colette grew tired or ran out of plums, and Fanny, stooping a little, edged her way down a small, quiet street, still holding her suitcase, hugging it to her body with her arms because the handle had broken off. She soon stopped to wipe her face and her bare arms. The flies, still numerous in summer although there had been no livestock in the village for a long time, were already clinging to her sticky skin. So I can't enter that house any more, thought Fanny. It's barred to me now that Grandmother is dead, as if my relationship with everyone has become nothing. And what about Mother?

At that very moment, Fanny looked up and saw her mother pass in the high street, at the end of the alley. As usual she was in a hurry. She was wearing a fresh white dress printed with big bouquets, and carrying her tartan suitcase. Fanny ran awkwardly. When she reached the street, her mother was going into Grandmother's house. She dared not call out to her for fear of making Aunt Colette appear. But seeing her mother go in reassured her, because wouldn't her mother feel it her duty to plead on her behalf when she heard Fanny was in the village, even if it meant turning her sister and brother-in-law against herself? Unless she thought it preferable to resign herself to Fanny's staying outside, to avoid what she called with disgust 'carryings-on.' Unless she did not put as much importance into Fanny's entry as Fanny herself did, or imagined that the current situation was of her daughter's own choosing and did not even speak about it to Aunt Colette. Or unless, quite simply, no one informed her that Fanny was here, which was very possible.

Fanny arrived at the only hotel in the village, the Plain's Inn. While passing through the fair, she had felt the enthusiasm with which she and Eugene — on holiday at Grandmother's at this time of year — used to rush from booth to booth, frustrated at not being able to do everything at once. Today the fair seemed gloomy to her, and the village, close up, seemed lacking in charm.

In the dark hall of the inn, behind the counter, Fanny made out a familiar silhouette.

'Isabelle!' she exclaimed, astonished. Isabelle acknowledged her with only a vague smile. 'It's me, Fanny, your old friend!'

They hugged each other, without Isabelle seeming the least surprised or disturbed that Fanny had changed her name. Isabelle and Fanny had played together as children. As far as Fanny could remember, Isabelle had never left the village. She was now married to the son of the former innkeepers, and her life was passing by in this small, barely frequented hotel, which she ran somewhat indifferently.

'I didn't see you at your Grandmother's burial,' said Isabelle, in an unusually severe tone. 'It made me wonder if you weren't dead too.'

'I was dead!' exclaimed Fanny, who felt horribly ashamed.

Over the counter she grasped Isabelle's cold, slender hands.

'Believe me, if it's true that I didn't attend her funeral — but are you

133

really sure? — it's because I was not even informed of Grandmother's death, or else I was dead momentarily, because how else could such a thing be possible? You know how much I loved and respected Grandmother. Wouldn't I have come to comfort her in her last moments? Wouldn't I have followed the funeral procession? You, who have always known me, can you even imagine such a thing?'

'It's true, you were very attached to her,' conceded Isabelle.

'You see,' said Fanny, still stroking Isabelle's hands. Then the extent of her misdeeds overwhelmed her. Grandmother had died knowing that Fanny had abandoned her! But, without a photograph on either her bedside table or the dresser to remind her of Fanny, was she even aware of Fanny's existence? Hadn't she, like so many people in the village, forgotten her or confused her with people in her dreams, dismissing her with a shake of her head, saying to herself: 'How absurd!' Unable to confirm Fanny's existence with her own eyes, had she had the slightest reason to believe in her still, surrounded as she was by Eugene and her many grandchildren who were all so perfectly similar to herself? Aunt Colette, perhaps, had whispered in her ear, taking advantage of a vulnerable moment: 'Fanny's nothing but a dream!' and Grandmother had departed believing it. Or believing, bitterly, that Fanny had forgotten her, an even more horrifying thought.

'I'll show you your room. It's a hundred and fifty francs,' said Isabelle to Fanny, who had lowered her eyes, her head slumped onto her chest. Fanny followed her friend up a dark staircase, then along never-ending, winding corridors and felt disconcerted to be led so far when the hotel seemed empty. When she saw the room, Fanny cried out, 'But that's Grandmother's furniture, and her quilt!' Grandmother's three large wardrobes embraced two whole walls.

'Your family let us have them,' said Isabelle, with satisfaction. 'They were in the way over there.' Some old clothes still hung in one of the wardrobes, among them an old yellow plastic raincoat which Grandmother had worn in the garden, its hem hardened with mud.

# TWO
## *A Childhood Friend*

Fanny visited Isabelle's little living quarters: she and her husband occupied two rooms on the ground floor of the hotel. Isabelle had recently taken pleasure in replacing furniture and carpets, to get rid, she said, of her in-laws' uncomfortable, old-fashioned things. She had only kept a spinning-wheel, which had been transformed into a plant stand, and a stained and varnished cart wheel which had been turned into an imposing ceiling light. Decorated with little lamp shades with multi-coloured pearl fringes, it was as wide as the table beneath it, which was plain wood protected by a sheet of sharp-edged glass. The mother-in-law's velvet armchairs had been dispensed with in favour of a rustic-style living room suite, which Isabelle and her husband had not yet fully paid for — their pleasure in seeing themselves seated on the plush fabric embroidered with flowers and scrolls which covered the rather rigid couch with jig-sawed legs, selected from a department store catalogue, was well worth the worry, the minor sacrifices, and, when all is said and done, even paying double its value to enjoy it immediately.

Fanny was particularly supposed to admire a long sideboard of dark lacquered wood, glazed with so much varnish that it appeared to be some odd material, some hard, common plastic, with green glass doors which were blown and latticed like a stained-glass window. Behind them, one could make out a complete collection of tankards, each with a different insignia. Isabelle modestly and proudly passed from one piece of furniture to another and told Fanny the brief history of each, where they had bought it and its price — which was always astonishingly high. That she had spent a large sum on a low smoked-glass table with metal legs, seemed to prove the aesthetic value of her purchase. Consequently, she could not spare Fanny this detail, without which Fanny — like Isabelle before she had asked the price of things — would undoubtedly have misjudged what she saw.

A beautiful kitchen fitted with light-coloured imitation pine formica — which Isabelle showed last, feigning indifference — was Isabelle's crowning glory. She paced up and down and round and round the kitchen for the pleasure of hearing her mules ring out on the intricate tile floor. Her apron fluttered and her cheeks flushed as she described the many facilities which enhanced her life as a housewife. 'She's so lucky! Oh, what happiness is hers!' Fanny thought over and over again, seated in front of the coffee Isabelle had served her.

The husband arrived, dragging his feet on the rugs. Although he had gained weight and his still youthful face had become puffed and red, Fanny recognized him straight away. As for him, he could not decide what to call her. It finally came back to him, and he uttered the name used for Fanny in the village. Since Fanny had been unaware of it until this day, she heard it with shock and dismay. Isabelle, a little embarrassed, rebuked her husband. So even when Grandmother was alive, they had secretly given her a cold nickname, meaningful and practical, without her even being aware of it and even though they knew her relation to Grandmother! This was how it was, no matter what she might do, no matter how she tried to please! Completely purpled with shame, Fanny bowed her head over her coffee. Isabelle came and went, and with exaggerated discretion pretended to want to respect Fanny's distressed silence. But, having snatched up a duster which she ran delicately over the clean, shiny furniture, Isabelle forgot and started humming. With her hands on her hips, she paused from time to time to gaze with a critical eye at the arrangement of her home, and put on a little annoyed look as she moved the gypsum flower on top of the television set an inch or two, or, with a sudden concern for perfection, corrected the angle of a deer hoof which hung from the wall; yet still she was only half-appeased, half-gratified in her artistic demands, her brow remaining wrinkled for some time. The husband had fallen asleep, sunk into his armchair. He suddenly awoke and — utterly surprised to see Fanny — muttered, out of professional courtesy, a few vague questions about the family and Aunt Colette, whom he hardly knew.

'Leave our friend alone,' said Isabelle, cautiously, and Fanny understood that she imagined she was helping her get out of answers which, in Isabelle's view, could only prove embarrassing, given Fanny's pitiable and impossible situation. Most probably, Isabelle, being kind-hearted, felt sorry for Fanny, and would for nothing in the world have changed places with her. Ugh! thought Fanny, suddenly feeling nauseated. But the village, with its self-satisfied narrow-mindedness, had her in its grip. Oh, it will eat me alive, it will eat me alive, thought Fanny as she watched Isabelle move about with indescribable pleasure.

# THREE

## *At The Cemetery*

Fanny bought a bouquet of French marigolds and — after lengthy hesitation caused by shame and dread — decided to go and put them on Grandmother's grave. She left the village under the noon sun and arrived at the cemetery, which was skirted by the newly-paved main road. In the corner where Grandmother had been buried, Uncle George was squatting, watering can in hand. He jumped up when he saw Fanny. Instead of turning to kiss her, he made do with mumbling a forced hello. Fanny knelt down beside him.

'I'm pleased to see you again, Uncle,' she said brightly.

'Eugene is going to get married, so...'

'Get married!' cried Fanny. 'To that girl I saw at your house?'

'Exactly,' he said, in a threatening tone.

'Are they going to live in Grandmother's house then?'

'Eugene's house now,' corrected Uncle George.

'Let me look through the house one last time?' implored Fanny.

'We'd rather not,' he said firmly.

Out of desperation, Fanny raised her skirt as if inadvertently, and gave Uncle George a glimpse of a good chunk of thigh, which she also pressed gently against his side.

'Nevertheless,' pursued Fanny, 'there wouldn't be any harm in it. Besides, you could keep an eye on me.'

'We'd rather not,' repeated Uncle George, moving away from Fanny with obvious disgust.

'I'm not dangerous,' mumbled Fanny.

'But you don't know how to behave!' exploded Uncle George, crimson. 'You couldn't care less about rules and customs and necessary family sacrifices and the duties of self-denial. Who on earth are you? Well, in the family's eyes you're nothing any more! Grandmother is dead. As for your mother, she regrets having brought you into the world and agrees with our complaints; she finally acknowledges her mistake. But you? What can you expect? Oh, disappear, that's the best thing you could do!'

'But the village is my home!' protested Fanny.

'How can we help it if you see it like that?'

This Uncle George, in a short-sleeved shirt and dungarees, was very different to the one Fanny had followed into his car, and even to the

137

Uncle George who, in his Sunday best, had pretended not to recognize Fanny on Grandmother's birthday. He finished watering, got up, and left without a word.

Fanny busied herself with carefully arranging her marigolds. A rustling made her turn her head. At the other end of the cemetery, which was dry and flat like a paddock, stood Aunt Colette, Fanny's mother and two women from the village, unmoving, stiff in the heat, all four in spruce summer dresses. The one Fanny's mother was wearing stood out because of its full skirt and abundance of white flounces. They were chatting and paid no attention whatsoever to Fanny. It seemed, from their strange position, planted right by the gate, that they were patiently waiting for Fanny to leave Grandmother's graveside. A big spray of roses dangled from Aunt Colette's hand. Fanny stood up and walked towards the gate. She brushed against Aunt Colette and fearfully exchanged glances with her mother, who stared into space and kept smiling, sweetly and politely. Fanny and her mother had not seen each other in such a long time! Uncle George told me the truth, thought Fanny, resignedly. For not the slightest emotion marred her mother's sweet face, and her pale eyes had met Fanny's dark ones like those of a stranger, with the amiable detachment she had cultivated at the hairdressing salon. Fanny was so distressed she tripped and almost fell. Neither her mother nor Aunt Colette held out a hand to help her, they simply headed slowly towards Grandmother's grave to put more flowers on it. Aunt Colette was lazily swinging the bouquet. Her mother's dress puffed out, revealing the hollows of her knees, where some veins showed through. They were walking side-by-side, their bare arms brushing against each other, as they had long before Fanny was born and when the possibility of her existence would only have inspired an outburst of disbelieving laughter, while they had no doubt felt touched by the thought of a future little Eugene, surely already similar in their dreams to what he had actually become. If only I could turn into Eugene! sighed Fanny as she left the cemetery. On the outside, the grey breeze-block walls were covered with graffiti and violent and obscene drawings. The cemetery was isolated on the edge of a field, and, like the huge public rubbish tip at the other entrance to the village or the supermarket which would soon open, it was difficult to reach on foot because the ditch between the road and the beet fields was narrow. Fanny, who for the occasion had donned court shoes, had to jump continually from the road, where indifferent cars passed at great speed, to the ditch, where she could not take a step without twisting her ankles. Soon her mother, Aunt Colette, and the two other women passed her on their bicycles. Aunt Colette was riding Grandmother's old blue moped, which had always been used as a bicycle. She was struggling hard. Not one of them looked at Fanny, although at risk of hurting herself she had jumped into the ditch to get out of their way. They ignored her without making a show of it, without it even seeming deliberate, and Fanny's mother was very cheerful!

# FOUR

## *Conversation With Eugene*

One night Fanny posted herself under Eugene's bedroom window, which looked out onto the street, and whistled softly. He soon appeared and cautiously opened the window. Fanny clung to the wall and stretched as high as she could.

'So you've forgotten me?' she murmured. 'It's me, Fanny, your cousin.'

'I'm not really allowed to speak to you,' whispered Eugene.

'What are they afraid of?'

'That you'll lead me off, like the first time.'

'Then I'd really be stupid, since you deserted me.'

'But look how you mistreated me!'

'So you're getting married, Eugene. Why not to me?'

'That's impossible!' he cried out.

'It's true I'm your cousin.'

'People would look at us. People would soon forget that you're my cousin, but not that...'

'Well, what?'

'Oh, you're getting on my nerves. Besides, I was asleep. Do you look like my cousin?'

'So that's it!'

'You have to give in to certain reasons.'

And he became stubbornly silent. Fanny tried to sound good-humoured, for fear of offending Eugene and driving him back to bed.

'Your fiancée, you love her of course,' she resumed, with effort.

'Of course.'

'So you love her more than me?'

'No more, no less than you,' he said firmly.

'You see!'

'I see nothing at all.'

'You'd marry me, if you had the courage.'

'Oh, perhaps. Only, it's like this, I'd rather not.'

'Oh, poor Eugene, you disappoint me.' Straight away, to keep him, she added, 'Tell me whether Aunt Leda will be present at your wedding.'

'How should I know?'

'But has she been informed of it?'

'No one knows where she is,' he snapped, yawning impatiently.

'What about my mother? Does she talk about me?'

'Never.'

'She saw me though.'

'She doesn't show it. Perhaps she's forgotten you.'

'Her own daughter?'

'The way people perhaps forget anything relating to a disagreeable or shameful memory.'

'Eugene, you're so perceptive!' jeered Fanny, practically fainting.

'Now, good-night.'

'Wait!'

But Eugene had closed the window and drawn the curtain. Fanny went back to the hotel, where Isabelle was watching out for her. Her friend stopped Fanny, her face cold.

'We would like,' she began, 'for you to pay for your room, for the time you've already spent here.'

'Yes, I'll speak to my family about it,' said Fanny, who did not have a penny.

As she started up the staircase, Isabelle grabbed her by the sleeve.

'Everyone knows you no longer have anything to do with your family. What would you do here? Anyway, is it really your family? That's what everyone in the village who remembers you wonders, and there are only a few who do, I assure you. Why would your true family reject you? It's inconceivable. Also...'

'Even if they have,' said Fanny, 'should that change anything between us?'

'But I don't know who you are any more!' exclaimed Isabelle, offended.

And it was as if she had suddenly persuaded herself that Fanny had always betrayed her trust. 'It's out of the question for you to spend another night here if you haven't settled up with us tomorrow,' she informed Fanny. Then Fanny's childhood friend crossed her arms and would not listen to another word.

# FIVE

## On The Premises

Shortly after noon, Fanny, armed with her suitcase, walked cautiously up to Grandmother's house. She skirted the little garden wall as far as the wooden door at the back, which she opened easily by hoisting herself up and drawing the bolt on the other side. She nimbly crossed the garden, reached the veranda, and opened the kitchen door. A hot silence, heavy with the odour of stewed fruit, reassured her — a full bowl of plums was still steaming on the table. She went in and hid her suitcase between the refrigerator and the wall. The same excessive cleanliness as in Grandmother's day made the kitchen unwelcoming. It was furnished with modest furniture and decorated with promotional barometres and painted plates, with a sort of important and abundant timelessness. Some fat, slow flies were wearily circling the plums. Fanny glanced into the living room: stretched out on the old, fluffy couch which smelt of dogs, her mother had fallen asleep in front of the television, which was mutely showing the touching images of an inane soap opera that Fanny and Grandmother had followed together in the past, when Fanny, snuggled against Grandmother on the then already threadbare and smelly couch, had to ask for the most simple explanations of the hero's crude motives. Fanny's mother's mouth hung open, her lips in a smile. She was smiling sweetly and peacefully, the same way as in the photograph on top of the television set, which Fanny was not familiar with, although it looked very old. Then she moved closer and recognized the snapshot which had belonged to her and which Uncle George had ripped up on Grandmother's birthday. It had been glued back together, all that was missing was a small part of Fanny's mother's foot and Fanny's own face, which was no more than a jagged hole on her mother's full chest.

Fanny quietly left the living room after turning off the television set, out of habit. Since she heard a soft noise coming from Grandmother's room, she gently pushed the door half-open and saw Aunt Colette lying on the eiderdown, with one of her sturdy legs hanging the length of the bed. Without the wardrobes the room seemed bare and desolate. Aunt Colette stared at Fanny with wide hostile eyes: Aunt Colette, as the whole family knew, had the peculiarity of always sleeping with her eyes wide open, as rich in expression as when she was awake. But Fanny had forgotten this characteristic, and she stopped in her tracks, not daring to take a single step forward, despite a strong desire to examine Aunt Colette's harsh face up close and penetrate its powerful influence. She noticed that the portrait of Grandmother, which to her knowledge had always hung over the bed, had been taken down and replaced with a snapshot of Eugene and his fiancée together, reeling with laughter and cutting an enormous cake which Fanny supposed was for their engagement. She wondered what had become of Grandmother's picture, skillfully painted during her youth by a local artist.

In the room on the ground floor, which had been Fanny's when she came, her mother's tartan suitcase lay open on the bed, carelessly crushing a little doll whose dress Grandmother had enjoyed crocheting. Fanny put it back in its place, cursing her mother's thoughtlessness. She also arranged the armchair antimacassars, which were lying crumpled on a seat, and smoothed out the quilt embroidered with big assorted flowers, whose pattern was repeated in a less bright pink on the ceiling, giving the impression that living in this bedroom was like living in a beautiful closed and padded box. Calmly, sadly, and with a sense of foreboding, Fanny gazed out of the window into the unimaginative garden, which was practical and orderly. She had often helped pick the strawberries at this time of year, and Grandmother, who abhorred waste, used to scrupulously check that not one remained unnoticed under a leaf, even though she was burdened every summer with too many.

Then Fanny headed for Eugene's room. He had closed his shutters and was resting on the bed with the girl. One of her legs, bare and glimmering in the darkness, was stretched across Eugene's thigh. It could have been Fanny's thigh weighing on Eugene's accommodating side; what a surprise that it wasn't! Fanny pinched herself. What a mystery that there she was, standing on the threshold, looking at the girl at the same time as her eyes asked: isn't that me too? Next to the crucifix they had left a tapestry of a woman reading, which Grandmother had stitched. Eugene's room had inherited the little glass bookcase where Grandmother had carefully arranged the books she had received from a club every month to which she had extravagantly subscribed — each book wrapped in transparent paper that meat had been delivered in, less out of respect for the books than the wish not to damage in any way a thing which had cost a little. She had soon regretted the subscription, because she became bored with having to read a book every month and even more with having to choose among books about which she knew nothing, whose stories were unfamiliar to her and aroused neither her interest nor her curiosity, both of which were dulled. Fanny noticed that each book was marked about a third of the way through with a bookmark — Grandmother had preferred the fatigue of beginning a book to putting something away which she had paid for without it serving any purpose, not even that of putting her to sleep. Careful not to wake the young couple, Fanny took out a book at random, *Lovers Without a Homeland*, and slid it into her belt. Nap time would soon be over. Aunt Colette would no doubt wake up first. If she came across Fanny, what violence wouldn't she permit herself?

In the hall, at the entrance to the kitchen, under the staircase to the attic, Fanny noticed a cubbyhole, hidden by a scrap of curtain, where Grandmother's dogs had been allowed to lie when it was freezing outside. She lodged herself in there as best she could, with her knees pressed against her chest and her chin lowered; her nose was assaulted by the persistent odour of wet fur which still permeated the folded blanket on which she crouched. After a minute she thought she could not endure such a position. Then her muscles became numb, the smell seemed less strong to her, and she felt almost comfortable.

At that moment, through an opening between the wall and the curtain, Fanny caught a glimpse of Aunt Colette, who came out of the bedroom, sat down at the table, in front of the plums, and started to eat noisily, straight from the bowl. She was wearing her beautiful blue dress printed with silver moons, which she had altered into a house-dress, probably deeming it too old now to make an impression on days of great occasion. The disfavoured dress was now being splashed with stewed fruit when only recently it had been taken out of its plastic twice a year and donned with self-conscious care. Aunt Colette put down her spoon when she heard Fanny's mother, Eugene and his fiancée coming. She quickly wiped her lips on the sleeve of her dress and busied herself with finding a plate for each person. As soon as he had sat down, Eugene, between mouthfuls, started talking about a dog he wanted to get. He wanted a big one which would bark loudly and terrorize visitors; with the house thus guarded, everyone would sleep peacefully. Aunt Colette approved of the idea. She nibbled elegantly, claimed she was not hungry, and insisted on giving away her share. Fanny's mother started to describe the outfit she would wear for the wedding; she would be dressed quite simply in mauve. Even the fiancée wanted to wear something very simple which could easily be worn again. Beige rather than white, without lace, and with low heels. For a hat, she would make do with a beret. As for Eugene, they would buy him a grey suit, the kind he would wear every day if he took up his father's trade, as Aunt Colette and the fiancée were planning for him. The wedding needed to be economical, although an abundance of food had been ordered; the wedding list being costly, they could not decently do less. The fiancée was thrilled with a set of stoneware fish plates, which Aunt Clemence intended to give them. She repeated its price with satisfaction, proudly, as though the three thousand francs bore witness to her own value. Aunt Colette, on the other hand, disdainfully named a particular relative who, under the pretext of financial difficulties, apologized for having to settle on the least expensive present, a pair of shoe brushes with imitation shell handles. She was scandalized that this individual, Eugene's godfather, worried more than anything about protecting his savings. Eugene was muttering; nothing could distract his thoughts from the dog he had decided to get. Fanny's mother was humming to herself as she leafed with one hand through the television guide, and not a word was said about Fanny; they showed not a single sign of embarrassment for having abandoned her.

# SIX

## *In The Doghouse*

To her great surprise, during the hour following dinner, Fanny found her mother throwing leftovers from the meal through the opening; some chop bones with fat still on them, some rind from the ham, a little piece of hardened cheese, an apple which was almost whole. She guessed from her mother's hurried movements that she was acting in secret. Then her mother adjusted the curtain on its rail so that the opening was as narrow as possible and nimbly moved away. She was wearing gold-coloured high-heeled mules, brand new. She did not address a single word to Fanny, although she was alone in this part of the room, yet Fanny was not really surprised because she understood that even if she still existed enough for her mother to worry about feeding her, she was no longer capable of making people speak to her. Besides, she was afraid that if she opened her mouth she would throw her mother into a panic, and then people would run up from all sides and discover her, Fanny, in this forbidden place.

Fanny gnawed greedily at the bones. Then she suddenly felt an urge to read the novel which she had spirited away from Grandmother's collection.

She read until morning, by the light of a moon-beam which came through the glass door from the garden, and she only remembered her predicament when she heard Aunt Colette emerge from her bedroom, clearing her throat and shuffling in her old slippers towards the bathroom. But Fanny felt exhilarated, enchanted by what she had read, unable to believe that anything more real existed. She settled happily in her nook — it was impossible for her to unfold her arms and legs or to raise her head — and squashed some fleas which had bitten her during the night. Fanny would gladly have given, there, on the spot, the rest of her life, however brief, for the certainty of a final emotion like the one she had just experienced, which was worth all her past joys.

Aunt Colette was washing with a lot of loud splashing and letting farts rip freely. What would life with Eugene have been, Fanny told herself, with his inevitable boredom and all his complaints, compared to the happiness that *Lovers Without a Homeland* had brought her in a few hours which seemed like years?

Aunt Colette reentered the kitchen as she fastened the last buttons on her blue dress. She scratched her stomach, making the nylon squeak;

Fanny shuddered in her nook. Aunt Colette made the coffee. Then she went off to drink it in the living room, in front of the television, which at this early hour was broadcasting a game show that had already been on the night before, but which Aunt Colette had undoubtedly missed. She rattled off the answers in an authoritatively loud voice, congratulated herself out loud for finding the right one before the contestant, lamented not being in his place, and felt bitter contempt for him. When the programme was over, she turned up the sound so she could listen to the television from the kitchen, where she started to peel vegetables.

Later, Fanny's mother threw the peelings into the nook; for lunch Aunt Colette had prepared one of her specialities, a shepherd's pie, none of which was left. Eugene in particular had made a pig of himself. His face was already taking on a reddishness, a certain purple puffiness which Fanny had always seen in Uncle George's face. He opened that morning's local paper and pushed back his chair to read more comfortably while the girl and Aunt Colette did the dishes and Fanny's mother settled down to watch her soap opera. He read out the names of the people who had died the day before. Aunt Colette, pretending to know everyone, would gasp, refuse to believe it, resign herself to it, and finally conclude in a satisfied tone, 'Who would have thought it, even yesterday?'

Suddenly there was a knock at the door and Fanny's father came in. He was accompanied by his servant with the brass buttons, who was carrying a heavy parcel. Everyone cried out in surprise. 'You're here?' exclaimed Fanny's mother, without leaving the living room. Aunt Colette bustled about. She pulled out chairs, offered coffee, got out the best biscuits. 'Uh, uh,' grunted Eugene, not knowing what to say. Fanny's father was dressed in an expensive white suit and his pale yellow shoes squeaked at the smallest step. He was proud, serene, a little haughty. He sat down in the kitchen and drank slowly. His servant remained standing, having placed the parcel at his feet. Fanny's father said nothing. No one dared speak. They all assumed an air of listening with interest to the determined voices coming from the living room, where Fanny's mother still sat, having contented herself with moving her armchair a little so she could see into the kitchen. That she did not put herself out to greet Fanny's father was no doubt less out of pride, since they had been on good terms for a long time, than out of reluctance to miss what might be a crucial scene from this episode — the soap opera had not been on for fifteen years, whereas she could visit Fanny's father whenever she wanted.

Aunt Colette could not remain still. She emptied the cupboard of all its biscuits and other delicacies, although Fanny's father had not touched a thing. She became hot and bothered, worried by the silence. At last he lifted up the parcel. 'I learned of your wedding,' he said, amiably presenting it to Eugene. 'This is for you, nephew.' Turning towards Aunt Colette, he added, 'It's the done thing, it seems to me.' And he smiled modestly, as did the servant, as happy as if the present had been for him. A little clumsily, Eugene unwrapped a long piece of thick, shiny material with an intricate pattern. It gave off a strong scent of spices, which overpowered the traditional smells of the house, smells risen from the cellar, exhaled by the ancient furnace, escaped from the wardrobes where lavender withered, descended from the attic cluttered with old things. The girl rapturously thanked him and draped the material around her waist, claiming that she knew of nothing more beautiful. 'You're spoiling them,' simpered Aunt Colette, her eyes transfixed on the servant's big brass buttons. Wasn't the servant's uniform even more imposing than the master's elegant and sober clothing? They all hugged Fanny's father, then no one could think how else to be nice to him. They asked him for news from his home, which he obligingly gave. When he had returned the courtesy, a warm affection prevailed on both sides such as there had never been between the family and Fanny's father. He agreed to stay until the next day, having made the trip by car, driven by the servant. Eugene went out to admire the limousine. The girl talked about making living room curtains out of the fabric. Leaning with dignity in his chair, polite and terse, Fanny's father was savouring his triumph. When as a young man he had crossed Grandmother's threshold for the first time on the arm of Fanny's mother, who was then sustained by her own strong will, cold looks had fallen on him, and Aunt Colette had not addressed a word to him except a few unfriendly, distrustful questions. Now Aunt Colette was bustling about, putting her best provisions together for dinner. She went down to cut the throat of a rabbit, while Fanny's mother went into the garden to gather raspberries; when she came back, she threw a handful of the least pretty ones into the nook. It seemed as though she acted absent-mindedly, out of a vague remembrance of duty rather than mercy. Did she even remember what she would have found in the nook if she raised the curtain? Probably not, considering how distracted and distant she was, crossing the hall in her pretty golden mules, stopping from time to time, by chance, in front of the cubby hole without a tremble of her ankle, without a little tap of her foot to let her daughter know of a thought in her regard, or a regret. And when she sacrificed a second of her time or went out of her way to offer some raspberries or the still warm tripe from the stomach of the rabbit under Aunt Colette's knife, she probably was not thinking any more than when the force of habit and a liking for neatness urged her to change the dried-out boxwood branch on the crucifix in her room. Would she even have wanted to believe that a daughter of hers could be in the nook? She was careful that no one saw when she half-opened the curtain, but it could have been out of a sense of propriety.

Aunt Colette cooked a vegetable soup and made a stew with the rabbit after catching its rich blood in the same chipped orange bowl as Grandmother had used for this purpose. Eugene, with nothing to do, hovered around her, although Aunt Colette pressed him to visit with Fanny's father who had allowed them to serve him an aperitif. Eugene seemed reluctant, suddenly shy — he was afraid he would commit some unforgettable blunder in front of this impressive man. Fanny's father was tasting his pernod with smackings of his tongue, which flattered Aunt Colette to the extent that she no longer saw in his uncommon nature anything other than a supreme, barely penetrable elegance. Having forgotten Fanny, Aunt Colette delighted in the idea that such richly adorned strangeness could only inspire admiration and respect. She promised herself to preserve the ties between Fanny's father and Eugene, who did not have a job and seemed less inclined each day to look for one. What would Aunt Colette have thought if she had suddenly seen Fanny, her niece, dart out from the nook under the stairs? Would her feelings towards her be changed by the new respect Fanny's father commanded, assuming that she recognized her and that the father himself acknowledged her as his daughter?

From a cabinet next to the nook, Aunt Colette took out jams and fresh onions for Fanny's father to take with him the next day. She counted them carefully, seeing no reason why one should ruin oneself to be kind. In the morning, she added half of a rabbit complete with its liver, and put the blood in a yoghurt pot closed with aluminum foil. Fanny's father left slowly. In the yard he met Uncle George, who was returning from a round. Not knowing how the father had been greeted, assuming that he had perhaps just been sent packing without further ado, Uncle George scornfully eyed him up and down from the top of his grey polyester summer suit, his lip taut and disdainful.

# SEVEN

## *The Wedding Preparations And Fanny's First Death*

The whole household got up before dawn in the greatest excitement. Fanny's mother paced back and forth in her mauve dress in search of a belt she could not find and forgot to toss what remained of breakfast into the nook, seemingly unaware of her absent-mindedness. She even happened to lift up the curtain as she explored every nook and cranny in a panic to find her belt, but her quick glance, concentrated solely on the image of the hunted object, swept the nook without alighting on Fanny. Her violet suede court shoes were clicking feverishly and heedlessly on the tile; she had put them on as soon as she got up, as she said, 'to wear them in.' Relaxed, Aunt Colette was getting glasses and bottles ready for the aperitif, which they would have at home, and clearing the dining room table where the wedding presents would be displayed. At last the girl appeared, dressed in a modest beige suit, followed by Eugene, constricted in his father's best suit which smelt slightly of mothballs. In its day, assured Aunt Colette, pulling at the too short sleeves, this suit had been a real extravagance, so Uncle George had only worn it for memorable occasions and had forced himself, successfully, to make it last. Eugene was already stifling and he loosened his knit tie. His movements were strained, the jacket was so tight on him. Hands in pockets, he dawdled from one room to another, feverish and at the same time not knowing what to do with himself. His cumbersome heaviness got in the way of the women, who were diligently bustling about. They complained at always finding him in their way, and jostled him, rebuking him with tender satisfaction. He suddenly left, promising to be back soon. Then Aunt Clemence made her entrance and they crowded around the fish service, which, with the stylized relief of a mullet head on each plate and its serving dish in the shape of a ship's anchor, proved to be just what the girl had dreamt. It was placed in the middle of the table and labelled with Aunt Clemence's name to avoid any confusion. But the guests were arriving in successive waves, the kitchen filled up, the presents piled up, and Aunt Colette arranged them in order of importance and expensiveness.

Such was the conversation:

'I'm afraid I'll be really hot in my shawl.'

'You can take it off after church.'

'No, she'll catch a chill!'

'You have to watch out in this weather.'

'It's the worst. Just last year a nasty breeze had me bed-ridden for three days and you never...'

'An escargot service! How spoilt they are!'

'The last ones I ate made me ill, but it was because they hadn't sweated enough.'

'And the butter! If the butter has soured...'

'Eugene doesn't even like escargots.'

'That's true. When he was little, he couldn't see a snail without...'

'They grow out of it.'

'Do you remember the escargots that your sister made for us, the year I broke my elbow while...'

'My sister knows how to prepare them perfectly too.'

'But not as well as our late mother...'

Then this strange circumstance occurred. Someone, perhaps the fiancée, cried out, 'There's Leda and Eugene!' and they saw Fanny jump out from the nook under the stairs and roll onto the tile floor, a little slaver on her lips and her eyes half-closed. A big, strong dog, which Eugene was holding, escaped from his grip and leapt upon Fanny, barking so hard that everyone backed off with fright. It seized her by the throat and started to tear her apart. It kept spitting out the big hunks of flesh that it had torn off, as if it wanted to taste all of her before deciding to swallow. It snarled, forbidding anyone to come near. No one moved. Eugene, dismayed and red with shame, was pulling at his sideboards. The dog had its four paws on Fanny's chest, her neck was almost severed. Fanny had not made a sound except a slight, very slight squeal! Now it was digging at her chest, looking for her heart. Suddenly it lost interest and returned docile, wagging its tail, to Eugene. Aunt Colette regained her quick-wittedness, and without distaste — just as she gutted rabbits or cleaned calves' heads — she wrapped what was left of Fanny in an old sheet and went out to throw the whole thing on the manure heap at the bottom of the garden. Aunt Clemence washed the tile floor and, not without enthusiasm, Fanny's mother took charge of serving the aperitif. Eugene went out to tie his dog up in the yard and conversation resumed about what they were drinking, although that never altered — a pernod for the men, for the women a drop of liqueur...

'Oh, oh this plonk would soon get you drunk!'

'Put a drop of water in then, you know.'

'She's trying to drown me!'

'This port isn't as old as...'

151

'But you know the one we brought back from our trip, we drank it in...'

'They make good ones there.'

'That depends, that depends, personally I...'

'Oh, but it's port wine country, and it doesn't cost anything. You should go there!'

Suddenly, George showed up, his handsome face sweating, a little distraught.

'Where's Fanny?' he asked Aunt Colette. He was puffing, having run all the way to the house. Aunt Colette had some difficulty recognizing George. When she realized who he was, she smiled coldly.

'In the garden,' she said, 'on the manure heap.' But the hens had already gobbled up all that the dog had left of Fanny. Finding nothing but a few scraped bones, a few bloody hairs, George thought Aunt Colette was making fun of him and that he had been mistaken to take her answer literally. The indifferent welcome accorded him by Fanny's mother, who used to be well-disposed towards him, convinced him to start back without delay. In any case, he had come on impulse; wasn't his love for Fanny passing?

He delighted in the fragrances of summer, and as he walked quickly towards the train station, his young, supple body seemed to him to drive away vigorously the hot air; it was as if nothing should ever resist him any more, for the infinite years to come.

# PART SIX

*Aunt Colettes's Account*

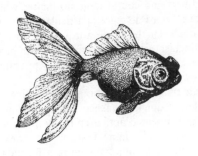

# ONE
# *The Wedding*

At last I put on my new dress, the one in the catalogue, which seemed to be made for large women, yet it restricts and suffocates me, not that it makes me ugly; it is black printed with little pink flowers. Except for my sister, the guests had hardly made an effort, as it seems is the custom more and more these days, out of a concern to economize and a desire to be natural and comfortable no matter what — which deep down I approve of. But I do regret, particularly this morning of course, that nobody, not even the bride and groom, any longer makes an attempt to distinguish a wedding ceremony from any old get-together where everyone comes wearing whatever they put on when they got up. Even my nieces were barely clean.

More than anything I love the moment of leaving the house!

Before we left, I quickly washed the aperitif glasses, otherwise I would have been tormented until evening by the thought of those dirty dishes waiting, free to sully, in my imagination, by extension, the whole house. Behind our backs objects acquire a formidable independence which must be quelled.

We rushed out into the street without any order whatsoever, without organizing ourselves into a procession. My son wanted to take his dog and refused to listen to me when I voiced my disapproval. He held the dog's leash in one hand and gave me his other arm, yanking and jolting me every time the dog threatened to dart off. My son would not stop talking about that dog. He wants to train it to hunt, so you cannot shake hunting from his mind. For his wedding my son was wearing one of his father's suits, which was too tight under the arms, but in it I thought I already saw his father himself when he leaves for work in this type of suit, especially because of the expressions my son is starting to get from his father, or which his father is passing on to him, which all have something very masculine in them. My son will also have that red face — from too much drinking and eating, and all that salted meat! From behind their curtains, the neighbours were watching us pass, and I regretted then that they were not seeing us in a stately procession, but as a crowd, separated into little groups of acquaintances dragging along behind us, spread out across the whole breadth of the road. My nieces had their hands stuck in the pockets of their canvas trousers and were talking about everything and nothing with my son's fiancée, whom no one could have picked out as the bride either by what she was wearing or any particular emotion, as she was extremely calm and moved without any grace whatsoever — she stooped a little, as if, instead of walking to the registry office, towards this irrevocable act of her own choosing, she was going on her morning outing to buy bread at the bottom of the village, with that vague boredom which she seemed to feel even now.

My son's dog started to howl, for no reason, and — since all the dogs of the street answered — we could no longer hear ourselves speak. My son let go of my arm to reach out and give the animal a good punch in the kidneys and almost got bitten. My son's dog was still wild and he had trouble controlling it. We arrived at the registry office amid a frightful chorus of barking. My son was pouting, upset because he had not known how to make his dog obey him, and his fiancée, noticing this, jerked the leash authoritatively from his hands and asked her young brother to take the dog back to the house, mortifying Eugene even more. He did not unclench his teeth until he uttered, without warmth, the ritual 'I do.'

'It's my dog, I forbid you to touch it!' he spat in his wife's face as soon as we had come out. Then she got angry and they argued all the way to the church, so annoyed with each other that it's a wonder they consented to take each other's arm. A few grains of rice which my sister — the only one to think of it — had thrown, stayed in their hair and they shook them out onto the porch with irritated jerks of the head, lost in their anger. They barely listened to the old priest's wise words, each muttering their own side of the argument in the other's ear. Would they have understood much of this language anyway, which few of the people around me really did understand although every word in it was simple? The sentences were long and by the end of one, we — being little used to working our memories so hard — had forgotten the beginning. The guests relaxed after their initial shyness and were chattering freely, talking about their hopes for dinner and working up one another's appetite. The hubbub of these voices managed to drown out the priest's interminable dronings, which no more impressed anyone enough to hold him in respect than did the high, dark walls of the church. We wanted neither to provoke him nor to flaunt our independence, but out of ignorance, a lack of education, we felt nothing more than boredom and an impatience to get out of there, to satisfy our more material desires. Even my son and his wife had no need of this ceremony. They had conformed to it spontaneously so no one could reproach them in the slightest. They were neither troubled nor soothed nor even irritated by what the priest said to them, who failed to penetrate their consciences. My son was probably thinking about his dog. My daughter-in-law was perhaps picturing a certain fish service that had been given to her. My son was standing poorly, resting on one leg. We used to have a sense of solemnity. My son and his wife smiled broadly when everyone, or almost everyone, took their photograph as they left the church. This smile definitely made them look rather simple, but people would have been worried if they had managed to stay serious. Lots of things were done incorrectly. For instance, it was at this moment that my sister should have thrown the rice, not after the civil ceremony. We vaguely remember traditions and the habit of respecting them, but we make minor mistakes. We smile with a little embarrassment, and in photographs we show a lot of teeth to confirm the happiness of the moment. It no longer matters to us to appear impressive; people would think we were being absurd or cold. So my son and his wife kissed each other for the photographs but with such violence that my son cut his lip on his wife's big teeth. Had they kissed gently, people would have judged them strangely indifferent and they themselves would perhaps have worried at not showing more eagerness, would perhaps have tried to find in it the sign of a complicated truth. Some drops of blood stained my son's shirt and his bad mood returned. Slowly we walked back to the house for the reception. To the guests were added numerous neighbours whom we had invited to this light refreshment. They were waiting patiently for us in front of the door, although manners would normally have required them to attend the church ceremony beforehand and would have forbidden them — their absence at the church not conforming to any principle — to show up at the moment for eating and drinking. If they had not put themselves out earlier, it was due to laziness and a fear of becoming bored.

My son eagerly untied his dog. He placed the dog's paws on his shoulders and got people to take his picture several times in this pose, his face beaming. He went into his house with the dog to show it off. He had fun trying to get it drunk — without success because the dog refused the wine — and we all laughed a lot to see it sneeze whenever the bubbles skimmed its nostrils. I have never seen my son as happy as he is in this dog's company. While he and his wife often have trouble thinking up a subject of interest to them both — since my son only has a passion for hunting and cars and the only thing that matters to his wife is the household — it seems that my son manages to talk better with that dog than with any other person, without ever growing tired. My son should have married his dog, not a woman, because what do they have in common? My son should have married his dog or some friend of his own sex to talk with endlessly about his dog! My son's wife couldn't care less about his dog! And his wife's little household concerns weigh on my son, who endures them out of duty. And what did my son do after teasing the dog? Tired, he went to lie down. Several long hours still separated us from dinner. The unoccupied guests wandered back and forth between the house and the garden. Some started a game of bowls. I joined a group that my sisters and some other women were forming in one corner of the kitchen. We chatted quietly about the family, each person's aches and pains and the remedies to use on them. We are peaceful and resigned and we only really have a good time among ourselves. If a man comes up, he bothers us; in his presence, we are reluctant to talk about ourselves. He moves away quickly, troubled simply by the sight of our gathering, where he is an intruder, where his body becomes heavy and clumsy. He goes off to rejoin the men in the garden or in the courtyard, where they stand, hands in their pockets, their stomachs protruding, conversing loudly about matters devoid of mystery, avoiding any subject which could put them too, like their wives, under suspicion of feeling affection, or pity, or fear. We stayed seated for a long time, with our hands in our laps. Only our mouths were moving. We could stay like that for whole days, as still as toadstools on a tree, because we keep trotting out the same remarks without tiring, without even giving the impression that we have made them before. Once the subject is really closed, we don't add anything which would disturb the learned observations already expressed; we are content with sending it back and forth from one to another like a hard, smooth ball, passing it, as the children say, without danger. We hardly worry about solving problems; we are preoccupied with translating facts into moral judgements. We have at our disposal numerous phrases or expressions composed by distant ancestors, which adapt to every circumstance in our calm lives. We understand one another perfectly that way.

My son finally got up, his handsome suit all crumpled. He gave the cream puffs, which were left over from the reception, to his dog, despite my disgust at seeing an animal spoilt in such a way. Then he made countless instant snapshots of all of us and his dog, and we were really amused by the strange, blurred and reddened faces, which appeared on the thick paper — although I thought it was a lot of money for ridiculous results. I was a little saddened that my son's wedding was being immortalized in such a mediocre way — to keep costs down, we had not hired a photographer, something I now regretted upon discovering that so few of the snapshots were any good.

Then we travelled by car to the inn where we were supposed to have dinner, a couple of miles outside the village, at the junction of the main roads. The doors to the cars were trimmed with satin ribbons, and my son sounded the horn all the way down the road, mainly, I think, to make everyone admire him in his godfather's new car, which he was driving. I took note that while my son's godfather was too short of money to give him anything more than a set of shoe brushes, he was still rich enough to buy himself velvet seat covers — some of the most expensive — and an alarm system which, a little earlier, had frightened us when it suddenly went off.

The noise from the road and the close proximity of the cars prohibited us from hanging around outside, so we surged into the banqueting room where we still had to wait for the tables to be set, our passive crowd getting in the way, so that the servers scolded us for arriving so early. We had done a lot of waiting the whole day long, some of us were yawning as if worn out by boredom. Our weddings always go on like this — everything leading up to the meal is just a long endurance test. We were hot, the room seemed low and already partly filled with smoke because it was directly adjacent to the kitchens from where strong fumes were escaping. There was no question of opening the windows, however, because of the din outside. My son took off his jacket and tie, and most of the guests followed suit. Some old people had even brought their slippers. After circling the tables, which were arranged in the form of a U, to find the menus bearing their names, everyone collapsed into their chairs with noisy contentment, knowing that they would not have to leave them for several hours, and relieved to have finally put their hands on something tangible, to be recompensed, finally, for the effort and expense they had gone to. We had devised the menu so that it seemed generous and sophisticated but was composed of inexpensive items; the terms used to describe them disguised their simplicity, we thought. Our experience of weddings had taught us that the guests are demanding and prompt to criticize the meagreness of a meal, even when it would have greatly appeased their hunger. We ourselves had considered another family stingy because they had served only four courses to their wedding guests. We wanted to spend as little as possible without it appearing so. It's hard to rid oneself of a reputation for stinginess.

We started the meal with white wine with a touch of blackcurrant juice. My son and his wife, seated at the centre of the cross-table, drank first, amid applause and wishes for their happiness. My daughter-in-law, red, tired, still a little angry at my son, stained her cream blouse with the blackcurrant juice. She was smiling with difficulty, as if this wedding had been a dreaded obligation she had not known how to get out of, yet I knew she had been overjoyed to be the leading lady in such a ceremony. She could hardly have imagined it to be any different — it was banal, like all of them. But she would soon forget the annoyance, the tediousness of this day in her pride at having organized it and having gathered around herself so many people who, for the first time, had made my son and his wife the centre of attention. I did not doubt that afterwards my daughter-in-law would sincerely see this day as one of the happiest of her life.

My son was laughing continually, although he bore a grudge against his wife and me for not letting him bring the dog to the meal, and he would occasionally sigh and cast resentful looks at us. My son's cheeks were crimson, and his half-unbuttoned shirt let his sleeveless undershirt show, completely damp with sweat and creased over his little fat tummy, which he had got into the habit of patting and stroking with visible pleasure when he had had enough to eat.

The hors d'oeuvre were brought in: two slices of pistachio mousse for each person and coquille de saumon sauce verte — boiled salmon, coated with pepper mayonnaise and presented on a beautiful lettuce leaf. People talked about the afternoon which had just passed, and made fun of the old parish priest and certain affectations in his language, which they decided were ridiculous mistakes that he made because he was old. The conversation turned towards old age, old people's homes, the vigour of the older people present. We talked about the prices of prescriptions and the misuses of medicine. Someone complained about his high taxes, and different means of evading taxes were assessed. Some excellent examples were mentioned. We returned to the meal since the meat was being brought in: a guinea fowl fondant on a nest of greens with garden peas which were a little on the large side. I congratulated myself that the food was good, although each of us present would certainly eat better at home, if less abundantly. Our mothers brought their daughters up in such a way that unless we had no natural ability we could not be anything but expert cooks, familiar with all the secrets of difficult recipes and having always known the best ways to prepare whatever came out of the garden or the farmyard. However, the special occasion of a wedding misled our expectations, we felt that what we were served should be exceptional, judging by the length of the menu, the reputation of the restaurant, and the servers' black uniforms. As far as I'm concerned, nothing I swallowed seemed anything other than ordinary, and I was seized by a slight regret at the thought of the cost of this meal, although we had kept the price down as much as possible. That's the way we are. We never go out to a restaurant for fear of having to say, 'It's better at home and less expensive,' and we do not get the slightest pleasure out of anything when we feel we haven't got our money's worth.

Pork loin with lentils followed the guinea fowl, which had seemed a little tough to me. A few spicy jokes had started to arise here and there. A cousin — the live-wire of the family — was getting ready for the festivities at dessert. My son was red and bloated, about to explode, and had undone his shirt down to his belt. Unable to wait any longer, this cousin stood up and, passing each person, organized the ritual game, wanting everyone to get up with a full glass, touch it to three spots on the body, then empty it in one gulp, one after another, amid the saucy remarks of everyone present. We did as he told us, although his interrupting dinner really annoyed us. My son was crying with laughter and shouting louder than everyone, having always loved this kind of entertainment. The air was so hot and so full of odours and smoke that I became dizzy. Some old people were sleeping already, worn out by the suffocating heat and the inactivity. We still had rabbit with olives, which almost no one touched. We complained, good-naturedly, about the hugeness of the meal. There followed cheeses, ice cream and the tiered wedding cake — of which my son and his wife had to take a bite even though they both seemed on the verge of becoming sick. My daughter-in-law climbed onto the table so we could play the garter game. Only a modest sum of money was collected, but the value of the presents which my son and his wife had received made up for it and, altogether, we perhaps reaped a slight profit out of this wedding.

# TWO
## *Heavenly Abode*

The supermarket which had been promised to us by the mayor and which we were impatiently awaiting — shops here being rare and poorly stocked — has just opened at the edge of the village, in the same area as the housing estates which it dominates with its considerable mass, tall and flat, visible, along with the gigantic letters of its name, from far away on the plain, marking out our village more clearly and sooner to travellers than the meagre church weathervane or the big marble cross in the middle of the cemetery. The building is actually nothing more than a sort of huge warehouse, with its corrugated walls painted blue, and a huge forecourt in front of it where cars and shopping trollies are parked. But, to us who emerge from the high street flanked by low and tightly-packed old houses, the building seems so long, so huge, so impossible to ever walk all the way around — the very idea of following just one of its walls on foot depressed us — that it seems to us much more than an unsightly warehouse, we see it rather as a fairy tale castle, the new pride of our village, and at last something to give potential visitors a reason to linger here. We have the pleasant and flattering impression that an important person has come to move in with us, and we will be its faithful subjects in return for its relieving our boredom and making our domestic life easier, while also bringing us each day larger and larger crowds from the neighbouring villages and market towns. Many of us had never seen so many people at once. Perhaps our village will soon lose its name to that of the supermarket — the two destinations are already mistaken for each other. While this prospect distresses me, I am too pleased with the presence of the supermarket not to resign myself to it quickly. My son, his wife, my husband and I cannot restrain ourselves from going there every day, at the slightest excuse. We get into the car with the dog — although the supermarket is hardly more than two hundred yards away — and drive slowly towards the housing estates as we carefully decide the programme for the outing. Our excitement makes us so extravagant that we try to make one another see reason and we promise not to buy anything that we haven't yearned for beforehand, that we haven't come to look at several days in a row, which, rather than being a restriction, is a joy for us, because it makes us return to the supermarket out of a sense of obligation.

We stop the car in the car park, in our usual spot, among the dozens of other vehicles and, to delay our pleasure a little, entertain one another by reading the license plates out loud. Then how small and suddenly almost intimidated we feel at the foot of the supermarket! It stretches endlessly across the plain, our eyes can never encompass it all. The brief sound of its name, painted in orange letters bigger than our house, rings in our ears like the name of a familiar person whom we particularly cherish. There is, indeed, no relative whose name we pronounce with so much warmth and hope. Even his dog now holds less interest for my son than the supermarket. But for some time now the dog has answered to the name of the supermarket just as if it were being called, perhaps realizing that this way it will please my son more.

At the entrance to the supermarket, we separate having agreed to meet two hours later at the first floor cafeteria, which is our favourite. We each grab a huge shopping trolley. We have a long way to go before exploring the supermarket in its entirety. Despairing sometimes of ever succeeding, we have agreed to each explore a different area before meeting up to describe in detail what we have seen. We never pass one another in the aisles. When we think we have become lost or plunged so far into the bright depths of the building that we are afraid of not having enough to come back to for the rest of our lives, a panicky fear makes our hearts beat fast, and then, to redeem ourselves, we are ready to swear that we shall never again set foot in the supermarket. But we always manage to find our way again, and it turns out that the ground covered is never so far that we cannot arrive at our meeting place at the proposed time. These terrors provide amusing fodder for our discussions. Now and again my son and his wife leave together when they need to choose some object indispensable to their new household. They buy little, it's so hard for them to make up their minds. Wanting a new bed, they suddenly find themselves confronted with a staggering quantity of beds of all styles and materials, and no longer know, looking at such diversity, what pleases them, not daring to set their hearts on any one of them, sensing that as soon as they point their finger at one model, another, not yet noticed, will catch their attention and they will regret having decided so quickly. I worry that these torments will never end, because though they assure us on the way home that they have finally looked at all the models and will at last be able to make their choice tomorrow with full knowledge of what is available, they forget that what they examined will undergo astonishing transformations during the night. In the morning they will discover models of an unimaginable design which were not there before, overturning any decision they might have made. They could not have imagined that such a colour, such a frame, such a strange and attractive material existed, and insisting on being familiar with everything, they continually postpone the moment of commitment, preferring the discomfort of this uncertainty to the aversion which they would most certainly come to feel for the object chosen under these conditions. I am afraid that one day they will pounce on the one furthest from their taste, and the most expensive, when their common sense has been completely scrambled. But the supermarket has given direction to their life, which it certainly needed, and has brought them closer together more surely than the shared love for a small child or dog.

My husband and I never explore the rows of shelves together, not being interested in the same products. My husband returns to the tools almost every time, where he discovers a multitude that he would never have dared to imagine, many of which disconcert him with a use which had never entered his head, filling him with the pleasant impression of spinning in a dream, where barely formed desires are fulfilled on the spot with the greatest perfection. He can rarely resist the temptation to purchase certain tools which it is unlikely he will ever use, but their surprising and specific functions suddenly make them essential. Then he feels as if he has lived in shameful blindness until now, having never felt the lack of this equipment conceived by a wiser mind than his own. My husband, who had always liked his job, has started to curse it because he cannot go to the supermarket as often as he would like. I think that when he leaves in the morning, my husband is often jealous of the rest of us who are going to go to the supermarket without him.

As for me, the sight of everything enchants me. I wander through the aisles in peaceful wonder at such a harmonious abundance. I have not experienced the pleasure of fine art, having never entered a museum in my whole life, but the spectacular stacking of thousands of colourful objects awakens a very special emotion in me, as does the perfect and never-ending check pattern of the shelves far below when viewed from the upper floors! Popular music seeps continually from the walls or even from the ceiling, though the ceiling seems too high in the sky for sounds to fall as far as us. A delicious heat always prevails throughout the supermarket; various fragrances fascinate the nose; we stroll along with a sense of freedom felt nowhere else with such intensity, because although hundreds of strangers circulate the shop at the same time as us, the area is so vast that we come across only enough people to remind us that we are neither lost nor alone. On the other hand, the check-outs are so numerous — a hundred? a thousand? even more? — that we never have to wait very long.

Around noon we meet in the cafeteria, impatient to tell what we have discovered or to show one another our purchases. We sit down every day at the same table near a large window overlooking the plain, and through it we see in the distance a modern water tower in the shape of a big mushroom, electric pylons with long, outstretched arms, plus the motorway, flanked at regular intervals by billboards. We make a game of them, trying to see who can decipher them first. When they concern the supermarket, they fill us with something like contented pride. We eat chops and rather greasy chips, breaking, here, our habit of not eating anything which is not made at home. But then we feel a great sense of well-being. The numerous brown formica tables quickly fill up again, and amid the noise of voices, the clinking of cutlery, we soon become silent, happy when we recognize a face. We stay there for a very long time, drinking coffee, looking out over the plain, dreaming about our next purchases if, despite everything, the shame at all this wasted time does not push us outside. We slowly head back to the exit, taking the longest way. We no longer understand how we did without the supermarket and we pity our ancestors, we feel stronger, happier and more clever.

# THREE

## *What Is Changing In The Village*

For some time, numerous transformations have been affecting our village — or, to be more precise, that of my late parents — which mean it will soon no longer resemble a traditional village, but just dwellings grouped together in a haphazard manner or chaotically scattered about. Our village is not a small city, nor even a market town, but can we still call it a village? In the centre where the church stands, the butcher's, the delicatessen, the grocer's, the bakery have all disappeared, and their shop windows, now smeared white, serve as backgrounds for publicity posters which — hastily stuck up and carelessly ripped down — have decorated them for a short time, extolling the advantages of shops located in the nearest town where most of us hardly ever go. If our tradesmen have closed up shop, the fault, of course, lies with all of us. I don't miss them for what we found in their shops, which the supermarket offers in greater quantity and at a lower price. But when we go down the high street in the morning, the desolate sadness of these closed shops, of the pavements where no one has any reason to stop any more, grips me painfully, and then I no longer know what I should prefer. Our butcher, now a public employee, collects the rubbish. Shouldn't we be ashamed, I tell myself, to see him employed like this? I avoid his eye, although, convinced of the inevitability of the situation and resigned to his new job, he perhaps takes my embarrassment and pity for some form of contempt. Even the church is closed more often than open; our parish priest visits several villages in the area. Consequently, no one any longer has any reason to direct their steps towards this dead village square, this deserted high street, and so, deprived of its heart, the village sullenly, lethargically, indifferently spreads outward. Here it is today, surrounded by housing estates — sprung up here and there without any organization — where those of us who live in the old part are certain to get lost, because all the houses look alike — aren't they all just one single design repeated over and over? We don't really know the inhabitants of these new neighbourhoods. Sometimes it seems to us that they too are identical to one another, without, however, any particular characteristics that could easily explain such an impression. Is it because they go for walks or to

165

the supermarket uniformly clothed in trousers and sports shoes — often hot pink for the women — and that we are not used to seeing our neighbours go out dressed in this way? Or is it that living in houses which nothing differentiates, common attitudes begin to permeate them all and give us the disconcerting impression of always meeting the same person, reproduced, like the houses, several dozens at a time? There is something about it which I cannot put my finger on. My son and daughter-in-law really surprised me recently by suddenly claiming they wanted to live in one of those houses as soon as they have sold this one, which they find old and impractical. 'Sell Grandmother's house?' I exclaimed indignantly. They dared not reply, but that only postponed the matter because they are attracted to the modern appearance of those houses, even though they know that they do not equal Grandmother's in charm or quality. How can we fight their appeal, when my son and his wife find gardens planted with daisies, and decorated with gnomes and a fake well, more stylish than their vegetable garden, which they hate to cultivate? They get just as lost as we do in these new streets, which they love to wander around on Sundays, despite the continual howling of the dogs who are sent into a yapping frenzy at the slightest noise. Would Grandmother herself still recognize her village?

The café-owner has stopped carrying newspapers. To modernize the appearance of his establishment, he has repainted the cream walls a light grey and changed the varnished wood furniture for grey metal tables and chairs. Loud, violent music now blares right out into the street, disturbing the old people who, to their great regret, no longer meet at the café to chat or play cards, but in the huge village hall, where a table has been set up in the middle, small and lost in that big empty space. I am afraid that the café itself might close, because the young people from the housing estates rarely go there; like us, they prefer the cafeterias at the supermarket and we bump into them sometimes without always recognizing one another. In truth, our village is now changing so fast that it seems as if an invisible hand is having a good time changing it behind our backs, but it would be more honest to admit that we are all responsible. A powerful movement is dragging us along, which, we are inclined to think, it would be pointless to try to stop, especially since we know how to take advantage of it.

Last Sunday we went to visit my husband's cousin, who runs a large farm with her husband in a nearby hamlet. Eugene, who has loved outings to the farm since he was a child, was overjoyed. We passed the supermarket and were surprised to arrive almost straight away. We had never before travelled the whole length of the building, and when we realized that the end of it almost touched our cousin's home, casting it in a shadow, we were deeply troubled, although in a certain sense we might just as well have delighted in this as a direct link between her and us. What's more, if the supermarket lavished her with the same joys as us, we could only be thrilled for her for being so near it. But Eugene was annoyed that the track to the farm was now so different to when he was a boy, when he could spot it from the village, on one side of the road, flat and winding, and without taking his eyes off it, saw it gradually widening through the huge, level and close-cropped field of beets. Not only did the supermarket prevent him from seeing the path from a distance, as before, but it also hid the broad panorama of the fields, which gave these outings their melancholic charm. In his disappointment my son held back his tears. I saw his eyes shining and rebuked him for his sentimentality, embarrassed that our cousin might guess what it was about.

We all sat down in the kitchen, around a plate of biscuits which we dunked in our glasses of sweet, sparkling wine. The cousins, who receive few visitors, were smiling contentedly. The room was immaculate, each object in its place, the furniture shiny, the sink scrubbed then wiped so that not a single drop remained (between two meals, to avoid wetting such a well-dried sink, we had to go and use the tap in the farmyard); a light odour of bleach lingered. The door was open onto the farmyard, which our cousin's husband had just resurfaced with cement, which was better adapted than the earth and gravel to the enormous wheels of his machines. Our cousin no longer raised livestock. They only had their old dog, which was basking on the warm cement. Our cousin had even parted with her rabbits. It was no longer worth their while to spend money on their upkeep, she explained regretfully. Oh, life is more peaceful like this... She slowly pushed the crumbs about on the oilcloth, while her husband crossed his arms over his stomach with a gesture of satisfied resignation. We spoke little, in clipped phrases. We listened to the clock and cried out 'already!' when it struck. My son got up and went out, saying he could be found in the barn. The cousin confided that they had bought a new television set at the supermarket. We went to gaze at it in the bedroom, where it sat imposingly at the foot of the bed. It was a handsome, modern set, so big that it was the first thing we noticed in the room, and our cousin turned it on so we could admire the brightness of the colours. We stayed planted lethargically in front of it for about an hour, without paying any real attention or showing any great curiosity in what we were watching, but seeing no need to return to the kitchen and unable to make up our minds to turn it off. We awoke from our trance when my daughter-in-law said, 'Let's go see what Eugene's doing,' and our cousin turned off the television with exaggerated care.

My son had headed for the building at the end of the farmyard where, when he was a child, a long swing had been hung for him, suspended from the beams and flying over the bales of hay which our cousin's husband stored there. The swing was still there and Eugene, squeezed onto the little plank, was swinging vigourously back and forth, his face serious. The barn was empty; our cousins no longer had any use for hay. Eugene's breath resounded loudly with the grinding of the metal rings, while our eyes followed him in silence amid the persistent smell of bleach, which prevailed here too. Eugene shouted out to hear the echo. For others to see my son entertaining himself in such a manner made me very uncomfortable and I surreptitiously glanced at our cousins, but they were simply watching Eugene, their legs spread wide and their arms crossed, just as in the bedroom shortly before. Their expressions were so devoid of the slightest feeling, of the least criticism, that one would have thought they did not see him any more than a television show which held no interest for them, in front of which they lingered out of laziness. My daughter-in-law, just as angry as I was, walked out of the barn. We set off after her and our cousin's husband offered to show us his machines. As for my son, he did not want to come down, so we left him, although it grieved us to let him shame us like that. We crossed the farmyard to the shed, our heels clicking on the cement. The wind was blowing violently, we moved forward, hunched; but in the farmyard nothing stirred.

# FOUR

## George's Betrayal

I had noticed for some time the interest that my husband seemed to take in a young cashier at the new supermarket. I was amazed since she was not at all pretty and handled our purchases in a glum or bored manner, which makes me think now that she was acting on my husband's orders. Before the affair was consummated, he no doubt wanted to divert any suspicion from my mind to give himself the option of coming back as if nothing had happened if things did not work out; but the way he arranged each time for us to wait for that particular cash register — along with abruptly postponed return visits and a suddenly changed schedule — was enough to convince me of his attraction to this woman. Besides, I hardly preoccupied myself with it, not being above reproach myself. I only worried that people might hear of it in the village. I feared my husband's lack of finesse and would have preferred to arrange his dates for him, as I considered myself more cunning. In truth, I had underestimated my husband's capacity for love, and in the midst of my present difficulties and serious concerns for the future, I cannot help regretting what our life might have been if I had recognized that quality in him from the beginning, or if I had been different enough to awaken it in him quite naturally when he was with me. Learning of his affair with that sullen woman, I had demonstrated an amiable condescension and only felt a slight annoyance at his poor aptitude for respectable discretion.

One afternoon, I went up to the window, saw my husband's car speeding past and glimpsed the supermarket cashier seated next to him. A little later I became aware that my husband had taken all of his underwear, several shirts and his handsome shoes which he wore on holidays. Bewildered, I stayed for a long time seated on our bed, then I rushed to the supermarket where I obtained the woman's name and address: she lived on the housing estate. I found her husband there, and her children, who were still waiting for her return to have dinner. After I had taken the man aside and explained to him what had just happened, he got so angry with me that I fled amid the barkings of a dog which he threatened to let loose on my heels if I came back. I told myself then that in the past no one in this village would have reacted like this, and I started to deplore such deterioration in manners. Then for a long time I walked around the estate, already ashamed at the

169

thought of the gossip the village would spread about our family.

A few days later, my daughter-in-law took the vacant position at the supermarket and swelled with pride at her importance.

# FIVE
## *A Walk In The Woods*

Not far from the village a clump of trees, spared because it did not obstruct any particular project, still stands between two fields. We used to spend summer afternoons there, although the foliage is sparse and offers little protection from intense heat; but we no longer ever think to take walks there, since the road leading to it, quiet not long ago, is now so heavily used and the little wood has been cut back. So I could not understand now what pushed me to turn my tracks in this direction, my mind being occupied, what's more, by serious problems — brought about by my husband's desertion and the destitution he has left me in. It had been many years since I had gone there, which makes me feel inclined to believe that destiny — not any intention on my part nor even chance — led me on that morning.

I walked briskly along the edge of the road, my shoulders huddled in my shawl, without bothering to step aside when a car came up behind and hooted for me to move over into the ditch. I had the feeling then, without knowing why, that I should hurry or I would be much to blame.

A thick fog, which seemed to my advantage, was curtaining the edge of the wood. In the surrounding fields, tractors were at work. Indifferent to the thickets, I plunged into the wood to hurry to a certain clearing where we used to go, and where, since it was my only possible landmark, I had to go first rather than circling in the thickets in search of I did not know what. Soon, an apparition guided me, comforting me in this choice: at the end of the path, my niece Fanny's changed face was smiling, floating, at the centre of a pinkish halo, and as I hurried forward, puffing and panting noisily, it would draw away, seeming to bounce, then would smile even more to encourage me, enticingly. I had recognized Fanny even though she was very different from what she had been and, to be precise, nothing set her apart any more, she was just as we had wished she would be in the past — without success because the core of her nature was so bad. Moreover, it was seeing this transformed face that made me follow without hesitation. For though I still called her Fanny, I found nothing to fault in that face and I even managed to find in it a vague resemblance to my own, which has the typical features of our family. Exhausted, I reached the clearing. A huddled form was lying in the middle, on the sprouting crocuses, with the same whitish colouring and as smooth as the crocus corolla. I kneeled down and shook her gently; Fanny awoke and immediately began to shiver. I wrapped her in my shawl, even though it was completely soaked with dew, to cover my niece's nudity which was already making her blush although she had just become aware of it.

'Aunt Colette,' she murmured with lowered eyes, 'may I call you that?'

'How can I deny that I'm your aunt?' I replied.

'But aren't you that even more now?'

'As I see you, you are perfect,' I said with conviction.

My niece's face seemed to swell with pleasure and I now found her extremely pretty — at least as pretty as her cousins who had lost a little of their freshness, while my niece's complexion glowed so sweetly this morning that it gently coloured my palm which I was holding out towards her. I told her to cling to my neck, hoisted her onto my back and carried her out of the woods. I hurried along the road, worried I might meet someone I knew; people had been talking enough about the family lately for me to be anxious to maintain the greatest discretion.

'Aunt Colette, am I forgiven?' whispered Fanny in my ear.

But not knowing what to reply, I remained silent.

'Aunt Colette, your silence will make me die all over again,' she insisted. And I thought it my duty to my niece to assure her that I did not see the slightest reason why she should not be accepted into the family again, but I didn't, in case such an extraordinary change of heart would subject us to further transformations. She would have to expect time to pass before gaining my confidence. She vigourously hugged my neck. I carried her right into our bedroom beneath Eugene's dumbfounded gaze; alone in the house, he was, as always, standing and gaping in front of the television screen. I laid my niece down. Then I left, carefully closing the door, after promising her that I would come back soon.

'Did you recognize your cousin?' I asked my son. 'It really is her!'

'She really has changed,' marvelled Eugene.

'She's now what we wanted,' I said, firmly.

'The way she is now, I might have married her,' he muttered. I was outraged and rebuked him, adding that we should still be on our guard with Fanny, because once we had admitted her, she could still return to her baser instincts and become the shame of our family again without our ever being able to get rid of her easily. Then, thinking of my sister's joy, I went to call her on the telephone.

# PART SEVEN

*Fanny's Account*

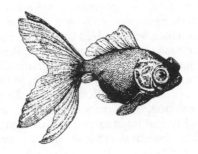

# ONE

## *My Coming To Life*

As I suddenly found myself full of self-confidence and no longer really afraid of anything, protected as I was by the change in my appearance, my first thought was to take the train to the capital to bring back George. Although I had looked down on him in the past and mistreated him, although I had wanted to dissuade him from thinking about me, I now deemed him a suitable companion for me in the village: his appalling distinctiveness could no longer humiliate me by drawing attention to how much we resembled each other, but would perhaps show to advantage my very pleasing new person. Besides, hadn't Aunt Colette wanted me to pursue relentlessly my relationship with George? It occurred to me to pity George for the torments he might be subjected to in our village, just as I had suffered them in the past, and for the family's silent coldness. The family might clutch me to its bosom, happy and proud to find me again, without even granting a glance to poor George. This thought didn't really give me any pleasure. But I wasn't about to give George up for so little. I felt very attached to him now that he couldn't harm me any more, and I was especially anxious to show Aunt Colette that from now on I intended to obey her in every respect. Besides, there was reason to hope that through prolonged contact with the villagers and members of our family, George, like me, would perhaps manage to lose this singularity — which was, according to Aunt Colette, nothing but the emanation of a presumptuous temperament, although we got it without asking for it and, in my opinion, through our parents' error and not our own. I wished with all my heart that the same good fortune would befall George. But would he ever understand the necessity of such painful self-sacrifice, which could only be achieved if it was so strongly desired that one was willing to die for it? For who can be certain of coming back? What did I owe it to, if not perhaps to fate's compassion, to Aunt Colette's mercy? Considering George's obstinacy and his great physical beauty, I felt that he would never feel ashamed of his own person or want to please Aunt Colette enough to give up features which, where he lived, added to his charm and had been passed on to him by his mother and father with natural and simple pride. If he could even imagine such feelings, I thought, ashamed, he would no doubt find it contemptible that anyone could yearn for such a transformation, though I respected the village and my own family so much that I didn't want to admit George was right.

I went to George's home, where his mother opened the door. Relieved to see that the little girls weren't there, I confidently entered the flat. Stiff and silent, George's mother politely offered me a seat; George said, 'Fancy that!' hardly surprised. He seemed happy to see me, hugged me, patted me on the shoulder and praised me for having come. These spontaneous demonstrations of pleasure and George's mother's calmness made me aware of this fact: neither George nor his mother noticed the slightest change in me. Piqued at first, I was soon delighted; deep down I had been afraid they might judge me with such severity that the only thing left for me to do would be to leave without opening my mouth. I silently prayed that they would always be the only ones to be blind in this way. Since I knew how to act warm and humble, George's mother — who had only been cold towards me because she remembered the discourteous way I had sneaked off the last time — became more relaxed. She seemed very grateful when I expressed my wish to return to the village accompanied by George. I promised that George would easily find a job at the new supermarket in our village. They were overjoyed because George had been unemployed for some time. He ran to pack his luggage and his mother cried on my shoulder a little. She continued to call me by my former name, which I had forgotten until she uttered it again, as if she had always kept it alive in a corner of her mind and had only waited to see me again to give herself the pleasure of pronouncing those three syllables with joyful emphasis. She asked for news of my father and was touched when I didn't reply, believing that I was overcome with emotion. And so George's mother clung to my neck, rubbed my skin with her damp nose, without noticing anything which would distance me henceforth from her beloved and sorely-missed village, a separation Aunt Colette had demanded of me. If Aunt Colette's flattering kindness had not convinced me of the perfection of my metamorphosis, George and his mother's lack of discernment would have overwhelmed me; instead I attributed it to an honest naivety, an inability to imagine desires such as mine.

George's mother checked his bag, her tears flowing more than ever. George did his best not to cry and, after she had detained us once more to give us some chocolate and bananas to take with us, we hastily set out. We heard her right to the end of the landing, lamenting that she had not been able to give George some little object to remind him of her, but she didn't have anything suitable in her modern flat. The rare knick-knacks placed on shelves or on the television set had been bought at the nearby supermarket, where the neighbours had also done their shopping. George was upset to leave without having kissed his sisters. I snatched sideways glances at him, surprised to find him so handsome when only recently he had filled me with distaste; I attributed this change in perspective to my certainty that no one would mistake us for brother and sister any more, or, what's worse, for one and the same person. I tried to console him.

'Your family,' I said, 'will come to see us in the village.' I thought, however, that while the indignity of George's face would no longer reflect on me, but rather enhance what I really had to call my own assumption, my total and perfect completion, I perhaps should not hope that his family's visits would have an analogous effect, but fear the opposite, because such acquaintances would be judged suspiciously and cast doubt on my new appearance. Although to question that I had changed was absurd, wouldn't people come to deny my transformation and then, in all sincerity, not even see it any more? I remorsefully pressed George's arm. 'Now,' I said, in an animated voice, 'let's go and pay our respects to my mother.'

'Who's there?' she shouted after I had rung on our doorbell. She softly came up to the door and whispered through the keyhole, 'Fanny, my poor child, it's impossible for me to open up for you. Your aunt told me, so I know how things stand with you now and, you see, my eyes can't take it. Why have you broken off with your parents like this? What will your father say? Oh, I'd rather suffer not seeing you!'

Dumbfounded, I didn't say a word. We heard my mother move away from the door with a long sigh and return to the living room, then brief, muffled whisperings.

'It's because she's not alone!' I exclaimed angrily, 'and she's ashamed to show her face! That's what it is! She's lying!'

I knocked violently and at the same time begged my mother to come and open the door for me, but there was no longer any sound. So I gave up, greatly humiliated, and dragged George outside, swearing that Aunt Colette would not let such an impropriety pass.

# TWO

## *Changes*

My return had provoked great commotion without my knowing it.
Several important decisions were made in great haste, but as they
seemed to suit those concerned, I felt free of embarrassment. My
sudden reappearance even seemed to the advantage of others because it
encouraged the implementation of plans which had been entertained
for some time. With the excuse that George and I needed to find
somewhere to live, Eugene and his fiancée jumped at the chance to go
and live in a house on the housing estate, leaving us Grandmother's
house which they didn't really like. In return, we kept Aunt Colette,
whom Uncle George's departure had left without any means of
support.

George immediately found a job at the supermarket gathering the
shopping trolleys. They were spread all over the car park, obliging him
to run left and right, which he didn't mind since he liked sports. How
did Aunt Colette feel about this situation? Did she feel embarrassed for
depending on us, or did she perhaps see it as an honour for us, or just
one of life's natural events, since she was my aunt and already getting
on in years? Was she grateful to me for my constant eagerness to see
that she didn't want for anything? In spite of everything, did she love
me as her niece, conscious of this duty to her sister's daughter? Or was
she feigning it, unable to feel any such thing? Who had created Aunt
Colette and would be capable of answering these questions? As soon as
I found myself apart from Aunt Colette, the mystery of her hold over
me exasperated me so much that I returned immediately to her side,
where, disappointingly, her presence taught me nothing. What was the
real link between Aunt Colette and myself? Was she really only my
aunt? We may die without ever knowing.

George and I tacitly agreed that Aunt Colette would continue to run
the house, where we would behave like respectful guests.
Grandmother's bedroom and the living room were reserved for her sole
use. At her request, we had them redecorated in a paper with large
mauve flowers on a purple background, and at the supermarket we
bought on credit a complete bedroom suite in a rustic style, which filled
the little room. Each morning I cleaned its carved decorations, which
had an interlacing design where the dust chose to settle. This purchase
put us deeply into debt. But we couldn't imagine doing any less for

Aunt Colette: for allowing us to live under her roof (although her own situation hardly permitted her to do without us) and for not considering us, George and me, a discredit to herself or the family, although in my new state I need no longer fear any snub, I sincerely thought that she could never be repaid enough.

# THREE
## *A Visit*

Since custom requires a woman who is about to settle down to introduce her fiancé to her closest relatives, I took George to the home of my cousins who lived on a neighbouring farm. To be honest, my initial intention was to study their reaction and draw from it the appropriate course of action. We took with us a bread cake which Aunt Colette, who approved of this step, had made with butter. George felt intimidated; he was becoming aware that he would not gain the family's approval solely on the strength of his qualities, which were obvious, but that he must hope the cousins, who were good people, would not notice a certain distinctive feature he possessed, which until now had only worried him slightly, even if it were impossible for it to escape the least discerning glance. But hadn't George and his mother failed to notice the obvious change in my appearance? As for that, George persisted in his blindness, strange as it might seem. George was increasingly affected by the misfortune that plagued his kind here and, including me in this misfortune, regarded me with compassion tinged with thoughtfulness. If I worried about him and tried to point out his mistake, he just pitied me more and tactfully did not even try to understand my obsession. Wasn't it insane, then, to expect that the cousins would not notice this characteristic in George, which would certainly make them cool if they chose to see it, and which, in any case, they couldn't fail to see?

They welcomed us with a rather detached kindness, a slight sadness. Their old dog, the last animal on the farm, had just died. My cousin had baked biscuits which would not keep and felt a little put out by the bread cake. It had to be eaten, though, to honour Aunt Colette. All four of us sat down around the kitchen table; my cousin got up again, wearily (to have to go down into the cellar!), to go and look for a refreshing sparkling wine. No one had shown the slightest surprise at the sight of me. They were aware of George's presence without even seeming to look at him and congratulated me, smiling, with a few appropriate words, without their tired eyes ever lingering on my face or George's.

Did they really know who I was? I wondered anxiously. They seemed so indifferent and their concern for the family so weakened. Far from their being offended by George's appearance, as I had imagined might be the case, and far from their noticing any change in me or their seeing me as I had been before, my cousins looked at us impersonally and politely, the way they would any stranger whose affairs did not concern them and about whom it would have been pointless and tiresome to form any judgement whatsoever. They recognized me, however, calling me by name, asking after my mother's and Aunt Colette's health. I was forced to admit, astounded, that they couldn't care less about the family, in spite of everything! It became more and more clear that my cousins showed no reaction whatsoever to George's strange face or to my appropriate appearance because it mattered little to them whether George became one of the family or whether I now looked like an exemplary family member.

'Doesn't anything matter to you any more?' I couldn't help blurting out just as my cousin came back from the cellar. Not understanding, they vaguely shook their heads. My cousin poured the wine into mustard jars, which were decorated with bright characters. A murmur escaped from the bedroom, from the television in front of which my cousins had seated themselves for lunch before our arrival. 'Where has your sense of family disappeared to?' I whispered. 'In Grandmother's day there was nothing you respected more.' My cousin's husband shook his head resignedly.

'The family has really broken apart, unfortunately,' he uttered, absentmindedly.

'What about George and me, do you really see us as we are?' I insisted.

'Yes, yes,' he said to placate me.

George was smiling, reassured, but I was upset by such a lack of affection and begrudged my cousins, now recluses, their indifference to the future of the family. I suppose, however, that their stubbornness would have done me harm in the past, since my cousins would certainly have proved to be more hard-nosed than Aunt Colette and had no doubt — seeing me die, devoured by the dog — felt a satisfied relief, though without any vindictiveness.

'We would have liked,' I insisted, 'for you to encourage our union with full knowledge of the facts, not out of complacency.'

'Oh, you're getting on our nerves,' sighed my cousin, as she headed towards the bedroom, her ears pricking up at the sounds of cheerful military music.

Her husband was fidgeting in his seat, so, to permit him to follow his wife, we in turn got up and moved in front of the television, where at this moment the thirty-third episode of a saga called *Castle Life* was showing.

# FOUR
## *How The Village Reacted*

In vain I paced up and down the little streets morning and night for no other reason than to show Grandmother's former neighbours that they could now have every confidence in me, with no other motive than to bring to their attention the sudden change in my situation. Whether they passed me or saw me from a window, they either didn't suspect that I was their departed neighbour's granddaughter — having known me to be different and not believing in metamorphoses of this kind — or, knowing who I was, they failed to ascribe any importance to it, not considering me any less a stranger to the village but even more so, because of the worry any kind of mystery provokes in people set in their ways. Whatever the reason, they met me without greeting me nor, what's more, showing any particular hostility. No one, when they saw me, called out 'Fanny!' If, of my own accord, I had introduced myself in this way, I probably would not have aroused the slightest surprise, no more than an 'Oh, yes!', full of memories. They would simply have politely acquiesced, without really understanding the significance of such a piece of information. One thing became obvious: as soon as I had disappeared, they had forgotten who I had been because they had never counted me as one of the villagers. To be honest, how could things have been otherwise? Why should they want to cling to the memory of throwing out such an offensive creature? While I no longer inspired the disagreeable comments which George now had to endure, I was someone unknown, about whom they cared to know nothing since people around here generally disliked new faces, as you could tell by the way they kept the new occupants of the housing estates at a cold distance.

# FIVE
## *My Mother Disowns Me*

Not long after we settled into the village, I received the following letter which distressed me for a long time:

My dear daughter,

I prefer to let you know immediately so that you make no mistake about it (I couldn't resist the pleasure of addressing you this way one last time, so you will understand how painful it has been for me to make the decision which you are about to read, and perhaps you will pity me as you pity yourself). Oh Fanny, why have we come to this? Am I to blame? But really, I can see no reason to blame myself. I have brought you up properly, and I have never tried to put into your head the harmful ideas (besides, I know nothing in particular on this subject) which have led you to your current highly regrettable situation. If only you had stayed dead! I would like you to explain to me why you find your present condition better than if you were no longer living, because, really, it's widely accepted that all suffering comes to an end there — I'll never believe anything else. Your obstinate nature has got the upper hand and according to Aunt Colette you have come back triumphant. But have you thought about your poor mother? No, I am certain you have not, not for a moment. Fanny, it is out of the question, such as I imagine you to be, for me to still consider you my daughter and for you to see me as your mother. You are no longer anything but the fruit of your own unbearable arrogance! What your father and I created, you have destroyed without scruple, and you have offended us more gravely than through any other act. That is why I believe that the decision I have made simply confirms your own choice. It makes me feel more sorrow but, equally, I must say, a kind of furious contempt in your regard. There, my tears are suddenly stopping; my anger is coming back! Fanny, do not attempt either to see me again or to write to me. Why would you, since from now on we are no longer anything to each other. Signed: Aunt Colette's second sister.

# SIX

## In The Mayor's Office

I made an appointment with the village mayor and went to meet him in his office on the first floor of a little house next to the school, where the teacher had his flat. In a tiny room with yellow walls, the mayor and his secretary were both working, their tables almost touching; he had just been elected. I approached, a little uneasy because of the presence of the secretary, an old lady whom Grandmother, I remembered, had spoken ill of in the past. She peered at me suspiciously — did she recognize me? I placed my hands flat on the mayor's table and inclined my face towards his, in the hope that the secretary would not be able to understand what we were saying. He eagerly leaned forward too.

'This is what brings me,' I whispered. 'I live in the village and would like this to be officially recognized. I intend to live here from now on.'

'You wish to become a citizen of our village?' queried the mayor in an approving tone.

'That's precisely it,' I said.

'Well, I don't think it's very complicated.'

'Oh, it *is* very complicated,' muttered the secretary, who had interrupted her work to listen better. 'It's not given to everyone to become one, certainly not. We apply the ancient laws here.'

'I wasn't aware of that,' said the mayor with surprise.

'We apply the new, much simpler laws, only when we are sure of the dependability of the person we are dealing with,' the secretary learnedly explained. 'Whereas, so many different rumours are circulating regarding this young woman, contradictory and almost impossible to sort out, that I really think it wise, unless you are opposed, to subject her request to the stringency of the old laws.'

'Where are these old laws?' asked the mayor, disconcerted and, I thought, somewhat unhappy to admit his ignorance.

'Although I know them by heart, I can show you the paper...'

'Yes, we want to see this paper,' I stated firmly.

And I stood up straight, walked across the room, my nose held high to show the young mayor that I no longer considered myself able to deal with him, and concentrated my gaze on the secretary, who was rummaging through the drawers in her desk and becoming ruffled because she could not find what she was looking for.

'If you have lost these old laws,' I said, 'how are you going to prove that they ever existed?'

But she suddenly dashed over to the mayor and snatched out of his hands a large sheet of pink paper on which, mechanically, for something to do, he was wiping the gilt nib of his pen.

'I've got it!' she cried out. 'Now let's see what we can apply in your case.' She held the sheet up close to her face and stood right in front of me, in such a way that I could not read the laws at the same time as her. However, I dared not complain, for it seemed to me that the secretary would not have hesitated, had she deemed it necessary to punish me in this way, to invent a particularly severe law on the spot, forcing me to leave without hope. The mayor was waiting, somewhat worried.

'Here it is for you,' said the secretary. 'Nothing could suit you better: "The stranger wanting to settle on a long-term basis or permanently in the village should obtain the written agreement of his legal mother or present himself in the latter's company at the office of the mayor of the village, between nine a.m. and ten a.m., excepting Mondays." Mr. Mayor, like me, will no doubt be of the opinion that you should conform to the second part of the article, which allows no ambiguity.' The mayor lethargically assented. As for me, I collapsed into a chair, overwhelmed.

I exclaimed, 'Doesn't the law say what the stranger who no longer has a mother can do?'

'As I told you just now, it is not given to everyone...'

I turned to the mayor and begged him to come to my aid; but, reddening, he protested that he could in no way oppose the law; he would make it all the more strictly respected since he perceived my readiness to try anything to get around it. And he suddenly became serious and cold, anxious to redeem himself in the secretary's eyes for his previous hesitation. Both of them pretended to forget my presence and I sneaked out, fearing that she might suddenly present some law which would make my staying in the village any longer illegal or — you never know! — make George's distinctiveness liable for a fine.

# SEVEN

## *New Thoughts Concerning Aunt Leda*

My visit to the mayor led me to reconsider my position in the village. I knew it was uncertain but had thought, due to my numerous relatives, that the simplest law could be applied in my case. On the contrary, the highest authorities mistrusted me as much as the first stranger to arrive, and instead of being honoured for my desire to make the village my home, they were inventing restrictions to discourage me. I started to wonder. Weren't they treating me even worse than any stranger, whom they would at least try to show proper respect? Weren't they reproaching me today for having obtained what they had previously looked down on me for not having? Consequently, didn't they look down on me even more now? What had I done wrong? Who really benefitted from my having changed, if not solely Aunt Colette whom my old appearance had always offended? Did I belong to the family any more than before, now that my own mother had disowned me, now that Grandmother would never see me with this face and other family members received me with cold indifference? What, what must I still do to deserve to be accepted by the village and the family, irrevocably? Why was it impossible for me to make the slightest decision without their moral consent?

I reported to Aunt Colette what the secretary had told me and explained the unexpected difficulties into which the old law had thrown us. Aunt Colette's face stiffened.

'I can under no circumstances replace your mother,' she said, 'that would be improper for Eugene. It is important that I remain your aunt, no more and no less.'

'Leda, perhaps, would do,' I timidly suggested.

'Oh, you're letting that take hold of you again,' she said tersely. With that she walked away and did not speak to me again about my suggestion, letting me interpret it as silent approval, which astounded me, but this was an attitude which Aunt Colette adopted more and more often now that she had resigned herself to not giving advice.

# EIGHT
## Among Family

The family had not assembled for some time, so for the anniversary of Grandmother's birthday, George and I decided, with Aunt Colette's permission — once again strangely tacit — to invite everyone to a huge lunch, as in the past. I travelled through the neighbouring villages to let each person know. While I had expected reactions of joyful excitement, I was greatly surprised to read boredom and annoyance on several faces, especially among the youngest, who, as I repeatedly heard, really had other things to do. Only an awareness of the respect Grandmother was due had made them come without too much fuss in the past, and it was very obligingly, no doubt, that they had come to my cousin Eugene's wedding, an official, solemn celebration which there was no question of missing without serious grounds. But the lunch which I was proposing was only artificially linked to the important occasion of the birthday, Grandmother no longer being with us. Giving various commitments as an excuse, many declined. People greeted me without seeing me, lethargically shrugging their shoulders; whether they recognized me or, having listened to me, contented themselves with the identity I claimed, I could not tell. More than likely, they couldn't care less what had become of the poor forgotten person that I had been. Such was their indifference, they accepted me as Aunt Colette's niece without thinking that they had never seen me like this.

My young cousins lived on the outskirts of the villages in prefabricated houses made of beige roughcast. The light, square rooms in all these dwellings, from the same manufacturer, were set out the same way. The rooms echoed, the walls were thin, the panes of glass were all one piece, lacking lattice-work. My young cousins, in great debt for the purchase of their house, worked hard. I could do nothing but beat a retreat faced with the excuse of continual work, which, neglecting to invite me in, they offered from their doorsteps to get out of the lunch. But, I thought, dumbfounded, we were from the same family and had felt the same unalterable attachment for Grandmother!

I felt utterly ashamed for George and worried that he would imagine himself the reason for these refusals, so I persuaded some old folks, great-uncles and great-aunts, to join us, though not without difficulty, as their memories had swallowed me into oblivion since the dreadful dog episode. I had never been so completely unknown to them! Aunt

Colette helped me to convince them and there ended up being about ten of us at the table, including Eugene, his wife and their dog. My cousin Eugene was so besotted with the latter that he could not resign himself to being separated from her; he had made her climb onto a chair next to him in front of a billy-can engraved with the dog's name and filled with a meat and bread mash. I walked carefully around that chair, although the nasty beast did not seem to recognize me. Right from the beginning of the meal, all eyes were drawn to an unexpected sight which, to my great horror, made the dog growl. It soon calmed down, however. It was a big straw and hessian doll, which I had made myself, perched on a chair at one end of the table. I had clothed it in a knotted tea towel; pumpkin seeds represented its eyes and mouth. George and Aunt Colette, from whom I had hidden during this task, looked at me, taken aback. Aunt Colette seemed unhappy, a fact which alarmed me immediately. I got up, placed my palms on the table and said in a strong voice: Here is Aunt Leda as I picture her. I wanted to see her among us today, in some form or other. Since no one remembers her facial features exactly, why couldn't they resemble these just as well as any others? But I hope that next year the real Leda will be here, that I will finally have brought her back and that she will know how to replace favourably my poor mother, whom a delusion has turned against me. Then I will belong to the village, and none of you will need to be ashamed of my situation any longer, although it has greatly improved since last year, as you can see.

I sat back down amid a heavy silence. Aunt Colette, her lips pursed, served the hearts of palm in vinaigrette. When she passed behind the doll, she flicked it onto the floor. Some dull conversations started, concerning the state of health of the old people present. Scared of being noticed, George dared not speak. Then Eugene turned on the television and everyone silently watched a game show which they were all thrilled not to miss — a frequent danger when they lunched away from home. The atmosphere mellowed. Even Aunt Colette was starting to smile, but what an icy look she gave me! Despite the limited number of participants, I had foreseen a great convivial pleasure in this day, but Aunt Colette's annoyance spoiled it for me; without knowing how, I had seriously let her down. It pained me to imagine that if, as in the past, Aunt Colette didn't recognize my right to take an interest in Aunt Leda, it was because she still considered me not responsible enough to the family. But what better could I accomplish, exactly, than to meet Aunt Leda, persuade her in some way or other to adopt me, then get full citizenship of the village and a place in the cemetery? Aunt Colette, I told myself, is decidedly too harsh and hardly reasonable. What more does she expect from me when I am already doing all that I can do, in all humility, to enter the family sphere from which I was most unjustly cast out?

The old people left early, as soon as dessert was eaten. Shrivelled silently into a corner, George did not seem to have been scrutinized by anyone and hardly seemed to have been noticed. Relieved, he straightened up gradually, although he was still trembling with the fear, which he had felt all the way through the meal, that people would notice his peculiarity and speak ill of him for it with that lack of restraint which old people sometimes have. His distinctive feature shone like a beacon to me and seemed, what's more, to have doubled in intensity, so that one could not begin to describe George without mentioning it first. George, however, in his straightforwardness, did not feel any shame but only the disconcerting, sad predicament of having to hide himself for not being what stubborn minds demanded of him in these villages. As for me, I congratulated myself every day for looking so little like George now and, pitying him constantly, loved him unreservedly.

# NINE

## George's Confession

Looking sad, George came to find me in the little yard where I was watering some fuchsia-coloured geraniums which Grandmother had planted. He sat down on a large stone at my knees and spoke as follows, more emotional than I had ever seen him:

'Fanny,' he said, 'I can no longer bear the way people treat me here. I can't find the slightest explanation for anything that happens to me. Who am I to deserve to be treated in this way? I am nobody but myself, George, and I understand nothing of the names people call me, which I hear whispered when I go down the high street. I know they are stupid, shameful names, but how can they attach such names to me? That's what I don't understand, since I am none other than myself, George, and these names that I hear as I pass are old and conventional; they weren't invented for me, yet I am forced, though astounded, to accept that they refer to me, so I blush and let my head hang as if some cruel truth had just been thrown at me, but I'm flabbergasted and can't believe that my face, George's face, draws these terrible words to people's lips. Am I then, without knowing it, something other than George, something, you know, to be hated and scorned? But I feel myself to be George, quite simply, and I tell myself every day to have nothing to do with those words, the meaning of which, unfortunately, I guess, because they are known words that I can't pretend never to have heard or to find pleasant.'

'What are they?' I asked lightly, but with my cheeks flushed and my forehead burning.

George turned slightly away and did not answer. Confused with shame, I carefully watered the last geranium.

George continued, 'But what if people are right to call me those names? What if I really am as unworthy of respect as people lead me to believe? Sometimes I don't know what to think any more, so I try to hang onto the certainty that I am the person Mother and my sisters love. Yet, since I am a long way from them, I become less and less certain of being that George rather than this one, worthless and to be made fun of since, without knowing me, just at the sight of me, people here are convinced that is what I am. Why, I tell myself, would so many people be wrong or why would they want to harm me? That can't be — I am, aren't I, an unassuming, good-natured boy. At the supermarket, my co-workers look down on me, and my boss doesn't hesitate to call me something other than my name, without, I think, harbouring any resentment towards me. I now answer straight away when he calls out to me in that grotesque, hurtful way, but, as time passes, the meaning of the term gradually fades in my mind and perhaps I'm even forgetting that I am George and not the person he makes me out to be. But I smile and hurry, not wanting to displease, well aware that I'm losing myself. So...'

Aunt Colette appeared at her bedroom window, inhaled the morning air, then withdrew, one hand holding back her hair in a bun, with the flabby curve of her white arm raised high, lightly and elegantly. George whispered, 'Even your aunt sees some kind of animal in me, something between a dog and a cat ... For all that, she is nice and doesn't bother me.'

Angry at his making fun of Aunt Colette, I looked at him severely. George gripped my knee tightly in his fingers and asked my permission to go home, back to his mother and his sisters whom he missed unbearably, for the reasons he had just mentioned, although he ran the risk of missing my presence almost as much, having become accustomed to living with me. I was painfully surprised and didn't know what to reply. George's face had an uncommon beauty — had anyone noticed?

# TEN
## *Last Days In The Village*

George's departure, because of the changes it brought to our situation, made Aunt Colette and I decide that we must move out soon, then I would leave on my search for Aunt Leda, which I would otherwise have willingly put off. The prospect of this trip already made me feel tired and listless, though I was well aware of the necessity of it. If I had not been leaving, it would have been wise to take George's place at the supermarket. But to continue to live like this, like a guest in the village, what was the point? Aunt Colette disapproved of this plan. Nevertheless, she obediently moved her things to Eugene's house. Her consciousness of being dependent upon her close relations seemed to make her deny herself the expression of any judgement or desire. Aunt Colette gave up her new bedroom suite, which would have cluttered her son and daughter-in-law's house. Eugene poorly concealed his displeasure at seeing her move in with them. To my great indignation he snubbed Aunt Colette, acted like a landlord and, through his abruptness, forbade her to feel at home. Aunt Colette stayed in the dining room, seated at the glass-covered table, vaguely watching television. She worried that she might be in the way and dared not indulge in any other activity; sometimes she watched the neighbours on the other side of the wire fence and commented on their way of life. Her heavy steps made the poorly-fitted windowpanes shake. While waiting to find a buyer for Grandmother's house, a thing Aunt Colette and I hoped would never happen, Eugene let it out to the young mayor.

The day before my departure, Aunt Colette gave me a piece of paper folded in half on which, she explained to me in a curiously cold and detached manner, I would find Leda's address, which she had actually always had. I was stunned and gratefully astonished that she gave it to me this time since she had disapproved of my venture. Aunt Colette looked down and didn't answer. I kissed her and she shrank back a little, ill-at-ease. But I was so happy that I soon forgot this strange embarrassment. Leda, Aunt Colette explained to me, lived in a village not far from here. Would I promise not to come back without her? I promised and Aunt Colette added that in any case, she would refuse to acknowledge me if I came back alone: having chosen to leave against her wishes, I must accept the consequences of my failure. Aunt Colette was still proving very harsh and I felt mortified.

# PART EIGHT

# ONE

## *Fanny's Father's House*

Fanny left the village in the early morning and took the direction Aunt Colette had indicated, which turned out be the one she and Eugene had taken the year before. After walking all day across ploughed fields and along trunk roads with continuous traffic, she arrived, somewhat surprised, in her father's village, where the sudden heat slowed her down. She had faithfully followed the route recommended by Aunt Colette without noticing, so far was the possibility from her mind, that her steps were leading her to her father's! Tired, she entered the village, which was so different from those she knew that she became lost there despite the smallness of the place. Villagers, seated on the sand in front of their doors to converse, stopped talking and silently and attentively watched her pass. Fanny hoped she was not recognized as her father's daughter because it would have embarrassed her if they knew of her transformation and the probable reasons for it. But, since her father enjoyed an unequalled prestige, it displeased her just as much for them to mistake her for a visiting stranger, whom they would not honour in thought as they should automatically honour the daughter of this man.

She stopped at last in front of her father's beautiful house and went straight into the garden, as barren and dry as the first time she had seen it, and poorly landscaped with an attempt at a lawn which was burnt and threadbare: her father had been over-ambitious. And Fanny remembered that in the past Grandmother had criticised her son-in-law for his big-shot style, and from time to time, for a certain coarseness in his manners. A little nervously, she tapped on the door.

'Well, fancy that! Miss Fanny!' said the servant, who had come to open the door. He forgot to move out of the way to let her come in, but gazed at her in astonishment. Fanny held her suitcase out to him, so he pulled himself together, apologized, and stepped aside. Fanny slid into the huge pink and white marble hall, where her father was just passing, coming out of a bedroom. A little piqued, Fanny noticed that it took him a second to recognize her. But then what a welcome he extended to her, such as Fanny had never received before and worthy of a visitor awaited for a long time, pined for and loved more than any other person, thought Fanny, overwhelmed. Her father walked towards her with his arms opened wide, his eyes glistening with pleasure and admiration; hugging Fanny hard, he expressed his joy at seeing her again. Her father had aged and become a little fatter. Who would have thought, to see them hugging like this, that they were father and daughter? Fanny's face was more like Uncle George's or Aunt Colette's and no longer had anything in common with her father's hard face. Next to his it provided a remarkable and disharmonious contrast. The servant was watching them and dancing from one foot to the other. He finally spat on the ground. Fanny's father, who had a lively look about him, saw him, drew away from Fanny and rewarded the servant with a flick on the nose, then ordered him to clean up his filth before serving them, himself and Miss Fanny, his daughter, a good dinner in the living room. The servant slipped away, his back rigid, contemptuous. The woman whom Fanny had glimpsed during her first visit was reclined on the couch in the living room. She wore a long, filmy white garment with a frothing train at her feet. As soon as he entered the room, the father waved his hands and barked, 'Get out, get out of here!' To Fanny's great embarrassment the woman fled, frightened.

'I'm anxious to be alone with you,' said her father in a warm, flattering tone, somewhat devoid of emotion. To look at Fanny more easily, he took a step back. Playfully, Fanny spread her fingers over her face, hiding it. But wasn't she happy, despite her confusion, to be so enthusiastically received by her father who until now had neglected to remember her and when he had seen her again after so many years, had been nothing but irritated, restrained and very impolite? Her father wanted to free her face; one at a time he pried her fingers away, keeping them prisoner in his hand. Fanny threw her head back with a little hoarse laugh, admitting her defeat, and suddenly remembered the photograph Uncle George had torn up at Grandmother's last birthday. In it her mother was smiling broadly, leaning over a little, serene and lively, similar, with her flowing hair, to Fanny at this moment. Fanny's father, who had looked down on Fanny, perhaps disappointed by her appearance, was kissing her on the forehead, the flat, slightly short forehead of Aunt Colette! Feeling delighted and sadly shocked at one and the same time, Fanny murmured, 'Come now, come now.' Her father responded with a clap of his hands to call the servant. The real Fanny felt offended, almost scandalized; hadn't her father seemed disgusted even to stand beside the person she had been when, looking for respect and affection, she had come to see him with Eugene, although there had been less doubt then that she was his daughter? Never would Fanny have imagined that her father would take pride in having for a daughter someone who looked so little like him but so much like people who, in the past, when Fanny's mother had introduced him to the family, had openly looked down on him, and whom he had surely found ugly and contemptible. Unless — this thought pained Fanny — her father had yielded to their judgement; unless perhaps he had made it his own and nothing had seemed better founded to him than Aunt Colette's distrustful low regard, than her cold condescension toward him. Now, in truth, Fanny's father was proud of her. His fatherly solicitude expressed itself in a thousand ways: although he had turned on the television, he turned the sound down so he could converse undisturbed with Fanny; he scolded the servant for having only cooked a very plain chicken and rice casserole when he would have liked to give his daughter a particularly refined welcoming dinner. They ate at a low table, sitting cross-legged, as was the custom at her father's. Fanny had sat down at some distance from her father's usual place, in vain, because he, far from understanding her sense of propriety, had sacrificed custom to come and sit right next to her, so close that they could not raise their forks to their mouths without knocking elbows or knees, which irritated Fanny but delighted her father. To please her, he pressed her with questions about herself, as if eager not to miss knowing anything about her. However, she had hardly started to answer before he asked something else, or else his gaze was suddenly drawn by the appeal of the coloured images on the screen and his attention visibly left, although he tried to be discreet. Discouraged, Fanny stopped talking without his noticing. Then he plagued her again, reproaching her for her silence, which he said was too cruel, like an old love. He fastened a keen, searching eye on her, filled not with desire but with a fierce nostalgia. Yet, Fanny wondered paradoxically, was it certain that her father's eyes perceived a change; weren't they, like George's and his mother's eyes, incapable of seeing it? Couldn't her father's attitude simply result from Fanny's new way of acting, which was more confident due to her certainty of having transformed in Aunt Colette's eyes? Her father was getting older; he had no child other than Fanny; perhaps he had mellowed, had felt regrets. Besides, wondered Fanny, did she have proof that anyone other than Aunt Colette had seen? Because no one, other than Aunt Colette with a brief remark about Fanny's current perfection, had mentioned the subject, and so Fanny was free to suppose that no one else had perceived what Aunt Colette, mysteriously, had seen straight away, it had so stared her in the face. She had become hospitable and lenient with Fanny, and perhaps Fanny herself had only seen the change under the influence of Aunt Colette's convinced eyes. It was likely that Fanny's mother would not have allowed herself to be mistaken in this respect: if, alerted by Aunt Colette, she had not seen anything that Aunt Colette claimed to see, she would have loudly made her surprise known and would have become determined, no doubt, to undeceive her sister. And then what would have happened? Fanny shuddered at the thought. But she was still convinced by the unquestionable image the mirror offered her eyes every morning, testifying to her complete transformation, and she found it difficult to imagine that the mirror had adopted Aunt Colette's view and imagination. And yet... Fanny dreamt, more and more persuaded that her father saw nothing.

Graceful in her long, delicate garment, the woman came to clear the table. She kept her eyes lowered and handled the dishes with polite gentleness. Fanny's father did not show the woman any more interest than he showed the servant, although she did not seem to be in the house as a domestic.

'Let's go out for an ice cream,' said Fanny's father, getting up. The woman, who was about to leave the room, stopped; Fanny's father, however, had only addressed Fanny, as the woman quickly understood. In the hall she covered Fanny's father's shoulders with a sort of tabard which matched the tunic he was wearing. Timidly she wished them a good evening then burst into silent tears. She withdrew quickly. Sighing, Fanny's father said, 'How that woman loves ice cream!' Fanny felt troubled but did not interfere.

Fanny's father took her arm. They crossed the village which was plunged into deep night, alive with insect calls, piercing sobs and high-pitched children's laughter. Often, behind the glazed lattice-work and the wire mesh of the windows, something was cooking in a lot of sputtering oil. At the foot of the giant trees, men were waiting to be called for dinner. Fanny's father returned their greeting with a haughty nod, then, with a great show of dignity, drew the pleats of his tabard around him. At the end of a courtyard he led Fanny into the little dining room of a café, only distinguishable from the other houses in the high street by its harsh white lights.

'Two lemon ice creams,' called out Fanny's father straight away, before leading Fanny towards an isolated table along a low wall which divided the room. Some people were there, eating ice cream. Since they were looking at Fanny, her father swelled with pride.

'My daughter,' he said to the proprietor in the loud voice of a master. This information did not seem to surprise anyone, yet they looked at Fanny with greater curiosity. To make an impression, she glanced over the low wall, towards the part of the room which was in darkness, and from where, perceptible to an attentive ear, soft sounds were arising: on mattresses on the floor, numerous children were sleeping. A wardrobe, clothing and a chair indicated that this was a bedroom, windowless, set up in the dining room of the café. Disconcerted, Fanny recognized among the sleepers her father's companion, whom they had just left! She had wrapped herself up in her satiny gown with only her face visible, and her closed eyes seemed to

Fanny to feign sleep; her lips were trembling slightly.

'She's there!' whispered Fanny to her father, suddenly trembling herself.

'Already!' he exclaimed, surprised. 'Before we left, I ordered her back to her parents' home for a few days, but she didn't need to run.'

He looked upset. 'I didn't want to feel her around us, hovering about, imagining who knows what,' he added, smiling. 'Because, imagine this, she refuses to believe that you are my daughter, the silly girl!' And her father burst out laughing, having spoken in a loud voice which could not have failed to reach the woman's ears. His whole bearing clearly revealed that, far from being indifferent to the attention being shown Fanny, he took care to preserve it, all the while pretending not to notice. If her father saw no change in her appearance, thought Fanny, that could not be the reason for his pride, and it must be aroused by some particular emanation of her person which proved, in her father's view and for the benefit of the village, that his daughter lived in a region incomparable to this one and indisputably superior. Because what would her father take pride in? Even Fanny's prettiness, inasmuch as it evoked these distant places, must be of great value to her father, as must her way of speaking (she now used some of Aunt Colette's expressions!) which established immediately that Fanny had not grown up in her father's village. To be honest, she swallowed her words and, like Grandmother, often ran her words together incorrectly, a habit her father started to mimic. The previous year, her father had treated Fanny with as much scorn as he inflicted on the woman stretched out behind the low wall. Now Fanny resembled Aunt Colette enough to be admired by her father, whom she charmed, and almost loved by him in a sudden rush of unchanneled affection! All the same, it's good, thought Fanny, to be esteemed by your father after having upset him for so long. She was enjoying her ice cream and put off speaking in favour of the woman, whose state had moved her to such pity. She feared annoying her father and did not want to disturb these gratifying feelings, an evening more pleasant than she had ever spent with him. In her behaviour she emphasized what she thought charmed him and especially stroked his vanity: a few of Aunt Colette's mannerisms and odd habits, which no one would have expected to find at all charming but which were so typical that they reminded her father of those dominant and attractive lands where he was not born, where he was despised in advance. It did not displease Fanny to imitate Aunt Colette, whom she visualized at this moment in Eugene's dining room, perhaps watching a foreign soap opera, her elbows on the cold glass table, in her dress with silver moons, now permeated with a light smell of burnt fat. It was to Aunt Colette that she owed her father's gentle amiability, while cousin Eugene did not even bother to show his mother respect and affection now that she was troubling him with her presence in his house.

Her father had gulped three little glasses of alcohol down one after another. Fanny asked for another ice cream, no longer worried that people were watching her.

'Oh Fanny, if you were my daughter,' murmured her father.

'But I am!'

Appalled, Fanny worried that someone might have heard him.

'Yes, yes, I didn't say that you weren't,' he stammered.

'Then it would be better for you to be quiet,' said Fanny, angrily. 'Anyway, what do you want me to be if not your daughter?'

'It's that you're so out of reach,' her father tried to explain. 'Is it natural to be so much less perfect than your own child, you know, to find yourself so vile next to her?'

'But that's why you love me,' interrupted Fanny, put out.

With that, she dragged her father outside, fearing the rumour would spread that he had publicly questioned whether this young person, presented as his daughter, really was. Could it be, wondered Fanny, as she held her father up, that he would go so far one day as to refuse to acknowledge me out of excessive humbleness? Then I would be really alone, strangely isolated!

A sudden exhaustion was transforming Fanny's father into a tottering old man. The servant put him to bed then led Fanny into a guest room. In the early morning, Fanny got ready to leave again, although her father was still in bed.

'He was hoping to keep you for a long time,' said the servant, who seemed to disapprove of such haste.

Fanny replied, 'I must find my Aunt Leda as quickly as possible.' On the tiled floor in the hall, she stretched out a geographical map of Grandmother's region and, with the servant's help, looked for the name of the village where Aunt Colette had disclosed that Aunt Leda was living. The name was simple and short; it had a familiar ring to both Fanny and the servant, but this may have been because of its banality. They could not see it anywhere on the map.

'This village must be so tiny!' sighed Fanny, discouraged.

'Yet I think I know it,' insisted the servant.

In the face of Fanny's uncertainty, he became more confident; and since she couldn't contradict him, he spoke with conviction. Fanny should get onto such and such a bus, go in this direction, and she would come across the village without needing any other information. He was sure of it now. Too happy to do otherwise, Fanny agreed to trust him. She made her escape without seeing her father. A vague shame took hold of her as she was crossing the desolate garden. But what wasn't her father capable of saying to her, which would slap her in the face like an impropriety? If, having dreamt along these lines throughout the night, he woke up to declare that Fanny could not under any circumstances be his daughter, finding himself too different from her now for this kinship not to be considered ridiculous, it would be better if Fanny did not hear him, if she left without knowing whether her father, disturbed by her, denied his status today, just as her mother had coldly done for other reasons. Must it be that at the very moment he finally received her correctly, he should of his own choice withdraw the right to call her his daughter and deny her the special happiness of being loved and protected by the one who had created her, even if it were to revere her more? Fanny thought that this painful situation, in which she bedazzled him so much that he no longer wanted to believe she could be his child, was still preferable to his being ashamed of her as he had been, when, although despising her appearance, he had not been able to disclaim her as his daughter.

# TWO

## *The Bus Trip*

Fanny thought she recognized the driver of the bus that she caught on the way out of the village as the one who had driven Eugene and she the year before. Some women got on with her, then got off after a mile and a half or so, on their way to the region's big market. For a long time, Fanny was alone. As her father's village was left further behind, the sky clouded over and a freezing cold wind filtered through the cracks. The brick red sand road gave way to a tarred trunk road, and gigantic stores towered over the flat fields. No one was waiting any more on the edge of the road for people to stop to buy cold doughnuts, a bag of roasted walnuts or peanuts; no young goat or stray animal crossed the road any more in the dust of the sparse traffic; but huge billboards lined the road with attractive, happy faces and oversized letters in vibrant colours, ready to jump out of the frame, drawing attention away from the dismal scenery. Didn't I come through here on the way to father's, wondered Fanny, a little worried. She reassured herself, however, knowing that everything looked like Grandmother's region and that she could visit several villages in a row always doubting whether she was not in fact coming back to the same one.

Then, on the edge of a beet field, far from any dwelling, the bus suddenly stopped, and Uncle George got on, appearing out of nowhere, a large bag in his hand. He was wearing his dark grey salesman's suit, he was so old and tired that Fanny, who had thought she could never forgive him for the nasty trick he had dealt Aunt Colette, was surprised to feel herself filled with emotion. Without noticing her, Uncle George collapsed onto a seat just behind the driver, and Fanny could no longer see any more than the top of his purplish skull. Deeply distressed, she hesitated to join him; at last she decided to go and sit next to him. Uncle George, however, hardly turned his head towards her, as if exhausted by the idea of the slightest movement.

'The weather is going to get better, they say, sir,' Fanny tossed out in a rather weak voice.

'So they say, yes. Oh, this region, I'd forgotten it could be so harsh...'

'So you had left it, sir?' asked Fanny, stunned that Uncle George did not react to her addressing him formally. And she understood that everything was over, although nothing proved it yet. She moved slightly away from her uncle, who was now opening up to the pleasure of chatting and even peppered his monologue with obvious lies; she closed her eyes with sudden despair. Uncle George was prattling on familiarly, addressing Fanny with a 'Miss' that seemed too formal from his mouth. He stopped bluntly when the bus stopped, straddled Fanny's knees and hastily got off, without bothering to take his leave from her properly.

'Terminus!' called out the driver. Fanny, troubled, inquired whether they were really at Aunt Leda's village, but the driver had never heard its name before. He did not travel the whole region, however, and could not swear that her Aunt's village was not outside the limits of his route. For the moment, it was to Grandmother's village that he had taken Fanny, a fact which at first she did not want to believe. She had no choice, however, but to recognize the church square, the empty high street, and the former butcher who, wearing the shirt with little blue and white checks from his former trade, was noisily lugging dustbins along. Alarmed, Fanny thought immediately that at no cost must she let herself be seen by Aunt Colette, whom she had promised she would not come back to the village without Leda; nor must she be seen by anyone who could inform Aunt Colette of her presence. Fortunately, dark night was falling, typical of this season. Where should I go? wondered Fanny, ruling out the possibility of someone giving her directions to Leda's village. She was gradually becoming suspicious of Aunt Colette's sincerity. Aunt Colette had led her strangely astray first by sending her to her father's house, then, with assurances that it was nearby, by giving her the name of a village which was not to be found on the map and which the driver had never heard of. But Fanny was ashamed of such wicked thoughts and refused to dwell on them. She felt little confidence in the future but did not know what she could do other than continue the search, even if Aunt Colette had gone to great lengths to make the task impossible for her.

# THREE
## *Fanny Gets Lost*

She walked towards the housing estates with the vague intention of putting distance between herself and the village, where she thought people would easily spot her. The cold had taken her by surprise and she was still only dressed in thin knitwear, which had been enough in her father's village. When I'm out of sight, I'll take a jacket out of my suitcase, Fanny told herself. In the meantime she went back and forth several times down the same streets without managing to leave the heart of the housing estate behind. She thought she was taking the right direction until the strange orangey shade of a kitchen curtain reminded her that she had just been here, and she finally got completely lost without stopping to turn around. Neither the houses, nor the cars parked in front of them, nor even the street signs with their never-ending bird names were any help to her. Fanny was becoming exhausted. She stopped next to a hedge just long enough to catch her breath. Suddenly, in the dim light of a window, she saw her mother's face in profile; she was leaning slightly towards Fanny and smiling a long, drawn-out and indulgent smile. Fanny had never seen this smile, even in the old days. While she smiled this beautiful, heart-rending smile, nothing remained of the nervous restlessness which often contracted her mother's features even when she was happy. Her mother seemed to hold this smile — a smile unknown to Fanny — forever, giving it to someone beneath her gaze, whom Fanny could not see. The light of the moon falling on the windowpane silvered her gleaming blond hair. 'That's Eugene's house,' murmured Fanny, sadly. She would have rushed there if it were not for the fear — even more powerful than the violent desire to see her mother's tender smile turn on her — of meeting Aunt Colette. Besides, would this smile have stayed for Fanny? Seeing her, Fanny's mother would probably have adopted an angry or even horrified look and the abrupt disappearance of this happiness, which must enchant those present in the room just as much as Fanny, would have been the first effect of her entrance.

With regret, Fanny set off walking again, numb with cold now. She advanced recklessly, turning off blindly, and gave up trying to find her bearings. Defeated by the cold, she was about to open her suitcase when the headlights of a car dazzled her. The driver braked; a man stepped to the ground and ran towards Fanny. It was her father, in a magnificent bright yellow garment; its reflection seemed to light up his face, as if her father were not in the same time as his surroundings, which were darkened by the night, but was floating in the golden gleam of a fragment of sunny day. Gasping for breath, he caught Fanny's arm and shook it.

'Oh, I'm sorry I left without saying goodbye to you. I beg your forgiveness,' said Fanny quickly, suddenly so ashamed that she thought her father had only hunted her down to make her admit her wrongdoing.

'It's forgotten, because now you are going to come back with me, you can,' her father exclaimed in a joyful voice. 'I just this minute saw your mother, and she confirmed that you are not my daughter, although I believed it until today. So, although it upsets me to have been fooled, I am thrilled, Fanny, for both of us. That woman you saw at my house, who really displeases me, I'm going to send her away without delay, and you...'

In his impatience Fanny's father was bruising her arm with his long, lean fingers, which she had inherited. Stunned, she remained silent while he tried to drag her towards the car; with a swift kick he shook free the hem of his flowing garment, which seemed impossibly golden and was perhaps the source of his boundless energy that evening. Without looking at her, he talked emphatically, describing their future life, the possessions he would shower on Fanny. She then perceived the servant, who was waiting for them behind the wheel of the limousine.

'Look, you must be reasonable,' she murmured, knowing that she could not drown out her father's voice. When he unthinkingly let go of her to open the car door, Fanny took to her heels. She jumped over a hedge, crossed a garden, jumped onto a path between two houses. She heard her father shouting, more and more faintly, and his entreaties were lost amid the howling of dogs. Still running, Fanny came across the way out of the housing estate, which she had searched for in vain a short while ago. Panting, she threw herself into the ditch. There she was free to think over what her father had said to her, which surprised her less now that she saw it as a misunderstanding. Recalling the terms her mother had used in the letter informing Fanny of her abandonment, in which she had expressed that she could no longer consider Fanny her daughter because of what Aunt Colette said Fanny had become, how had Fanny not immediately envisaged some mistaken interpretation by her father, whose imperfect mastery of the language spoken in Grandmother's region had led him to understand from her mother's ambiguous remarks what was hardly the case? Her mother had perhaps repeated that Fanny, under these conditions, could no longer be her father's daughter. Her father had taken the expression literally, no doubt imagining it a subtle means of confessing an old betrayal, and had shamelessly congratulated himself, proud to have guessed the day before what he thought her mother had disclosed to him today. Fanny was disgusted to discover that having a daughter mattered less to her father than a female companion true to his upstart desires. She did not deny that underlying his disinterest in the blood tie was the fact that her father could not think it natural to have a daughter so profoundly different and infinitely superior to himself, according to his mortifying set of values. Fanny now found her father repugnant and vowed not to see him any more. She did not know whether she despised him for wanting to replace the young, meek woman from his village with her or because he held himself in such very low esteem that he could not accept that Fanny was his daughter. She was no longer certain of being perfect, far from it, so her father's admiration seemed truly pitiful. It was as if, by failing to discern this breach of perfection, he, the father who revered her, was all the more absurd and unrefined.

# FOUR

## *In The Village M.*

It was already early morning when she came out of the ditch, not far from the last house on the estate, on the main road dividing the village. As was often the case in Grandmother's village, a low sky hung over the rooves, forbidding even the squat, sullen steeple to soar; it was hardly noticeable from the road, as if to dissuade travellers from approaching and strangers from feeling welcome in these parts. Fanny turned her back on the shapeless grey mass of the village and set off at a brisk pace. Because she did not know where to place Aunt Leda's village and for the moment had no means of obtaining information, she thought that by going in the direction not included in the bus route — the driver having never come across her aunt's village — she had more chance of meeting someone who knew it or of arriving there unexpectedly than by setting off again on the other side. If Aunt Colette had not misled her, as Fanny was now beginning to suspect, if this village really did exist and if it was located in the vicinity, it was impossible for Fanny not to find it unless she did not look hard enough.

That morning she passed through several little villages which straddled the main road, all steeped in the same idle silence of this dreary autumn day, schools and shops having closed everywhere. Fanny did not know whether she had already passed through these hamlets, it was so difficult to tell them apart. But around noon, when she entered the village M., she recognized it before she even saw the sign for the Coq Hardi. Troubled and annoyed at having come back there, she decided to put this mistake to some good by going to visit Aunt Clemence. Since her uncle was working, her aunt received her alone, somewhat surprised but not hostile. Remembering the poor welcome she had received from her the last time, Fanny told herself that Aunt Clemence's coldness may simply have been provoked by Fanny's disturbing her and was not necessarily, as Fanny had thought, a sign of intense dislike. Aunt Clemence invited her to share her lunch, a nice slice of heart, which she sauteed with slivers of onion. Sitting in the old kitchen, Fanny gazed gratefully at her aunt; while Aunt Clemence was serving her a generous portion, she dared to ask her what she thought of her now.

'What people think has changed about you doesn't fool me for an instant,' answered Aunt Clemence, casually, 'because I don't see it and am convinced there's nothing to it. However, you can give the impression of it, so you have changed enough after all to create the illusion of change.'

'That's exactly how it seems to me,' murmured Fanny, humbly.

Aunt Clemence, who had never been talkative, said nothing more. However, she obligingly answered a question Fanny got up the courage to ask about Aunt Leda; then, this question leading to others, she suddenly offered to tell Fanny what she knew of Aunt Leda, her sister, under the pretext that this was the only way to make Fanny understand how foolish it was to covet the protection of that particular aunt.

# FIVE

## *Aunt Leda's True Story*

Her young sister Leda, began Aunt Clemence, had always been, it had to be said, the favourite of the whole family, even of Grandmother, as well as each of the sisters who, consequently, had felt neither jealousy nor pique at this preference which they themselves held. Leda owed her popularity to the undeniable charm of her face and her behaviour, as well as to some more mysterious appeal which Aunt Clemence, not being used to telling stories, could not venture to describe, it was so difficult to put a finger on. From a very young age, Leda had been accustomed to getting away with all kinds of whims and strange habits, yet had, nevertheless, become the most talented of the four sisters, the one with the liveliest and boldest spirit. Fanny's mother and Leda, being the two youngest, were still living with Grandmother when Clemence and Colette had left home to get married. Fanny's mother introduced to the family the man who would become Fanny's father and who at the time was an unassuming and timid young man, nonetheless brilliant and strong-willed. But, for reasons Fanny knew and others besides, no one in the family wanted to hear anything of this marriage. All devoted themselves, keenly and with commendable determination, to persuading Fanny's mother of his inconsequence, to entreating her to abandon her plan, indeed threatening her; Fanny's mother responded to all these pressures with an impassive face and insignificant words which failed to convince them she had changed her mind. She never reacted in anger or said a rebellious word; but if she was going to admit defeat, give up, she never gave any sign of it. The family dug in its heels. All this greatly displeased Leda. She loved Fanny's mother with exceptional fervour and she took it into her head to come to her aid against the whole family, whom she had been taught to neither fear nor, above all, respect because of the indulgent fondness everyone had for her. As soon as some aunt or cousin arrived to give Fanny's mother a talking to, Leda strove to be present, answered before her sister and made remarks which scandalized everyone. Even Grandmother was powerless to stop her: Leda had always done what she wanted and she had never had such a serious motive for showing her determination. Sometimes it seemed as if she took the triumph of her sister's desire to heart even more than Fanny's mother herself. Fanny's mother, according to Aunt Clemence, had seemed insensitive to persuasion but would certainly have given in to the family's repeated attacks if it had not been for Leda, who had relieved her of the exhausting necessity of defending herself. Out of defiance, Leda even declared that if her sister gave in she would marry the spurned fiancé herself. She hoped this would force the family to surrender; but, on the contrary, it spurred them on. They now considered Leda the most to blame of the two sisters and almost forgot what had started the whole business. Their being against Leda, Aunt Clemence made clear, did not change the favouritism she had always been honoured with; it was simply a case of bringing her down a peg or two, of resisting the unexpected obstacle she had become to the higher wishes of the family, which, they believed, Leda was only disrupting on a whim, out of recklessness, blinded by her youth and the magnanimous education she had received. So, while they judged Leda severely, she was still loved with preferential affection, but Fanny's mother, who was viewed more leniently, was considered with much less sympathy and, since she had fallen in love with this man — a fact they found rather distasteful — was loved out of duty. Colette and herself, declared Aunt Clemence coldly, had actively participated in these attempts to bring her to reason. Aunt Clemence added without embarrassment that since Fanny's mother was their sister, they had only felt all the more intimately this repugnance towards the fiancé, who was, however, good-looking and clean-cut.

Fanny's mother's resolve gradually weakened. She became tired of so many complications and longed for the calm and harmony of the past. Seeing this, Leda decided to take desperate measures: she went to the fiancé's house and moved in with him, then informed the family that she would only come back once her sister was authorized to get married. Grandmother almost died of shame. Fanny's mother felt confused and unhappy, and no one doubted that she bore a grudge against Leda for this initiative, but, as far as things had gone, no longer able to back out, she allied herself to her sister's demand with new vigour. The family laid down its arms, thinking that if the situation dragged on, this scandal would have a more lasting effect than the indignity of such a marriage. Leda returned home and Fanny's mother's wedding went ahead. The family was divided: some wanted to continue to receive Leda; others deemed her inadmissable; the first invited her behind the backs of the second who, learning of it, gave them the cold shoulder. At last it seemed the only way of saving the unity of the family was to throw Leda out, whatever might be the cost to everyone. Even Fanny's mother did not protest against this measure. With no one to defend her, Leda had to leave. Out of pride she left without warning, without anyone being able to guess her destination. On this subject, imaginations ran wild. Some wanted to believe that she had joined Fanny's mother and her husband in their home, but that was never established. That was probably pure invention. Some went as far as to insinuate that perhaps Fanny's true mother... But Aunt Clemence, who had never had faith in these innuendos, was only mentioning them to give Fanny some idea of the depths the otherwise sensible family members stooped to as soon as Leda was concerned.

# SIX

## *Fanny Has To Reconsider What She Imagined About Aunt Leda*

Just as Aunt Clemence reached the end of her account, Fanny's uncle came back and no further mention was made of what had been said. Fanny was allowed to spend the night in the living room, on the couch which was identical to the one Grandmother had owned and which, with its fluffy fabric — she recognized the unpleasant feel of it on her skin as if it had long ago been imprinted in her flesh — upset Fanny, because she sorrowfully regretted not having known then to fully savour those moments when she would lean on Grandmother to watch a soap opera, while Grandmother gave an amusing running commentary, on long summer afternoons, in the room with closed shutters.

Fanny did not sleep. She needed to think about what her situation — greatly changed by what Aunt Clemence had told her — had now become. However, even before Aunt Clemence had begun her story, Fanny knew her aunt would achieve her aim and leave Fanny no other alternative, whatever she heard, but to renounce the search for Leda. The same went for the family's wish, which the best reasons could no longer oppose. If, carrying on regardless, Fanny insisted on wanting to find Leda, the family, without a word, without any indication, without perhaps even suspecting that Fanny was continuing her quest, would certainly always stop her from succeeding, would always steer Fanny to some village she would have the greatest difficulty escaping. But above all, Fanny now understood that all she had ever done was to cause herself a lot of harm; because, wanting to enter the family, what worse thing could she do to estrange herself from its benevolence than to try to bring back the very person whom the family, on reflection, had thrown out? That Fanny had not known the story did not excuse her: what the family hid must, in the family's view, remain hidden, although numerous clues allowed people to guess very precisely the matters they were not supposed to know about and to consciously stay away from them. Posterity came first, and Fanny had strayed from that duty, unable to claim that she had been unaware of it — besides, ignorance would have constituted an offence in itself. Sure of her right, she had not paid any attention to Aunt Colette's warnings! Not only did Fanny now have to flee any possibility of meeting with whatever Leda might be, but never again must she utter this name: only through the most perfect virtue could she redeem herself.

Trembling with anguish and remembering that Aunt Colette, after having given her that misleading address, had forbidden her to come back without Leda, she wondered if it weren't already too late. Purposely sending her to a nonexistent place, hadn't Aunt Colette wanted to let her know that she was banning her, quite simply, from ever returning, from ever appearing before her again? Hadn't she meant to make it clear that all that remained for Fanny, whose arrogance could not be subjugated, was to wander the villages indefinitely?

# PART NINE

# ONE

## *Aunt Clemence's Death*

Fanny was woken roughly by her uncle.

'She's passed away!' he exclaimed with alarm, then started pacing back and forth in every direction except the bedroom. He prepared his breakfast and gulped it down alone, while Fanny, incredulous and somewhat embarrassed that her uncle had appeared in his night clothes, went to Aunt Clemence's bedside. When she had confirmed her aunt's death, she joined her uncle in the kitchen. He was crying loudly. As Fanny had never seen her uncle show the slightest emotion before, she was almost surprised and, feeling sorry for him, cried a little herself.

'I'll take care of everything,' she gently promised. But she stayed at his side in the kitchen for a moment, reheated the coffee, served it with comforting words which the uncle listened to attentively, words based on something she remembered from a novel. Then she cleaned the table and advised her uncle to get washed, although she was no longer embarrassed by his half-dressed appearance. And the image of herself taking care of her uncle after his wife's death that morning, gently persuading him to do what had to be done, delighted Fanny who, having hardly known Aunt Clemence, felt no real grief. The kind welcome which her aunt had extended to her the day before counted for more in her distress than the visits made all through the preceding years when Aunt Clemence, having eyes only for Eugene, had never shown that she considered Fanny her niece.

When her uncle had washed and dressed, his good sense returned. He got busy and no longer needed Fanny's help, but he allowed her to stay as long as she wanted. Since Aunt Colette was expected, Fanny went down into the cellar. She thought it wise to avoid Aunt Colette under these unexpected and unfortunate circumstances, which might have made her aunt utter hasty, bitter words if she saw Fanny without forewarning. Certainly, meeting Aunt Colette again on that day would have augured badly. Besides, it was out of the question for Fanny to appear before her suddenly without having obtained permission, which, if she ever managed it, thought Fanny, would only be achieved through negotiation.

They hastened the necessary arrangements so that Aunt Clemence could be buried that evening. Aunt Colette, Uncle George, Fanny's mother and a few neighbours were the only people who had put themselves out; Eugene, Fanny heard Aunt Colette explain, had to apply for a job that afternoon. Aunt Colette had donned her black dress with the little roses, which was rather close-fitting. Fanny's mother was crying; Aunt Colette and Uncle George contented themselves with merely blowing their noses, while Aunt Clemence's husband bore a strange, contrite expression, as if he had to apologize to the two sisters for having let her die, for not having noticed until morning, and for no longer being able to shed a tear.

Fanny wisely followed the sparse funeral procession at a distance. It was as grey and cold as it had been the day before, and they walked quickly, with little tottering steps because the women were not used to court shoes, patent leathers with high, square heels. Fanny had prepared a letter for Aunt Colette in which she expressed her repentance and begged her, whatever the cost, to forgive her. Near the cemetery, she spotted a child about ten years old, who was curiously dawdling around. She pressed her to go and deliver the letter to Aunt Colette, to wait for the reply, and to bring it back to her as quickly as possible. Flattered, the child rushed over. Through the metal gate, Fanny saw her solemnly give the envelope to Aunt Colette, just as she was about to throw a clod of damp earth into the grave. The little roses on Aunt Colette's dress were merrily moving, dancing on the flowing material, fluttering in the wind. Against the dark sky, they seemed to flit about as if escaped from a bouquet.

The little girl soon came back and recited, importantly, 'The lady says that she can do nothing for you as long as your parents have not granted you their forgiveness. She says she knows that they both consider themselves offended for different reasons and she does not want to take the responsibility of acquitting you for them. After that, she said, we'll see.'

Fanny, relieved, noticed that the little girl had bare feet in her old trainers. Her pinched face was already marked with blotches and slight wrinkles. Fanny took her to her uncle's house, gave her a pair of woollen tights, and sent her off quickly, for fear that the family would return, because if they did she would have to go back down to her hiding-place in the cellar. The little girl would gladly have stayed: settled in front of the stove, stroking her new legs, she exclaimed over an embroidered canvas which in its gilt frame was, to her taste, the most stylish thing. Fanny had smeared the little girl's face with cold cream and, fussing over her, had almost forgotten Aunt Colette. Afterwards she remembered her with surprise. Had she ever stopped worrying about the family for fifteen minutes? Had she ever before let herself be enthralled enough by anything that she was surprised afterwards to remember that the family existed? Hadn't the family monopolized all the interest and emotion she was capable of?

# TWO

## *Fanny's Mother's House*

Shortly after Aunt Clemence's burial, Fanny carefully drew up an act of pardon, though it pained her to do it, then took the train to the capital. On the platform at the train station when she arrived, she suddenly bumped into her mother, who had no doubt got onto the same train as her after the funeral. Her mother was wearing the long fur coat, now threadbare at the collar and cuffs, and carrying her now outmoded tartan suitcase. Although she had seen Fanny, she would have continued indifferently on her way, but Fanny held her back.

'Oh, it's you! I didn't recognize you!' exclaimed her mother. She added, reassured yet puzzled, 'But it really is you. Because Aunt Colette told me that you had changed, I didn't recognize you at first, but I see that it really is you.'

'Your letter doesn't mean anything any more, does it?' asked Fanny, suppressing sadness and disappointment for her mother's failure to see how she had changed. Her mother agreed, not without visible pleasure, so Fanny took her arm and they left the train station. It seemed to Fanny that her mother was walking slowly, wearily. And while in the past her mother had moaned at Fanny, who used to cling to her arm, for not moving fast enough, now Fanny was slowing her pace to avoid giving the impression of pulling her mother, who seemed lost in thoughts which were hardening the crease of her mouth a little, making her lips narrow and colourless. Her mother must have forgotten long ago the rhythm of Fanny's steps. Having forgotten, thought Fanny, her daughter's own features, Fanny's mother now believed that she had not changed, as if she were alert to the most minuscule metamorphosis, like Aunt Colette; whereas, Fanny was now certain that her mother had forgotten all that she had known of Fanny out of lack of concern, loss of affection, receptiveness to the family's silent influence. If she seemed happy to be going home in Fanny's company, perhaps it was just because she preferred it to solitude?

They passed through several places which evoked specific memories for Fanny: on this little wall on the edge of the road she had loved to walk as a child, balancing herself with one hand on her mother's shoulder, laughing because she was a head taller than her and because her mother, playing along, called her 'Mum'; on this vacant lot one day, they had seen two llamas, escaped from some circus and had not been able to help feeling afterwards that they had dreamt them; here, Fanny had fallen... She would have liked to remind her mother of these little scenes or for her to mention them herself. But Fanny's mother continued along the wall at her slackened pace and crossed the plot without opening her mouth. Little wanting to learn for certain that her mother did not remember anything, Fanny stayed silent. Perhaps her mother felt too afflicted by Aunt Clemence's death at this moment to reflect on the pleasant past with Fanny. She had lived with her sister Clemence as long as with Fanny!

Once in the apartment, her mother heaved some long, drawn-out sighs. In Fanny's memory her mother had been a lively and cheerful young woman, now she was dragging her feet towards the kitchen and not once had she thought to turn and smile at Fanny. It seemed having her daughter come home with her was enough for the mother. In the same way, Grandmother, although she had often complained that they visited her too little, did not pay Colette or Clemence any attention when they came; making themselves at home, they did not seem to expect any, although Grandmother knew how to entertain a guest, to show him, out of deference, a warm affection which her daughters had no right to because she was sparing with it. Yes indeed, it was enough for her mother simply to have Fanny come home with her that evening. But did she ever miss Fanny's presence?

Fanny's mother prepared tea and served it in the living room. She did not give Fanny her usual cup but kept it for herself, without thinking, and poured Fanny's tea into a new, hard plastic cup. This tea was of a very poor quality, but Fanny's mother had bought it on special offer at the supermarket several years ago in such a quantity that she still had more than a quarter of a pound left. Fanny's mother hated waste and did not want to buy any better tea before this had been drunk; she always made it very strong.

After she had silently swallowed down her bad tea, from the cup she didn't know which end to grasp by because it was hot all over, Fanny took out her act of pardon. Her mother signed it without any problem or surprise at Aunt Colette's demand. Actually, whether Fanny got back into her sister's good graces or not did not matter to her.

'Is it true that people used to say that Leda,' Fanny suddenly asked, 'that, perhaps, my real mother...,' blushing, she was unable to continue. Her mother was looking at her in amazement. Tears started to fall from her wide, staring eyes, and Fanny's cup, with the little yellow heart design, trembled in her hand. Fanny wished she had never uttered these words; would she ever be an irreproachable daughter, an accomplished niece? Because now, although her mother had often behaved badly towards Fanny, even recently, here was Fanny again, through this one unfortunate sentence, the one carelessly giving offence. Her mother set down her cup, pushed it far away from her on the table, and lowered her head. She was sobbing.

'How,' she said, 'can you think such things?' Her voice, filled with disgust, convinced Fanny of her lowness, her basic unworthiness. In the past her mother had never cried. Fanny would never be allowed to know how much of what Aunt Clemence had told her was really true, she would never again dare to ask anyone. Her shoulders sunken and her body trembling, Fanny's mother seemed as slight and vulnerable, thought Fanny, distressed, as a fragile mouse caught by its legs. It was fortunate that Fanny's mother had just granted her official pardon; Fanny would certainly let some time pass before daring to visit her again. She felt annoyed rather than shamed by her tactlessness, and appalled to see her mother, who was not normally in the habit of crying, weep so much that she seemed ready to liquify on her chair, to leave this world, swept away in a flood of tears. Motionless, Fanny waited for her mother's sorrow to abate. The noise of traffic coming from the windows sounded like waves, and Fanny's mother seemed to be rocking to it, prolonging her pain and Fanny's awkwardness.

In a vase on a paper doily in the middle of the table, a bouquet of artificial daisies sagged under the dust. At Eugene's house Fanny had seen the exact replica of the new teapot her mother was using; it had a lid in the shape of some kind of water lily. Glancing around, Fanny noticed that several objects in the living room had been replaced by others identical to the models decorating her cousins' kitchen, George's mother's dining room, and Aunt Clemence's living room. Nothing that her mother now owned could be gazed on or inherited by Fanny with any emotion; because what did these interchangeable knick-knacks say about her mother, if not that she had common taste? Among these knick-knacks, even her mother's sorrow now seemed affected and trivial, but, due to lack of taste, her mother was unable to realize it. Her mother was crying, crying non-stop! Saddened and confused, Fanny turned her eyes away each time her mother raised hers. Fanny's mother loved comfort and had scattered cushions on the couch; on the wall she had hung engraved proverbs which, in gothic letters, praised the happiness of the home. She raised her swollen, aged eyes to Fanny, hoping, no doubt, to find Fanny's eyes damp too. But overcome with pity and embarrassment, her daughter, who had so cruelly hurt her, was looking elsewhere! That's how Fanny's mother must have seen it. But whatever is true that Aunt Clemence told me, thought Fanny, Mother, like the rest of the family, will always hide from me, and I'll be accused of having no respect, while they pretend not to be surprised, hearing it from me. Oh, I knew it! Why did I say anything! It would have been enough for Fanny to come back with her mother that evening, arm-in-arm. They would have slowly drunk tea, then dined on ready-meals, peaceful in her mother's average little home, casually watching the television, changing channel from the table every now and then to be always gazing at soap operas, which Fanny's mother was partial to. But Fanny made her escape as soon as her mother had calmed down; and, far from trying to keep her, her mother gave her approval with a tired gesture, as if, worn out by the suffering Fanny had made her endure, she could not wish anything more than to be rid of her.

# THREE

## *An Unpleasant Order From Aunt Colette*

Having nowhere else to go, Fanny went back to Aunt Clemence's house. Her uncle was still barely accustomed to solitude and did not know how to look after a home, so he willingly took her in — on condition, however, that Fanny leave him before too long because people would talk. Fanny pampered him; her uncle's grief diminished.

She quickly sent for the little girl who had already served as her messenger; she no longer had her tights. People seemed to care so little about her that instead of worrying when she disappeared for entire afternoons, they practically rebuked her for bothering to come back. Fanny thought she would have the little girl deliver her letters to Aunt Colette. Her aunt, she calculated, would surely be moved by the appearance of the little girl and would not have the heart to send her back with a disagreeable answer for Fanny. Besides, it was the most convenient way to contact Aunt Colette, and the direct route would not be difficult for the little girl to follow. Fanny dressed her up warmly, entrusted her with the act of pardon and a short letter saying this: since her father no longer believed Fanny to be his daughter, she requested Aunt Colette to authorize her to dispense with his pardon, which was no longer relevant. She slid the two papers under the child's hat and heaped advice on her before accompanying her to the road. Delighted, the little girl left at a run, and although Fanny had ordered her to walk in the ditch, she soon jumped onto the tarmac to run more easily, which worried Fanny, who stayed to watch her. In her impatience for her to come back, she could not bring herself to go home, despite the bitter cold. She imagined her on each stage of her journey, a little jealous when she pictured her at Aunt Colette's house. There was nothing this child could be reproached for! Touched by this child, would Aunt Colette perhaps make comparisons which would be to Fanny's disadvantage? Wouldn't she regret that Fanny, as a little girl, had not been as appropriate as this poor little child and end up fostering more grievances against Fanny, her eternal disappointment? She tormented herself like this, standing at the side of the road, until the child came back several hours later. She put her arms around her as she questioned her, bewildering the child as she tried to catch her breath. Aunt Colette had simply delivered her return message out loud and had not even made clear whether it was a reply to Fanny's note or a simple remark addressed to herself, but the little girl rejected this last hypothesis, having thought about it all the way back. Here's what Aunt Colette had said, or rather muttered: As it was not possible that Fanny did not have a father, whatever might be the doubts on this subject, concerning whatever father was in question, she must of course obtain his pardon for Aunt Colette to feel she had the right to receive her. The little girl recited with ease. As for the way she had been treated, Fanny did not manage to find out much. That she had been served a glass of grenadine was all that was certain. As for the rest, the little girl got mixed up, mistook a neighbour, who had probably dropped by for a visit, for Uncle George, could not describe either Aunt Colette or Eugene, whom she might not ever have seen, and the only thing she remembered about the house was the wallpaper covered with pheasants and ferns, which Fanny did not remember at all. But they must have dismissed her quickly. Did this lack of interest in the child, Fanny wondered, stem from their indifference towards herself? Knowing the distance that the little girl had covered — well, probably knowing it — they had not even bothered to offer her a meal, and now the little girl was famished. Did they despise Fanny so much that they couldn't care less if her little messenger girl fainted with hunger? Would they show no more concern over Fanny's own death? It seemed they had said nothing about her to the child, had not even asked where Fanny was staying; and, as soon as the child had held out her papers, Aunt Colette had muttered what the little girl had just reported, Eugene's wife had put a glass of grenadine into the child's hand, and they had pushed her outside, without a word, without accompanying her to the gate, without adjusting her little hat back over her ears. In short, they had received her with perfect indifference. Although Aunt Colette's new command made Fanny feel worn out already, she could still congratulate herself for having obtained clear and prompt instructions, thanks more to Aunt Colette's odd habit of thinking out loud than to her aunt's wish to make them known to her, because Aunt Colette had obviously lost all interest in her.

Fanny led the little girl back to her house, troubled to see her so unwilling to return, but she could not take it upon herself to have her spend the night with her at her uncle's house. She lived quite far from the village, between the main road and the track used by freight trains, in a narrow house with decayed roughcast, in a courtyard cluttered with rubbish. In front, the withered branches of an old, dead willow tree hung down into the scrap iron, miscellaneous pieces collected and thrown there for some improbable use. Fanny stopped several feet from the yard. The little girl had approached slowly, balking and sighing, still hoping she could go back with Fanny, but she let go of Fanny's hand as soon as she saw the house and dashed off without saying a word. On the steps she turned around to shout an obscene insult in a raucous voice which Fanny had never heard before.

As for Fanny's uncle, he criticized and complained about the soup which she had made for dinner. He must have treated Aunt Clemence that way all through their long life together.

# FOUR

## *Fanny's Father's House*

The servant was uprooting the scorched shrubs. The sweat, running down his forehead and off his soaked hair, had drenched a circle of earth at his feet.

'It's unwise,' said Fanny when she arrived, 'to toil at such an hour.'

'Oh, your father...,' he grumbled briefly.

Exhausted herself, Fanny knelt on the yellow lawn and as she watched the man work, noticed that he had kept on his heavy jacket with the metal buttons.

'Aren't you stifling, dressed so warmly?' she asked amazed.

'Well, the prestige of your father's house...' He straightened up, a little surprised by Fanny's question. 'What would people say if they saw me working with my chest bare like a gardener? They would say that your father is not even rich enough to pay a gardener and that he is obliged to have his majordomo, his trustworthy servant, dig up shrubs.'

'But isn't it actually you who are digging up the shrubs right now?'

'Pooh!' he snorted.

'Well?' she insisted.

'People will simply think that the majordomo, the trustworthy servant, in his handsome uniform has gone out to inspect the garden and he could not resist the temptation to put right two or three little things here and there,' explained the servant, puffing out his chest and raising his nose in the air.

'But,' Fanny argued, 'if you changed into a gardener's real outfit, with a big straw hat hiding your face, wouldn't that be a better idea? My father could make people think he has two servants.'

'But I don't want to be a gardener!' he protested indignantly.

'Well, you are digging up the shrubs,' said Fanny, shrugging her shoulders.

'It's not the same thing.'

Incensed, he started digging again, ignoring Fanny. Over the windows of the large, imposing house, the awnings were lowered for the siesta hour and nothing stirred.

'Is my father still convinced that I'm not his daughter?' Fanny murmured. 'Does he still want me to replace the young woman?'

The servant put down his spade, squatted against Fanny, and with a serious, pleased look, whispered, 'I think he's ready to lock you up to make you stay with him. He's so absolutely certain that you are not his daughter that he's considering adopting one of the village children because now he's upset at not having any offspring, although he's delighted with his discovery concerning you. He still hopes that you will come to him and can't wait to develop this new relationship with you.'

'Is he capable of keeping me against my will?' asked Fanny, alarmed.

'Who knows? Your father, you know, is not in the habit of having anything resist him.'

The servant seemed both resigned and proud to serve such a tyrant. But Fanny, having been disowned by her father, no longer thought it her right to be pleased with these characteristics and felt annoyed. Wasn't she jealous of the servant? He asked her curiously, 'What about your real father, do you know who he is now?'

'Oh, so you also believe...'

She despondently pulled up some blades of dead grass with the tips of her fingers.

'Oh, I don't know, I don't know,' he mumbled, confused.

'It would be best,' said Fanny, 'if I didn't let him see me for now. But hasn't he already noticed me?'

Nothing was moving behind the awnings. The village itself, during this, its hottest hour, was silent. Fanny took out the act of pardon which she was supposed to have her father sign and quickly read it to the servant.

'Since I have to give this back to my aunt as soon as possible, won't you sign it? As my father's trustworthy servant, you could act on his behalf,' said Fanny, thinking aloud.

'I could also take this paper to him on your behalf.'

'If he no longer wants to be my father, he will refuse to sign it, you know,' explained Fanny, sensibly. 'He can imagine any crazy thing he likes, but I can't let that stop me from obeying Aunt Colette.'

'All the same...'

'After all, if your master loses his mind, shouldn't you try to be sensible for him?'

And Fanny slid a pen into the servant's hand, who hesitated, then plunged in with visible emotion and worry. When this was done, they remained silent. Fanny carefully replaced the paper in her pocket, her eyes fixed to the ground. Suddenly, through the awning, her father impatiently called the servant. They exchanged brief waves, then they parted in their own directions, the servant heading towards the house, Fanny towards the bus stop. Although she was grateful to him for having complied, she vowed to do everything possible in the future never to see him again.

# FIVE
## *The Family Couldn't Care Less*

When Fanny got off in her uncle's village, snow had covered the rooves and the pavements. A loosely woven lace of frayed flakes, restrained in their dreamy fall, were catching on the coarse roughcast of the facades blackened by traffic. These walls had never seen climbing ivy nor purposeless wisteria; decorated with snow, they no longer seemed to belong to the village. Fanny passed her uncle's house without recognizing it. A fresh morning smell reminded her of winter holidays at Grandmother's house — hadn't she come back to Grandmother's village by mistake? She was reassured when she discovered the sign for the Coq Hardi. But the illusion of having come back to Grandmother's — as in the past when, coming from the train station with mother, arriving at dawn under a white sky, she would play at stamping the imprint of her booted foot onto the frost of the pavement — still vaguely imbued with her as she entered her uncle's house. Distinguishing the form of the fluffy couch at the end of the dark living room, she had to chase from her mind the thought that she was actually at Grandmother's house. What she was doing now, wasn't she dreaming it, stretched out on Grandmother's couch, similar to this one? Wasn't she changing places, right at this moment, in this dream about the couch where so many times in the past she had fallen asleep leaning against Grandmother? Because how could she really be at her indifferent uncle's house, so far from Aunt Colette and from Grandmother's village where she could not return? She would discover that she had dreamt Grandmother's death while resting on her shoulder, and how deep her shame would be when she awoke! If it was not a dream, thought Fanny, sitting on the couch, her situation would be extremely miserable. The rustle of the paper in her pocket both brought her back to her uncle's house and calmed her a little. Yet it upset her to realize that since the time when she used to trample the frozen ground joyfully, when her position in the family, even with Grandmother, had seemed painfully ambiguous compared to Eugene's, she had never been further from taking her place within the family group, in spite of appearances. Now that she was disowned by both her parents, she was supposed to beg for their pardon, beseech Aunt Colette, forget that Grandmother had been buried without her seeing her again. The more she had tried to get closer and the more strongly she had wanted it, the more she had found them short of even simple kindness toward her. She greatly regretted having ever left; she should have been content with the uncertain status time had granted her. The memory of the cold December morning when she had arrived in the village with her mother, stung her sharply as the image of what she should have settled for, of what, in hindsight, had been priceless.

Next door, her uncle was getting up, clearing his throat, spitting into the chamber pot. In the early morning he moved with melancholy slowness. Fanny prepared the coffee and reheated the food. Her uncle was waiting, his elbows on the oilcloth, his hair damp and dishevelled. Neither in the evening nor in the morning did they greet each other any more; they were so used to each other. Her uncle spoke in brief phrases. He did not say anything that wasn't necessary, that didn't have a practical purpose. His gaze, which rarely settled on Fanny, would fasten on the table, at the foot of the stove, on some detail of the tile floor. Before he left for work Fanny would outline the dinner menu to him. Her uncle would stroke his chin and utter approving 'hmms'. She would talk in a dry voice, her brow stern. Her aunts had addressed their husbands this way, hardly opening their mouths except to inform or to reprimand. Her uncle was saving his talkativeness for his colleagues. He would leave in silence, close the door behind him, and check twice that he had slammed it well.

After having made her uncle's bed, as every morning, turning the mattress and beating the bolster on the window just as he had ordered, Fanny ran to look for her little messenger girl. They hurried to the main road, already cleared of snow which was piled up in brownish clumps on the verge. Happy to have found Fanny again, the little girl was humming to herself. Fanny gave her the act of pardon signed by the servant, and a letter for Aunt Colette beseeching her to accept Fanny at her side; then, since the child knew the way and was getting impatient to leave, Fanny let her go without repeating her advice. She went back to her uncle's house, quiet at this mid-morning hour which she had loved best at Grandmother's house: after the housework was done and the vegetables for lunch were peeled, washed and waiting on the table, the newspaper swished gently as the postman slid it through a slot in the kitchen wall and it fell softly onto the tile, picked up by Grandmother every day with the same word of satisfaction. She would skim through it in the living room, seated on one thigh right on the edge of the couch, as if, although her morning work was done and Grandfather was no longer here to call her to order, she had wanted to show, nevertheless, that she was not settling down, that at the whistling of the kettle, the sudden sound of the doorbell, she could instantly jump up — she was still watchful, active, alert, faster than she needed to be.

Fanny sat down on a kitchen chair in front of a pile of society magazines which Aunt Clemence had been in the habit of reading and had kept intact and clean at the bottom of the linen closet. Fanny had also frequently bought this magazine, where the private lives of interesting people throughout the world were disclosed more accurately than elsewhere; but having been prevented from reading them recently, she was delighted to be able to catch up on the issues she had missed. She took in the articles and the interviews, examined the photographs — often taken without the knowledge of their subjects — in an excitement stirred by the regret of only now learning all these facts, when in past years she had followed each person's story step-by-step, day-by-day it seemed. Devouring these stories so late, she felt deprived, because surely they were at this very moment heading towards conclusions which she was missing.

Someone tapped faintly on the living room window. In the fever of pouring through the magazines, Fanny had thrown onto the floor the issues which Aunt Clemence had so meticulously cared for that it was hard to believe they had even been opened. In her haste to answer, Fanny trampled them and even spoiled some. She stopped to pick them up and quickly smoothed them.

'Fanny!' a frail voice called from outside. 'Fanny!'

'I'm coming!' she shouted, feeling lightheaded.

What Fanny had just read had pushed her surroundings to the back of her mind, and the living room furniture, small objects, frames and lamps, were a blur floating in the distance, as peaceful as in a dream, behind the carousel of images in the fore of her mind. It suddenly seemed to Fanny, walking to the door, that Aunt Colette's answer, whatever it might be, that Aunt Colette herself ... She kissed the little girl on her cold, pale cheeks. The little girl looked tired; Fanny, feeling sorry for her, took off her coat and hat, and cooked the little girl an omelette before questioning her. The child was mechanically leafing through a magazine, her inexpressive gaze coming to rest on the pictures. Fanny noticed a bulge under her sweater, between her neck and her shoulder.

'What have you got there?' she asked.

'Oh, nothing,' mumbled the little girl.

She pretended to lean with interest over an illustrated page and twisted a strand of hair around her finger. But Fanny wanted to see, and when she uncovered a thick bandage, she let out a cry of dismay. Questioning the little girl, pressuring her for a long time, such was the little girl's reluctance to tell, ashamed of who knows what, she managed to gather this: the child had become lost in the housing estate in Grandmother's village. When, after having wandered around for more than an hour, she had finally found Eugene's house again, they were just finishing lunch and Aunt Colette was getting ready to drink a cup of tea. Put out, they had greeted her coolly. However, seeing that she was exhausted, they had made her take off her coat and she had sat down and placed the two papers on the table. At this moment, a woman whose features she could not remember — Eugene's young wife? Some cousin visiting for lunch? — walked in from the kitchen carrying a pan of boiling water for Aunt Colette's tea. Without the little girl's understanding how it happened, whether she had knocked it herself trying to get out of the way or whether the woman had tripped, the water had poured onto her shoulder, burning her cruelly through her sweater. She had screamed, everyone had made a fuss, talking in all directions; Aunt Colette had led her into the bathroom, had carelessly smeared the wounded area with cold cream and hastily bandaged her up, as stingy with comforting words as with tender gestures. This the little girl did not complain about; she hardly mentioned it. But it was not very difficult for Fanny to work it out, in view of precisely what the child did not say Aunt Colette had done. Then they had let her leave without worrying about her any more, relieved to be rid of her. No answer for Fanny had been passed on to her — forgotten, probably. The little girl did not remember whether Aunt Colette had glanced over the papers. All that she could say on this subject was that there had been a piece of wrapping from fairy cakes lying on the table in the middle of other papers clearly destined for the rubbish bin; there was no way to tell whether Fanny's missives, discreetly folded in four, had not suffered the same fate. But as for an answer or even any observation, there was none. Disappointed, thinking herself to blame, the little girl was crying and Fanny could do nothing to console her. To keep herself busy, she changed the bandage and daubed the wound without the little girl seeming to notice; she was so hardened to pain that Fanny could have wept with pity, because all that tormented the little girl was the failure of her expedition. She took a short nap and as soon as she got up insisted on returning to Grandmother's village, despite Fanny's protests. She would not be held back; as soon as she had announced her intention she rushed outside. Fanny sat down in the most perfect distraction to wait for her. She had no doubt that the accident which had befallen the little girl was the manifestation of the family's feelings in her own respect, which the poor care the girl had received expressed so eloquently. It seemed that the family saw nothing human in the little girl, only the personified expression of Fanny's tiresome claims, which, as always, must be quelled or disregarded depending on the whim of the moment. All they saw in the child was an unreal fragment of Fanny's spirit! That they had permitted her to sit down and to speak instead of dismissively waving her away like a pure emanation; that Aunt Colette had bandaged her testified perhaps to some remaining generosity. But wasn't the family's patience at an end? What else can I do, Fanny wondered, without explicit authorization to visit them myself? Aren't I forced to have someone represent me? If she could have assured the family of the flesh and blood reality of her little ambassador, they might have listened to her more attentively and the little girl's visits might have been taken as a sign of tact on her part, of an absolute compliance with Aunt Colette's orders — who still had not pardoned her and had forbidden her from appearing again if she had not found Leda. But instead, they were more likely viewed as more of Fanny's pushiness and rejected as if Fanny were trying to invade their very dreams, a thing they perhaps believed her quite capable of.

Oh, thought Fanny as she got up and walked up and down, if only I could inform them that the child really is real! Feeling powerless, she clenched and unclenched her fists, suddenly suffocating in Aunt Clemence's dark living room. Night had fallen and her uncle would soon come home. He would be hungry, would want to eat dinner, and would scold Fanny for making him wait. She was about to set the table when the little girl pushed the door open. Fanny had to help her to a chair and make her drink a big mug of milk before the exhausted child could utter a word.

'I didn't even go in,' said the little girl straight away, her face turning crimson. She hid it in her hands and refused to say anything more. She cowered under her shame, her shoulders shaking. Fanny, who had hugged the little girl, suddenly felt suspicious; she rolled back the damp sleeve of her sweater and saw that a big hunk of flesh was missing from her right arm, clearly torn off by very sharp fangs. The wound was already clotting, but the little girl's arm now seemed as if it would break under the slightest pressure. Fanny let out a cry of horror and fright. The little girl sobbed, convinced of her disgrace. After many questions, interspersed with caresses and promises not to withdraw her trust in the little girl, Fanny managed to get her to tell what had happened. When the child had arrived in front of the house, which she found without difficulty this time, the gate was locked. She had rung the bell and called out; behind the living room curtain, one or two faces had appeared fleetingly, seeming to spy on her. The certainty that someone was there had made the little girl bolder, little wanting to come back empty-handed. She had jumped over the hedge, still calling out. As she walked towards the door at a determined pace, Eugene's dog had shot out from behind the house and lunged at her; she beat a retreat but did not manage to save her arm; the dog had torn off a chunk in plain sight of the people — who had run to the living room window, squeezed in there as if they were watching a show, with serious faces. But even after this frightful adventure she had tried to think of a way to get in again, though nothing remained but for her to come back since the dog was keeping watch in the middle of the garden. Her shame at having failed, at not even having managed to arouse the family's compassion, overwhelmed the little girl in spite of the kind words Fanny showered on her to forget her own discouragement. The child must leave soon so that she would not cross paths with Fanny's uncle.

'It feels fine,' she had said, irritated, when Fanny worried over her arm. And it seemed, in fact, that the little girl was not suffering, indifferent to her slight body, as impalpable as a shadow, an illusion of a little girl.

The next day, she was there as soon as Fanny's uncle had left. Although Fanny was thrilled to see her so lively and already eager, in spite of her wounds, to run to Aunt Colette's house again, she felt vaguely uneasy, as she would have felt if she could not manage to get some dangerous thought out of her mind. So she took it upon herself to slowly tuck in her uncle's bed, carefully sweep, wash the breakfast dishes, and ignored the little girl, who was waiting quietly, almost invisible in the darkest corner of the living room. The little girl remained silent and Fanny almost managed to forget she existed. The child seemed capable of remaining silent and hidden for as long as Fanny wanted or as long as it took for Fanny to find the strength to not give her another thought. If she was dying to go to Grandmother's village, it was only because Fanny could not hide her craving for her to do so.

Once all the housework had been properly done, Fanny opened the front door, flattened against the wall, and softly called the little girl.

'Go on now, run there,' she said, her eyes half-closed. From the breeze which blew on her gently, she guessed that the little girl had heard her, that she had left without a word, nimbly and obediently. And there she was already reaching the street at the end of the main road; the muddy, slushy snow squirting high around each side of her booted feet! They were short lace-up boots like Fanny had once had, made of burgundy leather.

Back in the kitchen where she now occupied herself with tidying up Aunt Clemence's magazines, Fanny noticed that it was only nine o'clock and reproached herself for having sent the little girl so early in the morning. Aunt Colette would no doubt not have finished her housework yet, which she was in the habit of doing while keeping one eye on a television show, and the child's interrupting at this moment would make her annoyed with Fanny: Isn't she going to end by hunting us down at dawn? What wouldn't Aunt Colette then be capable of to crush Fanny's troublesome thoughts, this clinging little cloud of demands which the little girl was?

But Fanny had just begun to worry when the little girl came back intact, although worn out from running, and her happy and triumphant face immediately reassured Fanny. She had found Aunt Colette alone, hanging washing in the garden beneath the dull winter sun. She had planted herself in front of her in such a way that Aunt Colette could not pretend not to see her; her dress with the little moons was hitched up on her hips, forming a pocket from which she took multicoloured clothes pegs. Her gaze distant, Aunt Colette had murmured, 'It's up to Fanny to make herself forgiven.' Then, jostling the little girl without realizing it, she had gone back in, on her way scolding the dog which could be heard howling behind the house. Delighted, the little girl repeated to Fanny what she considered to be a conclusive, as much as unexpected, message: It's only up to Fanny... 'What can I make of that?' murmured Fanny. Compassionately, she stroked the head of the child, who was dropping with tiredness. 'You see,' she continued, 'I now believe there is no hope.' With this absurd sentence, hadn't Aunt Colette meant that she couldn't care less about Fanny's little messenger? She no longer even thought of chasing her away or wounding her, caring little to find out the nature of her presence nor that possibly, dissatisfied, she would come back, each day, forever? Aunt Colette, having become used to it, no longer bothered being annoyed, no more than in summer when she let the irritating flies come and go, and if someone had pointed them out to her, would have said: 'Oh, are there flies?' It was clear to Fanny that the little girl could have spent the rest of her life in the garden without Aunt Colette, peaceful and sure of herself, if she even noticed her, uttering anything other than insignificant words, attending to household business, robust and confident, deaf to the appeals which she had decided once and for all hardly concerned her, forever unwavering. Thus without doubt had been Grandmother and Aunt Clemence, equally decent, honest, and impervious to pity. The same went for Uncle George, for the entire family with its sound good sense.

Disappointed in Fanny's reaction, the little girl had left without her knowledge. Fanny opened the door and scanned the main road, but she did not see anyone except the bread man who had stopped in his van and was about to sound his horn to let the village know of his arrival.

# SIX

## *Her Uncle's Decision And What Results From It*

'It's time for you to leave,' muttered her uncle, with some embarrassment, little used to expressing his feelings. 'It would not be fitting for you to stay any longer, so long after the bereavement.'

'But I don't know where to go,' said Fanny.

'What about the family?'

As he suddenly seemed suspicious, Fanny said nothing. She took her meagre luggage and walked as far as the little girl's house, not seeing any other solution. A man was coming out, furtively. Fanny asked him for news of the little girl.

'No child lives here,' he muttered, unhappy that she had noticed him. Pooh, thought Fanny, this gentleman is mistaken. A woman in an ill-fitting dress opened the door, surprised, but led the way into a room with closed shutters, scattered with indefinable objects, full of numerous threadbare cushions. Fanny asked after the little girl. The woman, misunderstanding, gave a crude reply and laughed hoarsely. There was, however, no child here to her great regret. She offered her a drink, and Fanny relaxed and accepted. She was not asked any embarrassing questions. The woman seemed pleased that she did not have the typical looks of the region, with features often over-pronounced. A few hours later Aunt Clemence's husband appeared, removing his jacket and his cap as soon as he came in; he was greatly surprised and annoyed to find her there.

# PART TEN

# Spring

In a grove of young willow trees which had been forgotten or ignored in the regrouping of lands and were the sole survivors next to a fetid brook, Grandmother's spirit nested, on the outskirts of the village. Since Grandmother had not been buried in the village M., and Aunt Clemence had passed away, Fanny knew that the spirit had left the village dear to Grandmother for her, to settle here, where it was out of place and alone.

It called to Fanny, as she went out one evening for a breath of fresh air, and gave specific information so that Fanny would recognize and trust it. She knelt down trembling at the edge of the water at the foot of the tree from where the voice seemed to come. On the horizon the street lights went out because it was past midnight, and although they would have emitted only a pale, lunar light, Fanny could no longer perceive the houses and started shivering. The spirit's voice sounded severe — would it have moved for any other reason than to reproach Fanny? According to general opinion, which Grandmother had shared, Fanny's conduct was blameful, even criminal, and on this subject the spirit's judgement would not prove any different.

For a long time it mumbled without Fanny's understanding a single word. The murmuring willow tree leaves were rustling in unison; if the spirit had not called Fanny just now, she would have thought the tree was only quivering because of its own tender young life. Then she remembered that Grandmother, talking to herself, had been in the habit of muttering like this.

'Why is your heart so cold?' it suddenly asked clearly in a tone unknown to Fanny. 'Why has your heart hardened and closed? Why has it become so cold? Don't you feel it through your chest? Is your skin still warm there? Why is nothing real in your eyes except whatever can help you with the family, everything else fades into insignificance, appears and disappears without your caring, lives and dies without your noticing? Even the trees... Why have you allowed your sense of community to perish when you want to be accepted into the family? Why does nothing move you except memories of me? Nothing binds you or shames you except the family as a whole and your failings in its regard... Do you love your uncle, your aunt, your parents? Did you love me? You neglected to come and see me on the last day, but all you care about is what people thought of your absence at the funeral. The same with my birthday; solely preoccupied with your search, you had forgotten it. As for the family, which you are more wrapped up in than

236

anything else, you hardly think of it except for its treatment of you. All you know about it is what concerns you. Have you got to know the soul of the family? Are you aware of each person's misfortunes, the good and the bad at the soul of the family? Have you patiently and attentively studied our family history? You boasted of knowing every event.'

The spirit sighed through the leaves which lifted and trembled as if in a strong wind, while the slender trunk gently bowed.

But is it fair that I have to make so much effort when all Eugene had to do was come into the world, thought Fanny, outraged and unable to speak to the spirit. Eugene once called you... A furious whistling shook the branches and abruptly interrupted Fanny's thoughts, making her blush. But she could not help remembering what Aunt Colette had confided in her on the lake: long ago even Grandmother had tried to conceal her connection with Fanny from the village, in vain, since everything was known before anyone thought to hide it. Learning of this had made Fanny irremediably bitter and resentful towards Grandmother. In the hostile and ugly cemetery, under the mound of earth, Grandmother's flesh was rotting, her frail old lady's bones were crumbling. Her plain black dress for special occasions, trimmed with a slightly yellowed embroidered collar, which Fanny knew she had been dressed in and which Grandmother had preserved with punctilious care, had rotted, an extravagant waste. Fanny's rancour had diminished and her deep, pitiful affection for Grandmother had not altered; whereas, Grandmother had been less than loyal to her. Grandmother's heart then had been no less hard than hers.

The willow tree had become silent, the branches softly bending, indifferent to Fanny. She laid her hand on the cool trunk, which was now casually straightening up. The spirit had left or was playing deaf. Fanny waited for a long while then, nothing coming, scraped impurities from the trunk and returned to the village.

When at daybreak she got ready to go to bed, the bottle of water which she kept at her bedside started to shake and oscillate, almost crashing to the ground. Fanny, drunk with fatigue, realized that it was the spirit again and pretended not to notice. Then she felt guilty and told herself that, in any case, the spirit would not be taken in by such a crudely human trick. In a bad temper, she took the cap off the bottle.

'At last,' exclaimed Grandmother's spirit, 'I couldn't take it any more! Are you really afraid of what I have to say? Or does the hardness of your heart make you prefer a good sleep to a few truths from your late Grandmother who, whatever you may think, has always striven for your happiness and suffered because of you more than any of her other grandchildren? All of the others are now settled in the situations they chose, more or less in accordance with their parents' wishes. They are married, have suitable jobs, work hard to make their houses nice. Those houses, no matter how flimsy they may be today, will pass down embellished and rich in memories to one or another of their children, whom in good time and in reasonable quantity they will bring forth into the world to the satisfaction of the whole family. (Could it be that Eugene had already...? wondered Fanny, upset. But the spirit did not answer.) You alone, although you long to carry out the family's intentions, revel in a deplorable situation. You failed to hang onto George and pursued no one but Eugene, who was not destined for you, as you were aware. The family does not exist without posterity. While you think any means are justified to force your way into the circle of your close relatives, while you complain of being unjustly excluded, having, in your view, almost the same rights as Eugene or the others, you have just as much duty to ensure its evolution as some of your cousins, who have the rights which you think you have. You do nothing but criticize their attitudes. Is that normal? Is it? Not worrying whether they are a part of the family or not, not questioning Aunt Colette's advice on this subject, your cousins conform to the family's few simple rules and prove much better than you their respect for this sacred institution. You wither away in futile ambitions, selfish and pointless quibbling, your heart completely absorbed in yourself... Is that the way to revere the family? Why, all it has ever asked of you is normal behaviour!'

But, since I unfortunately did not manage that, the family was quick to let me know about it, thought Fanny, who was having difficulty keeping her eyes open.

The spirit, spread throughout the whole room, muttered with annoyance.

'Don't think about anything except what you should do now!' it shouted.

'Since the family has rejected me,' explained Fanny, 'I can't think of continuing the line without feeling inconsistent. The family would not want to acknowledge anything or anyone from such a branch. So what's the point? For now, the situation being what it is, I can only work towards my own integration.'

'So?' asked the spirit.

'As for the family, that's exactly it,' answered Fanny, 'I no longer feel any hope.'

Unable to hold out any longer, she fell asleep. It annoyed her to give Grandmother's spirit such a poor welcome, but considering that all her failures and losses left her little to sacrifice now, she found the spirit's admonishments trivial and hardly worthy of such an extraordinary apparition.

A few days later, Fanny's daily walk led her to the outskirts of the cemetery, where she noticed Aunt Colette and her mother passing through the gate. They were each carrying a bouquet of blue dahlias and had no doubt come to put flowers on Aunt Clemence's grave, which was somewhat neglected by Fanny's uncle. Fanny's mother's lightweight dress, the same soft blue as the flowers, was fluttering, full and flowing, across the legs of Aunt Colette, who was holding her sister's arm. One would have said, from behind, that they were walking in one and the same dress, a square of chiffon cut from the spring sky. They moved slowly down the central path as if out for a breath of air; they would stop to look at a name and make comments. Sometimes Fanny's mother would laugh, her head thrown back, completely at ease. Fanny, who for a long time had not seen either of them, watched them tirelessly from across the gate. She soon moved away, however, to be on the safe side. Assuming they remembered who she was and agreed to speak to her, whatever Fanny might tell them of her current situation would shock them. Perhaps they would not even admit that they could know such a person, indeed that such a being existed. She would have become invisible to them, every memory of her vanished. They would start walking again without deviating from their course, and confidently cross Fanny's body as they would a simple heap of dust!

Noticing a fountain, Fanny went over to it to quench her thirst. She turned the tap, and the spirit's voice resounded, caught in the stream of water.

'My granddaughter is drinking at the village fountain, but has she earned the right? Has anyone ever said that she could take advantage of the village services like a true inhabitant?'

Even strangers, people passing through, thought Fanny with annoyance, are allowed to quench their thirst at the fountains!

'True, but you are not a visiting stranger,' the spirit cheerfully explained. 'Neither an inhabitant nor a visitor: what does the law provide for in your case?'

'I don't know.'

'See, you don't know the law! So, what are you to do?'

A man was approaching on the pavement. Fanny turned off the tap and jumped up, with feigned indifference. The man was not in a position, however, to hear the voice of Grandmother's spirit. Although Fanny hardly knew him, she smiled, her eyes lowered; he responded with irritable muttering. She dared not turn the water on again and left, hugging the wall of the cemetery. Old half-effaced graffiti sullied its whole length. As Fanny's glance landed on a big M painted in red, the downstrokes of the letter rocked as if trying to advance and the spirit's voice murmured, thin and laboured, as when Grandmother had the flu or when she had, as she used to say, a frog in her throat. Fanny was irritated but thought that nevertheless she must stop. If people saw her, what would they think of such unusual behaviour? The spirit's voice, imprisoned in the letter, was so weak that Fanny had to glue her ear to the wall, right where the two halves of the M joined.

'We've come to this,' whispered the spirit, 'because you were so cowardly in front of that man that you turned off the tap and shut me up. Had I voiced a single doubt about your right to exist in front of that villager, most probably, perhaps without your even noticing it, you would have immediately become invisible to his eyes. Later, you would not have tried to check what law I was talking about, you couldn't have cared less anyway to learn that there is no such law, any more than to know that there are a hundred more just as cruel. That's your whole attitude towards the village. If someone declares anything concerning you, there you go submitting to their judgement, no matter whom it comes from. There's not a base act, not a wrongdoing, not a mutilation that you would not be capable of just to be acknowledged.'

'But I've obtained more here than anywhere else, much more than in the family fold or in your village where, if you remember, without our knowledge people gave me this name...' objected Fanny.

'True, true,' admitted the spirit with, Fanny thought, a hint of embarrassment. 'But even though you would never realize it and for a long time would be misguided enough to find tranquility of the soul, it is my duty to warn you of this: here in this village, what you think you have gained — wretched as it is and so uncertain that your pride inspires incredulous compassion — is only a more pitiful aspect of what the villages and you yourself manage to make of a depraved situation, or, perhaps, what the villages create at your expense in their abhorrence of every form of strangeness. It would have been better, you see, for people to whisper behind your back in our village.'

'Pooh!' sighed Fanny out loud, suddenly tired.

She moved away from the wall, no longer caring whether the spirit still had things to tell her, and headed back, careful not to rest her gaze on anything which could serve as a refuge for an argumentative being, since it was obvious that Grandmother had never intended to do her anything but harm. It would deprive Fanny of any chance of not being in the wrong, whatever she did.

Ahead, her mother and Aunt Colette were turning the corner of a street, still pressed tightly against each other. Under their unified step, the pebbles were crunching in beautiful harmony. In spite of herself, Fanny called out to them. They were talking, did not hear her, and disappeared.

# PART ELEVEN

# The Cousin's Mission

I have been asked to conduct a little investigation in the village M. for two parties with opposing interests, as I am now aware — although at first I thought they merely represented two different means, one more cautious than the other, towards the same end. This will not make my task any easier. However, if both sides requested me for this little job, it is because I am known for my impartiality, and they trust that I will not, to favour the one, conceal anything from the other.

Here is the problem: my second cousin Eugene's wife, piqued because he will not settle into any serious occupation, has just left him. He does not seem too deeply affected by her departure but has taken it into his head to have his cousin Fanny with him. Although he claims to be in love with the idea, he does want to know exactly what she has become and what her feelings towards him are before making a direct request for her to join him. He particularly wishes to be reassured that her tendency to make herself distinctive in spite of everyone's disapproval has not increased. This tendency, even an appearance of it, would be damning for him. I have come to understand, however, that Eugene's desire to accept his cousin is strong. So although he begs me to be strict in my assessment, he most definitely longs for my eye to lack in sharpness so that he can get Fanny without being held responsible for such an escapade if she turns out to be unsuitable. My cousin Colette also wants me to discover all there is to know about Fanny because she is aware of Eugene's plan and, unable to forbid it, wants at least to control things. Although she was no less discreet than Eugene, I now know that Colette hopes to hear the most unfavourable report about Fanny so that, presenting it to her son, she cannot fail to convince him.

Apart from this, they both leave the matter entirely in my hands and have already resigned themselves to the truths that I will bring them, convinced that I will neither hide anything nor lie in any way.

I stayed with my late cousin Clemence's husband, who was delighted to lend me a bed for a few days. He is a taciturn man and fears that his words, incorrectly repeated and twisted, will come back to him disagreeably distorted. I questioned him about Fanny, but he made do with muttering a few trivialities and did not want to say anything to me, a member of the family and known for my reserve, which could be useful, except for one detail which I would have got wind of elsewhere: Fanny no longer uses that name in the village, but her former first name, the one her parents gave her. The syllables ring in an unseemly way to our ears; consequently, we find this name really ugly and complicated, not really a name at all. It is much closer to the name or nickname we would give to a dog or a cat. Animal names do not need to have meaning or remind us of something and should never bring to mind anyone in the family: Fanny's real name cannot make us think of anything. I expressed my surprise that she had chosen to take it back. However, my cousin did not answer, perhaps fearing that he had already told me too much. It seems that he sees little of Fanny and does not invite her to Sunday lunch; but, of course, he is a man living alone. He did not tell me where Fanny lives. What's more, he is very embarrassed and unhappy to be questioned about her, although he affects a surly indifference. I cannot rush him; where we are from, it is customary to keep things quiet, to stay silent about whatever appears doubtful or in its day provoked scandal or a stir; it is customary to act as if things which cannot be discussed openly, without embarrassment, without using vulgar or sentimental language, do not exist. That is why I am in the wrong when I question my cousin, and we both know it.

In order to glean some information, I went to the village café-bar, the Coq Hardi. Fat summer flies were eddying around the room; others were caught on flypaper and still trying to free themselves; they were buzzing so much in the general lethargy of the hot afternoon that they almost drowned out the sound of voices. Their little black droppings stained the walls and the oilcloths, and the neon lights were spangled with them as if for decorative effect. I perched in front of the bar, opposite the drowsy-eyed landlady who, at first, showed no reaction to the mention I made, as if in passing, of Fanny's name. She had already forgotten that Fanny had been called that. Then she pulled a contemptuous face, a vague, offhand movement, which two men seated next to me copied, letting it be known that Fanny was unimportant in their eyes. I could not help blushing a little, for one of the men had sniggered saucily, without, for all that, the contempt leaving his face. I thought of how embarrassed I would be to relate his reaction; we never speak of such things! Only married couples do sometimes, between themselves, after a little drop of something, and then only with the help of jokes. I myself have no idea what words to use. They continued to speak idly about Fanny; the landlady uttered a disdainful short phrase, which each of the men repeated, and they seemed to relish the taste on their lips, spitting it out with satisfied insolence. Although I do not upset easily, I was intensely ashamed at this instant: have we ever seen anything like it in our family? It did not take me long to understand that the contempt had less to do with Fanny than with what she is, than the stereotype these three people applied to her, knowing her occupation. In fact, they did not say anything about Fanny which could be hurtful or implied that she was not liked or even that they deplored her presence in the village. They despised her as people despise someone whose occupation is deemed unworthy, as in Grandmother's village we unanimously despise a certain neighbour who lives by reselling miscellaneous junk; this low esteem does not mean that we do not acknowledge his place in the village, nor that we would not be saddened to see him leave. So Fanny had her function here, as I quickly realized. When I thought of our family's decency for generations, this distressed me more than if she had seemed cast out on all sides. Only the fact that they had forgotten the name, Fanny, reassured me — it was no doubt difficult to imagine her connection to our family. I became saddened, admittedly, that it had become Fanny's lot to count as one of the villagers in this way, but I wondered with some embarrassment whether any other position in the village could be conceived of for her. Deep down, I had not approved of Eugene's ambition to live with his cousin. It seemed more natural, more reasonable, although this was cruel, for Fanny to remain a mistake without descendants or name, erased by the completion of her own life and having had no effect whatsoever on the unity of the family blood. These thoughts, nevertheless, must not influence the progress of my mission; I vowed to serve Eugene no more or no less than Colette.

Following a hint from the landlady when I had asked her where to find Fanny, I went that evening to the edge of a stream where young weeping willows stood, outside the village. I noticed Fanny seated at the foot of a tree, tightly hugging her knees. In order not to frighten her with my sudden presence, I softly called to her.

'Is that the spirit again?' Fanny murmured, surprised, without turning around.

'It's me, your mother's cousin,' I said, stepping forward.

Fanny's jump was no more abrupt than mine on seeing her. At first I did not think I recognized her, but after scrutinizing her features I had no doubt that this was Fanny like I had never seen her before. Embarrassed, I looked away. I sat down next to her; she seemed to be waiting with a kind of dread.

'Who sent you?'

'Your cousin Eugene,' I answered, staring at the stagnant water.

Relieved, I passed Eugene's proposal on to her. I remembered snatches of conversation overheard in the past and had assumed, as soon as Eugene had explained his wish to me, that it would fulfil Fanny's oldest desire and that there would be no reluctance from her. Her constrained silence made me realize that things were different today. I cried out with unintentional harshness: 'Oh, so that doesn't please you any more?' Fanny lowered her head, sadly. She began to explain her reasons to me in a clear and firm voice: if she had failed in this place and were still wandering without ties of any kind, regarded with distance and hostility, the chance of returning to the family in one leap through Eugene would have been miraculous. However, if, as was the case, she had found a role in the village and a place which was not denied to her, one that suited very well what she was, and in which, as a result of her appearance, she had even achieved some measure of success, why, despite the difficulties and the dishonour, would she abandon this unhoped for position for another, more precarious in view of Eugene's weak will and the family's feelings towards her? She had resolved to live excluded from the family and she did not want to throw herself into new hopes which, once disappointed, would leave her without any recourse. In any case, she did not consider herself badly off now but, on the contrary, favoured and prosperous. For a long time her love for Eugene had gone, irretrievably. Feeling a little nauseous, I then pointed out to her, as I would have done to anyone, that what she was talking about was a pitiful existence. I did not say anything more: weren't things better this way? Fanny calmly repeated that there was no other choice for her in the villages, and I admired the wisdom which had made her fulfill her plan of slipping into our region without going against the family's unspoken intentions that she remain apart — we have never, in fact, discussed it among ourselves. I congratulated her for having taken back her old name. It was with this one, she answered, that she pleased the most here. I wondered then, stupidly, if she really was, after all, the person I thought I was speaking to, I saw her so differently.

I returned home and passed on what I had learned to my cousin Colette, whose satisfaction I easily guessed. Then I informed Eugene first of the extent to which his cousin's appearance had changed, becoming, even in our unvarying, quiet region, resolutely strange. He seemed exasperated.

'Then she can't be trusted,' he moaned, seeming to consider that the responsibility fell back onto Fanny's obstinate nature. Extremely displeased, he nervously paced up and down the room. Thinking I would bring the matter to a close, I told him that in any case Fanny did not in the least want to live with him, and I repeated what she had said to me on the subject. Troubled, and I think a little embarrassed, Eugene found himself at a loss for words. But he could not permit himself to leave it at that; seeing him so annoyed, I had no doubt that his feelings for his cousin were serious. He earnestly begged me to go back and to inform Fanny of this final chance he was offering her: if she thought that she could change her appearance, if she had the willpower and the desire, he would wait for her for as long as it took; if she was so stubborn that she did not wish to hear any more of it or her desire was too half-hearted for any hope of success, she should forget him forever. I sighed at such stubbornness but left again anyway, persuaded to undertake a pointless trip. I found Fanny leaning against the same willow tree in the falling night, her bowed face invisible in the reflection of the water. She smiled with relief at the sight of me.

'What luck,' she said, 'that you came back.' It was not that she suddenly could not forego my presence, but, having really thought things over, she had changed her mind just after I had turned on my heels the last time and had regretted not being able to call me back in time. She now accepted, she admitted, Eugene's proposal. Worried, I dared not look her in the face. Her unbearable singularity seemed unknown to her! On the surface of the still water, I gazed at my own floating face, trying to make myself impassive. Then I informed her of Eugene's condition, as if this demand went without saying and she herself had lost all good sense. We remained silent for a long while.

This time, she murmured, if she fulfilled the condition, she would certainly not resist, she would die of exhaustion.

'Come, come,' I grumbled, overwhelmed with confusion.

# PART TWELVE

# Aunt Colette's Account

Since my son Eugene no longer had a wife to support him and George had returned to his job as a sales representative, we all three left the house on the housing estate, where my son had taken me for the duration of George's escapade, to move back to my mother's old home. Although the place belonged to him, Eugene was greatly disappointed — between his father and myself, he felt transported back to his adolescence. He knew that he was letting us down and worrying us with his laziness, his lack of aptitude or liking for any job whatsoever, his apathy towards the failure of his marriage, and an unfortunate tendency to ludicrous ideas which we strongly disapproved of for specific reasons. We had relinquished the house we had rented for a long time in a nearby village and our furniture was moved here; having always lived with it around us it would have been hard to part with. But we no longer had room to turn around. My mother's old furniture inconvenienced us, but it would have been scandalous for us to get rid of it; we already had three wardrobes for similar reasons. Quite understandably, the rest of the family would have resented it. Two lacquered sideboards, two heavy tables, two couches which were fortunately almost identical, three armchairs, a dozen chairs to match the tables, almost prevented entry into the dining room. In the other rooms, where no one went except us, we had stashed, higgledy-piggledy, living room and bedroom furniture, as well as piles of sundry objects which rose up from floor to ceiling in precarious stacks; narrow aisles allowed us to slip through to our beds where we slept as if in a tomb, overhung by some chest of drawers or writing desk which we had skillfully managed to shove over our heads, parallel to the mattress. We soon became used to the new arrangement and did not even think it unusual. Only Eugene still cursed, complained that he was suffocating, and sometimes, out of exasperation, foolishly jostled against some ingenious heap. He was happy, however, to take advantage of the three television sets, dividing his days between each one — since we were badgering him to take his future in hand, he thought he was giving us the impression of not spending all his time at home: in the afternoons he skillfully hid himself in front of the most secluded television set and swore afterwards, suddenly bursting in through the front door, sighing and feigning exhaustion, that he had just come home from a futile job search. To flush him out, we would have had to explore every nook and cranny, an impractical undertaking in this clutter. But I worried to see my son settle so complacently into shameful idleness. Without having spoken to his father yet, I was toying with the idea of sending him to my sister's husband, who had been brilliantly successful. As different from us as he still was, he no longer had anything contemptible about him, no disconcerting strangeness, and would perhaps succeed in making something out of our son. Eugene refused to become a sales representative. I regretted that at this moment no soap opera was playing whose hero, practicing this occupation, would have made Eugene want to copy him, as he always does. My son was not interested in anything without seeing it first on a popular series. This upset me, of course. However, I myself ... I really had to admit that the amiability I had recently felt towards my sister's husband, carried away in a girlish attraction to this man whom I had looked down on, was no doubt due to the influence of a particular television show which I had followed with a passion and whose moral was designed to encourage attitudes of this kind.

During the course of the morning, a neighbour came to look for the newspaper, which we were just finishing glancing over, an old habit from Grandmother's day: we shared the price of the subscription. She settled down in a corner, between two sideboards full to their seams with dishes for special occasions. In a shrill voice, she gave us the latest news from the village. Eugene, who had nonchalantly emerged from the bottom of the wardrobe where he liked to hide out in the mornings in order to listen, feigned contempt for all this gossip, lit up a cigarette, his gaze distant, and turned half towards the window to make us think he was concentrating on some spectacle outside. He never missed this neighbour's visit: she was a great supplier of scandal. As soon as we had moved back, he had asked her to come at exactly the hour when the game shows from the night before were being rerun, because he could forego seeing them again without too much regret.

The woman would chatter away, repeating herself; she would prop her feet on a chair and ramble on, looking at the toes of her shoes. Then she would open the newspaper and comment on matters pertaining to the village, not reading anything beyond that. I would listen to her with mixed pleasure. Wouldn't she gossip all over the village about what she could observe in our house — Eugene's laziness and the mess — tarnishing the excellent reputation our mother had established by dint of tact and neatness? Wouldn't people pity our mother, comparing her with us?

'Confounded gossip!' I would always mutter, a little angry, after she had left. At this moment the shame my son inspired in me was bitter.

Then we would leave for the supermarket to look at the new things. Eugene always spent a long time in the television department. A dozen sets would be turned on, and his stare would jump methodically from one to another, in such a way that he could follow each program without missing anything in the others, an experience which left him worn out. Oh, what to do with this child? I would think, seeing his indifferent face, the droop of his mouth. Sometimes the worry stifled me and tears would spring to my eyes. Yet Eugene wasn't stupid!

At this time of year a heavy heat, filled with acrid odours rising from the fields, soaked with showers of fertilizer, a white deluge in the distance, encouraged a nap after lunch. Eugene curled up in his wardrobe, and I headed wearily for our bedroom. A light bang made the front door shake.

'Come on in!' I shouted, remembering that we were expecting my sister. Then I shrugged, went to open the door, and at first saw nothing. Lowering my eyes, I perceived on the front door-step a long, unfamiliar form; the yellowish hue of the step where a stray clump of grass was growing seemed visible through this silhouette without name or equal, which, though it had trembled at first, was now as still as a corpse.

'Well what is it...,' I mumbled as I carefully felt it with the toe of my worn-out old slipper. I suddenly recognized Fanny's features, although they were so indistinct, so uncertain that I could not bring myself to call her that. What's more, I would no doubt never have remembered her if the idea had not crossed my mind that she alone knew how to cause such troublesome surprises. Fearing that my sister would arrive, I felt worried and did not know what to do; I lifted the faint silhouette and hurriedly carried it to the shed. There for a moment I shifted from one foot to the other. But not because my arms were giving way; they hardly felt like they were holding anything! Thinking it would not really be too hard a bed for her, I laid the body in one corner on a folded potato sack. Then I went out, carefully closing the door so the dog could not get in. At that moment the gate grated. My sister was coming into the yard, cheerfully swinging her little tartan suitcase. The intense light prevented me from seeing her face, but I watched with emotion the pale blue dress coming towards me, my sister's determined and well-rounded calves, her pretty city sandals.

Hello, her hem is coming down, I thought, as I leant against the shed door. Although when she was pushed on by some desire my sister still proved to be very resourceful, she had always been such that if we did not take charge of the slightest matters concerning her she would soon have veered off on the worst possible course. In her everyday life, out of laziness and thoughtlessness, she would have neglected the details which to us testified to the moral rigour of the whole family. So when we were kissing one another I did not tell her about her hem; but after dinner, when we were drinking herbal tea in a clear corner of the kitchen, I fetched my sewing box and began to stitch up her dress, leaning over her knees despite her protests. Next door, Eugene and his father were watching a detective film in complete silence. What will happen, I thought unwillingly, if the unimaginable form in the shed wakes up? What will my poor sister say? Was Fanny really dead at last? I could not help sighing; thank heavens our mother had departed before knowing all these new upsets. But my sister, who was very put out to see me kneeling at her feet, used it as an excuse, a little spitefully, to complain that I had not always taken such good care of her person or noticed so promptly other symptoms of her going astray. As a girl, my sister said, out of sheer folly she had started to read those little eight-franc novels with their titles wreathed in roses and their covers illustrated with a picture of an eternal couple locked in a languid embrace. She had always persuaded any neighbour or family member going to town to pick them up from the kiosk at the train station, where she had arranged to have a copy saved for her each week. Although the stories were self-contained, the mere thought, explained my sister breathlessly, of not having read every one of them contracted her stomach and brought sweat to her temples and forehead as if she were being forced to withdraw from some drug, which is what these little books, *In the Jungle of Love, A Fiancé for Bernice, For as Long as You Love Me*, written by ladies with English names, had become for her. With almost identical plots, they contained narrations rich with promises for herself, an ordinary reader, bored in an out-of-the way village (my sister sighed) with little education and no knowledge of love except the sensible marriage contracts which took place in our family circle. She had no way of knowing then that such passion only existed in books and that eccentric marriages such as these novels reproduced — invariably between beautiful young people from conflicting backgrounds — could not, in real life, lead to anything but disaster, as she now realized, having been to the depths of that failure. When she had plunged into the abyss of these flights of fancy, not only had no one around here put her on her guard or, at the utterance of the titles alone, led her to feel the slightest sense of their ridiculousness or, at the very least, of their absolute artificiality, but — she was still amazed by this — they had instead encouraged her with a sort of amused pleasure. Agreeing with her, I remarked that they did this because people take pleasure in encouraging a minor vice in someone, amusing themselves, convinced that they are not doing the person any harm. My sister said that people brought her these dangerous little books, but behind her back mocked her in front of the family, just as they would give a subtle wink when they filled to the brim the glass of some longtime drunkard who had come by the house. Our negligence had ruined her life, my sister accused. I protested in defense of us all. How could we have known what the end result would be? We had not even opened her precious books, not one of us. I guessed what she was about to add and felt confused and distressed. I had stopped sewing to listen to her more attentively and leaned my arms on her knee. From the living room violent noises from the television reached our ears at intervals, isolating us, my sister and me, in a rather dramatic intimacy. I hoped she would stop right there, but cruel — as she had often been during our childhood — she continued in a slight whine, kneading her hem without caring that she was pulling it out even more. My head was raised towards her and I was getting a pain in my neck. I sighed discreetly and rested more comfortably on her thighs. Such readings, uninterrupted, never criticized, had led her, continued my sister, to see the world through a rose-coloured filter which made every situation seem eternal and fantastic, every person elegant, beautiful, and noble. She had soon felt as out of place in this village as a princess who had ended up there by accident. A little short of breath, she explained with emotion how one day when she had gone into town and was just leaving the magazine kiosk at the train station with a new little novel under her arm, she had bumped into a man, the man who would become her husband, who was so obviously remarkable, so incomparable in his elegant strangeness to the dull young people whom she could meet. Arriving in town for the first time, fearing people's stares, he had possessed an air of unflinching determination, my sister remembered, contemptuous, a little too headstrong, just like the masculine expression of the hero with a strong chin, who was about to take the lips of a reclining blonde beauty on the cover of the little book my sister had just bought. When in her wild recklessness, falsely shy and blushing, she had dared approach him and speak to him, he had answered her without restraint, surprised and certainly flattered by such a prompt welcome, such an honour in an area where he was in danger of losing his mind with shame. She had immediately become convinced, said my sister, shaking her head with disbelief, that she could experience with him what people never experienced around here and what only she was made for. So, ended my sister, you are all somewhat responsible for the collapse of my marriage since, in spite of my being right under your eyes, you did not stop my imagination from running away with me.

I avoided answering, not because I did not think my sister frightfully unjust, but because knowing what lay below, lurking in the shed, I felt uncomfortable hiding it from her, and at this moment my pity for my sister was great. Let her be dead, I was begging inside, disappeared, dissolved. Let her never have existed or, likewise, let all memory of her having been here die!

But I could not help speaking about her to Eugene. It took him a few minutes to understand (which was, after all, still quick): feeling very ill-at-ease, I used unusual and vague terms to describe what I had seen. My son turned so violently red that I thought he was losing his mind.

'You know, I didn't ask that much of her!' he shouted. 'I swear!' He was stammering now, as if he had something to fear. I put on a serious air. I had decided to carry through my plan for him and deemed it best not to show the slightest leniency so that he would not think to protest. I asked him to look in the shed. But he was terrified and stubbornly refused. For two days he remained ashamed and disconcerted. I needed someone else, even Eugene, to confirm what I had seen. His impression would have helped me to get a clear picture of this freak, for I could think of no word to describe it and was beginning to doubt whether I had not dreamt it. I was still repelled by the idea of going back into the shed to check if there really was a semblance of my niece there.

A few days after my sister's arrival, without telling anyone, Eugene and I caught the bus to her husband's village, which I had never visited before. Although the houses in the village disappointed me at first with their general poverty, this man's house impressed me favourably; and in the huge hall made entirely of real marble, I felt intimidated and shocked at my own effrontery. The servant who opened the door asked us to be patient. Eugene was sulking but seemed proud to have been in this imposing residence before.

'It's really something, isn't it?' he repeated, strolling back and forth. He pressed me to answer, to go into raptures in turn, imagining, I suppose, that having seen the place before me he should collect a share of my admiration. But I stayed silently in a corner, out of politeness.

The man suddenly came out into the hall without seeing us. He was followed by the servant, who called us to his attention. He made a sweeping, irritated gesture. Then, the servant no doubt having told him who we were, he stopped dead and turned a flabbergasted and confused face towards me. He came forward, apologizing profusely; he was dressed in a splendid bright red garment, long and costly — next to it Eugene's little black jacket, which he was pulling even more out of shape by thrusting his fists into his pockets, seemed ridiculously tight-fitting.

'Oh, what a surprise, what a surprise!' exclaimed my sister's husband. He shook our hands in turn, several times. Then he gave a curt order to his servant; and although just now he had seemed to be rushing to get something done, he led us into the living room as if there was nothing more important than welcoming us and attending to our comfort. He straightened the cushions on the couch and plumped up the armchair. He turned on the television and lowered the sound, in order, I assumed, to entertain us with the stream of lively images. In our presence this man seemed as happy and feverish as if he were welcoming some celebrity, some superior spirit! As for me, I felt embarrassed to be treated with such consideration by someone accustomed to being the master, whose lifestyle, where we lived, would have made him the most notable person in the village, a position to which my husband's occupation would never lead us.

The servant brought us an orangeade, then he was dismissed with the click of a heel on the tile floor. At last, after a brief silence, came the moment to state the purpose of my visit. I complained lengthily of Eugene's inability to apply himself to anything whatsoever and of his indifferent ignorance; I explained that we were powerless to change him, since Eugene would not listen to a thing we said. Seated next to me, Eugene did not interrupt although he was definitely most offended; despite everything, I was grateful to him for it. Our host remained impassive. So, gathering all my courage, I said, 'If you could supervise him, lavish him with your advice, help him to find something to suit him... Oh, I see that I'm asking a lot of you, forgive me...'

I stopped speaking, frightened for having dared to trouble him in this way, all the more so since he now seemed astounded and embarrassed. He muttered something about money. I hastily set things right, 'No, no, Eugene doesn't need your money but your good sense, your example, you understand...' My voice died, and I lowered my eyes to hide my discomfort. An eloquent silence followed; he had even forgotten his duty as a host.

I understood him then in a flash of intuition: to see me appealing to him in this way cast him into the depths of turmoil and distress, in spite of the confidence he had acquired as the years went by. He could have been triumphant to see us lowered to the point of envying him; but even at this he was inept, leaving our glory intact. I wondered, seeing him troubled, if he would now implore me to withdraw what I had said, show me that, while he had felt able to give himself the little pleasure of a wedding present for my son, to allow himself this discreet victory over our hard-nosed contempt of the past, for us to appeal to his talent, for us to hope for moral protection from him, for his guidance, was inconceivable.

He got up and walked hesitantly towards the window — looking, in his flowing crimson robe, like the heart of an inferno. Eugene took the liberty then of turning up the sound on the television. I crossed my hands in my lap and patiently waited for our host's reply.